PENGUIN BOOKS

DRIVE ME
home

Carly Robyn writes contemporary romances with heat, heart, and humor. When she's not writing or reading, you can find her spending time with her family, scrolling through TikTok, exploring Chicago's restaurant scene with friends, watching a Grand Prix, taking a million pictures of her dogs, or binge-watching anything true crime related while drinking a Diet Coke.

Follow her on social media for updates: @carlyrobynauthor.

ALSO BY CARLY ROBYN

Drive Me Crazy
Ella & Blake's story

Drive Me Wild
Josie & Theo's story

DRIVE ME
home

CARLY ROBYN

PENGUIN BOOKS

PENGUIN BOOKS

UK | USA | Canada | Ireland | Australia
India | New Zealand | South Africa

Penguin Books is part of the Penguin Random House group of companies
whose addresses can be found at global.penguinrandomhouse.com

Penguin Random House UK,
One Embassy Gardens, 8 Viaduct Gardens, London SW11 7BW

penguin.co.uk

First published in the United States of America by Blue Dog Press 2025
First published in Great Britain by Penguin Books 2025
001

Copyright © Carly Robyn, 2025

The moral right of the author has been asserted

Penguin Random House values and supports copyright.
Copyright fuels creativity, encourages diverse voices, promotes freedom
of expression and supports a vibrant culture. Thank you for purchasing
an authorized edition of this book and for respecting intellectual property
laws by not reproducing, scanning or distributing any part of it by any
means without permission. You are supporting authors and enabling
Penguin Random House to continue to publish books for everyone.
No part of this book may be used or reproduced in any manner for the
purpose of training artificial intelligence technologies or systems. In accordance
with Article 4(3) of the DSM Directive 2019/790, Penguin Random House
expressly reserves this work from the text and data mining exception

Custom illustration by Lorissa Padilla Designs
Typeset by Jouve (UK), Milton Keynes
Printed and bound in Great Britain by Clays Ltd, Elcograf S.p.A.

The authorized representative in the EEA is Penguin Random House Ireland,
Morrison Chambers, 32 Nassau Street, Dublin D02 YH68

A CIP catalogue record for this book is available from the British Library

ISBN: 978-1-405-96926-0

Penguin Random House is committed to a sustainable future
for our business, our readers and our planet. This book is made from
Forest Stewardship Council® certified paper.

*For my Poppop Arnie.
Your love for Mimi is the kind that romance
books are written about.*

AUTHOR'S CONTENT NOTE

This book is written in a light and humorous style but does include explicit language, references to the death of a parent (past, off-page) and a main character who was adopted as a newborn. It is a slow-burn, open-door romance that portrays sexual content and is meant for readers 18+. Please take note!

The focus of this work is on the fictional characters and events within the Formula 1 racing world, and deviations from the current Grand Prix schedule and tracks are intentional for storytelling purposes.

PLAYLIST

Lover | Taylor Swift
Stick Season | Noah Kahan
Espresso | Sabrina Carpenter
Vienna | Billy Joel
What a Girl Wants | Christina Aguilera
Lose Control | Teddy Swims
From Eden | Hozier
Unwritten | Natasha Bedingfield
Beautiful Things | Benson Boone
Gorgeous | Taylor Swift
Dancing In The Flames | The Weeknd
Talk Too Much | COIN
Kiwi | Harry Styles

ONE
CHARLOTTE

I REALLY HOPE the person interrupting my dream is cursed to drink the wrong coffee order every morning for the rest of time. Groaning, I ignore the ringing of the hotel room phone and burrow deeper under the covers. Unfortunately, I told the front desk to call until I pick up, so a moment after it stops, it starts up again.

I'm not a morning person. At all. Quite frankly, I'm a grade-A witch until I've had two full doses of caffeine. *Minimum.* When I was a kid, my dad used to wake me up by saying "rise and whine" because there was absolutely nothing sunny about my disposition.

Giving up on my dream—where Jason Momoa is fighting Ryan Reynolds for the honor of buying me my first Birkin—I answer the phone with a groggy "'Ello."

"Good morning, Ms. Walker. This is Khan at the hotel front desk with your wake-up call."

"Yeah, thanks, got it," I mumble, rubbing the sleep out of my eyes.

There's a slight hesitation before he continues. "Shall I call back in ten minutes?"

Confused, I arch a brow. "Um, why?"

"To confirm your... alertness," he says, his tone uncertain. "Your husband requested that we ensure your timely arrival at the track. Your car will be ready in thirty minutes."

My stomach rolls. *Gross*. I sigh. "My brother."

"What?"

"Theodore's my brother, not my husband." Any future husband of mine better know not to use hotel staff to corral my arse out of bed. "There's no need to call back, though. I'm up. Thanks."

"Okay. Have a lovely day, Ms. Walker."

"You, too, Khan. I take back my wish about your ruined coffee order."

Once I've returned the phone to its cradle, I let out a string of expletives so colorful it would leave Shakespeare impressed and force myself out of bed. I get started on my morning routine at the speed of a crotchety, arthritic old man. Once my teeth are brushed, my skin is moisturized, and my curls are somewhat tamed, I stalk over to my suitcase. Ignoring the AlphaVite polo my brother gave me—there's no way I'm putting that polyester monstrosity on my body—I pull out the three potential race day outfits I brought with me. After a moment's deliberation, I decide on a cream knit midi dress. It's smart, casual, and perfect for Bahrain's weather, thanks to the lightweight fabric. I pair it with my beige Nike sneakers—I think the actual color is "light bone," but I find that anthropologic and weird—and shove my luggage to the other side of the room so it's not visible in the mirror picture I snap for my social media. Then I head downstairs and out the front doors to the waiting car.

By the time we pull up to the designated area at the track, I'm only running thirty-five minutes late. All things considered, like my jet lag, hatred of mornings, and problems with time management, I'm doing pretty damn good. I push my sunglasses up my nose as I approach the turnstile at the entryway of the paddock. It's only nine a.m., but the golden glow of the sun is already blindingly bright. A massive banner featuring the F1 logo and its sponsors looms overhead as I dig for my VIP pass. It's attached to a neon orange lanyard, so it shouldn't be difficult to find, but my purse is Mary Poppins' bag come to life. No cute clutches for me. Nope. This sucker is considered a carry-on by select airlines.

Once I've finally located my pass, I press it against the scanner, and the light on the turnstile flashes green, allowing me entry into the exclusive F1 paddock. Located behind the pit garage, the paddock is equal parts fancy and functional. F1 teams and employees do most of their work here, but it's also where sponsors, media, and special guests spend time before and after the events of the race weekend. The layout of the paddock is slightly different at every circuit, but it always resembles a tiny multi-million-dollar village.

I can't help but smile to myself as I make my way down the main path toward the AlphaVite motorhome and take in the details. The Bahrain Grand Prix is far from the first race I've been to. I attended my first grand prix when I was eight months old and have continued annually my entire life. As they always do, the faint aroma of engine oil and the mosaic of team colors lighten my mood. Along my way, I note the reporters setting up their cameras and equipment, the Formula 1 employees leading sponsors toward the hospitality areas equipped with champagne and caviar, and members from each team entering their respective motorhomes for meetings.

The outside of AlphaVite's motorhome is slate gray with large, tinted windows and their signature lightning-shaped logo stamped front and center over the door. One side of the ground floor houses offices, but the bulk of the space is packed with employees repping AlphaVite's signature cobalt blue while enjoying breakfast at the cafeteria tables. Drivers' private rooms are typically on the middle floor, so I make my way up there without slowing. I've just cleared the final step when my brother's booming voice echoes down the hall. I'd give him shit for it if I wasn't just as loud.

I consider knocking for all of 0.5 seconds before saying *fuck it* and walking in without announcing myself. Theo's manspread on the small couch in the room, chatting animatedly into the phone. Based on the goofy grin he's wearing, it's his girlfriend. I lucked out in the future sister-in-law department. I always make sure to tell my brother that the best thing that's happened to him as a Formula 1 driver has nothing to do with the world championships he's won. It's 100 percent Josie. She worked for the marketing team at McAllister back when he drove for the team, and at some point last year, they went from friends to adorably-slash-disgustingly-in love.

"Charlotte's finally here," he says.

I roll my eyes at the word *finally* because I know he hasn't been sitting here twiddling his thumbs.

"Yeah," he goes on. "Okay—sure. Miss you, too. I'll call you later, yeah? Mm-hmm. Love you, angel."

He ends the call, then greets me with a warm "you really should knock, you know."

"And you really shouldn't pronounce Worcestershire like it's a hobbit town from *Lord of the Rings*," I counter with a shrug. "But here we are."

At my comment, he whips his head in my direction and frowns. "Where's the shirt I got you?"

"I never wear team merch," I remind him, hopping up onto the edge of the desk.

I've loved fashion since I watched my first episode of *Sex and the City*. I had no interest in the trysts or rendezvous Miranda, Charlotte, Samantha, or Carrie had with the men of

Manhattan. Nope. The only love affairs I cared about included fabrics, the famous Fendi Baguette bag, and all the fabulous stores. As Rachel Zoe once said, "Style is a way to say who you are without having to speak." So as much as I support my brother's team, their awkwardly fitting, sort-of-itchy polo shirt isn't me.

"You ready for the race?" I ask. I have no interest in arguing about clothing today. "How are you feeling?"

"Don't look so concerned, Lottie." He chuckles. "Driving for a new team may be a bit intimidating, but my fans are still *my* fans, no matter what colors I'm sporting."

"True," I concede, drawing out the word. It's weird, encountering starstruck fans. But time and time again, they stop Theo on the street for his signature or a selfie.

He winks at me. "If I was brave enough to change your nappies when you were a kid, I'm sure I can handle this."

I roll my eyes. "I'm calling bullshit, Theodore. You once called emergency services while you were babysitting because I threw up and you wanted me away from you."

"That's only because—"

"Morning, Roo," comes a voice from the doorway.

Then a Greek god steps into the room. Lucas Adler. My brother's best friend and the bloke I've been crushing on for... well, for forever. I drink in Lucas's tall, athletic frame like he's a fine wine and I'm a world-class sommelier. His tousled, wavy blond hair brushes against his forehead, and his bottle-green eyes speckle with gold, thanks to the light leaking through the window. It takes conscious effort not to lick my lips in appreciation.

A lazy grin etches lines around the eyes of AlphaVite's other driver as he takes me in.

Lucas started calling me Kangaroo when I was a kid—because I was constantly hopping around like Australia's national animal—but over the years, the name has shortened itself to Roo.

A betraying sort of flush blooms across my cheekbones as I wave and say, "Hi."

"Theo said you were on your way over, so I grabbed a coffee and a croissant for you. Figured you could save it for later if your blood sugar's too high right now." He holds out an AlphaVite-branded coffee cup and a white pastry bag. "Double espresso with steamed milk and two pumps of sugar-free vanilla syrup, right?"

There's no use even attempting a coy smile. No, not when I'm this giddy. So I let an idiotic grin take over. "You know my coffee order?"

A slight pink hue spreads across his cheeks. It's utterly adorable, the way this grown man, with tattoos dusting his body and metal rings gracing his fingers, blushes. I make a mental note to do it more often.

He steps closer and hands me the coffee, the cup still warm even through the protective Styrofoam. "Good memory, I guess."

I take a sip and groan as the familiar flavor hits me. My ovaries do a choreographed can-can dance in appreciation. "You are seriously the best. If I didn't already have a list of baby names on my phone, I'd *so* let you name my first child."

Or let you father them.

"What about middle name?" Lucas counters with a chuckle.

Bringing the cup to my lips to hide my smile, I nod. "I can work with that."

I've made quite a few not-so-brilliant decisions in my life: Believing my ex when he said not to worry about that one girl. Thinking I could pull off low-rise jeans. Getting bangs. Paying to belong to a fancy gym with the hope that it would miraculously make me want to work out. The list is longer than a drugstore receipt.

But traveling the world with my brother for the Formula 1 season as I figure out what I want to do with my life and what's next after graduating from university? Not one of those kinds of decisions. Add in the bonus of spending my weekends with Lucas Adler, and hell, this may be the smartest decision I've ever made.

TWO
LUCAS

IF THERE'S one thing my mom excels at, it's laying on guilt thicker than schmear on an everything bagel. The first time I missed curfew, the speech she gave me was so lengthy and fear-inducing that I was never again late coming back from a friend's house. My brothers and I have dubbed it her "Oscar speech" because it's been known to bring tears to a person's eyes, though not in the same way.

I've already apologized twice for being hard to reach, but, ironically enough, she's barely acknowledged that I'm on the phone. Knowing I just need to wait her out, I make myself comfortable on the couch in my suite. Lord knows how long this will take, and the last thing I want to do after dodging her calls for a week is cut her short.

"I have better things to do than chase after you like I'm an annoying telemarketer," she huffs. I don't have to see her to know she's pacing the living room with one hand on her hip. "Is it so difficult to answer a call from your mother? Thirty-six hours of labor, and I talk to your voicemail more than I talk to you."

"Mom—"

"Oh, no, no, no. You don't get to *Mom* me, Lucas Noah Adler. It's been over a week since I last spoke to you. You barely even respond to texts."

Maybe because her texts consist of phrases like "hi" and "miss you," rather than anything of importance. Though I keep that to myself. But when she finally takes a breath, I gently remind her. "It's the start of the season, Ma. Things have been ridiculously busy, but I'm sorry, okay? I'll be better at keeping in touch."

"*Humph.*" Voice softening, she says, "I worry about you being so far away. I like hearing your voice. That way I know you're okay."

"I know," I reply, my heart heavy at the truth in her words. I twist the silver ring on my middle finger. "Promise I'll be better about answering."

"Good," she says. "Now that we've got that settled, have you looked into booking your flight home?"

I drop my head back with a thump against the back of the couch. *This* is why I've been avoiding her calls. "Yeah, I can probably make it in May or June."

She makes an obnoxious buzzer noise. The sound is so loud I cringe and pull the phone away from my ear.

"Nope. Wrong answer," she says. "You *can* make it. When was the last time you visited? Last summer?"

"You saw me in December."

She and my dad stayed with me in Monaco. We spent the week sailing like we did on the summer waters of Cape Cod when I was a kid. As one of five boys, I don't often get uninterrupted one-on-one time with my parents, but they make the effort, and I'll never take that for granted.

"Don't play coy with me," she says, her tone suddenly haughty. I can picture her standing in the middle of the room now with her chin raised. "It's time you came home for longer than a day or two."

My chest goes tight at the thought, and I rub at my sternum absentmindedly. "It's not as easy as you think, Ma. I have commitments here, and with the season—"

"I know, honey," she says with a sigh. "But it would mean a lot to us, especially *me*, if you could make the time to come home every once in a while. The whole family's driving to Montreal for the grand prix in May. What if you came back with us afterward? You could stay for the week. We all miss you."

I lower my head, sighing in defeat. I'm not one to air my dirty laundry, so my mom doesn't know why I've been avoiding Boston for the past few years. Taking a surprise trip back only to find my brother Jesse was dating my ex? The ex I was interested in getting back together with? Yeah, I'd say that's a solid reason to avoid my hometown.

But she's right. It's been far too long since I've spent time with my family. The ones I want to see, at least. "All right," I acquiesce. "I'll see what my team can do."

"That's all I can ask," she says, a pleased tone marking her words. "It'll be nice to have all of my boys home again."

My shoulders slump. Boston hasn't felt like home for me in quite some time, but I don't mention that.

"I won't keep you any longer," she continues. "Good luck today, little lion. We'll be cheering you on."

I try not to cringe at the embarrassing nickname. We all have them: Grayson the gentle giraffe, Lucas the little lion, Jesse the jokester jaguar, Ezra the elegant elephant (by far the worst of them), and Finn the ferocious fox. "Thanks, Ma. Love you."

"Love you more."

Once I've ended the call, I shoot off a text to Mitchell, my manager, and Natalie, my assistant, asking them to make travel plans. That way I won't be tempted to back out.

Then, putting the conversation out of my mind, I change

into my race suit, which is adorned with sponsor logos and hugs me like a well-worn glove. I only zip it up halfway, leaving the mandatory fireproof undershirt to cover my torso. With as scorching as it is outside, I aim to avoid overheating at all costs. My helmet coordinates with the suit, though it's got a few light blue accents on the side as well as the American flag and my lucky number seventeen. One side is already marred with scratches, thanks to one of the practice sessions, but like the tattoos that wind up my arms and my thigh, each one tells a story.

As I step into the garage, I take a moment to absorb the atmosphere. Mechanics and engineers adjust my car's settings, checking the tire pressure and fine-tuning every aspect of the sleek racing machine. The distant hum of engines rumbles through the air, welcoming me like a long-lost friend.

I exchange nods and brief greetings with familiar faces as I head toward Charlotte, who's standing next to my race engineer. She's curvy in all the right places, and her dark brown hair—a stark contrast to her fair skin and blue eyes—brushes past her shoulders. Her heart-shaped cheekbones are naturally pink as she listens to the engineer go on about something.

Objectively, it makes sense for her to spend the season with AlphaVite. Why shouldn't she take the opportunity to travel the world while she figures out her next steps? But subjectively? That's a whole different story.

Theo's an easygoing guy, and not quick to anger like Blake is, but if he knew I had a thing for his little sister? He'd go full berserker mode. Thanks to my actual brother, I'm all too familiar with how breaking bro code can ruin a friendship. I'm not about to screw up my relationship with Theo just because his sister's got a smile that can get me to say yes to anything, a laugh smoother than oak barrel–aged whiskey, and a body I'd like to map out with my tongue.

With a long exhale to shake off those thoughts, I approach

and greet Charlotte by lightly tugging on the end of one of her curls.

She whirls around, a less-than-pleased frown on her lips. But when my identity registers, her lips tip up into a smile. "Oh. It's you," she says, giving me a small wave. "'Ello. You ready?"

"C'mon now." I nudge her with my elbow. "I'm always ready for race day."

"I figured as much, but it felt like the nice thing to ask." She beams up at me, those blue eyes sparkling. "My fantasy team and I are rooting for you to kick some arse today, by the way."

I let out a chuckle. "What's your team name? Walker this Way?"

The mile-wide smile that blossoms across her face and showcases her dimples warms me from the inside out and makes me feel like I've won before the race has even started. "No, it's Holy Walker-Moly, but that's a good one. Honestly, the possibilities are endless. Walker on the Wild Side, Walker Flocka Flame, Walker-ness Monster. Oh! And Walker on Sunshine. That's an oldie but a goodie."

"Wow. My guess is lame in comparison to those choices."

"Not any lamer than your Crocs," she teases, lifting her brows and eyeing my feet, even though I'm not wearing my favored sandals.

"Hey, my Crocs are cool and comfortable." I waggle my brows. "You can't make fun of the guy who remembers your coffee order. Don't you know that's a rule?"

Her dimples wink. "Oh, is it, now? I talk a lot, so it's nice to know someone's listening."

I'm sure as fuck not about to own up to remembering nearly everything Charlotte Walker's said to me since well before I noticed her in *that* way. I know she enjoys her morning toast best when it's a little burnt, she doesn't like her toenail polish and fingernail polish to match, and she always chooses the purse when playing Monopoly.

Before I can come up with a clever response, a loud whistle, courtesy of our team principal, David Green, captures my attention. Several feet behind Charlotte, David is standing out on the pit lane in front of the garage with Theo by his side.

Ah. Time for his pre-race motivational speech, or as I've come to call it, his "Al Pacino in *Any Given Sunday*" speech.

"Good luck out there," Charlotte says, gently squeezing my bicep.

"You, too," I say, then immediately cringe when I realize that sentiment doesn't apply. *Oy vey*. "I mean enjoy... watching."

What the fuck?

Charlotte tips her head back and laughs. "Holy Walker-Moly needs you to score some major points, so get it together, Adler."

Spending all season in her proximity? Yeah. I definitely need to get it together.

THREE
CHARLOTTE

I BARELY HAVE the athleticism to wrestle my tits into a sports bra, yet my brother can drive a million-dollar car at 375 kilometers per hour like it's second nature. Genetics truly baffle me. On the monitor, Theo's car gains speed heading into a hairpin turn that will push him into a sharp kink in the track. My breath catches in my throat as his brake pressure spikes on the telemeter indicating the exceptional amount of pressure he's unloading onto his front left tire as he goes into the turn. As his car straightens out and he speeds toward the Ithaca car a few seconds ahead of him, I clap and release the tension riding in my shoulders.

"Great job," David says, complimenting my brother through the radio. "Hit DRS on the straight after turn eleven."

I adjust the chunky noise-canceling headphones I'm wearing as I turn to another screen. Each shows a different angle or portion of the track, which is one of the benefits of watching the race from here rather than the grandstands. When I was younger, I used to prefer watching the races from there. My dad retired from F1 before I was born, but he'd take me to the Melbourne Grand Prix every year. We'd sit with the fans like regular attendees, despite his status as a former world champion, and munch on popcorn and candy as we cheered and whistled for the cars barreling down the track. Without him, it feels strange, so I tend to watch in the garage now.

"Good race so far, yeah?"

I glance in the direction of the deep voice, then tip my head back, because the man strolling toward me is built like a fucking national monument. He has to be nearly two meters tall. Seriously. There's no way his three-piece charcoal suit isn't custom made. His broad shoulders would easily burst the seams of any department store ready-to-wear piece. Good lord, he must've been a massive baby. I shudder at the thought of his poor mother giving birth—*focus, Charlotte!*

"Uh, yeah, I reckon the team will have a podium win," I reply, giving him a friendly smile as I rack my memory for the bloke's name. Theo introduced me to every person on the team the day we arrived, like I was a show pony, and I thought I'd done well remembering, but I come up blank. It's surprising, really. I should remember someone this tall.

He sticks out his hand in introduction. "Mitchell Abramson."

"Lucas's mom-ager," I blurt out, pumping his hand energetically.

"*Mom-ager?*"

Heat creeps up my neck, but I give him a tentative smile. "Dad-ager works, but mom-ager rolls off the tongue a little better." Head tilted, I shrug. "Obviously, he's not your kid, but you've been with him since he was twelve, right? When he won the US Karting Championship, you saw his talent and potential. So you acted as his guardian so he could travel the world and compete, yada, yada, yada?"

He studies me for a moment, his lips downturned. "How do you know all of this?"

"It's on his Wikipedia page," I say, angling in conspiratorially. "And as his number one superfan, I stalk it every day, looking for new information. Did you know that Lucas prefers the red Gatorade to the dark blue one—which is blasphemy—and that he's allergic to feather pillows?" With a slow blink, I shake my head. "Not a very badass allergy for someone who rocks a leather jacket, but I'm not one to judge."

That's a lie, I totally am.

Mitchell's brows shoot into his hairline. "You—wait, what?"

"I'm taking the piss out on you, Mitchell," I say with a grin, straightening. "I know all of that because he told me. Duh."

Though I imagine some of that can be found online. Lucas is the only American driver on the Formula 1 grid, which makes him a unicorn of sorts. Most Americans focus on motorsports like NASCAR and IndyCar, since in order to gain experience and make a name for oneself in F1, a driver has to spend a significant amount of time in Europe, competing in karting events and single-seat series. Luckily for Lucas, Mitchell saw his talent early on, and here we are.

"You're Theo's sister," Mitchell says, snapping his fingers and pointing.

"Charlotte," I correct him, though I keep the usual vitriol out of my tone, considering I did just call him Lucas's momager. I swear if I had a penny for every time someone referred to me as "Theo's little sister" or "the other Walker," well, I wouldn't be rich, but I could definitely put down a deposit on a Chanel Classic Flap Bag. I've been living in the shadow of Theo's success my whole life. I don't begrudge his career or achievements, but it's hard to follow in his footsteps knowing I'll sprain an ankle even trying. My family has never made me feel as though I can't measure up. But with a brother as outgoing as mine? A man whose name and talent are known around the world? How could I compete?

Mitchell nods. "Right. Charlotte. Lucas mentioned that you'll be following your brother around for the season."

The irritation I've been holding back almost spikes at those words. Nose crinkled, I say, "Following him around sounds lame. I much prefer to say I'm taking advantage of him so I can eat, drink, and shop my way through the world."

He snorts at my deadpan delivery.

I'm not embarrassed about needing time to pull myself together, but I don't owe him, or anyone, an explanation. And although Theo is helping expense my travels, it's because he insists on it. I'm not kidding. He wouldn't talk to me for three days when I tried booking a hotel room with my own credit card. My brother's the only person in the world who can out-stubborn me.

Mitchell nods, the corners of his lips quirking up. "If I hadn't been tipped off by the blue eyes and smile, your charm definitely would've done it. The Walkers don't exactly fly under the radar."

I raise my brows and fight off a grin. "I don't know how to tell you this, but you don't fly under the radar either. You're built like Mount Everest."

When he tosses his head back, his booming laugh is loud enough to be heard over the noise in the garage. "Because I'm tall?"

"Um, yeah. I'd probably need an oxygen mask to climb you."

He makes a strangled sound, his brows shooting up again. Only then does my inadvertent insinuation hit me.

"Not that I'm interested in climbing you," I say, feigning nonchalance, despite the way my stomach twists. "No offense, but you're too old for me, and it'd be a little on-the-nose ironic for me to have daddy issues. What I mean is that it'd take me a while to get up there if I did."

For a moment, Mitchell just stares, but eventually, he shakes his head and chuckles. "I knew your dad back when he raced for McAllister."

A bolt of excitement works its way through me. "Really?"

"Yep. Worked for his driving partner's manager back then," he reveals with a small grin. "He was a great guy. Always had a smile for everyone."

"Yeah," I say with a beam of my own. Formula 1 is etched into the fabric of my family history. For my dad, it was a focal point. For Theo, it has been a borderline obsession. For me, it's always remained in the periphery. But I'd be lying if I said part of the reason I was so open to spending the season with AlphaVite was to experience the magic of the sport for myself.

As our conversation peters out, we both focus on the screen, catching the moment when Harry Thompson, an Everest Racing driver, overtakes Lucas during a tight turn.

I wish I could say the rest of the race is nail-biting. Instead, Blake Hollis, my brother's best friend and former teammate, maintains the lead. Theo struggles to overtake the car ahead of him, and Lucas and Harry duke it out for second place, with Harry securing the spot in the second to last lap.

Pride swells in my chest as my brother hops out of his car, smiling at fans behind the crowd barrier, then thanks his team for a job well done. Although he won't outwardly show it, he's not happy with his performance. Unless he's on the podium with a trophy in his hand, he doesn't think he's done well enough. I'm only competitive about board games, so I can't imagine the pressure that comes with the potential to win millions rather than Monopoly money.

Theo congratulates the other drivers and signs a few hats before waving me over. "The only perk of you not wearing blue is that you're easy to spot."

I grumble under my breath as I give him a quick hug. He's sweaty, and if I dislike my own sweat—hence the reason I despise working out—then I sure as hell don't want his on me. "You did great out there."

His brows crease as a hint of disappointment filters through his features. "Hardly, but thanks."

"Fifth place still earns points," I remind him. "And it's only the first race. You've got a lot of time to work your way onto the podium."

"I guess," he mutters. "But I should've been more aggressive."

"Grr," I tease.

That earns a grin from him, and this time, the smile reaches his eyes. "Weirdo. I'm going to call Jos really quick before I'm hounded for interviews. You good?"

I flash him a thumbs-up. "You don't need to hover, Theo. I'm fine on my own."

"Old habits die hard," he says with a chuckle. "Catch ya later."

As he heads off to call his girlfriend, I zero in on the man I've been covertly glancing at for the past fifteen minutes. It'd be hard *not* to notice Lucas. He's not broody like Blake or loud and outgoing like my brother, but he commands a room all the same. Standing by his car, which is parked in its respective place, he's focused on a reporter holding an ESPN microphone. Not wanting to interrupt, I stand off to the side, watching as he answers post-race questions in a smooth, calm, and steady tenor.

The pit area is a sea of organized chaos, full of people celebrating victories with high fives and cheers or chatting about improvements for the next race, so I don't expect Lucas to notice me. But as if he can sense me, his head jerks in my direction, and his eyes pin me to the spot. He nods to the reporter in a way that simultaneously says "we're done here" and "thank you so much" before strolling toward me.

Hello, handsome.

"Hey, Roo," he says, unzipping the top of his racing suit. Even though it only exposes the shirt he's wearing underneath, it feels like he's performing a strip show just for me. "How's Theo doing?"

Only Lucas would be more worried about how Theo's handling of placing fifth than celebrating his own win.

"How are *you* doing? Fifteen points in the bag to kick off the season is a hell of a way to start, Adler."

His face, already flushed from the race, turns a deeper shade of red. "Just doing my job."

"Modest as ever." I sigh. "I swear, if I had even a fourth of the talent you do, I'd be so fucking annoying about it you'd want to gag me. Not in… well, you know, *that* way." I wave a hand, going for flippant. "Or maybe you would. I don't know what you're into."

Did I just insinuate he may be into BDSM?

He arches his brows and coughs out a laugh. "You have talent, Char."

I shrug. "I'd hardly call the ability to recite every line in *The Devil Wears Prada* a talent, but to each their own."

"That helmet you helped design for Theo is sick as hell," he argues. "There's no way I could ever do something as artistic as that."

"Thanks." Now I'm the one whose cheeks heat. I've been helping design Theo's helmets for years. They're nothing ground-breaking, but it's a fun, creative outlet. This year his helmet fades from a black night sky in the front to a cloudy light blue sky in the back, with the Australian flag running through the middle. In the gold design swirled along each side are a few hidden *J*s and my dad's number.

"Do you need to get back to interviews?" I ask, nodding over his shoulder. "There's a blond reporter shooting daggers at me like I bought the last brioche bun at the bakery."

He cranes his neck, peering over his shoulder, and when

the woman spots him glancing her way, then turning right back toward me, her glare goes from menacing to murderous. I give her a smile anyway because I'm friendly and petty like that.

"That's Miranda," Lucas huffs. "Ella refers to her as Satin Satan."

I lift a brow and bite back a smirk. The satin part is obvious enough since she's wearing a satin shirt that's so tight across her chest, I'm shocked she hasn't popped a button. But the Satan part? Color me intrigued. "How'd she earn that nickname?"

Lucas runs a hand through his hair. Without his signature silver rings adorning them, his fingers look oddly naked. "She insinuated that Ella's success stems from her relationship with Blake and not her work. Something about getting the exclusive scoop during pillow talk."

I let out a scoff as a thread of irritation works its way through me on Ella's behalf. "Why the hell would Ella and Blake talk about G-force in bed when they could be focusing on the G-spot?"

Head thrown back, Lucas laughs, and I swear the sound could win him a Grammy. It's deep and inviting and rattles me straight to my bones. It comes to an end far too quickly, though, when a media person from the team—Alex, maybe? Alfredo? Anthony?—calls out to him, warning him that it's time for the press conference.

"Are you going to watch?" Lucas asks with what might be hope in his eyes. Before I can answer, he adds, "I'm sure you have better things to do, and Theo won't even be there, so no pressure."

Listening to drivers answer questions about differential throttle and torque would never be on my list of favorite pastimes, but there's no way in hell I'm turning down the opportunity to unabashedly admire Lucas for thirty minutes straight. "I'll be there."

FOUR
LUCAS

SIPPING my beer from my seat at the bar, I survey the hotel's ballroom. From here, it's obvious that no expenses were spared for this party. Not that I'm surprised. As far as glamour-drenched sports go, F1 takes the cake… and the doughnuts, eclairs, and macaroons. The high-top tables are draped in white tablecloths and decorated with elegant floral arrangements. A small band plays on a wide staircase on the opposite side of the room. And white-gloved servers weave through the partygoers, offering canapés and champagne. Like I said: fancy.

I undo the top button of my shirt and tune in to the argument Theo and Blake are having about how Everest's tire strategy played out during the race. Argue, I suppose, may not be the right word. It's more like Theo making grandiose claims and waving his hands around to accentuate his points and Blake rolling his eyes a lot and disagreeing on occasion.

I've just zoned out again when Theo nudges me with his elbow. "Mate, that bartender has been eye-fucking you for the past thirty minutes."

I don't need to look to know who he's referring to. The

woman has been watching me since the moment I sat down. Though I know where this is going, I sigh and take the bait. "So?"

"Are you going to get her number?" Theo prompts. "Celebrate your win on the track with a win off the track?"

His cheesy line makes me cringe. "I'm going to bed after this. *Alone*."

With a shrug, he says, "Okay."

That's it. No argument, no pestering.

His simple compliance creates an uneasy sensation in my gut. Not once in our twenty-plus years of friendship has Theo let a topic go without offering up his opinion.

Blake smirks like he's thinking the same thing. Like he knows Theo isn't done.

And he's right. A moment later, Theo drums his hands against the table and declares, "If you're no longer interested in random fucks, you should let us set you up on some dates."

My gut sinks. *There it is*.

Blake nods. "Ella has a few friends that you'd like." He lifts his chin and scans the crowd, looking for his girlfriend.

Ella travels with Blake not only to support him, but to interview drivers, engineers, and fans for her podcast, *Coffee with Champions*. It's why, instead of hanging out with us at the bar, she's off schmoozing and networking.

"I don't know where she is, but she's mentioned setting you up a couple of times," Blake says, bringing his rocks glass to his lips.

"Josie, too," Theo adds.

Blake sets his drink down on the lacquered bar top. "So you'd have options."

"And then we can triple date, so you don't feel like a fifth wheel."

I bite back a derisive snort. *Leave it to Theo to subtly point that out*.

"Jesus Christ," Blake mutters. "What this arsehole is trying to say is that if you're interested in a long-term thing rather than"—he nods toward the bartender—"a single-night fling, we can set you up."

Theo nods. "Not all girls will fuck you over like Kylie did, you know?"

Blake and Theo are the only people who know why Jesse and I had a falling-out. I told them while plastered after the Singapore Grand Prix last year. There's no good way to say "hey, my brother's dating my ex" while sober. Honestly, there's no good way to say it while drunk either, but vodka has thankfully dimmed that memory. All I know is that the next morning, Theo had a black eye, and Blake was sporting a split lip. Apparently, Blake tried to book a flight to Boston to "kill that knob-headed wanker" and Theo threw his phone at the wall to break it so he couldn't.

Honestly, I don't even blame Kylie for moving on so quickly. Though I do blame her for doing so with my brother, I can't deny that I wasn't a great boyfriend. I was never around, and when I was, it was on my terms. I never ingratiated myself into her life or went out of my way to bring her into mine. Hell, my parents didn't—and still don't—know I even dated her.

"There's no need for you two to play matchmaker," I say, annoyed by it all. "I'm fine."

"No, you're not." Blake hits me with his signature scowl, then eyes Theo as if to say *you're up*.

Theo, of course, wastes no time. He places his phone screen side up on the table and slides it closer to me. The live location sharing and tracking app we all use is pulled up, the dots representing Blake, him, and me overlapping.

I spare it a quick glance, then frown at him. "Dude, I don't know what the fuck you're trying to show me."

"Your location."

Irritation flares inside me. "I obviously know where I am," I snap. "So *why* are you showing me this?"

Theo snatches his phone back and levels me with what he probably thinks is an intimidating stare, but in all honesty, just makes him look constipated. "I'm showing it to you because it means I can *see* where you are at all times."

"You stalk me?" I ask, only half teasing. "Weirdo."

He's had my location for years, and I've never thought twice about it. He told me it was for "emergency purposes." Now I'm rethinking how wise it was to give him access to my whereabouts at all times.

"You do one of two things when you're not fine," he says, giving me a pointed look at the word *fine*. "You spend more time in Monaco or you get a new tattoo."

"And you've been in Monaco for the past two months *and* you got a new tattoo," Blake says, as if what Theo is insinuating isn't already clear.

I'm *really* not liking the way this conversation has veered toward intervention. Sure, I've felt a little lost and lonely lately, but overall, my life is great: my career is at its peak, my friends are happy, and my family is healthy and financially secure. So what right do I have to complain about being stuck in a rut?

"I appreciate your concern, but I promise I'm okay," I reassure them with a smile that feels more like a grimace. "You'll be the first to know if and when I'm not."

They're wearing matching *bullshit* looks when Charlotte appears at Blake's side, thankfully cutting the discussion short.

"Evening, boys," she says, her dimples on full display.

"What are you wearing?" Theo sputters, setting his drink on the bar top a little too forcefully.

"Oh, this?" Charlotte twirls, giving us a 360-degree-view of her outfit, her expression brightening further.

The form-fitting dress draws my attention to every curve. The curves only accentuated by the silver heels laced up her legs. It takes everything in me to bring my focus back to her face quickly and keep it there rather than peek at her cleavage, because *fuck*, she looks stunning.

"Isn't it adorable? I bought it while shopping with Mum last year but haven't had the chance to wear it yet."

Theo's eyes widen comically, and I swear he sways a little. "Mum let you buy that?"

"It was on sale," Charlotte says with a coy smile, "and you know Mum loves a good bargain almost as much as she loves us."

I cup my mouth to cover a laugh. She knows damn well Theo's referring to the neckline of the dress, not the cost.

"You were bitching about me not wearing AlphaVite's color," Charlotte reminds him, "and this is blue, so it's team appropriate." She shrugs those smooth, bare shoulders. "You should be happy."

"The color's the only appropriate thing about it," Theo grumbles, his brows drawing together. "Where have you been, anyway? You were supposed to be here an hour ago."

"Why do you make it sound like I was off doing something shady?" Charlotte huffs, crossing her arms over her chest.

My spine tingles at the way the move highlights her breasts. *Do not look at her tits, Lucas.*

"Because you're known for being reckless," he counters, clenching his fist on top of the bar.

"Reckless?" Charlotte rolls her eyes. "Really, Theodore?"

"You accidentally bought a plane ticket to New Brunswick instead of New Caledonia and *still went*."

She shrugs, the move easy and good-natured. "I had a fantastic time in Canada. And you can't complain. You loved the syrup I brought back for you."

"And then when you finally did go to New Caledonia, you had to pay an absurd fine—"

"The signs stating that beach was private were *not* clear," she argues, a crease forming between her brows. "They were small and easy to miss."

"Okay," he draws out. "What about when you stole a quokka?"

"I didn't *steal* it, Theodore. It hopped into my bag when I wasn't looking. It's not my fault it fell asleep there."

I bite my tongue so I don't burst out laughing.

Charlotte throws Theo a scathing look that would have my balls shriveling into raisins if it were directed at me and slides into the empty seat to my right. She flags down a waiter with a quick wave, effectively ending the conversation, and orders an espresso martini, which has me shaking my head in amusement.

With a nudge to my elbow, she gives me a teasing glare. "Don't even start, Lucas. There are way worse things to be addicted to than coffee. You know, drugs, cigarettes, porn."

"True," I concede with a chuckle. "I can't drink coffee past two p.m., or my sleep schedule is fucked."

"I'm a night owl, anyway," she says with a shrug. "I've always found it weird that coffee makes you more awake and active, but the whole point of coffee shops is to help you slow down and relax."

When Charlotte's drink appears in front of her, she takes a sip. The foam top leaves a small Charlie Chaplin mustache over her lips, and when she uses the tip of her tongue to wipe it off, I'm thankful as fuck to be sitting so no one can see the semi that move gives me.

"Good first race weekend?" she asks, completely oblivious to the problem in my pants.

I take a large sip of my drink to distract myself. "Mm-hmm. Strong start, minus the shit show of Thursday's press conference."

Blake stonewalled Satin Satan, refusing to answer any of her questions, and Theo, who's usually happy-go-lucky in interviews, was combative when asked about his relationship with his old team principal. It was as if neither remembered a thing they learned during the extensive media training we've all been through. I ended up answering the majority of the questions, which is fine, though I've never craved the spotlight like many drivers. I despise the pressure to say or do the right thing. I'm here to race. That's it.

Charlotte nods, but her eyes dart to the side. "Yep. That was something, all right."

"Can't believe the two Ithaca drivers almost came to blows," I lie, testing a theory. "Especially over a woman."

Her eyes widen, and she shakes her head so fast I worry she'll give herself a headache. "Oh, that was wild. But you know what they say: boys will be boys."

Brow cocked, I stare her down. "What's even more wild is that the fight never happened."

"Well—" She pauses. "Shit."

I chuckle, my chest warming at her adorable reaction. "What's shit is your poker face, Roo."

"A for effort, though, right?" Wincing, she angles forward, sending a wave of her honeysuckle- and summer-smelling perfume my way. "Can you keep a secret?"

For her? There's no question. "Scout's honor."

"You were a boy scout?" she queries, her voice skeptical.

"Yep." I dip my chin. "I even have the merit badges to prove it."

"Huh." She tilts her head to the side, her attention licking over me like flames. "I wouldn't have pegged you as one."

"Why not?"

She waves a hand in front of my body. "Don't get me wrong, the tattoos and rings and such are hot, but they don't exactly scream wilderness life skills, ya know? They give off more *Sons of Anarchy* than *Survivor* vibes."

A hearty laugh bursts out of me as I toy with the sterling silver ring on my thumb. "You think I look like a biker?"

"Not a biker, per se, but you definitely exude a bad-boy-bad-arse aura. You've got the whole *look at me the wrong way and I'll snap your neck* thing going on."

I snort. "I donate to charity and recycle, Char. I'm hardly badass. My bar mitzvah theme was *Star Wars*, for fuck's sake."

She wiggles her eyebrows. "Was Princess Leia your first crush?"

"Maybe," I say with a wink. There's no way in hell I'd admit that Princess Fiona from *Shrek* was actually my first crush. In her human form, not her ogre form, thank you very much. "So what secret am I keeping?"

Peering over her shoulder to make sure Theo's still engrossed in conversation with Blake, she admits, "I wasn't at the press conference."

"Yeah, I figured that out, Roo. I'm just not sure why it's a big deal."

"It was Theo's first big interview as an AlphaVite driver," she says with guilt tainting her words. "He was nervous and asked me to stick around for it."

Despite my surprise, I keep my features schooled. Theo hasn't mentioned his nerves to me, and the guy's MO is oversharing.

"And that was the plan," Charlotte continues. "But my blood sugar started to drop. I usually keep glucose tablets or a bar in my bag, but I switched purses at the last minute and forgot to swap those out, I guess." She swipes at a rogue piece of hair. "So I power walked to the paddock—because running is for marathons and being chased by serial killers—and on my way there, I ran into that photographer bloke. The one who takes really good paddock photos."

"Kyle," I confirm with a nod.

"Right. Kyle. So I introduced myself to him and asked if

he'd take a picture of me. Not with his professional camera, obviously, but with my phone." She inhales a deep breath. "But I wasn't about to let the neon VIP lanyard ruin my photo op, so I took it off and then totally forgot I'd set it on the ground. Security wouldn't let me back into the media room after I found a snack, and I couldn't find my original lanyard, so I had to get a new one. By the time I finished with that, the press conference was wrapping up."

I take a sip of my whiskey to hide my grin. "Sounds like quite the adventure."

She huffs out a sigh. "Yeah, but I feel guilty. Theo—"

"What are we gossiping about?" the man himself interrupts as he flags down the bartender. "Blake ditched me to find Ella."

"I'm not surprised," Charlotte says with an innocent smile. "She's prettier than you."

"Ha." Theo nudges her with his elbow. "So what's the tea? Have people been talking about how good I look in my blue driving suit? Have they noticed the way it brings out my eyes? Or were they discussing how Lucas accidentally left his fly unbuttoned at the event last night and didn't notice until a photographer told him?"

I'm going to throat punch him.

"We most definitely were not talking about that," I say, exasperation gnawing at me. "Thanks for bringing it up."

"What are friends for if not reminding you of moments you wish you could forget?"

"We were talking about how I met Mitchell at the race," Charlotte says easily. "I swear his height's the eighth wonder of the world."

I smirk. "He did say you were impressed by his… climbability."

Mitchell's not a dick, but he also doesn't give much time to people who don't bring value to my career. Sounds shitty, but there's a reason he's good at his job. Charlotte can't secure a sponsorship deal for me or help me train, but she sure as hell can win just about anyone over. Her dimpled smile is sweet and her eyes are sunshine on a rainy day. Not to mention, she's got an aura that gives an instant sense of familiarity, as though she's a lifelong friend, even to those who've just met her. It's disarming but charming all the same.

"Oh," Theo says with a frown. "Definitely thought it'd be something juicier."

The last thing I need is to keep secrets from Theo, but I simply take a sip of my drink and shrug.

FIVE
CHARLOTTE

"ARE YOU EVEN LISTENING TO ME?" Theo asks through a mouthful of food. It's a wonder he can talk, since he's shoveling eggs into his mouth like it's a competition.

"No." I rub my eyes, careful not to ruin my makeup. "As I've already told you, I need more coffee before I can listen to you."

Lucas looks up from his phone and chuckles but leaves it at that. It's too early for conversation for everyone but Theo. It took a plane, a train, and an automobile to get to the race in Japan, and jet lag is kicking my arse. Considering I can barely form a coherent thought, let alone sentence, I have no idea how they'll handle being interviewed in less than an hour.

"I thought you were being sarcastic." He forks another bite of his omelet. It's so loaded with veggies that it could probably qualify as a garden. Access to a private chef—who makes preapproved meals for the drivers, each one meticulously planned out by their performance coaches—is a major perk and one that I'm definitely taking advantage of.

I swallow back most of my crankiness. "I don't joke about coffee."

Especially not at six fucking a.m.

He shrugs. "What are you doing today?"

"Sightseeing," I say vaguely with a dismissive wave. "Touristy things."

"Wow. Spare me the details, why dontcha?"

I take another sip of my coffee. "You know me, Theodore. I'll figure it out."

"Yeah, because that's worked out so well for you in the past," he teases.

Regardless of the lighthearted tone, the words still bring my insecurities to the surface. Making and following a plan has never been my forte. Hell, I changed majors three times and took nearly five years to graduate from college. I'm rarely obstinate or contrary. Planning has just never been one of my strengths.

"I'm jealous," Lucas says, his voice raspy from sleep. "I swear every minute of our day is planned for us. It's got to be nice to explore without any agenda."

"To each their own, I guess," Theo says to his friend before zeroing in on me. "Will you share your location with me so I know where you are?"

Oh, hell no. There is no way I'll allow Theo access to my whereabouts at all times. He already takes "big brother" way too far. Being nine years older than me, he already thinks he has a say in what I do, even though we haven't lived in the same city, let alone house, full time since I was five years old.

"You had my location, but not hers?" Lucas straightens, his lips pressing into a white slash. "What the fuck, Walker?"

"Why did you say *had* instead of *have*?" Theo gasps and drops his fork. "Did you remove me as a follower?"

"Yup," Lucas replies, head high and unremorseful. "I have no interest in listening to your thoughts on where and how I spend my time."

Sipping my coffee, I study both men. Lucas usually has the

patience of a saint when it comes to my brother, so watching them bicker is pure entertainment for me. They go back and forth for another minute before I step in and say, "Mum has my location. You don't need it, too, Theodore."

"What's Mum going to do if there's a dire emergency? She's a ten-hour flight away."

He has a point. Not that I'll admit it. That'll only fuel the flames. My brother's overprotective intentions may come from a good place, but fuck if they aren't intrusive at times.

An idea forms in my mind, and nerves skitter through me. Bouncing my legs beneath the table, I blurt out, "Um… I'll share my location with Lucas."

The second the words are out, I wish I could suck them back in. Talk about intrusive. *Damn*. Why would Lucas want my location? He may like me, but in the grand scheme of things, I'm just Theo's younger sister, a fact his manager aptly pointed out. I open my mouth, scrambling to come up with a way to backtrack, but before I can, Lucas simply shrugs.

"Sure," he agrees. "That way if Theo needs to know where you are, he can ask me rather than stalk you."

"I wasn't stalking you, Adler," Theo says with what I'm sure he thinks is an intimidating scowl. "Sorry for being a caring friend who wants what's best for you."

Usually, I'd be nosy as hell and try to get to the bottom of their little bromantic lovers' quarrel, but it's too early for sleuthing, and it's better that I leave while Theo's attention is set on something other than me.

Standing, I swallow the final dregs of my coffee, savoring the bittersweet flavor. "It's been lovely, gentleman, but I'm off. People to see, things to do, and all that."

"You're not going to wish us luck at practice?" Lucas asks with a playful smirk, fingers drumming against the table.

Shaking my head, I wink. "That implies I think you need it."

• • • •

I EXPLORE Suzuka for a grand total of forty-three minutes before I end up on a train to Osaka. I blame the tourists I met in line at a local café. Yes, I headed straight from breakfast to a nearby café. One cup of coffee wasn't going to cut it. I was simply minding my own business, waiting to order, when I overheard the couple behind me chatting about their recent day trip. *It's not eavesdropping if they're talking that loudly.* I shifted so I could hear better, and as I did, I caught sight of the woman's pants. I gasped like Taylor Swift had dropped an Easter egg about her next album because the pants were to die for. Not literally, but I'd consider selling a kidney for them. *I only need one kidney to survive, right?* The cargo pants embroidered with blooming cherry blossoms were a piece of art. So, coffee in hand, I headed for the train station, and before I arrived, I already knew how I wanted to style them.

The train ride to Osaka gives me ample time to research the top need-to-see attractions for tourists, so by the time I arrive, I have a general idea of how I want to spend the day.

Throughout the labyrinth of alleyways outside the station, vendors sell their wares from colorful stalls. Brightly decorated bicycles weave through the crowds, and tourists gawk and take photos of the vibrant street art that adorns every available surface. The air is alive with the savory aroma of street food—something a vendor calls *takoyaki*. Octopus isn't my favorite type of seafood, but fried in a dumpling and covered in sauce? I can get behind that.

My first stop is obviously the boutique where the woman at the coffee shop purchased her pants. As I enter, I'm greeted with a wave of soft sandalwood incense and upbeat music. The interior is a study in contrast. Rustic wooden shelves adorned with handcrafted ceramics and pottery line the walls, along with a curated selection of contemporary streetwear brands.

It only takes a moment to spot the linen cherry blossom pants—and about ten other pieces I'd love to add to my closet (or suitcase, whatever). I waste no time loading my arms with potential purchases. I've never been good with numbers, but if what I know about the exchange rate from a Japanese yen to an Australian dollar is correct, these are a damn good deal.

Adjacent to the modern fashion section is an alcove housing a collection of silk kimonos in rich jewel tones. They hang delicately from wooden stands to highlight the intricate patterns and embroidery so there's no mistaking the artistry that went into each one. These aren't mass-produced fast-fashion kimonos, but individually handcrafted. Drawn to them, I brush my fingers against the rustle of the silk. It's incredible. This kind of work is tedious and time-consuming. I have a few rough spots on my fingers from the needle pricks I accumulated when I learned how to sew, thanks to my habit of losing thimbles.

I leave the store with the pants I came for, two kimonos, a new skirt, and directions to a local vintage store. As I stroll along the street, taking in the sights and smells, my phone rings in my purse. When I pull it out and see that it's my mum, I can't help but smile. The flight time between Australia and Japan may be long, but the time difference itself is only an hour.

"Hi, Mum," I answer, eager to tell her about my finds. "You'll never guess what I just bought. Okay, maybe you can, but I'm impatient, so don't bother. I found these beautiful handcrafted kimonos in a store in Osaka, so I bought one for each of us. Yours is emerald, with patchwork designs and embroidered butterflies that represent hope. I think. It may be good luck. I'll have to look it up later. The shopkeeper told me about this vintage shop nearby, and I'm headed there now."

"Well, hello to you, too, Charlotte," she says, her tone

amused. While Theo's always called me Lottie, my mom never has. "Did you say you were in Osaka?"

"Yes."

"Isn't the race in Suzuka?"

"Also yes."

A brief moment of silence passes before she bursts out laughing. My mom has one of those ridiculously contagious laughs that has me grinning like an idiot as I continue my trek. "You always did have an adventurous spirit."

I snort. "That's one way to put it."

"Thank you for thinking of me, honey. I'm sure the kimono is beautiful," she says, her voice warming me from thousands of miles away. "Where are you off to now?"

"A vintage store."

"Oh," she practically squeals. "I'm sure that'll be a treasure trove. I still wear that jumper you reworked for me and get compliments on it all the time."

"Mum, no," I groan, a wave of embarrassment washing over me. "It should be illegal for you to leave the house in that."

Growing up, I constantly had bolts of fabric, sketches, and sewing equipment cluttered around the house. I've always loved taking vintage clothing items and accessories and turning them into new and unique pieces. Over the years, I've had many hobbies, from scrapbooking to gardening to photography, but fashion design has always been my true passion. I planned to study it at university, but then my dad passed, and I chose to stay close to home, attending a university where the nearest fashion-adjacent degree was photography.

The jumper my mum's referring to—if it can even be called that—was one of the first things I upcycled, and it shows. The stitching on the thrifted dress I reworked into a cardigan is lopsided, the pattern atrocious. It resembles a garment created from spare linens sometime in the 1800s.

"It's beautiful," she argues in a tone that brooks no argument. "I'm allowed to be proud of you, and there's nothing you can do about it."

It's both endearing and exasperating, how she sees the value in the smallest aspects of my life. "Fine," I say with a sigh. "But don't be surprised if someone asks you to churn their butter the next time you wear it."

We catch up for the rest of my walk, and I end the call with a promise to send her a photo of the kimono when I'm back in my hotel room. If I hadn't been looking for the vintage shop, I probably would have passed right by it. The storefront is plain, and the wooden door opens with the faint jingle of a bell.

Grinning, I take in the highly curated shelves and racks. I love a good treasure hunt, but the lack of disorganized piles of clothing and bins filled with nondescript items is a relief. As I spot a pair of pre-loved vintage Chanel trousers, I know I need to check the train times again because I won't be leaving anytime soon.

SIX
LUCAS

FORMULA 1 IS one of the few sports where, in the offseason, a driver can't train in a traditional sense. Sure, we work on endurance and strength and use simulators to prepare, but as far as actually being in the car? That's reserved for race weekends. Before qualifying and the actual race, we're given three free practices to test and refine the car setup and familiarize ourselves and find a rhythm with the track. That means I have to make each moment I'm in the car count.

The Suzuka circuit is shaped like a figure eight, though there are several smaller curves throughout. The challenge makes it a driver favorite. My heart pounds as my engine roars and I launch into the straight, the rush of acceleration pushing me back into my seat. As I approach the first turn, I brake, and the weight of the car shifts, the tires biting into the asphalt. With practiced finesse, I navigate the curves marking sector one. My instincts guide me as I thread the needle through fast, sweeping corners.

With each lap, the rhythm of the track becomes second nature, my movements fluid and instinctual. The feeling of commanding such a powerful machine with precision and finesse is unparalleled. Sometimes I wonder if pursuing my dream instead of doing normal teenage stuff like sneaking girls into my room and applying to college was the right choice, but the moment I put on my helmet and grip the wheel with my glove-clad hands, any second-guessing ends. The freedom that engulfs me as I push the limits of what's possible on the track makes everything I gave up worth it.

David waits at the entrance of the pit garage with his signature clipboard in his hands as I pull myself out of the car after the hour-long practice.

"Great lap time, Adler," he says as a nearby team member tosses me a water bottle. "Only three-tenths of a second behind Hollis."

I take a long sip, then tug off my helmet and nod. "Not too bad."

Blake's a fucking speed demon on the track. I may be a great driver, but Blake's on a whole other plane. If he wasn't one of my closest friends, I'd probably hate him a little.

Before leaving the track, the team meets to debrief; the engineers have access to the data from my car, but my feedback and feelings about how the car reacted to each portion of the track are what give significance to the numbers. With that information, the engineers can refine and enhance the car's performance for the next practice.

"Wanna grab dinner and drinks with Martin, Christopher, and me?" Theo asks on our way back to the hotel. "Char's running late, per usual, so we have an extra spot."

I like Theo's manager and performance coach, but a night out on the town with that trio sounds exhausting.

"Thanks for the invite, but I need a low-key night," I reply, yawning for emphasis. "I'm beat."

"No dramas," Theo slaps me on the back. "I'll text you when I'm back. I've been practicing my Madden skills and think I'm finally ready to kick your arse."

Nudging him in the ribs, I joke, "So says the guy who doesn't know the difference between a tight end and a wide receiver."

He rolls his eyes at me, but he's wearing a grin all the same. "Whatever."

Back in my hotel room, I luxuriate under the heavy pressure of the shower spray. The pounding water relaxes some of the tension that developed in my upper back during practice. Even with the hours I put into training, the physical exertion of driving a car at high speeds takes a toll on my body.

When the water temperature dips to lukewarm, I force myself to shut it off. As I dry off, I consider texting Blake to see what he and Ella are doing for dinner, but I quickly nix the idea. Third-wheeling doesn't sound particularly enticing tonight. I love them as individuals and as a couple, and they never make me feel unwelcome or inconvenient, but, as strange as it sounds, being alone feels less lonely than being the token single friend with a couple.

Maybe it's the adrenaline still rushing through my body from practice or the image of Charlotte in that floral sundress this morning that I can't shake loose—the one that made her look like the goddamn goddess of spring—or maybe it's because I know she doesn't have dinner plans. Regardless of the reason, I decide to shoot her a text. We've had plenty of meals together over the years. The only difference tonight is that Theo won't be there.

LUCAS ADLER

> Hey. Want to grab dinner? No worries if not, but if you're interested, there's a spot near the hotel that has great reviews online.

THE MOMENT after I hit Send, I rub my brow and let out a

groan. What is it about Charlotte that turns me into a fumbling, bumbling teenager?

Thankfully, her response is nearly immediate.

CHARLOTTE WALKER
> Yes! Definitely.
>
> My blood sugar's low, so I'm eating sweets I bought from a street vendor, but I should be ready to eat dinner by the time I get back to the city.
>
> Should be about forty (ish) minutes.
>
> Does that work?

TYPICALLY, receiving multiple texts in a row irritates me, but it's cute when Charlotte does it. She texts like she talks: a full stream of consciousness. I chuckle at her messages, though when I reread the phrase "back to the city," the sound dies off.

LUCAS ADLER
> Are you not in Suzuka?

CHARLOTTE WALKER
> I took a detour.
>
> Of about a hundred and one miles.

LUCAS ADLER
> Lol. No wonder you didn't want Theo to have your location.

CHARLOTTE WALKER

I didn't even think about that... oops.

I have to change trains now, so I'll see you in a bit! 😊

I KILL time watching highlight clips of the Michigan v. UCLA March Madness game from yesterday before heading down to the lobby. It's been an hour since we made plans, yet the lobby's empty, minus a group of guys checking in at the front desk. I'm not the least bit surprised. Charlotte may have said forty minutes, but I've never known her to be on time.

I'm settling into a plush chair tucked off to the side when my oldest brother, Grayson, calls. Whether he's calling to catch up or to talk business is always a crapshoot. He's a lawyer and handles all my negotiations and contracts, so it's possible he's calling about that, but my spidey senses tingle as I study his name on the screen, considering we spoke about both yesterday.

Curious, I hit Accept on the call. "Hey, man."

"Hey, little bro," Grayson greets me with a yawn.

"You know, that's not the personal greeting you think it is, considering you have four little bros."

He snorts out a chuckle. "Sorry. Hey, Lucas. That better?"

"Yep, now I feel loved," I confirm. "How's everything? It's what, six a.m. for you?"

"Mm-hmm. Madison woke us up an hour ago, ready for breakfast."

He's the only Adler brother with a kid, although it's a wonder Finn hasn't gotten anyone pregnant yet.

"At least Mads is cute."

A muffled *humph* echoes through the phone. "That she is. Looks more like her mom every day."

"So what's going on? Always happy to hear from you, but I feel like you're not calling to tell me about pancakes."

He exhales, causing a staticky sound that has me pulling the phone away from my ear. "Jesse and Kylie broke up."

My breath whooshes out of me when the words register. It's a good thing I'm already sitting. My ass would be flat on the floor if I wasn't. I thought I'd be punching the air the day they broke up, but instead of basking in the vindication of karma bitch-slapping him, I'm pissed. My brain won't stop shouting "was it worth it?" Maybe it's fucked up, but the idea that he'd damage our relationship in order to get his happily ever after is far more acceptable than knowing he was willing to cause the strife he did over a connection that didn't even last.

"You there?" Grayson asks.

"Yeah," I reply. "Sorry, I'm just surprised. Was it mutual?"

My brother sighs, the sound scarily similar to the sound our dad makes when he's wondering how mad my mom will be if he smacks one of us upside the head for doing something stupid. "You could call him and ask for the details, you know."

My gut twists. "You called me with this news, remember?"

"If you just talked to him—"

"Can we not do this right now, Gray?" I bite out more harshly than I should.

I've kept what happened to myself, never bad-mouthing Jesse or doing anything that could strain his interactions with our brothers. Instead of causing a major family rift, I quietly removed myself from the situation, letting the cracks in our once-close relationship grow big enough to be considered a natural disaster.

"Okay, okay," Grayson says. "Sorry. He came over for dinner last night and seemed upset. He's still your brother, even if you two aren't close anymore."

I massage my forehead with my free hand, taking a

moment to collect my thoughts, but am disrupted by a commotion in the lobby.

Shaking my head and chuckling, I watch as Charlotte wrangles herself through the revolving door, shopping bags dangling off her arms like Christmas ornaments.

She always did know how to make an entrance.

She scans the open lobby for a moment before she finds me. When she does, her eyes light up in a way that feels like a sucker punch.

I lift my hand and stand, then use her arrival as an excuse to end the call with my brother.

"Hi," Charlotte says as she approaches, nearly out of breath. "I'm so sorry I'm late. I got on the wrong transfer train, and I couldn't text you because my phone died, which, yes, is really stupid and dangerous. But in my defense, I wasn't planning on venturing outside Suzuka. I wrote out the directions on my arm once I realized my phone was dying, but still. At least I had my glucose meter and test strips on me. But I should've brought my portable charger—"

"Roo." I gently lift two bags from her arms. "It's fine. Apology accepted. I haven't been waiting long, and the extra time gave me a chance to catch up with my brother."

Granted, the phone call was anything but fun, but there's no need to make her feel worse.

"Oh, okay, good." She puffs out a relieved breath. "Which brother? You have enough of them to form a rugby team."

I chuckle. While it's not technically true, we could start a basketball team. "Grayson."

"He's the oldest, his wife is named Jaclyn, and he's Madison's dad," she says, as if reciting it from a notecard.

"Yep," I confirm, my chest expanding with satisfaction and a bit of surprise that she remembers. "Instead of going out, why don't I pick up food while you drop off your bags and charge your phone? We can meet at my suite to watch a movie and chill instead."

Chill instead? Holy shit, get it together, man.

"Are you sure that's okay?" she asks, nibbling on her lip.

Relieved she didn't pick up on my inadvertent invitation to Netflix and chill, I scratch at the back of my neck and quickly reply, "I wouldn't have suggested this if I wasn't on board."

"Okay, then let's do that," she says, readjusting the bags on her arms. "I love this dress—it's from this boutique in Sydney—but I have to wear a strapless bra with it, and they're the absolute worst. I don't know what the hell I was thinking when I put it on this morning. Well, I mean, I do, but"—she straightens, her eyes going wide—"oh, I should clarify that I will be putting on a bra for dinner, just a different one. One that won't try to cut off my circulation or strangle me. If I go around with the girls unsupported, I'll be at risk of knocking someone out. Death by D-cups, can you imagine?"

My lungs seize, and I choke on air. *Oh, for fuck's sake.* It's hard to miss how well-endowed Charlotte is in the chest department, but I didn't need to know her bra size. That's catnip to a breast guy like me.

"Anyway, what are you thinking for dinner?" she continues as if she hasn't just casually talked about her tits for an entire minute. "Sushi? Ramen?"

Benjamin, my performance coach, would be banging his head against a wall if he knew I wasn't going to eat the grilled mackerel, baked potato, spinach salad, and yogurt topped with mixed berries that he had sent up to my room when I told him I was staying in.

Now that I can breathe again, I pull my head out of my ass long enough to ask, "Anything you're craving or want in particular? I'm open to whatever."

"You can surprise me," she says. "Wait, no," she adds in a rush. "I don't know why I said that. I do love surprises, don't get me wrong, but I hate shrimp. I think I may be allergic to it since my throat gets kind of scratchy when I eat it. Sort of like I just did four hours of karaoke. So don't surprise me with shrimp, please. Other than that, everything's fair game."

"No shrimp," I repeat, biting back a laugh. "Copy that."

"Oh, oops. One more thing. I love soy sauce, so feel free to get a lot of that. Like whatever you'd usually get, double that, and then add some more."

"Anything else?"

Her cheeks flush the prettiest shade of pink. "Um... please and thank you?"

The grin that spreads across my face stays there all the way to the restaurant and then back to the hotel.

SEVEN
LUCAS

THE PLAN WAS for me to text Charlotte once I returned with the food. I'm tidy by nature—it comes with the territory for a person who lives out of a suitcase for half the year—but I want to do a last-minute sweep of my room, put the toilet seat down, that kind of thing, before Charlotte comes over. That plan crumbles to dust, though, the moment I step off the elevator on the sixth floor, three bags of food in hand, and find her standing outside my suite, wearing a gray sweatsuit and holding a massive lilac-colored stainless-steel water bottle.

I can count on one hand the number of times I've seen her wear sweats, and I like that she feels comfortable enough to relax around me—in a bra, of course. What worries me is that she looks just as stunning in loungewear and gym shoes as she does in a dress and heels.

"Hey," I call out, going for chill, despite how wound up the sight of her makes me.

She gives me a tiny wave, her lips tipping up on one side. "Hi. I felt bad about being late and wanted to make sure you didn't have to wait on me again, so I sweet-talked the concierge into giving me your room number."

Ahh. It's worrisome that the staff so easily gave out my information, especially because I've dealt with stalkerish fans before, but Charlotte has that kind of effect on people, so I suppose it doesn't surprise me.

"It's really not a big deal, Roo," I reassure her as I tap my key card to the sensor on the door.

"No, it is," she insists, shifting her weight from one foot to the other beside me. "A lot of people would've bailed, but you didn't."

"I knew you'd show eventually," I say, holding the door open with one arm and motioning her to step inside. "And some things are worth the wait."

As she passes me, I silently chide myself for that statement with a shake of my head. Then I follow her in. It's a beautiful hotel, but then again, almost all of our accommodations during the season are five stars. I may only sleep and shower in my hotel room, but AlphaVite makes sure we're treated like royalty. Eating in the fancy kitchen seems too formal, so I move the vase of welcome flowers off the coffee table in the living room and set the food down there.

I picked up a little bit of a lot, including sushi and sashimi, a few skewers of yakitori, a variety of soups and ramen, a couple of soba noodle dishes, and mushroom tempura. As we sit on the overstuffed oddly patterned couch, Charlotte slips off her hoodie. Beneath it, she's wearing a black shirt printed with a collage of images featuring Shrek—yes, the green ogre who's married to my childhood crush, Princess Fiona—with the phrase *I'm Totally Swamped* written in the center.

"What?" Brow creased and lips turned down, she crosses her arms over her chest. "I'm wearing a bra, Lucas. I told you I would."

Head tossed back, I bark out a laugh. "No, it's not that. I just never envisioned you wearing a *Shrek* shirt."

"Oh." She drops her arms to her sides and grins, her blue

eyes dancing. "It's great, isn't it? I like to sleep in punny shirts. I have a whole collection of them. My friend got this one for me a few years ago."

Opening up a container of egg drop soup, I hum. "I never knew that."

"Duh. It'd be kind of weird for you to know what I wear to bed, wouldn't it?" she jokes, opening up another to-go box.

Yup, I walked right into that one.

"I thrifted one today that says *my favorite type of men is ramen.*"

As we eat, Charlotte fills me in on her day in Osaka. She raves about the streets filled with trendy boutiques and quirky souvenir shops, the bustling market, and the neon-lit signs mixed in with the traditional architecture.

As she goes on, I'm hit with conflicting emotions. She's so animated and entertaining, and that makes it hard not to feel the excitement that emanates from her. But there's an underlying disquiet there, too, because I genuinely can't remember the last time I said "fuck it" and did whatever I wanted for the day. No plan, no destination, no real purpose. Every aspect of my life is so strictly regimented, from workout sessions to sponsorship commitments to meetings with AlphaVite, that when I do have a second to myself, all I want to do is take a nap. It's lame, but that's what happens when a person hits thirty.

"Damn," I mutter. "I think you've seen more of Japan in a day than I've seen in all the years I've been coming here."

Head tilted, Charlotte swipes a salmon avocado roll from the container in front of me and drowns it in soy sauce. "Really?"

"Yeah," I admit, rubbing the back of my neck. "I've been racing competitively since I was a kid. I'm grateful for the opportunities it's given me, and I've been all around the world, but truth be told, I rarely do much more than just race."

"And party," she teases, her dimples making an appearance.

I grunt in response. She's not wrong. I spent a large chunk of my twenties at fancy parties in foreign cities. I don't regret the fun I had with my friends, but my priorities have shifted since then, thank fuck. That shit was exhausting.

"That, too," I admit, lowering my attention to the yakitori in front of me. "I'm realizing I probably missed out on a lot."

"You're thirty-one, not geriatric." She gives me a lopsided smile. "You've got time. And I'd argue that you're in a better position than I am."

"How's that?"

"I'm traveling and exploring because I don't know what else to do," she says, her smile fading. "I'm lucky that I can afford to do it, of course, but it's not as fulfilling as it seems. Not when I'm trying to figure out what to do with my life. But you've known that you wanted to drive professionally since you were how old? Five? Six?"

"Six," I confirm. "I had a car-themed birthday party, and this kid, Robby Anderson—hate that prick, by the way—kept saying that *Hot Wheels* were lame in comparison to Formula 1 cars."

"What a dick," Charlotte mutters.

"Oh, he definitely was." *And still is.* "Anyway, I made my mom take me to the library the next day so I could research Formula 1."

"The library?" Charlotte asks, brows raised.

"I grew up in the '90s, Roo. We didn't have Google." I chuckle. "My mom checked out a few books for me, and I became obsessed. I hid them so she couldn't return them to the library, then ended up grounded for being irresponsible with other people's property." Shrugging, I hover my chopsticks over the take-out buffet in front of us. "But it was worth it."

Charlotte sips from her bottle of water and smiles. "I wanted to be a tooth when I was a kid."

I smile before I process her statement, but when I do, I can't help but scoff. "A *tooth*?"

"Yep."

"Like a tooth in someone's mouth?"

"Unless there's another type of tooth I'm unaware of," she quips. "And don't ask me why. I couldn't tell you. When I was about eight or nine, my life goals changed, and I wanted to be one of those dogs that sniff out contraband at the airport. I don't know whether that's better or worse."

Laughter bubbles out of me. *Damn, this woman is hilarious.* "Hey, no shame in being an imaginative child."

"Moral of the story is you're living your dream." She absently wraps a curl around her finger. "I'm pretty jealous of that. I'm glad I'm not someone's molar or incisor, but you know what I mean."

If I'm living my dream, then why does my world feel so incomplete?

A knock on the door interrupts that thought. Frowning, I look at Charlotte, whose expression is just as perplexed.

"Maybe the concierge gave your room number out to someone else," she suggests, a twinkle in her eye.

"If they did, this place is getting a horrible Yelp review," I mutter as I stand.

When I open the door, I find another blue-eyed Australian, although this one doesn't have dimples. Theo pushes past me —because he doesn't do polite things like wait until he's invited inside—but stops dead in his tracks when he catches sight of his sister. "What are you doing here, Lottie?"

"Hi, Theodore." She gives him a small, ridiculously cute wave. "How was dinner?"

"What are you doing in Lucas's hotel room?" he repeats, completely ignoring her question. There's no malice in his tone, just genuine confusion.

"Seducing him," Charlotte says with a straight face. "Obviously."

We all know she's fucking with him. Even so, Theo's face turns a shade of red that I'm 99.9 percent sure is not healthy.

"No." He slashes his hand through the air. "Absolutely not."

"You can't fight the facts, big bro." She straightens, her shoulders pulled back and her chin high. "Why do you think we're eating sushi? The omega-3 fatty acids in these salmon rolls help in the production of sex hormones and are linked to more intense orgasms." Turning to me, she says, "I spend a lot of time on Google. Unlike your ancient arse, it's been around since I was a kid."

I press my lips together to hold back a laugh. "Noted."

"Please never say the words *orgasm* or *sex hormones* in my presence again," Theo begs. "Or Lucas's."

"Your girlfriend's mum is a sex therapist who gifted you a cock ring." Charlotte points her chopsticks at him, one brow arched. "I highly doubt me saying org—"

"Lottie," he practically growls, clenching his fists at his sides. "So help me God, if you don't stop talking in the next two seconds, I'm going to curl into the fetal position and start screaming bloody murder."

That threat has me cringing. If there's one thing Theo does well, it's drama.

With a deep breath in, then back out again, I say, "I don't want my neighbors to file a noise complaint."

Charlotte winks. "Unless it's from a very loud orgas—"

With his head tipped back, Theo lets out a battle cry worthy of a Norse Viking. *Fucking hell.* There's no way the guests next door aren't calling the front desk. Or security. I snatch a pillow off the couch and toss it at him.

"I think someone's at the door," Charlotte tells me, an amused glint in her eyes.

Turning away from the yodeling idiot, I eye the suite's door and tilt my head, listening. Sure enough, I notice the knocking.

I can tell it's Blake by the knock alone. It's always the same: three short taps, a pause, and then an aggressive bang with the heel of his palm.

Theo pulls his shoulders back and grins. "Blakey Blake is here."

Eyes closed, I massage my temples. "You do know you can't invite people to *my* hotel suite, right? That's not how hospitality works."

Ignoring me, he throws the door open, welcoming Blake in like this is his room instead of mine. "'Ello, Blake. You're just in time."

"In time for what?" Blake asks, taking in the details of the room. "Oh. Hi, Charlotte. What are you doing here?"

From the couch, she shrugs. "Trying to seduce Lucas with sushi."

His eyes widen for an instant, but then he merely shrugs like this is nothing out of the ordinary. "Okay."

"Okay?" Theo spits out. "You're *okay* with that?"

"Calm down, she's kidding." I shoot Charlotte a chastising look.

She grins back at me like the cat that got the cream. Sure, it's funny to see Theo riled up, but she's not the one he'll beat the shit out of.

"I don't really know how seduction via sushi works, mate," Blake says. "Can we focus on the nine-nine-nine text you sent me? What's the emergency?"

"Lucas," Theo replies. "He's upset."

My jaw drops, and I puff out a deep breath. "If I'm upset, it's only because you're giving me a headache with your yelling."

Theo points his finger at me. "See? He's only feisty when he's upset."

Charlotte giggles, and Blake curses under his breath. I stay quiet. I'm honestly not sure how to approach this situation since I don't know what in the actual fuck is going on.

"Okay, so it's a Theo emergency, not a real emergency," Blake notes, some of the tension leaving his shoulders.

"My emergencies are real emergencies," Theo counters, crossing his arms over his chest. "And Lucas being upset over his ex *is* an emergency. Unless you want a repeat of—"

"Theo," I bite out. The last thing I want is to have this conversation in front of Charlotte. I'm not exactly proud of how I handled the situation. I'm used to being the peacemaker, not the shit-starter, and boy oh boy, did I start a lot of shit when Jesse and Kylie started dating. I couldn't take my anger out on him since he was thousands of miles away, so I took it out on anyone and everyone in my proximity. The only positive is that I found boxing, which is now my favorite way to train.

"Grayson called me," Theo says. "Told me about the breakup and said you reacted poorly."

My stomach twists into a painful knot. *I'm going to kill my brother.* I've been racing against Theo and Blake since I was a kid, so they've known my family for years, and Theo has a bit of a case of hero worship for my oldest brother. The two of them text regularly, sometimes about rugby, and other times Theo asks Grayson random legal questions like "if my suitcase is identical to someone else's, and I accidentally take theirs, is it considered stealing?" I don't mind their friendship except when they talk about me as if I'm not an adult capable of communicating on my own behalf.

"Ah. I think this is my cue to head out," Charlotte says with a grimace. "Let you fellas have a boys' night."

"You don't have to leave, Roo. They—"

"It's okay." Giving me a small smile, she stands. "I'm getting tired, anyway." She nods at the canvas bag hanging from Theo's shoulder. "And Theo has his video game purse on."

I internally groan. I don't always mind playing video games with him, but he's a sore loser and a cocky winner, and I'm not in the mood for his antics.

"Satchel," he corrects her, his brows pulled down and his expression stern.

She tilts her head, an innocent gleam in her eyes. "That's what I said."

He *harrumphs*. "Whatever. I'll come check on you later, yeah?"

Charlotte opens her mouth like she wants to argue but sighs instead. "All right. Good night. Thanks again for dinner, Lucas."

The moment she leaves the suite, Blake spreads out on the couch. "Why are you checking on her later?"

Theo's already taking his Xbox out of his "satchel" so he can hook it up to the TV, but at the question, he stops. "Her blood sugar's high."

"What?" I bark, my stomach sinking. "How do you know?"

"When her levels are high, she gets super thirsty," he says, turning back to the task at hand. "She chugged about half a bottle of water in the few minutes since I got here."

Teeth gritted, I chastise myself. *Fuck. I should have noticed.* I didn't even know that was a sign her blood sugar was high. Or is it a symptom? I encouraged her to eat more since I ordered so much. Was that why it's too high? Did she not take the right amount of insulin?

"I didn't know that," I say, roughing a hand down my face. "Will you make me a list?"

"Of what?" Theo asks over his shoulder. "You already know what I want for my birthday."

Blake sighs up at the ceiling. Theo regularly sends us an updated list of items he wants for his birthday and/or holidays

—and yes, that includes Valentine's Day because it's "bromantic."

"No," I huff. "A list of signs that Charlotte's glucose levels are dropping or rising."

Turning to face me, Theo shakes his head. "It's a nice idea, but she won't like it. You know how, if a woman is cranky or moody, it's offensive to ask her if she's on her period? Watching for her symptoms is like that. You'll think she's tired because her blood sugar is low, when, in reality, she slept like shit or had an early morning wake-up call."

"That… makes a lot of sense," Blake says, taking the words right out of my mouth.

"I guess, but I'd still like to know." While I respect and understand his point, I still don't like being in the dark about something as important as her health.

Blake gives me a funny look, but rather than questioning me, he changes the subject, going with one far less enjoyable. "Were you going to mention Jesse and Kylie or simply keep it in the vault?"

I collapse into a plush armchair, the force of the move knocking the wind from me. "It's not a big deal."

He sits up and cocks a brow. "That doesn't answer my question."

"Which doesn't really matter since you know, regardless." I turn my attention to Theo. "It wasn't Grayson's place to tell you."

"I don't think he meant to." Theo frowns. "I called him because I wanted to chat about the Wallabies game, but he thought I was reaching out about that."

"He doesn't know that my issue with Jesse has anything to do with Kylie."

"Your brother's smart." Blake rolls his eyes. "If you think he hasn't figured it out by now, you're seriously underestimating him."

I puff out a slow breath. Dammit. He's right. He's probably pieced enough clues together to have a pretty good idea. *Fuck his Harvard law degree.*

"Can we not do this tonight? I appreciate you guys checking on me, but this is the last thing I want on my mind during a race weekend."

Blake gives me a slow nod. "Fair enough."

"Fine, let's talk about my sister instead," Theo says.

Well, fuck. Maybe Jesse was the safer topic.

"I should have brought this up earlier, but don't feel obligated to do dinner and shit just because we're related."

I blink at him, a little stunned. That was the last thing I expected Theo to say. I very rarely know what's going to come out of his mouth, but this time? I'm at a loss for words. If anything, I feel obligated to *not* spend time with Charlotte simply because she's related to Theo.

"Don't get me wrong," he continues, oblivious to my confusion. "I think it's cool that you guys get along and all, but I don't want her to be a distraction for you. She can be a lot sometimes, so don't feel like you have to spend time with her simply because she's my sister."

"It's not a problem, man." I sit forward and rest my forearms on the armrests of the chair. "I like Charlotte." *And there won't be a problem as long as he doesn't know how much I like her.*

"Me, too," Blake says with a smirk. "She's my favorite Walker, actually."

"If that changes, just give me a heads-up," Theo responds, ignoring Blake's jab. "Do you want to play *Madden* or *Call of Duty?* And if you don't put your all into playing, I'm going to be pissed, since I'm missing phone sex with my girlfriend to hang out with you."

And just like that, the mood shifts into one of brotherly banter and bullshit.

EIGHT
CHARLOTTE

A PRISON CELL has better lighting than Theo's suite does. At least I assume that's the case. I've never been to prison, but I imagine the lighting would be decent. If it weren't, the inmates could easily hide things and do sketchy stuff without being seen. I know that's what I'd do. For a motorhome that costs millions, AlphaVite dropped the ball on this. I'm surprised my brother hasn't complained, since he live-streams himself more than a beauty influencer does, and there's no way anyone can look good with shadows dancing across their face the way they do in here.

Good thing I've got a travel ring light. In a pinch, it works well as a flashlight. Crawling across Theo's room like it's an underground tunnel, I use the ring light to illuminate the space beneath his couch. All I find is ugly carpet. *Fuck*. Groaning, I stand and fan my face. The motorhome is air-conditioned, but even working nonstop like it is, it barely puts a dent in the São Paulo heat.

My VIP lanyard, wallet, and purse lay scattered on the desktop, but my phone is still nowhere to be found. It's not uncommon for me to misplace things, especially when I'm in a rush—which, honestly, is often—but rarely do I end up playing *Where's Waldo?* with my phone. I tend to keep track of it more than just about anything I own. And for a good reason. I can't survive without it. Not in the stereotypical, generational way of being addicted to social media and texting, but because my phone's a lifeline for me. Literally.

Despite my forgetful tendencies, I'm meticulous when it comes to my health. I've been a Type 1 Diabetic since I was four, and from a very young age, I've understood the importance of checking my blood sugar levels throughout the day. Even with my wireless pump and the small wearable glucose sensor on my arm that communicate with one another to adjust my insulin delivery, I still need to manually add doses when I eat and monitor my levels because the fluctuations in glucose can be rapid and unpredictable. And, of course, I have to use the app on my phone to do it.

Running a hand through my hair, I scan the room again. It has to be here. *Ugh*. Climbing onto Theo's couch—which isn't easy in a dress—I slip my hand between two cushions and run it along the length. While I don't find my phone, I do find an earring I thought I'd lost at the last race, which I'll consider a win.

"Am I interrupting something?" a feminine voice asks from behind me. "Because I can come back later."

Without turning, I know it's Ella. There are only two Americans in existence who would waltz into Theo's room without knocking. And since Ella's voice is feminine while Lucas's is raw, unadulterated sex, it's more than a little easy to distinguish between them. I quickly untangle myself from the awkward downward dog position I'm in. I may have a good arse, but no one needs to see it that up close and personal.

"Hi," I say, smiling. "I didn't hear you come in."

"Probably hard to hear when you've been muttering 'fuckity fuck' under your breath for the past minute," she says, her own smile only growing wider. "Which, by the way, is one of Theo's favorite phrases, too."

Chuckling, I swipe my hair out of my face. "Our mother would be happy to hear that."

Her laugh is light and easy. "Whatcha doing? Yoga?"

"Hell no." I shake my head hard enough to give myself whiplash. "Being left alone with my thoughts in silence? While sweating? That's my biggest nightmare." I click off my ring light. "I'm looking for my phone. I know it's here because I haven't left since I spoke with my mum thirty minutes ago. Well, I did pop out to go to the loo, but I already checked there, and unless I accidentally flushed it, it's not there."

Ella raises her brows and side-eyes the desk. "You mean the phone by your purse?"

I snap my head in that direction, and sure enough, the damn device is peeking out from under my purse. Oh my God. The tension in my chest loosens instantly. "If I wasn't worried your boyfriend would come for me, I'd totally kiss you right now."

Grinning, she shakes her head. "Any interest in watching quals from McAllister's rooftop? The view from there is incredible, and I've been surrounded by way too much testosterone today."

I eagerly agree. Not only am I desperate to get away from the criminal lighting of Theo's suite, but I love hanging out with Ella. She's easy to talk to and funny as hell. Plus, I respect how she's made a name for herself in such a male-dominated sport.

As we step outside, the Brazilian heat hits me hard. And by me, I mean my hair. For the most part, my curls behave well. I use enough fancy product to maintain a beachy-wave style most of the time, but when heat and humidity come into play in such a powerful way, it's every strand for itself. Not wanting to deal with the impending frizz, I flip my head down and wrangle my hair into a messy bun. Of course, that's when Lucas appears out of thin air like he's Harry fucking Houdini. With my hair secured, I snap back up, earning myself a major head rush.

"Hey," he says, the corners of his lips quirking up. *That fucking smile.* It's simple and sincere, which makes it all the more sinful. Like a warm hug from the sun after a month spent camped out in the Arctic. It's impossible not to want to bask in its glory while simultaneously stripping off every item of clothing.

Instead of greeting him with a *hey, hello*, or *hi*, I blurt out, "Did you ever have braces?"

Is it really any wonder that I'm single? Having a nonexistent filter is tough. I learned that lesson the hard way. Apparently, telling a man he reminds me of my grandpa isn't a compliment. Asking a surgeon what she wears under her scrubs is inappropriate. And inquiring about what hair color people who are bald put on their licenses is invasive. There's no winning.

Lips parted, he rubs the nape of his neck. "Um, yeah... when I was nine. Why?"

"You've got good teeth," I continue. The train has left the station at full speed. "I bet you could charm a leprechaun out of a pot of gold if you flashed him your pearly whites."

I don't comment on how leprechauns are always a *he* and never a *she*. Oh God. My heart jumps into my throat. *He probably thinks I have a tooth fetish after I admitted that I wanted to be one as a child.*

With a chuckle, Lucas shakes his head. "No one's ever complimented me on my teeth before, so thanks... I think. My parents will be happy to know that their investment paid off."

"I always picked ligature bands that would match the outfits I wanted to wear that next week." I shrug. "I had to take into consideration any pieces of jewelry I might wear, too, and my skin tone, of course, and that can change depending on the season, you know?"

Ella snorts. "It doesn't surprise me at all that you managed to style your braces."

"Me neither." Lucas stuffs his hands into his pockets. "We should get AlphaVite fans with braces to get blue bands as a subtle way to support the team."

"Yes," I exclaim, clapping. "Subtle support is great. It's exactly what I do."

With a single brow raised, Lucas gives my outfit a once-over. "I don't see any type of subtle blue on you today, Roo."

"Just because you can't see it doesn't mean I'm not wearing it," I say with a wink. *Yes, way to flirt with the guy moping over his ex. Good job, Charlotte.*

Lucas's face goes slack for an instant, then he bursts out laughing. The rumbly, deep sound does something entirely illegal to my body, and despite the humidity, goose bumps cover me like a blanket. He's still laughing when Mitchell appears to herd him into the garage for qualifying.

Once they're gone, Ella hooks her arm through mine and pulls me toward the McAllister motorhome. With wide eyes, she asks, "Are you really wearing a blue thong?"

When I finally realize she's referring to my underwear and not what Americans call flip-flops, I snort. "Nah, but he'll never know that."

Unfortunately.

McAllister's motorhome, like AlphaVite's, is composed of staff offices, drivers' rooms, a coffee bar, an actual bar, and a dining space, but with a way better rooftop. *Not that I'll ever tell Theo.* The balcony doubles as a VIP lounge, but it's not too crowded today. Thank goodness for that because packed people plus heavy heat equals me stressing about not applying enough deodorant.

Ella and I claim a table in the far-left corner where we have the perfect view of the track. From here, the whirs of the mechanics from the garage and the announcer over the loudspeaker are audible, but the balcony is a pocket of peace.

Putting on my sunglasses, I turn to Ella. "All right. Spill the tea. How have things been going with Blake and Cooper?"

Blake can be a major dickhead when he wants to be, and from what I've seen, he's been avoiding his new driving partner's company like the bloke's got cooties *and* the chicken pox.

Ella lets out a low, long sigh. "It's a work in progress."

"That bad?"

"It's not that he dislikes Cooper." She clasps her hands on the table between us. "He just doesn't know what to make of him. And you know Blake. I wouldn't exactly describe him as warm and cuddly."

"Who would?" I laugh.

The only reason he puts up with Theo is because, when they were kids, my brother wouldn't stop pestering him until he agreed to be friends. Cooper and Blake don't have to be besties, of course, but they'll be driving partners for at least the next two years, so finding common ground would do them a lot of good.

"I'm interviewing Cooper for the podcast next weekend, and Blake hasn't complained about it, which I'll take as a good sign," Ella tells me. With a mischievous smile, she adds, "I'm dying to ask him about—well, you know… but Blake would kill me. Honestly, I'd probably chicken out, anyway."

Curiosity fully piqued, I slide my sunglasses down my nose and arch my brows. "Know about what?"

Her cheeks go pink. "About his thing."

"His *thing*?"

"His *thing* thing," she whisper-yells. She peers over one shoulder, then the other, to ensure no one's eavesdropping. They aren't. Qualifying may not be as exciting as the grand prix itself, but this is where the starting order of tomorrow's race is determined, so the crowd is still invested. "His one-eyed wonder weasel. His tadpole torpedo. His lap lizard. His boney macaron—"

"I seriously don't know if I'm more interested in hearing about Cooper's dick," I tease, "or why you have so many alternative names for the body part."

The flush in Ella's cheeks darkens. "Let's focus on the first one. There's a rumor that it's, well, that it's"—she glances around once again and then lowers her voice—"pierced."

My breath catches in my throat. "He has junk jewelry?"

Grinning, Ella nods. "According to the rumor mill, he's rocking some major junk jewelry."

"You *so* have to ask him." I wiggle in my seat. "I used to hook up with a guy with a frenum piercing, and the sex was *unreal*. Obviously, it's more about the driver than the make and model, but *phew*, that man could deliver where it counted."

"I don't know where a frenum piercing goes, and I'm 100 percent okay with that," Ella admits, shaking her head emphatically. "Oy, that sounds painful. I wouldn't want a needle or a tattoo gun anywhere near my nether regions."

"Tattoo gun?" I perk up, my spine snapping straight. "He has tattoos down there, too?"

"No, not him. Shit, Jos didn't tell you about the other one, did she?"

I blink at her, racking my brain. But... nope. I have no inkling of what the other one is, and now I desperately need to know.

"You *can't* repeat this to anyone," Ella warns me.

"I won't." I place my hand over my heart for emphasis. I'm a fantastic secret keeper. No one knows that when we were babysitting my aunt's dog and had to pick her up from the groomer, my mom brought home the wrong dog. Or that when my best friend Willow broke her hand, it's because she fell out of a tree trying to spy on her ex-boyfriend. Or that Theo once thought our parents were hiding another sibling from us because he found my Cabbage Patch doll's birth certificate and thought it was real.

Ella holds out her pinky, her expression nothing but serious, so I link mine with hers and give it a shake.

"Okay," she says, once she's satisfied I won't repeat what she's about to tell me. "There's absolutely no proof whatsoever that this is true, but according to the friend of a friend of a cousin's ex-wife—or something like that—Lucas has a tattoo... down under."

I gasp, my lips forming the perfect O as her words sink in. Of all the things she could have told me, I would've put money on it being anything but *that*. Now that I've heard this rumor, how am I supposed to look at Lucas and not imagine his potential dick tattoo? I shudder at the thought of how badly that had to hurt. What kind of tattoo would he even want in a place like that? And how does tattooing that body part work? Does he have to be hard or—*nope! Stop thinking about it.*

"I know," Ella says, though I haven't said a single word. "That was my reaction, too. I honestly don't think it's true, since all of Lucas's tattoos have meaning, but the *does he or doesn't he* rhetoric is fun to think about."

"Oh, it's all I'm going to be thinking about."

She throws her head back and laughs, clearly thinking I'm kidding.

I'm absolutely not.

"Maybe it's his ex's name."

"Ex?" Ella frowns, her brows furrowed. "Lucas doesn't have an ex."

"According to my brother, he does." I shrug.

She presses her palms against the table and adjusts her legs so she's sitting crisscross on the chair. "Huh. As far as I know, Lucas hasn't dated anyone seriously in the few years I've known him."

My heart squeezes at that, but I ignore the sensation. "Maybe I misheard."

I definitely didn't. I'm sure his ex is gorgeous, and her left boob isn't slightly bigger than the right one, and her hair doesn't look like Medusa's when she wakes up.

"You can ask him," Ella suggests, leaning forward, her forearms resting on the table.

I waggle my brows, going for light and easy. "About the ex or the tattoo?"

"The ex," she clarifies with a *humph*. "You've known him longer than me. You'd have the better shot at getting the tea."

"Yeah, maybe." I shrug noncommittally. "I'll think about it."

I can't recall a time when I didn't have a crush on Lucas. It's a constant in my life, like my love for pickles or the way the scent of lilacs makes me smile. I don't remember when or how it started, but my feelings have never gone away. It's not like I plan to act on them—a woman has her pride after all—but knowing he's caught up on his ex makes my crush seem silly. While he's been living his best life, I've been secretly pining for him, measuring every guy I date against the impossible standard he's set.

Not that I'd admit any of this to a soul. If I'm good at keeping other people's secrets, I'm exceptional at keeping my own.

NINE
LUCAS

AS THE COLD, bubbly splash hits me square in the face, I startle back. *You've got to be joking*.

I enjoy a glass of sparkling wine as much as the next guy, but I prefer sipping it from a glass over wiping it from my eyes and nose. The top three finishers pop bottles and spray fans and one another—it's all part of the podium ceremony—but usually, we don't aim for the face. Unless you're Theo, who always claims it's "an accident."

"Aw, shite, man," Cooper says, his Scottish accent peeking through. "Sorry about that. I swear I've opened one of these things before, but the adrenaline's making my hands shake."

"No worries, man." I use my sleeve to wipe the liquid dripping from my face.

Cooper's second-place finish was well-earned. The Interlagos circuit is full of high-speed straights, technical corners, and steep elevation changes. Add in the rare counterclockwise direction of the course, and it's one hell of a challenge. And since it's his first time on the podium as a Formula 1 driver, I understand his overzealousness with the champagne. Though a first-place finish never gets any less exciting—and I'm buzzing about my win today—we learn to contain the exhilaration it brings to avoid coming across as cocky.

Theo barks out a laugh at my wine-soaked face as he waves his bottle around like it's a water gun. It's better than the last race, when he held the bottle in front of his crotch, making it look like he was pissing sparkling wine. He's an idiot, but it's impossible not to love him.

The rest of the podium ceremony passes without incident, and soon we're ushered into a room adjacent to the stage. The space is cool, thank fuck. Racing in this heat means my balls are practically glued to my thighs and I have sweat in crevices I didn't know existed. We get a few minutes to cool off, and I take advantage of every damn one, chugging water and wiping the sweat and wine from my face.

The TV interviews and press conference go off without a hitch, much to Mitchell's delight. To say he's on edge about Theo's new position as my teammate is an understatement. He likes the guy well enough, but he's worried that his love of attention will overshadow my unassuming attitude toward it.

In my time as an F1 driver, I've indulged in plenty of the luxuries that my status grants me. I've dated award-winning actresses, I own a boat that costs more than my brothers' college tuitions combined, and I attend Fashion Week as a guest of Gucci every year. I'm a lucky son of a bitch. But I've never felt the need to flaunt my status. Maybe it's because, unlike most of the F1 drivers, I don't come from money. My parents did well enough, but I grew up in hand-me-downs instead of Hermès, and I learned to drive in my dad's 1997 Toyota Corolla, not a brand-spankin' new Ferrari.

Fame and notoriety are fickle. Both can vanish as quickly as they come, so I do my best to enjoy the opened doors quietly. Mitchell respects this, but he also worries that I'm robbing myself of opportunities by sticking to the sidelines.

"I'm surprised Theo let you answer so many questions,"

Mitchell comments as the two of us stand off to one side, far from the reporters, after the conference.

Taking a sip of my water, I roll my eyes. "Because he knew they were directed at me. He can be a professional."

"Hmm…" Mitchell purses his lips. "Is that why he mouthed 'suck my dick' to his trainer mid-interview?"

"I said he *can* be a professional." I bite back a laugh. "Not that he always is."

Chuckling, my manager undoes the top two buttons of his shirt, the only indication that the heat is affecting him. "Oh, I got the tickets you asked for, by the way. Forwarded them to your email, so you should be all set."

"Ringside, right—" My question is cut off when Ella wraps her arms around my waist and squeezes tightly.

"Congrats!" She takes a step back. "That was such a well-deserved win."

"Thanks." I swallow thickly, suddenly a little less enthusiastic about it. "How's Blake doing?"

I have a feeling I already know, but I still want to get a pulse check. He was handed a five-second time penalty when he caused a collision trying to overtake another driver. Those five seconds cost him a podium finish.

With a grunt, she punches my arm. Hard. "Can't you just accept my compliment and bask in the glory?"

My stomach twists. "But Blake—"

"Is fine," she says, wearing a genuine smile. "He's on the phone with his sister, and Champ's keeping him company."

Champ, short for Champion, happens to be the cutest dog I've ever met. He's twenty-five pounds of caramel-colored fluff and boundless energy. He also has the funny habit of bringing objects to people when he greets them. He's brought me shoes, socks, empty chip bags, a tampon (unopened, thankfully), and Gatorade bottles as welcome presents over the months. Although they didn't get him with the intent of training him to be an emotional support animal, he acts like one for Blake all the same.

I hold up my hands in surrender. "Fine. Winning is nice, so I appreciate the recognition."

"Winning is nice," Ella repeats, her face a mask of disbelief. She turns to Mitchell and shakes her head. "I don't know how you deal with his modesty."

Mitchell shoots me a victorious smirk. "I don't know either."

"Are we talking about Lucas's modesty?" Theo, suddenly appearing on my left side, swings his sweaty arm around my shoulder. "Because I have a lot to say on the matter. For starters, I know Americans love their board shorts, but there's nothing wrong with tailored, fitted shorts. They'd show off that epic thigh tat of yours, mate."

"Not what we were talking about." I shrug him off. "But your input is duly noted and ignored."

"Your loss," he says with a shrug. "Where's Charlotte? Did she leave already?"

She left about ten minutes into the press conference, but rather than tell him that and throw her under the bus, I shrug. "Maybe she went back to the hotel."

Chin lifted, he surveys the room as if she'll magically appear. "Will you check her location?"

"Sure."

I already know she's at the hotel because I've already checked the app—I was worried; don't judge me—but I'm definitely not mentioning that. Once the app loads, I show Theo the small dot indicating Charlotte's approximate location.

"I'm heading back now. Want me to check in with her? Make sure everything's good?"

Nodding, Theo slaps me on the back. "That'd be great. I've

got another interview before I can head out. These reporters just can't get enough of me, mate."

Ella ducks her head to stifle a laugh. Theo's *post*-race interview was originally supposed to be a *pre*-race interview. It had to be rescheduled after he went thirty minutes over his allotted time with *SkySports*, and it threw off his entire media schedule.

I wish him luck before catching a ride back to the hotel with Mitchell.

While he spends the car ride going over my sponsorship obligations for the next few months, I check my notifications for the first time since the race ended. There are two missed calls from my mom, a missed call from each set of grandparents, and a fuck ton of texts in The Gentleman's Club—the ridiculous name for the Adler brother text thread.

GRAYSON ADLER
Congrats on the win, bro!

JESSE ADLER
Holy shit.

That was an unreal race.

Great fucking job, Lucas.

FINN ADLER
My favorite part was when Cooper Fraser hit you in the face with champagne. There are already memes circulating.

EZRA ADLER
How pissed off is Blake?

And congrats!

FINN ADLER

After that win, you're definitely Mom's favorite again.

EZRA ADLER

What do you mean Mom's favorite again? I'm always the favorite. As the baby of the family, it's my birthright.

JESSE ADLER

You're younger than Finn by two minutes, idiot.

FINN ADLER

He bitches like a baby, though.

GRAYSON ADLER

You're Mom's second favorite, Ez. Lucas has been the favorite since he bought her that Bvlgari bracelet for Hanukkah.

EZRA ADLER

Ah shit. I forgot about that.

Sort of dickish for you to do that, considering I'm a jeweler, but whatever.

JESSE ADLER

There's a Red Sox game the first weekend Luc's in town. Anyone want to go?

FINN ADLER

BROS' NIGHT OUT. LET'S FUCKING GO.

EZRA ADLER

I don't know how we shared a womb. You're so weird.

GRAYSON ADLER

Jaclyn's out of town that weekend, but if Mom and Dad will babysit Madison, I'm in.

EZRA ADLER

Mom would kidnap Madison from you if she could.

Pretty sure she'll agree to babysit.

GRAYSON ADLER

True. Someone else needs to give her a grandkid soon.

FINN ADLER

There's a chance I'm someone's baby daddy and just don't know it.

EZRA ADLER

I bet that's exactly what she wants to hear.

LUCAS ADLER

1. Thanks! Was a good race, for sure.

2. The Bvlgari bracelet was from all of us, considering you assholes also signed the card (and forgot to write my name on it).

3. I'm Mom's favorite because I'm the only one who knows how to properly do laundry without fucking everything up.

4. Down for the game. Will Dad want to come with us?

A NEW TEXT from Theo comes in as we're pulling into the hotel. It's nothing but four digits, though I realize quickly that it's Charlotte's room number. Good thing he remembered I'd need it. I don't think I'd have the same kind of luck she did if I tried to sweet-talk the front desk into giving out guest information. I chuckle when I arrive at her room and see the Do Not Disturb sign hanging from the handle.

I knock, then slip my hands into my pockets while I wait for her to answer. Amusement works its way through me when I hear muffled swearing, then an object clattering to the floor and more choice words. When the door finally swings open, I find myself face-to-face with Charlotte, who's wearing a T-shirt that says *olive you*, with two olives positioned where her nipples are.

Oh hell.

"I wasn't expecting the stripper for another"—she flicks her wrist, as if to check an imaginary watch—"hour or so, but come on in."

I can't help but grin. "I'll take that as a compliment."

"As you should." With a wink, she pulls the door open farther and waves me in. "I've got high standards when it comes to strippers."

Unsure of how to reply to that, I shake my head and change the subject. "I saw you left the conference early."

"Are you stalking me?" she asks, splaying one hand over her chest. "Because if you are, that's definitely the most romantic thing anyone's ever done for me."

A huff escapes me. "Did you just insinuate that stalking is romantic?"

"There's a whole fan base for it in romance books," she tells me with a wave of her hand. "Willow loves a good stalker romance. I'm more of a forbidden love girlie, but to each their own."

I met Charlotte's best friend at the Australian Grand Prix. The woman is as fiery as her hair color suggests. Her fondness for stalker romances doesn't surprise me as much as it probably should. "I remember Willow. She's the one with—"

Charlotte perks up and grins. "An attitude and a great arse?"

Affection for this woman and her ridiculous commentary warms my chest. "I was going to say auburn hair."

"Oh." She nibbles on her lower lip. "Well," she hedges, "yes, she also has auburn hair. She'd love you for saying auburn instead of red, by the way. Now let's get back to you stalking me. I find that way more interesting."

"I'm not stalking you," I chuckle. "I told Theo I'd check on you."

If I hadn't been watching her face closely—to avoid accidentally looking at her olives—I would've missed the way her smile faded almost imperceptibly and the subtle dimming in her eyes. "Ah. Well, you can tell him I'm right as rain."

"That's not the only reason I'm here," I quickly clarify, my chest tightening at the idea that I've upset her. "I have two tickets to a fight tonight."

The beginnings of a playful smile dance on her lips. "Is that an invitation or simply a status update?"

"An invite. You are, after all, the one who reminded me that I'm not geriatric and can still check things off my bucket list."

I've wanted to attend a professional match since I picked up boxing, but the timing has never worked out. I train with the legendary retired boxer Kelsey "the Hitman" Wells a few times a week, and when he texted me that another one of his clients had a match out here tonight, I decided to be spontaneous. For me, at least. It's not the same as seeing the sunset at Praça Pôr do Sol or checking out the street art in Beco do Batman, both things Charlotte did while I practiced on Friday, but it's a small step out of the rut I've found myself in.

"I have been known to give rather sage advice from time to time." She flips her hair over her shoulder. "This isn't the kind of fight where two blokes wear Speedos and wrestle in a kiddie pool filled with Jell-O, is it?"

A grin curves up my lips. "No, not exactly."

Charlotte nods. "That's unfortunate, but I'll still go. Why the hell not? When should I be ready?"

With a glance at my watch, I do a quick calculation, considering the buffer I'll need to add, since there's no way she'll be on time. "An hour."

"An hour?" Her gasp is so animated, one would think I've just revealed the existence of extraterrestrial life forms. "Okay, I can make that work." She turns in a circle, inspecting the room. "I think. Hopefully. Maybe."

To my surprise, it only takes her an hour and eleven minutes to "make magic happen." Her words, not mine. And holy hell, does she abracadabra herself into a walking wet dream. I swear I mean that in the most respectful way possible. She's always beautiful, but the knee-high black boots and a short leather skirt make me desperate to bend her over the nearest surface and fuck her until my knees give out.

Charlotte's shoulders tense when she catches me staring. "What? Is it my outfit? Do you think it'd look better with a white shirt? That's what I originally had on, but then I got foundation on it, which is particularly annoying because I did my makeup *before* getting dressed so this exact scenario wouldn't happen. But how was I supposed to know I had extra contour powder on my hand? Do you reckon I should change?"

Clasping my hands in front of me to hide my dick's painful attempt to join the party, I manage a grin that may or may not resemble a grimace. "No, sorry. You look… great."

Great? Who am I? Tony the fucking Tiger? She looks phenomenal.

"Thanks." Her body deflates in relief. "You don't look too bad yourself. It's giving suave instead of stripper," she says, hiking her purse higher on her shoulder. "Ready for fight night?"

"Let's do this," I say, holding a hand out and gesturing to the elevator.

Little does she know that the fight I'm more focused on is the one occurring in my briefs.

TEN
CHARLOTTE

WE'RE SITTING SO close to the ring—not the stage, I'm told—that there's a 90 percent chance we'll be hit with either blood or sweat from the boxers. The security escort who led us to our seats made it sound like an honor rather than an expensive dry-cleaning bill. *Thank God I wore the black shirt and not the white.*

As Lucas takes a photo with a few fans who approached him, I squint against the blinding glare of the overhead lights and take in the arena. Nearly every seat is filled, and the crowd is chanting and roaring for their favored fighter. The announcer practically shouts into the mic, his booming voice over the loudspeaker hyping them up. The massive screens hanging from the ceiling will broadcast the fight and real-time stats, but for now, trainers and cameramen swarm the ring, prepping for the boxers' introductions.

As Lucas sinks into the empty seat beside me, I get right down to business. "So which fighter has the cooler nickname?"

Resting his forearms on his thighs, he tips forward, head turned my way, and grins. "You tell me. We've got Daniel 'the Polka Puncher' Novák versus Aaron 'the Toybreaker' Zale."

I tap my fingers against my chin. "Hmm... tough call. Maybe I'll just cheer for them both. Spread the love and all that."

Lucas straightens, looking appalled by my suggestion. "You can't root for both opponents, Roo. That defeats the whole purpose."

I raise a brow and shift so I'm facing him. "Why not? I root for both you and Theo."

"No, you don't," he says, though his voice is adorably uncertain. "That's... well, that's not how it works."

"Do you not remember when I told you that you were the number one pick for Holy Walker-Moly?"

He takes a swig of the beer he ordered, doing a poor job of hiding the way his cheeks have reddened. "Point taken."

The lights suddenly dim, and the attention of every person in the place is diverted to the ring, the only area still illuminated under the spotlights. The announcer standing in the center, microphone in hand, speaks, his deep voice echoing through the arena. I don't speak Portuguese, so I have no idea what he's saying, but there's a commentator from America, as the match is being broadcast there. When the crowd erupts, the sound nearly shaking the foundations of the building, and every person gets to their feet, I don't need the English-speaking commentator to tell me that the fighters are being announced. With our ringside seats, we get an up-close-and-personal view of the Toybreaker's muscular frame and the Polka Puncher's confident swagger as they climb through the ropes.

The fight is relatively anti-climactic to start. The two men circle each other, looking for weaknesses or an in. Then, out of nowhere, *bam*. The Toybreaker charges forward like a man with a vendetta. I watch in stunned silence as the fight plays out in front of us. By the third round, I'm truly clueless as to *why* people subject themselves to this. I complain when

I sleep wrong and wake with a small kink in my neck, yet these men are voluntarily pummeling and injuring each other for fun.

The bloke next to me screams something that I don't think is anatomically possible. I mean, maybe if the fighter were double-jointed, but even then, it'd be pushing it. I step an inch closer to Lucas, hoping to avoid the man's spittle. He's making my middle finger twitchy, and the last thing we need is me telling him to lower his voice. I can't see that ending well for anyone.

Lucas tears his attention away from the ring and regards me with a concerned expression. "You good?"

"If he doesn't stop shouting 'get him a body bag,' there's a very high chance I'll try to put him in one."

I'm only half kidding.

As if on cue, the guy screams his signature line. It was funny the first few times, but now that he's uttered the phrase one hundred and eight times, it's lost the bulk of its charm. I widen my eyes at Lucas, silently saying "see?"

Lucas stifles a laugh, but the corner of his mouth quirks up. In a move that surprises the hell out of me, he wraps his arm around my waist and gently tugs me over until I'm parked in front of him. I wait for him to switch spots with me, but nope, he stays right where he is, his chest brushing against my back. It's intimate in the best kind of way.

"Better?" he asks, his breath tickling my ear.

A shiver of raw desire flows through me like lava, but I will my body to remain relaxed. "Mm-hmm."

I can't say I was paying super close attention to the match before, but now? It's background noise. How am I supposed to focus when Lucas's tattooed forearms keep brushing against my waist and the rumbles of his cheers for the Toybreaker vibrate through me?

Needing to break the tension, one that's probably

completely one-sided, I ask, "Why do they call it a boxing ring if it's actually square?"

"No idea." Lucas shrugs. "I'm sure Kelsey would know. I can shoot him a text."

Kelsey Wells, a very badarse boxer who owns a private high-profile gym, ventured into the hospitality scene last year, and Theo's girlfriend, Josie, heads up his marketing team. He's built like a brick house, though he's not as big as Mitchell. Lucas's manager is still in a league of his own.

"How'd you get Kelsey to train you?" I ask over the noise. "Not that he shouldn't train you, but I can't imagine you plan to go pro or anything. You're more of a boxing... hobbyist? Enthusiast? Amateur?"

Lucas takes a sip of his beer, then sets it in his cupholder again. A bead of liquid lingers on his lip, but I hold myself back from angling in and licking it off for him. *Self-control, baby.*

"We were introduced at a poker game." He shakes his head. "I've never met someone with so few tells."

"Everyone has tells. You touch your eye or eyebrow when you're irritated," I inform him. "And you fiddle with your watch when you're getting impatient. You have a nice watch collection, by the way. And eyes." Though nerves skitter down my spine, there's no stopping the flood of words escaping me. "They're a good color; not super common. Sort of a pickle green. Gherkin, not the bread-and-butter kind."

Lucas opens his mouth, but before he can speak, I gasp and spin to face him completely.

"Wait, did you say poker game? I *knew* there was a secret underground celebrity poker ring. You've seen *Molly's Game*, right? The woman who ran high-stakes games—"

"This was a charity poker game." Lucas gives me a wry smile. "And I'm not a celebrity."

With a huff, I roll my eyes. "And I'm not a serial shopper. Let's be real, Lucas. You're a public figure. Calvin Klein didn't approach you to strip down and star in their latest campaign because you can win a grand prix."

"I can't believe Theo told you about that," he grumbles, more to himself than me.

I try not to grin at his reaction. Actually, Theo told Josie, and Josie told me. Though I don't tell him that. He'd probably dislike it more. "We're getting off topic."

"The story isn't all that exciting," Lucas warns me. "He invited me to check out Wells Gym, so I did."

"And it was love at first punch?"

"Something like that. I was"—he pauses, his brows lowering—"going through a lot at the time. Needed an outlet, and boxing became that for me."

My head jerks back. "You were angry?"

The closest I've ever seen Lucas to angry is when a reporter wouldn't stop grilling him about a strategy gone wrong that resulted in him being unfairly red-flagged. He doesn't lash out or say things in the heat of the moment. It's more like controlled annoyance that never tips the scale to angry.

Sighing, he peers back at the ring, where the boxers are taking a break between rounds. It takes him so long to answer that when he finally says, "I had a falling-out with my brother," I've all but forgotten the question I asked in the first place.

"That sucks," I reply simply. It takes a lot of willpower to not ask a million questions, including who, what, where, when and why, but based on the way his expression has shuttered, it's clear he wouldn't welcome that line of inquiry.

He exhales, and his frown eases. "Yeah, it does."

In my periphery, the boxers appear to be hugging. I spin and study them. "Is that the end?"

"Hmm?"

Tilting my head to the side, I confirm that I am not hallucinating. They're indeed embracing. "They're hugging. Is it a congratulatory hug? Like a 'good job, man, you did great' kind of thing?"

Lucas's laugh rings louder than the bell that announces the end of a round. "It's called cinching, but I see where you're coming from. It's a defensive technique."

He walks me through a few more tactics as the next round begins. I don't care a bit about the strategies, but I do love the way Lucas's eyes light up and his smile widens as he talks about his second-favorite sport, so I do my best to absorb his words like a sponge.

"So you're telling me," I say with a hand in the air between us, interrupting him, "that it's considered rude to punch someone in the dick?"

He takes a slow sip of his beer before responding. "It's considered illegal, and it'll earn you a five-minute breather."

I roll my eyes. Men are such babies.

"You should do more of this," I tell him, taking a swig of my water since watching men beat the living crap out of one another has me working up a sweat.

"More of what? Explaining boxing to you?" he says with a tilted grin.

"Spontaneous, fun activities in every city you visit," I clarify. "I'll gladly serve as your tour guide any time you want to tag along on my adventures."

"Such a generous offer," he teases, giving my hip a quick squeeze.

As my ovaries explode and my heart trips over itself, I glance toward the medics on standby, wondering if I should flag them over.

The match ends during the ninth round when the Toybreaker knocks the fuck out of the Polka Puncher. Not just a small knockout, but a lights-out, *no one's home and we should probably make sure he's breathing* knockout. Instantly, the press storms the ring to celebrate Aaron's win. I don't particularly care who the victor is; I'm just glad we made it through the match without being hit by bodily fluids.

Apparently, the tickets were courtesy of Aaron "the Toybreaker" Zale, or maybe his manager, so before we leave, we head to the locker room to congratulate him and say thanks.

Clearly assuming I'm nervous about this meet and greet, Lucas gently nudges me forward with a palm splayed over my lower back. In reality, I just don't have a strong urge to spend an extended period of time in closed quarters that smell like sweat and liniment and have horrific fluorescent lighting.

Only moments after we've entered, thankfully, the Toybreaker stalks through the door with a towel slung over his shoulders. He's mid-conversation with his trainer, but he stops in his tracks, and his expression morphs into first confusion, then surprise.

"Adler," he says through a bloody smile. "Thanks for coming out, man."

Lucas dips his chin. "Thanks for having us."

They do one of these complex masculine half handshake, half high five with a one-armed hug-slash-shoulder bump and a brief pat on the back.

"This is Charlotte," Lucas says when he steps back. The man doesn't need more brownie points, but he's instantly earned them by introducing me as "Charlotte" rather than "Charlotte Walker, Theo's younger sister."

Unsure if I should hug him or high-five him or not touch him at all, I settle on a simple wave. "Hi. Congrats on your win."

He takes me in from my head to my toes, a smile slowly building. "Hey, gorgeous. Nice to meet you."

I'm too focused on the massive cut on his lip and the bruises forming under both of his eyes, not to mention the ones scattering his torso, for the compliment to register. "Um... do you need medical attention?"

He flexes his fingers and shakes his head. "Nah. I'm sure I'm fine, but thanks for worrying about me, sweetheart."

"My friend didn't initially get her sprained thumb checked out and nearly tore the ligament as a result," I warn him. "To be fair, she didn't realize it was sprained because, honestly, who in the bloody hell sprains their thumb at the nail salon? But the technician didn't like when she fidgeted during her manicure and yanked it hard. So it's always better to be safe than sorry and get checked out by a medical professional. Anyway, do you mind if I ask how you got your boxing nickname?"

The Toybreaker tilts his head and smirks as if I'm a magician and he's trying to uncover my latest trick. "I like to play with my opponent before I go in for the kill."

Um, okay. "Well, that... makes you sound like a bit of a sociopath, if I'm being completely honest."

Lucas tucks his chin into his chest and snorts, but the Toybreaker is completely unperturbed by my comment. In fact, his grin gets even wider. *Weirdo.*

He invites us to celebrate with him and his team at some exclusive nightclub, and while that sounds like my version of hell on earth right now, I turn and silently defer to Lucas. I slept in, spent a couple of hours in a local market, and showed up just in time for the race. He's the one who's been up since six a.m. and raced for two hours straight. This is his adventurous night, anyway. I'm just along for the ride.

"Thanks, but I think we'll head back to the hotel," Lucas says with an apologetic smile. "It's been a long day."

Completely ignoring him, the Toybreaker turns his attention to me. "Why don't you give me your number? If you change your mind, you can reach out, and we can play, just the two of us."

Did he seriously say that? Compared to Lucas, the guy has the sexual appeal of a cactus.

"I—"

"She's not available," Lucas bites out.

Mouth agape, I slowly turn and blink at him. *I'm not available?* There's no way in hell I was giving him my number, considering he probably sends two to three dick pics a day and just referred to sex as *playing*, but that doesn't give Lucas the right to make that decision for me.

The two of them have a silent conversation that involves narrowed eyes and clenched jaws. Then, as if that weird interlude never even happened, they go on to chitchat about the match, leaving me utterly stupefied.

By the time we've made it outside, my annoyance is simmering, on the verge of boiling over, and my thoughts have morphed from *what just happened?* to *what just happened was completely unacceptable.* As soon as we're far from prying ears, I turn on my heel and cross my arms over my chest. "I can speak for myself, you know. I don't need you stepping in."

His jaw goes rigid, and his green eyes go hard. "Were you planning on giving him your number?"

I huff out an exaggerated breath. "That's beside the point."

"If you weren't planning on it, I did you a favor."

"So if a woman asked for your number, and I stepped in to turn her down on your behalf, without consulting you first, you'd be okay with that?"

"Yes," he says without hesitation, as if this is the obvious answer. "Why would I care about other women when I'm out with you?"

Fists clenched at my sides, I let out a disgruntled noise. He's still missing the entire point. "Next time, let me deal with it. I have a tried-and-true method for rejecting a guy without having to be mean about it, okay?"

He cocks a brow. "Tried-and-true?"

"Yes. I simply tell them that they can have my number on the condition that they correctly answer a riddle," I explain, propping a hand on my hip. It's a technique I perfected in university and have been using ever since. It isn't as if men ask for my number right and left, but it's a nice technique to keep in my pocket, just in case. "Then I ask them a riddle that doesn't actually have an answer because I made it up myself."

Lucas stares at me for a beat before he doubles over, laughing. He's so loud, and it goes on for so long that passersby start to stare. "The man you end up marrying will be one lucky guy, Roo."

Usually, it's *the man you end up marrying is going to need a lot of patience* or *the man you end up marrying is in for it*. But not for Lucas. I never have to worry that I'm too opinionated, too direct, too loud, too *much*. For him, I'm just enough. And shit if that doesn't make me so warm and fuzzy I forget why I was even mad in the first place.

ELEVEN
LUCAS

AS THE BARCELONA sun sets over the beach, casting a warm, golden glow across the sand, the breeze carries the salty scent of the Mediterranean Sea onto the deck. The city lights twinkle in the distance, blending with the stars now appearing in the darkening sky. I love the beach. Always have and always will. When I was a kid, my family would spend summer weekends at Martha's Vineyard, and I'd spend every spare moment in the water. The ebb and flow of the waves have a unique way of relaxing my brain. And with a cutthroat, high-pressure job like mine, I'll take all the relaxation I can get.

"What do you think?" Mitchell asks, reminding me that I'm here to socialize. "Would you do it?"

"Definitely," I reply, although I have no clue what the hell I'm agreeing to.

Mitchell purses his lips and nods. "So you'd fuck a goat in public for a million dollars?"

There's no point denying I wasn't paying a lick of attention, so I shoot him a guilty smile.

My manager, decked out in a black tux, simply chuckles and shakes his head. "I know it's been a long day, but you only have to schmooze for an hour or two more before you can hit the hay."

I grin at those phrases. The first time Theo and Blake heard me say "schmooze" and "hit the hay," they stared at me like they were concerned I was having a stroke. Blake asked if "schmooze" was the way we say "booze" in Boston, and Theo assumed that working with hay was typical for Americans, since the country has so much farmland. In all fairness, I had no idea what the hell Blake meant when he said "it's brass monkeys out," (it's cold) or when Theo told me "you'll be apples" (you'll be okay). That's the fun of having friends from other countries.

I salute Mitchell with one hand while taking a sip of my drink with the other. Today started with a five-a.m. workout and ended with a practice that was delayed by two hours, thanks to debris on the track. If this party wasn't taking place at our hotel, there's no way in hell I would've attended.

"Adam from Nike is headed this way," Mitchell says, swirling the liquid in his glass. "You met him briefly at the Bahrain Grand Prix and bonded over football."

I hum. "American or European football?"

He hits me with a look that would have anyone else hiding under the nearest surface. "European. Obviously."

"Just checking," I say, plastering on a smile. "He's the global head of partnerships, right?"

"Good to know you listen sometimes." Beside me, he lifts his hand in greeting and calls out, "Adam, my man. How the hell are you?"

"You sound like Ari Gold from *Entourage*." I straighten my shoulders and dig deep for that smile again.

Forty-five minutes later, I'm burned out and in desperate need of a new drink. Spotting Ella and Blake at a table by the bar, I excuse myself from the conversation and make my way over.

"Hey, Lucas." Ella hits me with a warm smile. "Do you want my seat? I'm headed back to our hotel."

"To hit the hay?" I ask her, although my grin is at Blake's expense.

"I have a FaceTime date with my friends at home, plus we can't leave Champ unsupervised for too long," she explains. "But then I'm definitely hitting the hay."

Blake mutters something along the lines of "bloody Americans and their stupid sayings," which has Ella and I exchanging an amused look. It's nice having another American around to say "trash" instead of "rubbish" and "sneakers" instead of "trainers." Though Ella actually says "gym shoes," but that's because she's from the Midwest. I don't hold it against her.

Blake kisses Ella goodbye, making her promise to text the moment she's in her Uber and then back in their room.

I slip into the seat beside him, and I'm ordering an old-fashioned from a passing waiter when Cooper approaches us. I sneak a glance at Blake to gauge his mood, noting that he seems relatively calm. Ella interviewed Cooper last Saturday when we had an off weekend, so with any luck, he and Blake called a truce. Getting Blake to give someone new a chance is hit or miss, but if they get Ella's approval, he tends to warm up a little more easily.

"Hey, Coop," I greet the Scot.

He's dressed like a coastal Abercrombie model in a linen suit.

"Coop?" Blake mouths, rolling his eyes. Ah. They aren't besties yet. Noted. At least he hasn't told him to fuck off.

Eyeing Blake and apparently deciding it's safe to join, Cooper slides into the one stool left at the table. "Hullo, fellas. How's your night going?"

Cooper's easy to get along with. He's in his mid-twenties, but his maturity far surpasses his age, and he's ambitious in a way that doesn't make me internally cringe. We quickly fall into conversation about this afternoon's practice and the recent FC Barcelona win, the dynamic comfortable. That is until he asks about Charlotte.

I lift my beer to my lips and take a long swig. "What about her?"

"I see her around the paddock sometimes but wasn't sure what her deal was," he says while peeling the label off his beer bottle. "It's kind of hard to meet someone when you're traveling a lot, so…"

Hell fucking no. In a panic and not wanting Blake to speak up before I can, I blurt out the first thought that comes to mind. "She's in a relationship."

Blake chokes on his drink, and when he collects himself, he stares at the side of my head with wide-eyed censure. His disapproval barrels into me as I angle my body toward Cooper.

"I can definitely put out some feelers for you, though. With other women. Not Charlotte, since she's, you know, taken and all."

"That'd be great," he says, wearing a genuine grin that makes me feel like an absolute asshole for lying, but whatever. He may be a good guy, but he's not good enough for Charlotte.

Blake waits until Cooper's gone back to the party before fixing me with an accusatory look. He doesn't say a damn word, just stares at me until I'm squirming in my seat.

"Stop looking at me like that."

"Like what?" he challenges, his jaw tight.

My chest constricts. "I'm too tired to play this game. Say what you want to say and be done with it."

With a slow sip of his drink, he considers me, and even after he sets the glass down, he's silent. Uncomfortable, I fist my hands on the table, listening to the waves gently lap at the shore in hopes that it will soothe me.

Finally, Blake breaks the silence, his tone more serious. "Be careful, mate," he says. "That's all."

I dip my chin, the gesture noncommittal. The conversation ends there, diverting to lighter topics. I'm finishing up my drink when a pineapple cocktail appears in front of us and is thrust into Blake's hand. And I don't mean a cocktail that is simply pineapple flavored. No, this drink comes in a hollowed-out pineapple with a pink umbrella sticking out of it.

"Hold my drink, mate?" Theo phrases it as a question, but without waiting for Blake to answer, he dashes off.

Everyone else at the party is drinking beer, whiskey, sangria, or chilled wine, so I have no idea where Theo got a drink that looks like it belongs at an all-inclusive resort in Mexico. But I learned a long time ago not to question the things he does.

Blake glares at the drink like it's personally offended him.

"You too scared to try it?" I tease, nodding at the festive drink.

He takes the jest as a challenge—of course he does—and sips from the straw. Instantly, his face blanches, and he takes a dramatic sip of water. "Christ, I don't know how Walker enjoys this crap. It's pure sugar."

I chuckle. "I think that's the idea."

We stick to balanced diets for the most part, but we all have our weaknesses. Blake discovered Girl Scout cookies and goes through a box or two of Thin Mints every week, and I'm a straight-up slut for chicken wings. Theo? He loves fruity, sugary drinks.

After another twenty minutes or so, Blake calls it a night. He stayed this long because, according to him, he wanted to give her some time to catch up with her friends. In reality, Ella's friends overwhelm the hell out of him.

Not wanting to sit at a table alone, I head to the beach. I pick up Theo's lonesome pineapple cocktail, set to find a passing server to hand it to, because knowing him, he forgot he handed it off to us. But first, I take a small sip. I'm expecting a flavor similar to a Sour Patch Kid, so when the sweetness of the coconut rum and tartness of the pineapple hit my tongue, it startles me. The flavors balance one another out well and make for one hell of a good drink. Maybe Theo's on to something with these things.

Outside, with the cocktail in hand, I slip off my shoes and roll up the hem of my pants, then wander to the water's edge. My bare feet sink into the cool, damp sand with each step I take, and the occasional splash of water laps at my feet, cooling me down. I've been wandering for a few minutes when a familiar unabashed laugh tinkles in the night air.

It only takes a moment to spot the lone silhouette sitting in the sand, talking animatedly into a phone screen. Like a Pavlov-trained dog, I can't help but smile. Then my feet are moving in her direction.

At my approach, she squints against the glare from her phone, and almost instantly, her features soften.

"Hey, you," she calls out.

"You?" a familiar voice asks. "Who's you?"

Charlotte turns back to her phone. "Lucas."

"Lucas is there?"

She lifts a brow, smiling at me. "Mm-hmm. If I had to guess, he's stalking me again."

"How romantic," Willow says, a note of wistfulness in her voice.

With her lips pressed together, she shoots me an "I told you so" look. Apparently, she wasn't kidding about Willow's feelings on stalking. But hey, to each their own.

I squat, knees cracking, and settle in next to her, then twist my pineapple drink back and forth in the sand so it stays upright. Tilting close so that my face appears in the small square in the corner of her screen, I greet Charlotte's best friend. "What's up, Willow?"

"Just taking a lunch break and hiding out from the twenty gremlins who constantly make me question why I became a primary school teacher," Willow answers, stabbing her fork into her salad. She's sitting behind a desk, the wall behind her decorated with colorful posters. Australia's thirteen hours behind Brazil, making it late morning in Melbourne. "Do you know how hard it is to pull an eraser out of a child's nose? That's rhetorical, by the way. It's very bloody difficult."

Amusement winds through me. "Your day sounds more eventful than mine."

Charlotte huffs a sardonic laugh. "So says the guy with the second-fastest lap time at today's practice."

I hold back a grin and tamp down on the pleasure building in my chest. She wasn't at practice today, so she must have been keeping tabs. Willow opens her mouth, but before she speaks again, she holds up a finger and mutes herself. She briefly talks with someone offscreen, then she's back, telling us she has to go separate two kids who are fighting over something one of their imaginary friends did. Then, with a wave, she's gone.

"So why were you taking a long, romantic walk on the beach by yourself?" Charlotte asks as she locks her phone screen.

"I could ask you the same thing." I plant my hands in the sand behind me and stretch my legs out. "But since you asked, I wanted to get some fresh air before heading in for the night."

Resting her chin on her shoulder, she gives me a sweet smile. "Party wasn't fun?"

I let out a noncommittal grunt. "It was fine. What'd you end up doing today?"

In one long sentence, she tells me about researching the top things to do in Barcelona, then about her trips to the Sagrada Familia and the Picasso Museum. From there, she shopped and ate her way through Las Ramblas. In usual Charlotte style, she took a few detours. While I was in a team meeting about tire strategy, she was at Granja La Pallaresa, indulging in churros dipped in a thick, dark, hot chocolate with freshly whipped cream. When I was in my third media interview of the day, being asked the same questions worded in twenty different ways, she was wandering through a maze designed to mimic the Greek myth of Theseus destroying the Minotaur to get to Ariadne in the Parc del Laberint d'Horta. And when I was schmoozing my way through a team dinner before this party? She was clapping and cheering at one of Barcelona's famous flamenco shows.

She's appalled when I admit I've never seen a flamenco show. "That's blasphemy. You can't come to Barcelona and not experience the beauty of one of their time-honored traditions. It's so much more than just dancing and singing. It's... honestly, it's art."

"I'm not against going to a show," I say, feeling a little defensive. "I just don't appreciate dancing like you do."

Charlotte scoffs. "That's a bald-faced lie if I've ever heard one."

I raise my hands as if that'll fend off her accusation, biting back a grin. "No, it's not."

"If you've been to a strip club, you're a fan of dancing," she says, her expression and tone far too serious to accompany those words.

There's no holding back now. I bark out a laugh that doesn't stop until I'm grabbing at my sides. She's got me there. I've been to my share fair of strip clubs around the world, so yeah, I guess one could say I appreciate a good dance.

Playfully, she smacks me in the arm as I'm wiping a tear from my eye. "It's not funny. Do you know how much work and practice go into those pole routines? A lot."

I waggle my eyebrows. "You speaking from experience?"

She nods, surprising the hell out of me and making my stomach plummet straight into the sand. I don't judge anyone for how they make their livelihood, but if I don't like the idea of Charlotte flirting with Cooper, I sure as fuck don't like the idea of her taking off her clothes for strangers.

"What do you mean?"

"Calm down, you drongo." She rolls her eyes. I'm certain drongo is an Australian insult of some sort, but I'm too impatient for her explanation to care.

"Willow and I took a pole dancing class last year at this place called Stiletto Siren. It was for beginners, so we only learned basic spins, a bit of choreography and some floor moves. I was horrid, considering I have the core strength of a noodle, but we had a blast. After the first few times I used the pole, I had more bruises than the Toybreaker did the other night. I kept falling flat on my arse."

"Oh."

Great job articulating, Lucas. A-fucking-plus. My mind's too busy imagining Charlotte swinging around a pole in sky-high red-bottom heels and nothing else that I can't form a single coherent sentence.

Her eyes dance with humor at my single-syllable response. "Stripping isn't in my future. Not when I bruise like a peach. But I do have a hell of a lot of respect for women who do it. Willow and I went to the strip club a lot last year to support our instructor. If you're looking for a recommendation, I highly suggest the Leggy Lady. Great dancers and even better sweet potato fries."

"I don't even know what to make of that." I drop my head forward and give it a shake. "Thought I knew everything about you, Roo, but you're full of surprises."

She cocks a brow. "There are plenty of details you don't know about me."

"Name one," I challenge, pulling my knees up and resting my forearms on them. "And keep in mind that I know your favorite non-domesticated animal is a Pallas cat and that you're wildly good at untangling necklaces. Oh, and you can recite every word of *Elf* and *The Devil Wears Prada*."

There must be more rum than pineapple juice in this cocktail. Why the hell else would I admit to knowing all that?

Charlotte narrows her eyes at me, looking more annoyed than impressed by my wealth of knowledge. "Those are entry-level facts," she says. "The same as me knowing that you hate tomatoes, but love pizza and spaghetti sauce. That you enjoy putting together Ikea furniture and get emotional during every single Olympic ceremony."

A bolt of pleasure courses through me. Damn. While she tilts her head and hums like she's running through a mental Rolodex of facts about me, or maybe about herself, I revel in the knowledge that she knows so many of my quirks.

Digging her toes into the sand, she says, "There's one detail about me that no one knows, so you can't tell anyone. Not even Theo."

Heart rate picking up, I nod. Maybe I should feel guilty for so easily agreeing to keep a secret from Theo, but everyone's entitled to their own shit. Unless it's something that puts her in harm's way, I can respect that.

Charlotte takes a deep breath, her shoulders and chest rising, then slowly exhales. "I got into FIT."

Like I've been smacked in the face, I jerk back, eyes wide. "The Fashion Institute of Technology?"

What the hell else would it stand for? Fun Imagination Trust? Fuck, I'm Tropical?

"The one and only," she confirms, wearing a small, amused smile. "I was planning on living my best Carrie Bradshaw life."

"I didn't even know you applied there."

"Exactly," she says, nudging me with her elbow. "You asked me to tell you something no one else knew."

"Touché. Why'd you decide not to go?"

"It's complicated," she answers with a defeated sigh.

"More or less complicated than explaining all the rules and regulations to someone who thinks F1 is the same as NASCAR?"

"More," she admits, although my question does ease the tension in her shoulders a bit. "Long story short, I found out I was accepted the week after my dad passed."

"Shit." I drop my head between my arms, heart aching for her.

"That about sums it up," she says with a laugh. "My mum was really struggling, and I know it wasn't my burden to take on—and she would kill me if she knew why I stayed—but leaving Melbourne wasn't an option after that."

Focus averted, she scoops up a pile of sand and lets the grains slip through her fingers. "I was okay with it. I always thought the details would work themselves out eventually. Probably depended on that mindset a little more than I should've, considering I still haven't figured fuck all out."

I angle closer and nudge my shoulder against hers. "My brother Finn majored in psychology and now works in finance. And Jesse? He majored in music theory and now works for a tech start-up. You can work in fashion without having the degree."

Pulling her knees to her chest, she wraps her arms around them. "I wouldn't even know where to start." She swallows audibly and clears her throat. "Enough about me. You should tell me something about you that no one else knows. Like… do you have any secret tattoos?"

I scratch at my cheek as I consider the question. Sure, I have tattoos that even my friends probably haven't seen, but that's only because I don't announce every new piece of ink. For a moment, I mentally shuffle through my choices. I mean to tell her that I failed my drivers' test the first time around because I couldn't parallel park, which is absolutely mortifying, but what comes out instead is "My brother started dating my ex after we broke up."

My heart lurches as the admission registers. *What the fuck?* Yeah, there is absolutely too much rum in this damn drink. There's no way I'd admit that willingly otherwise.

Charlotte's hair brushes against my shoulder as she whips her head in my direction, her features etched with pure horror. "You're lying."

I huff out a breath, ignoring the slice of pain that hits me. "I wish I was."

"Holy shit," she says, shaking her head. "That's so unbelievably fucked up. If I were you, I don't think I could ever forgive him, but I also hold grudges like it's an Olympic sport. Ingrid Nevins? She pressed the *close doors* button on the elevator, even though I was only a few feet away, and I ended up being late for class because I had to sprint up seven flights of stairs instead. The professor wouldn't let me take the final exam because of my tardiness, and I failed the course. Do I still curse her name? Absolutely. And Jamie Dieter claims he got the high score on *Pac-Man*, but I *know* he had his older brother rig the game so he could manually enter his name above mine. Wanker."

I snort, thankful for the way her babbling eases the tension gripping me. "Yeah, I can't see myself forgiving and forgetting any time soon."

"Nor should you," she says with a resolute nod. "Don't worry, though. Your secrets are safe with me."

I freeze, confused. *Secrets? Plural?*

She nods at the pineapple drink I've mindlessly picked up again. "It's okay to admit that you like drinks other than beer and whiskey. Enjoying fruity cocktails is nothing to be ashamed of. Really."

Standing, I wipe the sand off my pants, yank the straw and umbrella from the drink, and throw the now-empty pineapple like I'm Travis Kelce. "I have no idea what you're talking about."

"Mm-hmm," she says, her eyes crinkling as she laughs. The sound brings me more peace than the waves lapping at the beach ever have. Maybe it's the drink talking, but it's taking the last strands of my sobriety to not kiss the fuck out of her. Forget pineapple drinks; I'm ready for a taste of something much sweeter. And that would be a secret just between us.

TWELVE
CHARLOTTE

THE KNOCK ECHOING through my room has me groaning into my pillow. What the hell's the point of putting a Do Not Disturb sign on my door if no one is going to respect it? Grumbling, I drag myself out of my pillow cocoon and shuffle to the door.

Swinging it open, I grit out, "Can you not read, or did you willfully ignore the sign?" It's definitely not the friendliest greeting I could have gone with, but I've never once claimed to be a morning person, and everyone I know has been warned that I'm a bitch before I've had my caffeine.

As if my visitor has read my mind, a steaming Styrofoam cup is thrust into my hand. Even knowing it'll singe my taste buds, I take a sip. I'm enjoying the smoky notes of the blend when something wet brushes against my foot. Cringing, I peer down. And there, at my feet, Champ Hollis-Gold sits, his pink tongue hanging out the side of his mouth. After he gives me a smile—I swear he does—he lowers his fluffy head and once again licks my toes.

If the coffee wasn't enough to wake me up, that would've done the trick.

It's hard to maintain my grumpy frown when an adorable creature with big brown eyes is watching me. Blake has always seemed like a German Shepard kind of guy. Yet he ended up with a twenty-five-pound cockapoo that looks like a stuffed animal.

"Morning." Ella greets me with a dimpled smile.

She steps past me and into my suite with Champ at her heels. She's dressed in her signature outfit: trainers, athletic shorts, and oversized T-shirt. Not many people can wear athleisure and manage to look professional, but Ella's mastered it.

"Stop smiling," I say, shutting the door behind her. "It's too early to be happy."

If anything, her smile widens. "It's nearly noon."

I vaguely remember the front desk calling to wake me up at nine, but I must have gotten right back into bed after brushing my teeth. The plan was to go to bed early so I could watch this morning's practice before heading into the city center to shop and explore, but I couldn't sleep. How could I when I couldn't stop thinking about which of Lucas's brothers is dating his ex? Is this ex the one Theo and Blake were referring to in Japan?

"My point remains," I reiterate. "It's too early to be smiling."

"I brought you coffee so you wouldn't bite my head off." She eases herself onto the couch and crosses one leg over the other. "And I figured Champ would soften you up."

Taking another sip of coffee, I close my eyes and savor the flavor. It's exactly how I like it. Eyes open again, I squint at her. "How'd you know my coffee order?"

"Lucas."

My surprise must show on my face, because that perma-smile widens.

She tries to hide it by looking away and patting the spot next to her. "C'mere, Champ."

The pup bounces toward her, but halfway there, he gets distracted by the clothing strewn around the floor. To him, my shorts and bras look like new, exciting toys. He picks up a dirty sock and drops it at my feet, then looks up at me expectantly, his tail moving from side to side so fast his whole butt goes with it.

"Am I supposed to throw it or something?" I love dogs, but I've spent little time around them. I'm not sure of the proper etiquette, but I know they like fetch.

"No," she says with a laugh. "He's just bringing you a welcome present."

"He's bringing me my own sock as a welcome present?"

Her shrug is easy. "I can't say why he does it, but yeah, that's exactly what he's doing."

"Thank you, buddy. That's very thoughtful." I crouch, careful not to spill my coffee, and give him a few scratches on the head. "I mean this in the nicest way possible," I say, eyeing Ella, "but why are you here?"

I won't complain, since she did bring coffee, but that can't be the only reason she showed up at my door.

Her responding laugh is light. "I interviewed your brother for the podcast this morning, and he mentioned you were shopping today. Since I desperately need something to wear for Monaco, I wanted to tag along."

"But how'd you know I was still here and not already out and about?"

She hums. "Yeah, I wanted to ask you about that." Petting Champ absentmindedly, she tilts her head. "Why does Lucas have your location but Theo doesn't?"

Rather than answer, I lift my brows and wait for her to come to that conclusion by herself.

It happens a moment later. "Okay, yeah. Much safer option," she says, nodding. "Anyway, I've ordered a bunch of shit online, but hate all of it, so I'm in desperate need of your expertise and assistance."

A squeal escapes me at the prospect, and I do a small happy dance that has Champ barking and running in a circle. This was so worth being woken up for. I'm fine shopping on my own, but it's so much more fun with company. It's like being in an episode of *Sex and the City*. And since Ella's vibe is so different from mine, I get to browse pieces and options that I'd never consider otherwise. Finding the perfect item for someone else is like solving a puzzle. I have to pair their tastes with items they'll feel comfortable in while simultaneously styling in a way that challenges them to step out of their comfort zone.

Settling down on the floor next to Champ, I ask, "Do you need something for a specific event?"

"I desperately need something for the Dom Pérignon party." She sighs.

I've never been to the Monaco Grand Prix, or Monaco at all, for that matter, but I swear more celebrities and photographers attend the event than even an award show. The Dom Pérignon after-party is the crème de la crème. It's invite only, and not every driver is invited. Even plus-ones have to be vetted beforehand.

"Didn't you meet Nicholas Galitzine at that party last year?"

"No, but Blake did," Ella says, scowling. "I didn't know until I saw a picture of them in *Vogue* the next day. Blake thought he was a fan and didn't understand why I was freaking out about it."

I burst out laughing. Only Blake would think one of the hottest actors in Hollywood right now was a fan rather than an A-list celebrity.

After I've finished my coffee and given Champ all the belly rubs, I stand and head into my room to get dressed.

"How long is it going to take you?" Ella asks. "Do I have enough time to catch up on last week's episode of *Law and Order: SVU*, or should I just scroll through TikTok?"

It looks like my longer than usual morning routine precedes me. "You can catch up on the episode."

With a thumbs-up, she kicks off one shoe, then the other, and pulls her feet up under her.

IT'S clear right away that Ella's shopping strategy is "one and done" whereas mine is "shop till you drop." Thankfully, she gets a second wind once we've refueled with gelato. We went to the shop she and Blake visited just before their first kiss, and once she had a double scoop of vanilla in hand, she was ready to hit more stores.

We found a dress for the party at the first place we popped into post-gelato. I forced her into trying on a stunning emerald green dress with a fitted bodice and short A-line skirt. She was convinced it would make her look like a "lumpy bag of Idaho potatoes"—*whatever that means*—but, of course, she looked like an absolute goddess. Once she got a look at herself in the mirror, it didn't take any extra convincing for her to make the purchase.

I drag her and Champ into boutiques and markets, grand department stores and artisanal shops until even I'm ready to call it quits. With bags adorned with local shops' logos draped over our arms, we trudge into our final vintage shop of the day. Inside, the scent of perfume mingles with the aroma of freshly ground coffee from the adjacent café. Like most stores of its kind, it's a charming mix of nostalgia and chic, with racks of vintage dresses with intricate lace, tailored suits with sharp lines, bold hats, and patterned scarves.

Ella ventures over to the shoes, which I find risky, since Champ has a penchant for anything with laces, while I start at the front of the store. Immediately, my attention catches on a stunning watch. I don't wear watches—although I probably should—but that doesn't mean I don't appreciate their artistry.

"Holy shit," I mutter, running my fingers over the face of what has to be the *Mona Lisa* of timepieces.

A nearby shopper shoots me a dirty look, but I pay no mind. This gorgeous accessory deserves a stunned, dramatic reaction. Squinting, I angle closer to get a better look at the watch brand, but it doesn't ring any bells. Not that my unfamiliarity means anything. My knowledge of designers doesn't extend into watchmaking.

"Ooh," Ella says from my left. "That's a nice watch. Are you thinking about buying it?"

With a sigh, I pull my hand away. "No. It's gorgeous, but it's a man's watch."

"So? Maybe you have a special someone in your life who'd like it," she says, bumping her hip against mine.

"Oh, you mean Bob?"

"Bob?" Ella's tone is one of confusion and excitement. "You're dating someone named Bob? I didn't realize that was still a popular name. How'd you guys meet? How long have you been dating? Does—"

Grinning, I grasp her hand. "Bob stands for battery-operated boyfriend."

With a sharp intake of breath, she throws her head back and cackles. "Okay, so no actual boyfriend."

"He gives me more orgasms than my ex ever did, so do with that information what you will," I reply. "And it's kind of hard to date when you're living out of a suitcase and spend four out of seven days a week in the company of your overbearing brother."

"Yeah, that'd definitely be a cockblock," she sympathizes. "You could always go out with Cooper. You know he's into you, right?"

"Cooper Fraser?" I ask, shock weaving through me, making my heart stutter. I met the Scottish driver at the first grand prix of the season, and we've spoken briefly a few times since then, but I've never gotten anything more than friendly vibes from him. Regardless, it's nice to be noticed.

"Mm-hmm. Blake said that Cooper asked about you last night. Of course, he gave me zero details. God forbid a man remembers a conversation. But he said there was definitely interest."

Huh. "Did you ever find out if he has a penis piercing?"

The same woman who glared at me for swearing makes the sign of the cross, then shuffles out the door of the shop.

Ella bursts out laughing, which has Champ yipping, too.

"I couldn't figure out a way to casually bring up frenum piercings, but that doesn't mean you can't do some research and figure it out," she teases, her lips tugging up on one side.

I laugh. "You're the journalist, not me."

"You're the single one," she argues. "Not me."

"True." I scan the pieces in front of me, once again ensnared by the watch. I'm far more interested in finding out whether Lucas has a tattoo down there, though I won't admit that to her. My attempt to get that information out of him was derailed when he revealed that his brother had dated his ex. My heart aches at the memory, at the hurt in his expression. No wonder he got into boxing.

Ella heads over to a table with neatly stacked piles of T-shirts while I pick up the watch and admire the small details I missed the first time around. Lucas isn't my special someone, but he is a friend, and he happens to love watches.

While Ella's trying on a new band shirt to add to her ever-growing collection, I quickly purchase the watch and slip the small box into my purse.

It's not until I'm standing in front of Lucas's door that I consider it might be weird for me to have picked up a gift for him. A few years ago, Willow and I took the quiz that determines a person's love language. While mine is words of affirmation (to absolutely no one's surprise), I show my love through gift giving. Not that I love Lucas. I simply enjoy giving people gifts. I love the way they light up. Because c'mon, who wouldn't want a surprise present?

Fuck it.

I knock on the door, then anxiously shift my weight from one foot to the other while I wait for Lucas to answer. Is he even here? He may have my location, but he didn't share his with me, so I have no clue if he's in his hotel room. He and Theo have a team dinner in an hour, so he could have gone out to drinks beforehand. Or out to do some sightseeing? What if he met a really hot fan and went back to her hotel room to—

The door swings open, and at the sight that greets me, I nearly choke on my tongue. *Lord have mercy.* Lucas stands in the doorway wearing a pair of gray sweatpants, with a towel draped around his neck. A few droplets of water trickle from his chest, and holy shit, the man has so many abs I could play a game of chess on them. I've seen him shirtless before, sure, but I've never been this up close and personal with his nipples.

"Hey, Roo," he says, his voice scratchy from overuse after media interviews.

I drag my eyes away from the tattoos that twist up his left side and focus on his face. "That's porn."

Instantly, my face flames. *Seriously? Why can't I ever say hello like a normal person?*

Because Lucas is normal, rather than a person who greets others by announcing "that's porn," his brows scrunch together. "Excuse me?"

"Gray sweatpants are girl porn." How does he not know this universal truth? "It's like the female equivalent of men thinking a woman's arse looks good in yoga pants."

With a smirk, he dips his chin. "Interesting."

Needing to focus on something other than his porn pants and chiseled chest, I root around in my purse and pull out the navy box the woman at the store packaged the watch in. "I got you something."

"You got me a present?" He blinks at the box, studying it like it's a compass that will lead him to the lost treasure of Atlantis. "What is it?"

"Cocaine," I deadpan. Why ask when he can simply have the answer himself?

He tears his attention from the box and zeroes in on me. "What is it really?"

I toss it at him. I hate opening gifts in front of people. It's too easy to tell when I'm not enamored by something. I'm grateful for any gift I get, but people expect recipients to act like they've just been given floor seats to a Taylor Swift Eras Tour show even when it's a gift card to a local coffee shop.

Lucas absentmindedly licks his lips as he eases the top off the box. With more gentleness than a man with that many muscles should possess, he takes the watch off the cushion it's wrapped around. Then he turns it over in his hand, examining it from all angles. "Holy shit. This is… I don't even know the right word. Saying 'it's sick' seems lame as hell."

I swallow thickly, unsure of whether I'm pleased or embarrassed. "I know you like watches so… yeah."

Great fucking sales pitch, Charlotte.

"Thank you, Roo." He slips it onto his wrist and grins down at it. "Looks good on me, right?"

Even Crocs look good on this man, so yeah, this looks great.

Breathing past the pressure in my chest, I nod. "It looks great. Very distinguished."

"Thanks for thinking of me."

I always am.

THIRTEEN
LUCAS

ONE WOULD THINK it'd be obvious that a person should not jump off a moving boat, right? Clearly, it's not to Theo. Unless it's an explicitly stated rule, he doesn't understand why it's frowned upon. So now, every time he sets foot on my sailboat, I have to spend fifteen minutes going over rules that should be common sense to anyone over the age of five.

"Theo, shut the fuck up and pay attention," Blake snaps, taking the words right out of my mouth. "We're only listening to these bloody rules because of your dumb arse."

We're in Monaco early so we can relax for a few days before our obligations start, but Blake looks anything but at ease. If it weren't for Ella rubbing calming circles on his back and Champ sitting on his lap—wearing a life vest with a shark fin on it—he'd be shoving Theo into the water.

The Australian simply rolls his eyes. "Says the guy who sunbathed nude on this very boat last year."

"Because you fucking pantsed me," Blake growls, a vein in his temple throbbing.

I tip my head back, begging for the Monaco sun to give me strength. Would it really be so bad for Theo to jump off if it meant I'd be spared from arguing with him over why turning the sail the other way won't make us go backward?

"Only as payback for—"

"I'm not going to apologize for stopping you from climbing the mast like you were in *Pirates of the Caribbean*."

Theo doesn't understand the first thing about boating, and that's okay. But he's a grown man, and he could at the very least not treat it like a jungle gym or playground. This boat was the first item I splurged on. It may not cost as much as Blake's two superyachts, but it's my pride and joy. The *Blank Check* is my escape, and every time I step aboard, a sense of freedom I only ever find here and from the cockpit of my car overtakes me.

Ella raises a polite hand. "Can we skip going through the rules if Josie promises to keep Theo on his best behavior?"

Theo waggles his brows at his girlfriend. "How are you going to keep me in line, princess?"

She's too busy trying to coax Champ out of Blake's lap and into hers to pay him any mind. With Josie working a normal nine-to-five job in London, it's hard for her to travel to races, but she took some time off to spend the week in Monaco with him. She's coming to the Australian Grand Prix next month and a few more later in the season, too.

"No," I tell Ella. "While I trust Josie, I don't trust Theo. Do I need to bring up what happened after the grand prix five years ago?"

"How many times are you going to make me apologize for that, man?" Theo says with a frown. "Rose and Jack make it look so easy in *Titanic*."

I hold up my hand and continue with my rules. "No pushing me out of the way and yelling 'I am the Captain now.' No jumping off while the boat's moving. Or pushing people off while it's anchored. No climbing on anything. If you see a bird, leave it the fuck alone. Do not try to feed it or befriend it. No pantsing or nudity. No—"

"That's hypocritical, considering I can see your nipples," Theo quips.

The irritation simmering in my gut heats to a steady boil. *Murder is illegal. Murder is illegal. Murder is illegal.*

"Because I'm in a bathing suit, you annoying piece of shit," I state calmly, despite how badly I want to throttle him. Turning to Blake, I say, "You have my full approval to push Theo off the boat whenever you feel like it."

Finally finished with my spiel, I leave my friends and move through my pre-sailing checklist with practiced efficiency. Lines neatly coiled? Check. Sails securely furled? Check. Deck clear of any loose items? Check. I confirm that the engine oil and water tanks are full before moving to the stern, where the marina staff has nearly finished untying the mooring lines. I nod to the dockmaster, and she throws me a thumbs-up, letting me know we're good to go.

With a deep breath in, I tune out my friends' chatter and soak up the soft sounds of the morning activity—the gentle clinking of rigging, the distant hum of engines, and the occasional call of gulls—then I climb up to the helm. I start the engine and relish the low, satisfying hum, then expertly guide *Blank Check* away from the dock, navigating through the narrow marina passage with ease. As we slowly make our way out to open water, the opulent Monaco skyline recedes. The grand façade of the Monte Carlo Casino, the elegant Hôtel de Paris, and the colorful buildings of the old town all wave goodbye as we sail farther into the deep, inviting sea.

Clearing the harbor, I cut the engine and move to unfurl the sails. The mainsail goes up smoothly, catching the gentle morning breeze. I adjust the jib, and immediately, the boat leans slightly and gains speed. The sound of the engine is replaced by the peaceful rustle of the wind through the sails and the rhythmic splash of water against the hull.

I fill my lungs with sea air and exhale the tension from my body. *Now we're talking*.

Charlotte climbs across the spacious cockpit toward where I'm stationed at one of the twin helms. She greets me with her signature wave, then settles in to watch me with quiet curiosity while the rest of our group noshes on breakfast from a local bakery around the alfresco table.

After several quiet minutes, she speaks. "How long have you had your boating license?"

"In Monaco?" I ask. "Nine years now, I think. I've had a boating license in Massachusetts since I was thirteen, though."

"Thirteen?" Her eyes widen in surprise. "Christ, the most complicated thing I was doing at thirteen was figuring out how to put in a tampon."

As the words register, I abruptly jerk the wheel, causing a chorus of *whoa*s to erupt from our friends. *Oops*. With a sharp breath, I readjust the wheel.

"Sorry, that was probably too much information." She grimaces. "That's young to be driving a boat, though, right?"

"I never really thought about it," I admit. "It's sort of a tradition to get your boating license once you hit thirteen in my family. My mom's parents lived on Martha's Vineyard until they retired, and they had a boat called *Blank Check* that we took out every summer."

While one grandpa taught me about watches, the other taught me about boats.

"*Oh*." She sits straighter. "That's where the name of your boat came from. I was wondering about that."

The scrutiny in her tone has me raising my brows. "You don't like the name?"

"No, I do. It's adorable, and you know I'm a sucker for a

good pun. But without the backstory, it seemed a little pretentious for you."

I snort. "It's an homage to childhood summers with my family."

Head tilted, she surveys me, her expression soft. "Have you considered getting merch made?"

"Merch for a boat whose only passengers are my friends?" I arch a brow. "No, I haven't."

"Fine, don't make merch. Just make a one-of-a-kind special-edition shirt for me."

"Ah, to add to your collection."

"Mm-hmm." She unscrews the cap of her giant water bottle and takes a few large sips. "I've decided to get one from each new city I visit, but Monaco's punny shirt scene is seriously lacking. The only touristy stuff I've found are magnets and mugs, and they're disgustingly expensive."

Charlotte stays at the helm with me as I navigate along the coast. Even when everyone heads out to relax on the deck, she stays put, asking me questions about the boat, the places I've sailed, and anything else that pops into her head.

We've been on the water for a good hour when I ask, "Want to give it a try?"

She looks up, her lips parting in surprise. "I thought the 'no asking to sail the boat' rule extended to all Walkers, not just Theo."

"Unless you plan on racing my boat like we're escaping from a diamond heist, we'll be fine."

Adjusting the tiller, I find the perfect angle to catch the wind, and the boat responds instantly, cutting through the water with a sense of purpose.

"Are you sure?" She takes a hesitant step forward. "I don't want to fuck anything up."

"I'll be right here with you," I reassure her. "It's easier than it looks, I promise. Come on, give it a go."

It's definitely not easier than it looks, but I'll do all I can to make this a good boating experience. And I'm eager to see how hot she'll look behind the wheel.

At my words, she bounces over, her face split into an eager smile. Though when she lifts her hands, she holds them so they're hovering over the wheel uncertainly. Smiling to myself, I move behind her, close enough to guide her but leaving enough space for her to feel in control.

"Okay, place your hands here," I say, gently grasping her wrists and positioning her hold. "Feel the way the boat moves with the wind and the water. Don't fight it, just guide it."

She nods, gripping the wheel more firmly. The sensation of controlling the sailboat is clearly as exhilarating for Charlotte as it is for me. Beaming, she peeks over her shoulder. "Am I doing it right?"

"Mm-hmm," I say with a smile and an encouraging nod. "Now gently turn to the right. Just a little."

She follows my instructions, and the boat responds, smoothly changing direction. "This is amazing. I can't believe I'm actually doing it. Can we go a bit faster?"

With a laugh, I appease her. "Let's trim the sails a bit and catch more wind."

As I walk her through how to adjust the sails, explaining each step, she follows my lead, and soon the boat picks up speed, slicing through the water with a little more momentum. Unable to resist touching her, I place my hands over hers once again and guide her with subtle movements. The warmth of her hands under mine and the steady presence of her back against my front fill me with a warmth the sun can't compete with.

"You're wearing your new watch," Charlotte says, just loud enough to be heard over the flapping sail.

I grin down at the item in question. I haven't received a gift from a woman that wasn't a family member since… Kylie. And her presents were lingerie. Sure, they were enjoyable, but they didn't hold any kind of meaning, really. This gift? It's rife with it.

I've always liked accessories—hence my rings and bracelets—but I started collecting watches as a kid. My grandpa was a jeweler, and my dad now runs the business, with Ezra working under him. For my bar mitzvah, he gave me a Celestial Chronos watch. More accurately, I suppose, he gave me the parts of a Celestial Chronos that were necessary to restore it. We spent the next year tinkering with it in his shop when I wasn't racing. In a lot of ways, watches are like Formula 1 cars. Both require several mechanical processes that underscore their engineering precision, performance, and craftsmanship. They're technological works of art. Masterpieces in their own right.

I'm particular as hell about my watches, though there is no specific criteria for what makes one stand out to me. It's more of a *when you know, you know* sort of thing. That's why no one ever bothers buying them for me. Sure, if I did receive one, I'd be appreciative, and I'd wear it on occasion. But it's unlikely that I'd feel the need to add it to my treasured collection and show it off like a proud parent.

This watch? It's a clear fucking winner. When I texted Ezra a photo of it late last night, he immediately recognized it as a Longines from the early '80s. It features a manual wind, luxury leather strap, elongated hour markers, and sleek hands finished in gold. It's easy to read while maintaining a sophisticated look. There are a few minor scratches and dents, but that only adds to the vintage character. I felt a bit like Don Draper when I put it on this morning.

"You'll teach her how to drive your sailboat, but you won't teach me?" Theo asks, interrupting my tranquility.

"Yes," I reply with absolutely no remorse. Though my heart lodges itself in my throat when I realize how close Charlotte and I still are. I take a subtle step back, dropping my hands back to my sides.

Theo, luckily, seems unfazed.

I don't even trust the man to water my plants, so he definitely has sun poisoning if he thinks I'm letting him anywhere near the steering wheel of this thing. Theo's way too competitive to drive anything but a Jet Ski on the water. There are unspoken rules out here that he blatantly ignores.

Though it shouldn't, my succinct answer throws him off, and instead of replying, he simply waves his arms around and sputters in frustration. He knows Blake will take my side, so he doesn't bother roping him in to the conversation.

Finally, he answers in a way that throws *me* off. "How are you going to name me your kid's godparent if you won't even let me take care of your firstborn?"

A bark of laughter erupts from me. "I've quite literally never told you that. Ever."

"It's part of the plan, Lucas," Theo says, rolling his eyes as if I'm an idiot for not knowing this. "I'm your kid's godparent, you're Blake's kid's godparent, and Blake is my kid's godparent. We'll reverse the order for our second kids."

"This is news to me," Blake says, approaching us with Ella at his side.

Oh great, now everyone's joining the party.

"After you nearly killed Champ, I can't say I like the idea of you anywhere near my future kids."

"You said to give him treats when he was being a good boy," Theo pouts. "It's not my fault he was a good boy the entire weekend."

Ella playfully shoves him in the chest. "It is your fault I had to pick up fucking dog shit for—"

"Fine," I interrupt. "You can be my kid's godparent."

I'm not sure who's more surprised by my easy acquiescence, but it stuns the hell out of both of my friends.

As if he's worried I'll take it back, Theo spins and heads down into the salon level of the boat.

"Are you dehydrated?" Blake asks, wearing a concerned frown.

"Godparents aren't a Jewish tradition," Ella answers for me. "Theo can have the title, but it's honorary only. It has nothing to do with legal guardianship."

She throws me a wink, knowing neither of us will have to worry about Theo having any legal claims over our kids. I have no doubt he'll be a great dad when the time comes, but that doesn't mean he'll have the right to tell my kid to do anything.

Theo returns a few minutes later with an armful of snacks, so with the whole group here, I fill them in on my plan to drop the anchor so we can swim and hang out for the rest of the day. When Charlotte slips out of her crochet coverup, it's a damn good thing that we're in the middle of the sea without another boat in sight. That's the only reason we don't fucking crash. *Christ Almighty*. Her bathing suit is a simple cobalt blue triangle bikini, but it leaves little to the imagination. A simple pull of one of the ties, and she'd be—*get it the fuck together*.

Blake's been on *Blank Check* enough to help me anchor with ease. He holds the boat steady from the helm, then slows and points the vessel into the wind before gently easing off the throttle so I can release the anchor, letting the heavy chain rattle through my hands and into the water below.

Anchored and secured, I do a quick stretch and dive off the boat. The cool saltwater is invigorating, and I resurface with a grin on my face. Blake sets up an inflatable beer pong table while Theo blows up giant pool floats shaped like jungle animals, Ella plays water fetch with Champ, and Josie connects my phone to the speaker system and puts on a playlist. Surveying my friends one by one, I scan my surroundings. When I catch sight of Charlotte, a thread of concern weaves its way through me. She's sitting on the edge of the boat with her feet dangling off, barely grazing the ocean.

"You don't want to cool off?" I call out.

Peering into the water, she shakes her head, causing her curls to sweep over her shoulders. "I'm good right here."

"Is it because of your pump?" I ask, nodding to the wireless device to the left of her belly button. I'm grateful for my sunglasses, otherwise I'd surely get caught checking her out longer than what's considered friendly.

"No, this bad boy's waterproof," she tells me, giving it a gentle pat. "It's more of a me thing. I don't like swimming in water where I can't see what's around me. I love pools, but oceans? No, thanks."

I still for a second, processing her words, but kick below the surface again quickly to keep from going under. "Wait. You're serious."

"Eighty percent of the ocean hasn't been explored yet, and the 20 percent we know about is scary as fuck. Do you know what a deep-sea dragonfish looks like?"

Wincing, I rake a hand through my wet hair. "Uh, no."

"You're lucky. I don't recommend googling it unless you want to have nightmares for the next five years."

I can't help but laugh. "Fair enough."

We spend the next few hours swimming, then break for lunch. No one came close to convincing Charlotte to get into the water, especially after she saw a jellyfish. As I towel off and let the sun warm my chilled skin, she slaps my phone into my hand.

"You have a text," she says, eyes darting down and to one side.

Curious, I take a peek at the device. All that appears on the lock screen is the Spotify icon showing that "Shirt" by SZA is playing. "Are you—"

"I read it," she blurts out.

A chuckle threatens to escape me, but I bite it back. I really hope she never commits a crime. The cops would have to do absolutely nothing to wring a confession out of her.

"Okay," I reply, one brow arched. "It's not—"

"I wasn't reading your messages or anything," she interrupts, her expression dripping with guilt. "It popped up on the screen when I was trying to change songs, so it's not really my fault."

Confused, I ask, "How'd you unlock my phone?"

Sunlight dances in her eyes as she rolls them, turning them the same color as the sea we're sailing on. It's like looking into the waters. They draw me in, urging me to dive deeper. "It's tattooed on your arm in Roman numerals."

"Huh." Amusement flickers through me. And here I thought I was clever using 052384 as my password. Who would guess my parents' anniversary date as a lock code? Charlotte, apparently.

"Who's it from?" I ask as I hold my phone in front of my face to unlock it.

"Jesse."

At those two syllables, my stomach drops farther than the anchor of our boat. *Shit.* Quickly opening the *Messages* app, I find the text from Jesse sitting there like a ticking time bomb.

> **JESSE**
>
> Hey. I'm on a ridiculously tight deadline right now, so I can't make it to Montreal next weekend, but I'll be finished when you're home. I'm hoping we can talk one-on-one.
>
> I miss you, bro.

I press the heel of my hand to my forehead. At least in Canada, I could claim to be too busy for the heart-to-heart he seems hell-bent on having, but now he's going to double down on "talking" when I'm in Boston.

"My money was on Finn," Charlotte says, interrupting my doomsday spiral.

Dropping my hand, I assess her. "What do you mean?"

"You can't drop a bomb like your brother being a douche canoe general and expect me to not want to know which one. I'm nosy by nature, Lucas."

"And you thought it was Finn?" I ask, fighting a grin. Finn's got a lot of game, but he's allergic to commitment and condoms, which makes him a walking red flag for most women.

"Yeah," she admits. "Process of elimination. Grayson's married, and since he just posted about their seven-year anniversary, I couldn't imagine it was him. The next closest to you in age is Jesse, but I ruled him out, since the two of you have always been so close."

Her words are like a knife to the chest.

"That leaves the twins. Ezra and Finn," she continues. "Ezra has less game than a dead Nintendo, so I can't exactly see him being Mr. Steal Your Girl, which leaves Finn. While he's the most likely to have illegitimate children, I can't see him sneaking behind your back. He's definitely the kind of guy to boast about who he's slept with."

Fuck. How the hell does she know so much about the twins' flirting styles? Jealousy rears its head, but I press my lips together to tamp it down.

Charlotte tilts her head, as if reading my thoughts. "I met them at the Austin Grand Prix last year. Watching Ezra try to flirt nearly sent me into therapy for second-hand embarrassment, and there's no way Finn works full time, since he spends half his days sliding into my DMs."

My lungs seize, and my phone clatters to the outdoor carpet beneath us. I quickly pick it up and affect a neutral expression, although playing it cool left the boat about twenty nautical miles back.

"My brother is in your DMs?"

She hits me with an affronted frown. "You don't have to seem so shocked that a good-looking guy is in my DMs."

I can't exactly tell her she's mistaking my anger for surprise, so I focus on the last part of her sentence. "You think Finn's good-looking?"

Ezra and I take after our mom, with blond hair and green eyes, but Finn, Jesse, and Grayson take after our dad in the classic tall, dark, and handsome way.

"Every member of your family is good-looking," she says, looking at me in horror, as if I just admitted to loving jellyfish. "Five boys, and all of you could easily be Abercrombie models? That's got to be a world record."

I'd normally preen at a compliment like that, but being lumped in with my brothers in her eyes spoils it. Until this moment, I couldn't imagine Jesse being replaced as my least favorite brother, but Finn is quickly worming his way to the top of that list.

"What's Finn saying to you?" I press.

"Nothing of importance," she reveals. "He mostly just sends me fire emojis, the GIF of Leonardo DiCaprio in *The Great Gatsby* lifting up a glass of champagne, and random dad jokes."

That little piece of shit.

"I'm glad I didn't end up ordering that voodoo doll for you," she muses, more to herself than to me.

I jerk back so quickly that I nearly trip over Champ, who's curled into a doughnut-shaped ball behind me. "Did I get water in my ears, or did you just say voodoo doll?"

She nods, her expression serious, as if that was a completely normal question. "Mm-hmm. I was going to order this custom voodoo doll with your evil brother's face on it."

There's a lot to unpack in that statement, but I start with "Custom voodoo dolls are a thing?"

Maybe Charlotte's pettiness should weird me out, but it's honestly sort of a turn-on.

"Clearly you've never been on Etsy," she says with a disappointed sigh. "Yes, of course custom voodoo dolls are a thing. But it would've been super confusing if I presented you with one sporting Finn's face when you two don't have any beef."

Considering he regularly DMs Charlotte, I'd say we have beef.

"Based on that text and the way you looked like you wanted to throw your phone into the bottom of the sea when you read it, I'm going to go with Jesse being the culprit," she continues. "It's a good thing he's not coming to Montreal."

"Hmm." I keep my response noncommittal. It may be obvious now that Jesse's the brother I had a falling-out with, but that doesn't mean I want to outright admit to it.

"Not for your sake," she clarifies. "For his. Boxers may be forbidden from punching people in the dick, but I'm sure as hell not."

An unexpected laugh rumbles out of me, and Charlotte's lips quirk up playfully. I've never craved attention or the spotlight, but one smile from her and I understand the temptation.

FOURTEEN
CHARLOTTE

AS A PERSON with a flair for the dramatic, I'm used to exaggeration. Monaco being the height of luxury? No embellishment whatsoever. The harbor is filled with enormous superyachts with sleek designs that boast of wealth, and the streets are lined with designer boutiques, each with elegant window displays showcasing the latest haute couture from brands like Chanel, Dior, and Louis Vuitton. And the Monte Carlo Casino? None of the James Bond movies did it justice. Every detail, from the impeccably groomed gardens and fountains to the interior architecture featuring intricate frescoes and gold-leaf detailing, screams "I'm part of the 1 percent."

Add in the film stars, directors, musicians, and athletes who swarm the principality for the grand prix like bees to honey, and it's no wonder this place is considered the billionaires' playground. Ironically, the race all the celebrities show up for is the one with the least amount of action. But considering Monaco is one of the most expensive countries to visit in the world, it makes sense that the rich and famous would rather watch the race here than in, say, Spielberg. The Austrian Grand Prix is beautiful, with the picturesque mountain background, but it's two hours outside of Vienna, so it's not nearly as convenient as many others.

Josie, Ella, and I watch as celebrities meander around the pit lane, taking photos and chatting with reporters like it's a red-carpet event. I nearly melt on the spot when I spy Joe Jonas chatting with Anya Taylor-Joy in front of the Ithaca garage, but I manage to keep my cool. Okay, not really, but Ella's absolute fucking panic over the man far supersedes mine. Apparently, she created mock wedding invitations to the ceremony where she'd say *I do* to him—had them printed out at FedEx and everything—when she was thirteen. And when Josie sees Rose Leslie and Kit Harington from *Game of Thrones*? She goes apocalyptic. She's only stopped from asking for an autograph—which is a big no-no at Monaco—when Theo's manager corrals us into the pit garage. According to him, he's on "fangirl duty," a.k.a. making sure we don't do anything that would embarrass Blake or Theo. *Rude*.

But we oblige and find a grouping of chairs to settle into on AlphaVite's rooftop, then watch from afar as the rich and famous mingle amongst themselves.

I rummage through my purse and grin when I find the bingo cards I made yesterday and the pens I swiped from the hotel. I pass copies to Josie and Ella before I get to work crossing off the box that reads *Joe Jonas wearing a half-buttoned linen shirt*.

"You made a Formula 1 bingo?" Josie asks, mildly impressed.

I swallow down a sigh. "Yeah, it's a mixture of celebrity sightings and race predictions."

"Oh." Ella straightens beside me. "I saw Emily Ratajkowski wearing a triangle bikini as a top earlier." She marks an *X* on her board.

Giddiness rushes through me at her excitement. I spent a

lot of time working on this over the past few days, so I'm glad it's being properly appreciated.

"You should have put Blake complaining about his tires as the free space." Josie giggles. "What did he say last year during the race? That he drives faster—"

"On the freeway during rush hour," Ella finishes for her, a smile teasing her lips. "He can be such a dick."

"But a lovable dick," Josie says.

Ella breaks into a saucy smirk. "I do love his dick."

I narrow my eyes at Josie. "Think very hard before making any comments about your boyfriend's dick. I don't want to be scarred for the rest of my life."

"Thanks to being scarred for life by my own mother, I try to avoid talking about genitalia in general."

Laughter bubbles out of me. Much to Josie's embarrassment, her mum is London's leading sex therapist. When Mrs. Bancroft spoke at a conference called "Sex in Suburbia" in Melbourne last year, she and Josie's dad went to dinner with my mum and her boyfriend, Richard. Mrs. Bancroft gifted my mom gummies formulated to enhance sexual arousal and stimulation, and Josie still hasn't forgiven her for it.

After people watching for an hour or so, the three of us wander up to AlphaVite's rooftop so we can view the race from there. This race is by far the least exciting. It's a street circuit, which means the track winds through the actual streets of Monte Carlo. That attribute leaves very little room for overtaking, so it's more like a procession of cars than a competition. The winners have already been decided based on qualifying times. Theo's starting the race in P5, and Lucas is starting in P7. He initially placed P4 but then received a three-grid penalty after impeding a Catalyst driver during Q1.

As the five gantry lights go out, the roar of the engines echoes through the narrow street, mimicking the way my heart pounds against my sternum. I'm always consumed by a mix of exhilaration and fear as I watch a race. The cars take off and speed uphill toward the Massenet hairpin turn, the slowest and most challenging corner on the circuit. Lucas and Paolo Gallo, a Catalyst driver, battle for position, which is risky, given such a tight turn. Gallo tries to assert his position, but Lucas maintains his line and doesn't yield. In the next second, Gallo runs out of space on the inside and makes contact with Lucas. Their wheels tangle and their cars violently collide with a sickening crunch.

Horror and panic engulf me as debris scatters across the track, causing Lucas to lose control. When his car spins, then slams into the barrier, I clutch my chest and gasp, though the sound is lost in the collective surprise of the crowd.

The stewards immediately red flag the race, bringing everything to a halt while emergency crews rush to clear the wreckage and ensure the drivers' safety. Cameras zoom in on the damage, broadcasting the image on the jumbo screen. It's immediately clear that Lucas's car took the brunt of it. Three of his tires are trashed and no longer connected to his car, and the damages to the front suspension and left side make it impossible for him to continue the race.

I shoot to my feet, gripping the railing so tightly my knuckles turn white. My vision tunnels, and I focus solely on the wreckage, praying, begging, for Lucas to move, to emerge from the twisted remains unscathed. The seconds drag on, each one an eternity, as fear claws at my chest. Tears well in my eyes, blurring my view.

Come on, get out. Please get out.

I've seen my fair share of crashes over the years, but it never gets easier watching someone, whether it be a family member, a friend, or simply another driver, sitting helplessly in a mangled car. Adrenaline surges through my veins, making me lightheaded as I wait with bated breath until, finally, Lucas staggers out of his car, unharmed but visibly angry.

As I slump back in my seat, the only thing I can think is: *that certainly wasn't on my Bingo card.*

EVEN IF I didn't have a penchant for eavesdropping, it'd be impossible to ignore the raised voices coming from the back of the garage. It's not surprising that the team is upset that the crash not only ended Lucas's race but marked a significant setback for AlphaVite. They have to spend who knows how much repairing the car while also dealing with the points lost in the championship standings.

While Blake has won seven championships and Theo has won two, Lucas hasn't won the coveted Drivers' Championship yet. He's a phenomenal driver—these guys don't get paid millions a year for being okay or average—but there're only so many opportunities to win, and the competition is tough. So far this season, he's been in a great position to compete for the title, but this upset will dent his chances.

I wait until Lucas is done talking to Mitchell, David, and his performance coach before approaching him. As I do, I survey him, from his shoes to his tousled blond hair. Other than a small scowl, he looks like his usual gorgeous self.

"Are you okay?" I ask. He's no doubt been asked this fifty times by now, but I can't help myself.

"Yeah," he confirms, his tone gruff and his green eyes swimming with frustration.

"You may want to try that again if you want anyone to believe you."

The strain of his frown lessens, his shoulders lowering a fraction. "Noted."

"Do you have to stay here, or can you clock out?" I ask, a plan forming in my mind. And by plan, I mean a very ill-thought-out, last-minute idea.

"Clock out?" Lucas repeats.

"Yeah, when you're done for the day and—"

"I know what clock out means," he clarifies. "I've just never had anyone use a nine-to-five phrase in reference to my job."

I transfer my weight from my left foot to my right and cross my arms. "Is that a yes or a no? Because I have a feeling you haven't taken my advice and done something new in the cities you've visited. And since your afternoon just opened up…"

He doesn't respond right away. Maybe my request is batshit crazy. It's not a hard and fast rule that drivers have to stay and watch the rest of the race if they're unable to finish, but I can imagine it's frowned upon if they leave for shits and giggs. Even so, there's a chance he wants to dip out early, and I've always been a believer in shooting my shot. But maybe he thinks it's weird that I'm insinuating he should ditch the race to spend time with me. I don't—

"Monaco's the second-smallest country in the world, Roo," he says. "There's not much I haven't done here."

Perking up, I counter that statement. "Have you ever been to Èze?" The medieval hilltop town on the Côte d'Azur is thirty minutes outside of Monaco. "Everyone says it's the prettiest village, and I've been dying to go."

"For dinner, yeah, but there's not much to do there."

"That's kind of the point," I tell him. "You're the one who said you never explore without an agenda. Now's your chance."

Lucas smiles, but it doesn't reach his eyes. "Don't worry about me, Roo. You should stay and watch the race."

"We're already thirty minutes into the red flag, with no update," I remind him. "And no offense, but Monaco isn't super exciting, anyway."

"Unless another driver is stupid enough to box you out for a lead that's clearly not theirs, and then your car ends up looking like a fucked-up can of vegetables."

I let out a laugh at his deadpan delivery but quickly slap a hand over my mouth. "Sorry, it's not funny. Your crash did mess up my entire bingo card, by the way."

"Your bingo card?"

I take the folded-up game from my purse and hold it out.

As he peruses it, the tension in his jaw softens, and some of the lines next to his eyes disappear. Focus still fixed on the bingo squares, he says, "I'm going to have a shit ton of interviews once the race is over."

Ah. We're back to the "can you clock out?" question. "Have Mitchell get you a doctor's note saying you have a headache and need to see the medical team. No one questions those. It's what got me out of having to run the mile in phys education every year."

The corners of his lips turn up. "Okay."

"Okay?" I repeat.

"Yup," he confirms. "My car may be wrecked, but that doesn't mean my day has to be, too."

FIFTEEN
CHARLOTTE

ÈZE IS A FAIRY TALE, with its picturesque ancient stone buildings draped in ivy and flowers. Normally, the village would be teeming with tourists, but thanks to the Monaco Grand Prix, it's mostly deserted. Lucas wore a baseball hat—which is a close second to gray sweatpants in the girl porn clothing competition—to keep a low profile, but he quickly realized it wasn't necessary.

We spend an hour meandering down alleyways and cobblestone streets before we end up in a small square surrounded by charming shops. Their windows display an array of handmade soaps, tiny perfume bottles, and delicate ceramics, all untouched by the usual throngs of visitors. It's at one of these shops that we learn about Parfumerie Galimard, a local perfume laboratory. To my surprise, it's Lucas who suggests that we check it out, claiming it sounds like a "fun activity." I think he's more interested in having a plan than the actual perfume, but I'm on board. I've been on the lookout for a new scent since my last perfume bottle shattered when Theo tossed my carry-on luggage into the back of an Uber like it was a sack of grain. *Lesson learned: travel with your perfume bottles in plastic baggies unless you want your clothes smelling like nectarine blossom and honey.*

Despite the very specific hard-to-fuck-up instructions the shopkeeper gave us, Lucas whips out the *Maps* app on his phone. The perfumery is in a beautifully preserved historic building. The entire village has been around for thousands of years, but while many restaurants and stores have updated interiors, this structure still holds a sense of old-fashioned elegance. When a woman greets us in French, dread washes over me. I hate having to ask people whether they speak English. But as it turns out, that's unnecessary, because Lucas replies in perfectly accented French.

Excusez-moi?

The two of them volley back and forth while I stand there in stupefied silence. Every time I think Lucas has reached peak hotness, he outdoes himself. There's something undeniably sexy about a man who's bilingual. Maybe because it hints that he's good with his tongue?

"I am Élisabeth," the perfume lady says, turning her attention to me. "Your boyfriend says you would enjoy a private tour and workshop. Yes?"

Boyfriend? Maybe Lucas's French isn't as good as he thinks. Clearly, something got lost in translation. Even so, I confirm the tour part before turning to Lucas and smacking him in the stomach. On contact, pain radiates through my hand. I can only imagine the hit hurt me more than it hurt his abs.

"I can't believe you speak fluent French while I've been walking around making an arsehole of myself, tossing around the phrase 'parlez-vous anglais' like a typical tourist."

"Your French accent is cute," he says with a laugh that has my heart rate increasing. "And I wouldn't say I'm fluent, but I know enough to get by."

"My French accent sounds like silverware in a garbage disposal, you liar."

With a grin, he holds out a hand, signaling for me to follow Élisabeth, who's patiently waiting to start our tour. She guides us through the mini museum, pointing out the gleaming vintage machinery and the star of the show, an antique perfume organ used by master perfumers. Although Élisabeth probably does this tour a thousand times a week, she answers every one of my questions with enthusiasm. The tour ends in a sleek, modern area filled with bottles and ingredients for our workshop.

She seats us at a workstation with droppers, pipettes, small glass beakers, and scent strips, along with a selection of essential and fragrance oils, and explains the architecture of how to create perfume. The variety of scents is impressive to say the least—everything from corn and nectarine to ones I've never heard of, like *seriguela* and *cloudberry*. She encourages us to try everything rather than going with a preconceived idea of notes we will or won't like.

"Smell this one," Lucas says, holding out a test strip.

I lean down and sneeze at the mossy, woodsy smell. "That smells like a national park."

"In a bad way or a good way?"

I scrunch my nose at him. "My idea of outdoorsy is sitting on a patio with a cocktail in my hand. What do you think?"

He lets out a loud laugh that echoes off the walls. "Okay, so it's a pass."

"Don't skip it just because I don't like it," I tell him with a wave. "It's your cologne."

"Why would I create a scent you don't like?" he asks, arching a brow. "If I did, then you'd be less inclined to hang out with me."

Swoon.

"I think your ability to speak French cancels out smelling like a forest."

Grinning, he gets back to work, so I follow suit. While I

stick to testing out fruity and floral scents, Lucas strays toward the spicier ones, avoiding anything that I deem smells like camping. I don't actually know what camping smells like, since I've never been, but one can assume.

"Oh, I love this one." I shove a test strip in front of him. "Isn't it good?"

He jerks his head back, his face scrunched up adorably. "That doesn't smell like you."

Head tilted, I fix him with an inquisitive stare. "Well, yeah. It's supposed to smell like"—I turn the bottle around so I can read the label—"heliotrope."

Whatever the fuck that is.

"It's too vanilla," he says, tossing a rejected tester into the small container on the table.

"What's wrong with vanilla?" I ask, offended on behalf of the world's most beloved flavor. "It's a fan fave. You've got vanilla ice cream, vanilla cake with vanilla frosting… hell, even vanilla sex can be top tier if you know what you're doing."

Élisabeth lets out a squeak and drops a small vial of thyme to the table with a clatter. Clearly, she understands English. I shoot her an apologetic smile, but Lucas simply chuckles.

"I'm not saying vanilla is bad," he insists. "It's just not you. You smell like honey and flowers."

My cheeks heat, and Élisabeth's are pink as well. She quickly locates a few scents that she thinks will best represent my "boyfriend's description." He doesn't correct her, so neither do I. In the end, I choose black orchid, lemongrass, and sage. Élisabeth notes the selections, including measurements. That way the recipe will remain on file in the event that I want to order more in the future.

"What are you going to name yours?" I ask Lucas.

"Um…" he hedges, lips pushed to one side. "Èze cologne."

With a groan, I drop my head back. "That's like naming your dog 'dog.' You need something more creative."

I lift his beaker, savoring the refreshing yet smoky and leathery smell. If it wasn't toxic—not to mention socially frowned upon—I'd drink this stuff straight off his body. "How about Scent-sational?"

"Absolutely not."

"Nose-talgic?"

He grimaces, which has me laughing.

"Oh, c'mon... have a *scents* of humor."

Rubbing his brow, he asks, "You have a serious hard-on for puns, don't you?"

"Monaco has no punny shirts, Lucas." I let out an annoyed huff. "Not that I could afford them, anyway. Even the cheapest bottles of water here are glass. I'm all about being hydrated, but I'm not about to pay a bloody ransom for natural spring water if it doesn't promise eternal youth, you know?"

A chuckle rumbles through his chest. "What are you naming your perfume?"

"I was thinking something simple, like Wildflower or Bloom."

"You get those, yet you suggest Nose-talgic for mine?" He shakes his head and sighs. "I vote for Wildflower."

With warmth blooming in my chest, I nod. "That's what I was leaning toward."

Now that my name has been officially picked, I hand the bottle over to Élisabeth so she can make it look legit enough to earn a spot on my bathroom counter. Lucas looks utterly perplexed, as if I asked him to name his firstborn child—which, if I have anything to do with it, will be Riley, girl or boy—rather than a cologne.

Groaning at his indecisiveness, I brainstorm quickly and blurt out the first name I come up with. "Velvet Desire."

He lifts a brow but simply shrugs. "Sounds like a porno from the '80s, but sure."

Élisabeth leads us to a softly lit showroom with strategically placed spotlights highlighting the stunning bottles displayed on sleek glass shelves. Each area is dedicated to a different fragrance family, with a curated collection of perfumes artfully arranged to showcase their unique characteristics. She leaves us here, encouraging us to sample whatever we want before disappearing to bottle our final scents.

"Thank you for doing this," Lucas says as we wander toward a shelf holding heart-shaped crystal perfume bottles.

"Helping you create a cologne that doesn't make me want to take an allergy pill?" I tease.

"Ha ha," he says. "But seriously, I appreciate it."

"Of course." I wave off his thanks. "It's no biggie."

"To me it is," he admits. "If it weren't for this, I'd be spending the day in a shitty mood, pissed at the world. Not everyone would go above and beyond to make sure I'm okay like you did."

Not everyone wants to have your babies either.

"You're my friend," I say simply.

It sounds juvenile, but it's true. Sure, I'm outgoing and social and know a lot of people. But friends I can sit in silence with because I miss my dad and want company without the expectation of conversation? The ones I can call in the middle of the night to help me bury a body with no questions asked? I can count those on one hand. Lucas would definitely have a lot of questions about the body, but I'm almost positive he'd do it. I think. I have no actual confirmation that he would show up with a shovel and tarp, but in the 0.03 percent chance that I end up in a situation that would force my hand, I think he would.

"You're my friend, too," he says, bumping my shoulder.

"You're not just saying that because I'm Theo's sister?" I affect a teasing tone, though underneath, the question is a serious one. I've had one too many people enter my life solely because of who my brother is, rather than who I am.

"I don't have to pretend around you," Lucas says casually, as if that statement doesn't melt me on the spot. "That has nothing to do with Theo and everything to do with *you*."

"And I smell like flowers," I add.

He throws back his head and laughs. "That definitely helps."

I pick up a round perfume bottle that's painted with delicate roses and has one of those old-fashioned atomizers. I spritz one wrist, then rub the other against it. Before I've even set the bottle down, I'm engulfed in the scent. *Damn*. If a perfume can be described as provocative, then this is it. It smells expensive and sexy, yet clean and classy, with subtle notes of lavender and bergamot. Because I'm an all-or-nothing type of girl, I pick the bottle up again and hit the pulse points behind my ears and then my collarbone.

Curious about what Lucas will think of it, I motion him over from where he's checking out a cologne shaped like a rearing horse. I extend my arm, expecting him to smell my wrist, but *nope*. He gets all up in my space and dips his head until his nose is nearly brushing the crook of my neck. I'm too stunned to do anything but stand still as a statue, my heart fluttering in my chest. He smells sinful—like fuel, exhaust, sweat, and minty deodorant.

When Lucas lifts his head, he doesn't step back, leaving our lips nearly touching. From here, the specks of gold in his eyes are visible, and his warm breath ghosts across my skin like a tantalizing promise. His lips part slightly, as if on the brink of forming words, but none come. Instead, we stand in silence as time holds its breath. I can't help but drop my focus to his lips —soft, inviting, and so temptingly close.

Breath held, I somehow muster up the willpower to not ask "are we about to kiss?" and leave the ball in his court. I'm not afraid to make a first move, but I don't want to make things awkward if I'm misreading the situation. *Maybe he just really likes the smell of the sex bomb perfume?*

A sudden noise from the hallway breaks the spell, then Élisabeth returns with our perfumes in organza bags and cute little diplomas of participation. Lucas steps back ever so slightly, as if I'm not covered in fuel, ready to ignite, and he's holding the match.

I may have learned that Lucas speaks French today, but it looks like I won't be finding out if he French kisses, too.

SIXTEEN
LUCAS

THE SKY DARKENS OVERHEAD, the heavy clouds gathering into an ominous mass. *Shit.* It's been raining on and off for the past two days, ending our practice sessions early and pushing back today's qualifying. According to the forecast, the rain's supposed to hold out for the rest of the afternoon, but the gray skies say otherwise. I pick up my pace as we head to our destination, hoping to beat the impending storm.

Only a few grand prix tracks offer fans the chance to ride at full throttle in a supercar driven by an F1 driver on the circuit during a race weekend. Canada is one of them. Hot Laps give spectators a unique glimpse into what it feels like out there on the track. It's also a huge reminder of just how elite the sport is. This experience can cost upward of twenty grand. Yup. One lap with an F1 driver costs the equivalent of a year's college tuition.

My parents opted to spend the afternoon at the Montréal Insectarium with Madison so she can "meet butterflies" while Jaclyn takes a much-needed break. Wrangling a five-year-old while pregnant with twins isn't for the weak. Grayson looks like he's about to drop at any moment. If it weren't for the promise of a Hot Laps experience and Theo's stream of ridiculous questions like "can you get a DUI for skiing drunk?" and "can you legally domesticate a pigeon and keep it as your pet?" I'm sure he'd be sleeping behind a pile of tires.

A smack to the back of my head has my tunnel vision fading.

"What the fuck? What was that for?"

Finn rolls his eyes. "You're not listening to me."

We're still on this?

Since the moment my family arrived in Montreal, Finn's been relentless. And since it took 2.5 million dollars to get my car back to racing standards after it was crushed like a soda can last week, the last thing I want is Finn sitting in it and fucking something up just so he could get a cool photo for his dating profiles.

"You're not getting into my car," I tell him. Again. "Even if I wanted to let you—which I don't—you're not allowed to."

That may or may not be true. No one's ever asked. Requesting to sit in an F1 driver's car is akin to asking to ride a cowboy's horse or a biker's motorcycle. You just don't do it.

"Your fat arse wouldn't fit, mate," Theo adds with a shit-eating grin aimed at Finn. "Your hips are too wide."

Finn stops dead in his tracks and whirls around, getting in Theo's face. "Are you body shaming me?"

"He totally is," Ezra says in a serious tone.

"Your shirt *does* look a little tight today, man," Grayson agrees.

"It's a fitted shirt, asshole. It's supposed to be snug," he growls.

"Snug, not suffocating—"

Finn smashes his fist into Grayson's stomach, causing him to double over with an *oof*. Before things can escalate, I step between them. "I'm not body shaming you, Finn. Walker wouldn't comfortably fit in my seat either."

Each cockpit setup includes a custom seat made from a body-model carbon-fiber shell. Even drivers on the same team wouldn't simply swap cars without bringing their own seat and steering wheel.

Finn has mostly stopped begging by the time we make it to the Hot Laps area five minutes later. I'm not surprised to find Blake is already here, having volunteered to take out one of my brothers—most likely Ezra, since Theo "shot-gunned" Grayson, and Blake can only deal with "one loudmouthed fucker at a time" and Finn would put him over that allotted amount.

I *am* surprised to find Charlotte standing with him, though.

I figured she was off sightseeing, since she wasn't at breakfast, but not wanting to invade her privacy, I haven't checked her location. *I'm not a stalker, after all.* She looks like an office siren in her kitten heels, pleated skirt, and button-up vest with a lapin neckline.

Damn, she looks gorgeous. She always does.

If it hadn't been for Élisabeth's interruption, there's no doubt in my mind I would've given in to my overwhelming urge to kiss Charlotte that day in Èze. She turned a terrible day into an unexpectedly enjoyable one. A day where I could almost forget about lost points and damaged car parts. Because all I thought about was her.

"What're you doing here, Lottie?" Theo asks, sidling up next to his sister.

Her smile turns haughty. "I'm here to take a Hot Lap, something you failed to tell me you were doing this morning."

"I tried," he defends himself, spinning to face her and holding his hands out. "But you weren't speaking to me."

Running a hand through his hair, Blake turns to Theo and sighs. "What'd you do this time?"

"Nothing," he exclaims with a huff. "I merely pointed out how wearing another team's color isn't very nice."

The color of her outfit *is* an uncanny match to Blake's racing suit, but she simply waves him off. "I missed the part where McAllister had a monopoly on the color red. Anyway, Cooper offered to take me on a Hot Lap, so it all worked out."

As if on cue, the auburn-haired Scot steps out of the Hot Laps tent with waivers and pens in hand. When Charlotte gives him one of her little waves, my gut twists. I don't like that one bit. I feel oddly proprietary about them. Another thing I don't like? How his smile grows at her greeting.

Nope.

"I'll take you," I tell her, leaving no room for argument. "Cooper can take Finn."

"Are you sure?" the Scot asks, wearing an easy smile as he approaches the group. "I don't mind taking the lass out. I figured you'd want to spend time with your brothers."

Damn. It's impossible to dislike Cooper. He's a genuinely good guy who says shit like *lass*. It's really fucking annoying.

"I'm sure," I confirm, trying and failing to keep my voice neutral. "You can take Finn."

The corners of Blake's lips twitch up, but he doesn't say a word. And for once in his life, Finn goes with the flow instead of making an idiotic remark and putting up a fight. He shrugs at the change of plans and sticks out his hand to introduce himself to McAllister's new driver. "I'm Finn, Lucas's favorite brother. You're the one who hit him in the face with champagne, right? That was epic."

And there's the idiotic remark. The irritation I just pushed down comes roaring back.

Cooper blushes, his cheeks matching the color of his hair. "Accidentally."

"You're not his favorite brother," Ezra argues.

Finn slips his sunglasses down his nose so Ezra gets the full effect of his incredulous look. "Well, it certainly isn't Jesse anymore, so I claimed the spot for myself."

The tension in my jaw intensifies so severely I worry my teeth will crack. We've managed to steer clear of any topic of conversation that involves Jesse for the past day, but leave it to Finn to bring it up in front of a crowd. At least Jesse isn't here. Finn would no doubt make the weekend exponentially more awkward. Plus, if he were here, I have no doubt Blake and Theo would join Charlotte in the whole punching him in the dick thing.

"At least you have multiple to choose from," Charlotte quips, breaking the tension. "My only option is Theo, and he made me a bullet point list of all the ways I've betrayed Alpha-Vite this season by not wearing merch."

The group erupts into laughter at Charlotte's revelation. Theo's drama with a capital D.

"Please note that my lovely sister made a presentation in response titled *From Racing to the Runway*," Theo says. Despite his attempt at annoyance, his expression is filled with affection and pride. "Included photos and shit, too."

With a shrug, as if it's no big deal, she turns to Cooper to get a waiver. In a matter of minutes, the forms are all filled out, and we're led onto the track. Charlotte lets out a squeal of appreciation as we approach a spider-black McLaren. I specifically requested this car because I love the way it drives. Every aspect of it urges me to push it to its limits like I'm striving for a podium position. And there's no denying the car itself is sexy as hell.

"Okay, you know *Ocean's Eleven*?" Charlotte asks. She barely gives me time to nod before she goes on. "This looks like a car they would use to get away after emptying out the casino's bank. Not one they were planning on using, but one they had to steal to make a quick escape because their first plan went sideways. Don't you think?"

"I've never thought about it." I head over to the passenger side and open the door of the sleek supercar so she can slide in.

Charlotte chatters away about how she can "totally imagine George Clooney behind the wheel" as I ensure her helmet's strapped on snugly and her seat belt is secure. Only then do I shut the door and head to the driver's side. I tend to my own helmet and seat belt and relax into my seat while I wait for the signal. When it comes, the engine roars to life with a throaty growl and I ease out onto the track. The moment we're clear, I floor the accelerator. The car surges forward with an incredible burst of speed, pressing us back into our seats. The world outside the windshield becomes a blur of colors and motion, the sound of the engine a deafening roar. Charlotte's gasp of surprise quickly turns into a laugh of exhilaration as we rocket down the straight. Approaching the first corner, I brake hard. The car responds with precision, as it should, and the tires grip the asphalt with unyielding determination.

"You okay?" I ask, assessing Charlotte out of the corner of my eye. I wish I had a full-frontal view of her expression, but I have no interest in crashing this car.

"*Yes*," she shouts over the noise, her voice full of rapture.

I accelerate out of a turn, causing the supercar to leap forward like a beast unleashed. Each corner is a dance of speed and control, and I won't lie and say I'm not testing the car's agility to show off my skill. But that ends abruptly as a blinding flash of lightning splits the sky, turning night into day for an instant, and a torrent of rain begins to fall.

Fuck.

"Hold on," I tell her, my voice barely audible over the pounding rain and engine's roar.

Instructions to pull over crackle through the built-in helmet radio, but I've already reduced our speed significantly as I maneuver to a runoff area farther up the track. The McLaren's tires struggle to maintain their grip, and my visibility drops to almost nothing as the rain comes down in sheets, turning the world into a blurry haze.

I'm no stranger to driving in the rain, and I have no trouble improvising as the racing line, which was previously built up with rubber for better grip, becomes a slippery adversary instead of a reliable guide. But in those instances, Charlotte isn't my passenger, and the car I'm driving has wheels specifically built for any weather conditions.

Shoulders tense, I guide the car off the track and into a safe area. The engine's roar fades into a steady purr as we come to a stop. The rain hammers down on the roof, the sound deafening in the sudden stillness. Pulled over and safe, I check in with the team over the radio. Their weather radar indicates the rain should taper off in the next twenty or thirty minutes. While I could safely get us back to the start line, I don't want to risk it. And sure, I'll take the extra one-on-one time with Charlotte.

Beside me, I realize, my passenger is clutching the edge of her seat with a white-knuckled grip. Her cheeks, rosy only minutes ago, have drained of color, and her pupils are blown out, her body going into fight-or-flight mode.

"Roo?" I ask, keeping my tone gentle.

She spares me a glance before looking back out the window. "Hmm?"

With a soft touch, I pry her fingers from the leather seats and place them loosely into her lap. My intention isn't to hold her hand, but when she intertwines her fingers with mine, I roll with it.

"You don't like thunderstorms," I observe.

"Hate," she corrects me. "I don't know how in the flying fuck people find this relaxing."

As if demonstrating her point, a jagged bolt illuminates the swirling clouds, casting stark shadows over the track.

"When I was a kid, I was scared of people in costumes," I reveal, hoping to distract her. "Jesse used to be obsessed with PowerRangers, and for his sixth birthday party, my parents hired someone to come dressed as the red one to take pictures with the kids and teach them some cool moves."

She finally shifts her body, angling my way slightly rather than rigidly facing forward. "Did you freak out?"

"Lost my ever-loving mind," I say with a chuckle. "My dad thought having the guy take off his mask so I could see that he was a real person would help, but that made things ten times worse because I thought the PowerRanger was a body snatcher."

"At least you grew out of it," she says, a hint of a smile breaking through.

"Sure, I can be in the same room as a mascot, but there's no way in hell I'll ever take my kids on a family vacation to Disney World. Fuck that shit."

Charlotte lets loose a giggle, and the death grip she has on my hand loosens. "Did you know that Theo's scared of kangaroos? He thinks they look like humans wearing animal costumes."

Theo may be my best friend, but half of the details I know about him have been forced on me against my will. There's no need for me to know his plan for the zombie apocalypse—because it's a when, not an if, according to him—or that it is indeed possible for a man to get a yeast infection. But his kangaroo phobia is news to me.

"He also thinks they're creepy and manipulative," she explains, color returning to her cheeks. "And doesn't understand how it looks like they're on steroids."

I shake my head at her description. Yeah, that sounds exactly like Theo. "Did you really make a PowerPoint presentation for him about fashion and Formula 1?"

"Of course I did," she tells me, her tone holding a hint of exasperation that I would second-guess this. "Wearing team merch is great for the grandstands, but in the paddock, it's about personal style and making an impression. It's like

Fashion Week. You can show off your outfits and the latest trends. Hell, the paddock is how fans keep up with the drivers' street style."

I snort. "I would hardly call Blake's black T-shirts, jeans, and bedhead 'street style,' but point taken."

"Okay, not *every* driver, but there are tons of social media accounts dedicated to your outfits."

"Yeah?" I ask, playing dumb. My publicist has kept me well apprised of the countless fan accounts dedicated to highlighting nearly every piece of clothing in my closet. I'd be creeped out if I wasn't secretly pleased that people appreciate my style. My stylist knows my tastes and preferences and curates looks to perfection. On top of that, she sorts through all the PR I'm sent and highlights emerging artists along with well-established brands.

"Mm-hmm," Charlotte says, oblivious to my duplicity. "There's definitely been a shift in the past few years. The personalities and culture of the paddock have come to the forefront. Even big brand names are getting into it—Chanel had that viral F1 Monaco T-shirt, and A$AP Rocky's first collection as the creative director of Puma was a collaboration with F1 and sold out immediately."

"If anyone can blend team support with style, it's you, Roo," I tell her, squeezing her hand.

She smiles, and my chest expands. The fear is almost nonexistent now. True to her nature, rather than continue that line of conversation, she changes the subject. "Has it been nice having your family here?"

"Yeah." I chuckle. "Nonstop chaos, but a lot of fun. I swear each and every time my mom comes to a grand prix, she acts like she's never seen me race before."

"She's proud of you," she tells me, her expression soft. "It's sweet."

"Hmm."

"Are you ready to go back to Boston?"

I puff out a breath, considering. I've successfully avoided extended amounts of time with Jesse over the past few years. My mom sticks to me like a starfish when I'm there, which helps keep the drama tempered, and I've got three other brothers to spend time with. Jesse, thankfully, has respected my need for distance, but now that he and Kylie are done, he thinks things can go back to how they were? That pisses me off.

"I'll take that as a no," Charlotte says. She regards our hands, which are still intertwined.

It's only then that I realize how tight my grip is. I don't extricate my hand from hers, but I do ease up.

"Short answer: no. Long answer: fuck no."

Charlotte lets out a throaty laugh that has goose bumps traveling down my arms. "Well, I'll only be a train ride away in New York if you need backup."

She's headed to NYC after the grand prix to do some sightseeing and shopping. Her agenda includes all the Big Apple classics: Times Square, the Statue of Liberty, a Broadway show, visiting Carrie Bradshaw's apartment, and bagels.

"You'd come to Boston to save me?" I ask, teasing.

"Of course," she says, though her demeanor is far more serious. "If you wanted me there for support, I'd come in a heartbeat."

Without second-guessing the thought, I say, "I want you."

She tilts her head, like she's waiting for me to add, "for support," but I leave it at that. I do want her there for support, but I also want her more than I want a first world championship win.

And that… well, that's more dangerous than driving in the rain.

SEVENTEEN
CHARLOTTE

WILLOW

You better wear something sexy to bed!!

And before you ask, your T-shirt that says I have a P.H.D. (Pretty Huge Dick) does not qualify, although I will admit it's funny.

CHARLOTTE

I think you've been reading one too many of your smutty romances, Wills.

WILLOW

There's no such thing as too many smutty romances!!

CHARLOTTE

LOL.

Considering Lucas is a millionaire and has a penthouse, I can't imagine we'll be forced to share a bed.

WILLOW

Hahaha. Fair.

> New plan: pretend to get lost on your way back from the bathroom or sleepwalk into his room.

I ROLL my eyes at her message. Definitely not happening. I'm here because he needs a friend. I was serious when I told him that I'd happily visit Boston while he's there, but I didn't think he'd take me up on it. And what I never would have expected? The way he wasted no time in having his assistant book me a first-class train ticket. I haven't said anything about it to Theo, and to my knowledge, neither has Lucas. It's not that I'm hiding it from him, but my brother tends to make a mountain out of a molehill. Rather than seeing this for what it is, he'd act like we were going on a couple's retreat to the Bahamas.

I'm typing back a response when a loud shuffle catches my attention, and when I look up, I come face-to-face with the Adler twins. Though I suppose it's more like face-to-crotch, since I'm sitting on one of the couches in the VIP lounge in the motorhome.

Finn and Ezra make themselves comfortable across from me, and suddenly, I feel like I'm about to be interviewed on a topic I haven't been prepped for. It's painful how attractive they are, though they look nothing alike. Ezra shares Lucas's blond hair and green eyes, but Finn's got darker features, like a mini-John Travolta in his *Grease* era. If Lucas loaned him his signature leather jacket, he'd be golden.

"Hey, Charlotte," Ezra says with a smile. If Finn's spice, then his twin is everything nice.

Returning the expression, I tuck my phone back into my bag. "What's up?"

"My heart rate now that I'm looking at you." Finn gives me a flirty smirk.

With a groan, I shake my head. "You're way too cocky for someone who dresses like they're color blind."

Ezra whoops and smacks his twin on the back. "Told you those shoes didn't go, man."

The quintessential fuck boy glares at his brother. "Fuck off."

"You're wearing so many shades of blue, you look like a quilted baby blanket," I tell him.

I'm all for team spirit, but Finn's navy shorts, sky blue Sambas, and cobalt-colored team shirt make him look like Grumpy Care Bear.

"At least I'm wearing color," Finn says, giving my outfit an exaggerated once-over.

If he expects me to feel self-conscious, he's got another thing coming. My outfit's kick-arse. A white Rhode dress with a ruched ruffle accent at the skirt and thrifted Chanel kitten heels. Kyle the photographer—who captures everyone's outfit—even threw me a compliment, which is as rare as lightning striking twice.

"White contains every hue on the visible light spectrum," I tell him. "And if you think I'm dressing to impress the likes of you, you're wrong. There's a higher chance that the Statue of Liberty will step down off her pedestal and wade through new York Harbor than there is of me dressing to impress a man—or woman."

"Do you think I should change?" Finn asks, tugging at his shirt, his expression uncertain rather than rakish. "Lucas has a plain black shirt in his room."

I shake my head, partly to mediate his distress and partly because it's ridiculous how concerned he is over the outfit now. "No, I think it's really sweet that you guys are supporting him."

Yes, the F1 paddock is about the glitz and glamour rather than sporting a baseball cap with a favorite drivers' number on it, but the Adler family walking around in AlphaVite attire? It's adorable. Even if Lucas's dad is rocking cobalt Crocs that make my eyes bleed. And yes, he did offer to buy a pair for me when I'm in Boston, but I politely declined, much to Lucas's amusement.

"Thanks," Finn says, puffing out his chest. "Found this bad boy on eBay a few years back."

"eBay?" I confirm with raised brows.

He nods. "Yeah, it's an online marketplace where you can sell stuff and then bid—"

"I know what eBay is," I tell him. "I'm from Australia, not the lost city of fucking Atlantis. What do you mean you bought it there?"

"For someone who claims to know what eBay is, you certainly don't understand how it works."

"I'm a pro at hunting things down online," I explain, crossing my legs. "I sourced a discontinued Louis Vuitton Pochette Twin GM Monogram crossbody bag for my mum in less than two days. And my ex-boyfriend? I could tell you his aunt's cousin's primary school teacher's address. If there was AlphaVite merch that didn't make me want to gouge my eyes out with spoons, I would've found it."

He lifts a brow. "This is vintage Alpha Arrow, not AlphaVite."

"What the fuck's Alpha Arrow? A superhero?"

Ezra chuckles, but when I only give him a deadpan look, he snaps his mouth shut. Brows furrowed, he says, "You're F1 royalty, and you don't know Alpha Arrow?"

"Is my 'what the bloody fuck are you talking about' facial expression not explanation enough? No, I have zero idea what you're talking about."

"I'm just surprised," Ezra says, holding his hands up. "They've been around forever."

While I know all the current Formula 1 teams and drivers, and a bit of McAllister history, since both my dad and Theo drove for them, I'm not a fucking F1 history book.

"ViteRomeo, too," Finn adds.

Ezra snaps his fingers, his eyes lighting up. "I forgot about that. They were both on the starting grid, right?"

"ViteRomeo sounds like the name of an Italian mobster from the '80s," I say. "Now what does any of that have to do with your shirt?"

Finn shoots me a salacious grin. "What will I get in return if I tell you?"

"I won't smack you so hard, you forget your favorite color," I say, pasting on a saccharine smile.

He coughs out a surprised laugh at that and lurches forward on the couch. "Don't bully me, Charlotte. It'll only make me fall in love with you."

I look to Ezra for an answer because my already limited patience is reaching its limit.

He doesn't disappoint. "Both teams have been around since day one, but Alpha Arrow's team ownership changed in the mid-'90s due to a shitty track record. That's when they dropped *Arrow* and became Alpha Racing. Similar thing happened with ViteRomeo. The team came under new leadership and changed their name to Vite Racing, and the two teams eventually joined and renamed themselves AlphaVite."

"Did you really not know this?" Finn asks, his brow furrowed.

"Do I need to rent an airplane and write *no* in the sky for you?" I huff, crossing my arms over my chest. "Why do *you* know all this?"

"Our hometown bar hosts F1 trivia night when Lucas is in town for Thanksgiving every year," Ezra explains, his cheeks flushing. "It'd be super embarrassing if we lost, so we study. The team color for both Alpha Arrow and ViteRomeo was blue, though different shades. So AlphaVite's is a combination of the two."

A bolt of excitement courses through me as an idea hits. I slam my hand against the arm of the couch, my spine snapping straight. My takeaway from this history lesson? There's an entire untapped marketplace of AlphaVite-adjacent clothing out there.

"Everything good?" Lucas asks, sauntering into the lounge area. He's holding Madison in his arms, and her face is buried in the crook of his neck.

This is her first race, and she's not a fan of loud noises, including my brother, which he's taking extreme personal offense to. I don't particularly care whether people like me. Everyone's entitled to their opinion—even if it's wrong—but Theo's lifelong mission is to win over everyone he meets.

"Finn tried flirting with Charlotte, but she told him he looks colorblind," Ezra replies.

"I wasn't flirting." Finn glares daggers at his twin. "It's called having a conversation."

"A conversation where you make more eye contact with her tits than her—"

"Dude," Lucas hisses. He shifts Madison from the right side of his body to the left. "Little ears listening."

"Big ears," Madison mumbles.

Lucas tucks his chin and regards her. "Hmm?"

She lifts her head, her brown eyes wide as she takes in the space. "Mommy said I have big ears."

"That just means you like to listen to grown-up conversation when you're not supposed to," Lucas explains, his voice teasing. "She doesn't think you look like Dumbo."

"You're silly, Uncle Lulu," Madison giggles, her round cheeks plumping up in a smile.

Her adorable nickname for Lucas melts my heart into a puddle, but Ezra and Finn snicker into their hands.

"Do you want to say hi to Charlotte?" Lucas points to me. "Remember what I told you?"

I smile and wave and leave my greeting at that. While I've never considered myself an intimidating person, I am loud, which very well may be too much for a shy child. And yes, I do want her to like me. *Sue me.*

She turns to him and cups a hand over his ear but doesn't lower her voice as she asks, "Is she the one who plays dress-up? Like a Barbie doll?"

"Mm-hmm," Lucas confirms, his eyes dancing as they zero in on me.

I'm not nearly as smooth or proportionate as a Barbie doll, but I'll take the compliment. "You like playing dress-up, too?"

She nods emphatically, then she wiggles in Lucas's arms in a nonverbal bid to be put down. The moment her tiny pink sneakers hit the ground, she swallows the distance between us and climbs into the open spot to my right.

"What about butterflies?" she asks, her hands clasped like she's begging for my answer to be *yes*. "Do you like them?"

"I do," I confirm with a nod. "Did you know that they taste with their feet?"

She looks down at her shirt, which is covered in rainbow butterflies, and pets them as if they're her friends rather than sparkly embellishments. Since I shared a secret butterfly fact with her, she takes it upon herself to tell Finn, Ezra, Lucas, and me all about what she learned at the butterfly museum yesterday. The kid's got to be a genius. That's the only reasonable explanation for why she recalls that butterflies have a long tube-like tongue called a proboscis that allows them to soak up their food rather than sip it. *Gross.*

As Madison chatters on, my vision starts to blur, and a wave of dizziness washes over me. And on cue, my glucose sensor beeps, telling me what my body has already recognized: my blood sugar is dropping. *Shit.* I've been ignoring my monitor all morning because I felt fine. Though I did have a headache when I woke up—a classic symptom—I figured that was from the rain.

"Are you a robot?" Madison asks with all the innocence in the world. "You beeped."

The noises my continuous glucose monitor makes are relatively quiet, but she said it herself—she has big ears. Finn and Ezra look at the two of us blankly, but Lucas, who's perched on the arm of the couch, considers me with an expression full of understanding. He turns toward Madison and then me, as if he can't decide whether he's more embarrassed by what his niece insinuated or worried about my blood sugar.

"I'm a type 1 diabetic," I tell her, opening my purse up so I can find my glucose tablets. "So I have a robot part that helps me stay healthy."

She nods, her lips pressed together in a line, as if that makes all the sense in the world. "Oh. That's cool. Uncle Jesse was a robot for Halloween last year and had buttons that light up. Do you have those?"

"No buttons," I tell her with an exaggerated pout.

"Maybe he'll let you borrow some of his."

That's all she has to say on the matter before she's back on butterflies and how they can see ultraviolet light. Her reaction is refreshing. When most people discover that I'm diabetic, they suddenly treat me like I'm on the brink of a health crisis all the time. It's frustrating because it feels like they're questioning my ability to manage my own health, and I live a fairly healthy lifestyle, thank you very much. Well, I'm not very active, but that's due to my dislike of sweating rather than any physical limitation.

Lucas, who's been stationed like a sentry on the arm of the couch, stands up and casually crouches in front of me. His moves are smooth and understated, drawing little attention, which I'm appreciative of.

In a low tone, he asks, "What do you need?"

"A new pancreas," I joke as I pop another tablet into my

mouth. *Ugh.* It's my least favorite flavor, but the local pharmacy only had cherry-pineapple, and beggars can't be choosers.

"I'll start scouring the black market," he teases. He gives my knee a light squeeze, and all I can think is *thank God I shaved my legs today*. "Anything in the meantime?"

"Orange juice," I suggest. "Or a lemonade?"

"You got it," he says, unfolding himself and looming over me.

He strides away, so I focus on chewing my glucose tablets and listening to Madison rattle off butterfly facts, her enthusiasm never waning, while I wait for a glass of orange juice.

It doesn't come.

Nope.

When Lucas appears, he's holding two *jugs* of Tropicana orange juice like they're dumbbells.

"What is that?" I ask, my jaw dropping.

"Orange juice."

I cough out a laugh. "Yeah, and if you found a couple of bottles of champagne, you could make mimosas for the whole team."

"Now we know what to do with the leftovers," he says. Sitting beside me, his thigh touching mine, he unscrews the cap of one jug. "Drink up."

"I'm not going to chug it," I warn, because the way he's waiting with the other jug ready to go has me thinking he's expecting exactly that.

He snorts and waves in a way that signals that I should get on with it. Rolling my eyes, I take the juice and lean forward to take a sip so I don't spill OJ on my cream-colored dress. Twenty minutes, three glucose tablets, and a quarter of a jug of orange juice later, my blood sugar's back to normal. Well, normal for me.

"Now we can focus on more important things," I say, screwing the top back on the juice. "Like butterflies."

Madison is still spitting out facts like she has a doctorate degree in entomology.

Lucas's relieved smile drops into a frown. "There's nothing more important than you, Charlotte."

I'm so used to hearing him call me Roo that I get caught up on the use of my name. Unable to form a verbal response, I tap the butterfly tattoo on his forearm. I don't have all his tattoos memorized, I swear. And even if I did, there are probably several I don't even know about—possible dick tattoo included—but the simplistic butterfly is inked next to the delicate bouquet of tulips on his arm. Since they're my favorite flower, my attention tends to stray there, and muscular forearms are apparently a turn-on for me. *Who knew?*

Lucas's phone buzzes with a text, and when he glances at it, his jaw clenches. With a long exhale, he tilts the screen in my direction. Considering I've had boyfriends who guarded their phones like medieval knights, the ease with which he just shows me is surprising.

JESSE
Good luck later today. See you soon, bro!

I CRINKLE MY NOSE. The text reads more like a message a person would send to an acquaintance than their brother. Not liking the tension bracketing Lucas's lips, I once again offer to punch Jesse in the dick. "It's a big offer, considering I'll probably break my hand and a few nails in the process."

The frown lines framing his mouth relax. "Let's keep that off the itinerary for now."

"Itinerary?" I ask, blinking in surprise.

He chuckles. "Yeah, I'm making an itinerary, scheduling activities for us while you're in Boston."

Did you hear that? No? Oh, well, it was the sound of my heart exploding.

"You don't have to do that," I tell him. "I don't want to be a bother."

"It's no bother." He shrugs, his lips quirking up on one side. "I like making schedules."

"You like making schedules," I repeat slowly.

He presses his leg farther into mine as he tosses his head back and lets out a hearty laugh. "Maybe say that again but try not to make it sound like I just told you I have an incurable rash."

I grimace, because yup, that's exactly how I said it. "As you know, I have the time-management skills of the White Rabbit from *Alice in Wonderland*, so schedules aren't really my thing, but I appreciate the thought. And the orange juice."

I always thought my love language was words of affirmation, but I'm starting to think I've been wrong all along, and it's actually acts of service.

EIGHTEEN
LUCAS

I HAVEN'T PLAYED tourist in my own city since I was on a school field trip in seventh grade. We walked through Boston's historic neighborhoods on what's dubbed the Freedom Trail. It was a memorable experience, and not because we saw Benjamin Franklin's statue or the Old Law House, but because Rebecca Steinberg let me feel her up on the bus ride home.

I planned on showing Charlotte my version of Boston rather than the historical one—the ice cream parlor we'd stop at after Finn's baseball games, the park where my friends and I would spend hours kicking around a soccer ball, the amazing Chinese restaurant we go to every Christmas. Similar to how Americans don't learn much about Australia's history, they don't learn about ours, so I figured Paul Revere's house and Ben Franklin's statue wouldn't be that exciting for her.

But, of course, in usual Charlotte style, she manages to surprise the hell out of me.

In her quest to find a punny shirt, she stumbles across one featuring John Adams and John Hancock sitting on the Boston Harbor, sipping cups of tea, with a speech bubble above Hancock that says *Spill the tea, sis*. That leads to a redacted version of the event known as the Boston Tea Party, which she finds wildly amusing and hilarious given the "absolute genius level of pettiness" and insists we learn more.

So yeah, that's how we end up spending our entire afternoon at the fucking Boston Tea Party Museum.

I drag her out after three hours, but not before she buys a shirt from the gift shop that says *Time to Par-Tea!* with two tea bags dancing on it.

"How upset are you about going off schedule?" she asks as we walk back to my car. I parked in an area that would be central to the places I planned to take her, which is not at all near where we are now.

"I'm not." Stopping in the middle of the sidewalk, I turn to face her, my pulse ratcheting up. "Why would you think that?"

She nibbles on her lower lip, and if I wasn't holding her shopping bags, I would reach out and stop her. "You had our whole afternoon organized, and I completely disregarded that and went off course. I don't want you to think I don't appreciate your planning or that I ruined things."

If her vulnerability at this admission wasn't written all over her face, I would scoff at the ridiculousness of it. "You didn't ruin anything, Roo. So we didn't stick to the original plan. That doesn't mean the detour was any less fun."

She studies my face, eyes wary, as if looking for deception. But it only takes a moment for her shoulders to relax. "Learning about the tea party *was* fun."

I love how she says *tea party* as if it's afternoon tea at a hotel rather than over one hundred American colonists protesting against British taxation by boarding ships and dumping their tea into the Boston Harbor.

"Lucas Adler?"

At the sound of my name, I turn, finding the six-five captain of the Boston Panthers jogging our way.

"Cole Barrett." I shake my head and grin at the hockey star. "What're the odds?"

He chuckles, his expression mirroring mine. "How are you? I didn't realize you were in town."

"Keeping it quiet," I admit with a shrug. If anyone gets it, he does. "This is Charlotte, by the way."

"Hi. Nice to meet you." Charlotte smiles, but then her jaw drops and she claps loudly. "Oh my God, I know you."

Cole scratches the back of his head and grimaces. "Uh—"

"You're TikTok famous," she announces, her lips twitching up into a mischievous smile.

I can't help but chuckle. I didn't think Charlotte was a hockey fan, so I figured she wouldn't recognize Cole for his three Stanley Cups wins and being one of the best centers in the NHL, but I definitely didn't think it'd be because of TikTok.

"Well, not you, but your dog," she clarifies, her eyes dancing. "Goose, right?"

Cole coughs out a laugh. "Um, yeah. I'm Goose's dad."

Charlotte squeals and does a little happy dance. "Oh, he is so adorable. The videos your girlfriend makes of him choosing her book club's next read with his paw literally make my heart melt. Did she teach him to do that?"

Cole's posture eases, and his expression is pure amusement as she goes on. Clearly, he appreciates Charlotte's love for his dog and lack of interest in his career. The two of them chat about Goose, the golden retriever I had no idea even existed, for the next twenty minutes as I listen, chuckling internally the whole time.

Only Charlotte.

The conversation ends with Charlotte working to convince Cole to take Maya on a date to the Boston Tea Party Museum. While I didn't find the experience romantic in any way, shape, or form, it also wasn't a date. *Unfortunately.*

The drive back to Brookline and my childhood home takes about twenty minutes. It wasn't my first choice of places to stay while Charlotte's here, but Finn and Ezra live in my penthouse downtown. I stayed with them for the first few days of my visit, since the master bedroom still has my shit in it, but I doubt Charlotte would enjoy the experience. The twins may be twenty-seven, but they've turned my professionally decorated *Architectural Digest*-worthy home into a frat castle. They seriously have a poster hanging on one wall that says *Don't Do Coke in the Bathroom*. So yeah, I'd rather deal with back pain from squishing into a twin-size bed than subject Charlotte to that.

Also, I don't need to give Finn additional opportunities to flirt with her. I don't blame him for shooting his shot, but that doesn't mean I have to like it.

Of course, that backfires because he's lounging with my dad in the backyard when we get back to the house and greets Charlotte with a "Hey, gorgeous. Are you a parking ticket? Because you've got fine written all over you."

She gives him a cursory once-over. "Are you a fire alarm? Because you're loud, obnoxious, and hurting my eyes."

Finn throws his head back and laughs, but Charlotte simply turns to greet my dad and chats for a moment before announcing that she's heading inside to shower and get ready for dinner. Dinner is beer, chicken wings, and nachos at a local sports bar with my brothers and some friends, but for Charlotte, dressing up is practically a requirement, regardless of how small the occasion.

Once the back door slides shut, I narrow my eyes at Finn. "Stop being weird and checking her out."

"Last time I checked, you weren't my parent, and therefore can't tell me what to do," he says with a smug smirk.

My dad clears his throat and straightens in his chair. "As your parent, I don't appreciate you making Charlotte uncomfortable in our home, so I'm telling you to stop."

Actually, Charlotte finds Finn's cheesy pickup lines "endearingly lame" and takes zero offense to them. But I keep that information to myself. If my dad can get him to stop, I'm all for it.

"You can't tell me what to do either," Finn argues. "I'm a grown-ass adult."

Dad simply arches a brow. "Then you can do your own taxes next year."

With a grumble, my brother shifts in his seat and rests his forearms on the armrests, suddenly not so combative.

"What are you doing here, anyway?" I ask, settling into the open lawn chair next to my dad. "I thought we were all meeting at the bar later."

"Got off work early and wanted to come hang," he says, feigning an innocence he hasn't possessed in more than two decades.

My dad chuckles. "That's code for he knew your mom made chocolate chip cookies for Charlotte and wanted some for himself."

Finn shrugs, completely unashamed. Can't say I blame him. Our mom's chocolate chip cookies are legendary and were always the most popular item at school bake sales, even beating out Robby Anderson's mom's superhero-themed cake pops. *Take that, fucker.*

"What'd the two of you do this afternoon?" my dad asks, leaning back in his chair. "Mom mentioned you were going to take her to the Charles River Esplanade."

I readjust my watch—the one Charlotte got for me. "Uh, we ended up going to the Boston Tea Party Museum instead."

My dad and Finn whip their heads in my direction in perfect unison, their mouths hanging open. Their reactions are warranted. If anyone else wanted to visit that museum, I'd be throwing myself into the Boston Harbor, posing as the tea and reenacting that infamous day to avoid it, since American history was always my least favorite subject in school.

But I never could, and probably never will, say no to her.

THE BARREL IS the stereotypical neighborhood bar. Neon beer signs line the walls, and there's a pool table standing proudly next to a jukebox that only plays '80s rock and jazz. The high tops and booths that have seen better days are chock-full of patrons with their attention glued to TVs mounted throughout the room. Every eye in the place shifts, though, the moment Charlotte, Finn, and I step into the bar, and for once, it's not because of me. Not to be cocky, but people get excited when a professional Formula 1 driver visits a local haunt, even places I've frequented for years. But with Charlotte beside me, I may as well be Casper the Friendly Ghost.

Not only does she look gorgeous, but she's wearing a ruffly pink romper and strappy silver heels in a bar that's known for their cheese curds. I would expect nothing less.

Automatically, I rest my hand on her lower back, in part to warn others that she's unavailable, but also because I like touching her, and this is about all I can get away with without raising eyebrows. Finn scans the space, and when he doesn't spot "our crew," his words, not mine, he offers to grab a table while we get drinks. That's his subtle way of telling me to start a tab with my Amex.

The Red Sox are playing the Yankees tonight *and* an NBA final is on, so the bar's packed with fans eager to cheer for their team while indulging in local stouts. I grab Charlotte's arm so she doesn't get lost in the crowd, but when I'm met with cool, hard plastic rather than warm, soft skin, I jerk back. Thrown off by the placement of her insulin pod and not wanting to accidentally knock it off, I reach out again, this time grasping her elbow to guide her to the bar.

"It's not contagious," Charlotte says, lifting her arm, motioning to the small pump that's no bigger than a case for wireless earbuds. "Nor will it bite you for touching it, so you don't have to act like it's a monarch butterfly."

"A monarch butterfly?"

"Madison says they're poisonous."

When the comment registers, I burst out laughing. *She can't be serious, right?* When her brows lower and her eyes go icy, I realize that yes, she is serious, and yes, I did just make a bad situation worse by laughing. She turns and takes a step, then another, her movements harsh, like she's going to storm off, but the sticky floor prevents her from getting far before I pull her back and spin her around using her belt loops.

"I'm not laughing at you." I tug her closer so she can hear me over the ruckus around us. "I'm laughing at how ridiculous it is that you think I care about your pump."

If possible, those eyes go glacial.

"Let me rephrase that." I inhale a deep breath and let it out slowly. "I care about your pump because it keeps you alive, but I don't care that you have to wear it. I just didn't realize it was there, and it caught me off guard. My first instinct was to move my hand so I wouldn't accidentally knock it off."

Her body softens against mine. "Oh."

"You seriously think I'd care about that?" I ask, my chest aching at the idea.

"No." She sighs. "It's a reflex, I guess. I dated this guy once, and he asked me if I could take it off 'just for sex.'"

Instantly, red crowds my vision. "You're fucking with me," I growl. Who in the ever-loving fuck would ask a question like that? Not only should it not matter, but her pump should be the last fucking thing on his mind if she's naked in front of him.

"Unfortunately, no." She shrugs. "Don't worry, though. I got even. I use his email when stores ask for one, so he's been getting junk emails for years now."

Some of my anger fades at this, though I rub at the pain in my chest that hasn't subsided. "Still fucked up."

"Yep," she agrees. "I change the location of my pump depending on what I think I'm going to wear."

I study her, dumbfounded by the information. "What do you mean?"

"I have to change it every three days," she explains. "So, if I know I'm going to be wearing jeans in the next few days, I won't put it on my thigh, since I don't like how bulky that looks. If I plan to wear a tighter shirt with a skirt, then I'll put it on my thigh rather than my stomach."

"I had no idea."

"Why would you? You're not exactly privy to my closet." She laughs. "But yeah, my outfits are about the only thing I plan ahead of time, and that's only because I want to make sure my pump sits comfortably. Wearing it on my stomach while in high-waisted jeans is not a good move, you know?"

"Huh," I note.

Charlotte's low key about being diabetic. She doesn't hide it—hell, her pump and glucose monitor are visible most of the time—but she doesn't let the disease stop her from doing what she wants. Because of that, I've never put much thought into where she wears her pump.

"Anyway," she says, moving on from the topic. "What's good to drink here? Is there anything they're known for?"

I chuckle at the question. "Cheap beer is what they're known for, Roo."

She crinkles her nose. Like Theo, she doesn't like beer, but she doesn't enjoy sugary cocktails either. "I'll take a glass of wine, then, please."

There's a good chance this bar doesn't serve wine, but I bite the bullet and ask for it anyway. Turns out that not only do they have it, but they have options. The bartender is so excited by the order that she offers to make Charlotte a flight of her favorites.

As we approach the booth Finn commandeered near the pool table in the back, we find the rest of our group has arrived, and they've taken over a second booth. They all look scandalized by the wine flight I'm holding, considering they all drink Sam Adams Boston Lager like it's water, but my friends are more interested in meeting Charlotte than commenting on her drink choice. I go through the introductions quickly since I don't appreciate how they're all staring at her with a little too much interest. Conversation is easy between us as we watch the game—minus Charlotte, who doesn't even pretend to have interest—and shoot the shit. A few drinks in, Grayson stands and announces that he wants to play pool.

"Charlotte, you're with me," he says, making teams without anyone's input. "Finn, you're with Ezra. Rack up."

That motherfucker.

While there's ample space for players around the pool table, there's little room for an audience. Grayson set it up this way so Jesse and I would be forced to stand off to the side. Alone. *Fuck me.*

I take a deep breath and turn to the brother I've done my best to avoid. We've been in the same room, sat at the same family dinners, laughed at our dad's corny jokes together, and salivated over our mom's home-cooked meals, but talked? We haven't done that.

"Let's get this over with," I say, crossing my arms. Maybe the look comes across as hostile, but I'm feeling defensive. "Say what you have to say so we can be done."

He flinches and scans the crowded bar. "Oh. Here?"

"It's as good a time as any." I shrug as a mix of pain and irritation swirl inside me. "You wanted to talk, so talk."

As much as I would love to *not* have this conversation, I can't evade it forever, especially now that Grayson has involved himself. And at least here, there's crowd control in case it gets... heated.

"What do I have to do?" Jesse asks, his shoulders slumping. "How do I get you to forgive me? I never wanted things to go down the way they did, and I regret how I handled it, but—"

"See, that's the thing," I interrupt him. "You regret how you handled it, but not what you did. How the hell do you expect me to forgive you when you're not even sorry? Exes are off-limits, and you *knew* I was still into her."

His dark eyes narrow, and his chest expands with a harsh breath. "Be fucking honest, Lucas. You were barely dating. You fucked her when you were in town, but barely referred to her as your girlfriend. I was one of a handful of people who even knew you were seeing her. You wanted to have your cake and eat it, too."

"How I define my relationships is none of your business, and not the point," I snap, clenching my free hand at my side. "She was still my ex. How did you think I was going to react? Say congrats and get you a gift? Ignore how you went behind my back to hurt me?"

"I didn't date Kylie to *hurt you*. Not everything is about you. Did you ever think that maybe I was in love with her long before you got with her? Did you ever consider how I'd feel when you started dating one of my friends? No. You didn't. You may have been interested in getting back together, but that's only because you liked the idea of having someone. It had nothing to do with who she was."

There's a lot to fucking unpack there, but anger rises in me like a tide, making it impossible to think of anything but my hurt. "So after I date her is when you decide to make a move? Sure, maybe I wasn't in love with her, but what you did was still shady as shit."

Jesse takes a step forward, invading my space. His lips twist into an ugly smirk. "What *I* did was shady? That's really hypocritical, considering you're fucking your best friend's little sister behind his back, Lucas."

"I'm not sleeping with Charlotte," I bite out through gritted teeth. "And she has nothing to do with this, so keep her name out of your mouth."

Jesse tips his face up and barks out a laugh. "She has nothing to do with this? You're pissed that I broke bro code, yet you're doing the same shit, man."

"There's nothing going on between the two of us," I hiss, poking him hard enough in the chest that he stumbles back a step. "So fuck you."

Definitely not my greatest comeback, and I'm sure something more profound will come to me later, but I stick with it.

"No, fuck you, Lucas," he says, his voice harsh. "I'm sorry I hurt you. I truly am. But you've been punishing me without looking at your own role in all of this. I love you, man, but I've lived in your shadow for *years*." His voice wavers a little on that last part. "Yeah, going for Kylie without speaking with you was shitty, and yeah, I could've handled it better, but rather than give me the benefit of the doubt, you make me the villain and don't give me five fucking seconds of your busy life to try to mend things."

I can read Jesse well enough to know he's about two breaths away from either turning and taking off or driving his fist into my face. Grayson must sense it, too, because suddenly, Jesse's being pushed toward the pool table while I'm pulled farther from it.

"You good?" Grayson asks, his hand resting on my shoulder.

Shrugging his hand away, I round on him. "I told you not to get involved."

The flicker of a wince wrinkles his forehead. "Can't blame a guy for trying."

I shoot him a droll look and take a long sip of my beer. The caramel sweetness and the bitter, spicy hops do nothing to alleviate the tension in my shoulders. The sound of pool balls shuttling into pockets and breaking against the sides, darts thunking into the dartboard, and the good-natured ribbing and cheering as a team scores become background noise. I'm not sure what I expected from my conversation with Jesse, but it certainly wasn't that. I had no idea he had a thing for Kylie before I got with her. They had been friends for years, and yet he never once indicated that he had any romantic interest in her. Hell, he's the one who introduced us. I don't—

"Oh, fuck," Grayson says, shoving past me and hightailing it to the pool table. My mind jumps to Charlotte, and I follow him blindly, in the dark about what's happening, but needing to know that she's okay.

A cursory once-over reveals that she's fine, but Jesse? He's doubled over, staggering backward while clutching his groin and groaning. Fuck, does that have to hurt. A phantom pain hits me, almost causing me to double over, too.

"I did warn him to back up when I lined up for my shot," Charlotte grumbles.

Huh. It wasn't Ezra or Finn who hit Jesse in the nuts. There was no brotherly annoyance involved. It was Charlotte and her pool cue. And based on the way she looks about 15 percent apologetic and 85 percent pleased with herself, I don't think it was an accident.

Lowering my head, I sidle up next to her and say, "I thought we agreed to no dick punching."

She peers up at me, wearing an innocent smile. "I thought that was just a suggestion, not a hard and fast rule."

I duck my head to hide a grin. I might not want my brothers involved in my issues with Jesse, but I've got to admit it's nice knowing Charlotte has my back. She's one hell of a beautiful ballbuster.

NINETEEN
CHARLOTTE

"IT'S NOT GOING to fit, Roo." Lucas sighs.

I puff out a frustrated breath and glare at him through the strands of hair falling in front of my face. "Yes, it is."

A choked noise comes from his lips. "Be serious. It's way too small to fit this much."

"You're not trying hard enough," I argue, lifting my chin.

"One more shot," he negotiates. He takes off the rings adorning his fingers as if that will somehow help and sets them on the dresser. "And then we're doing this my way."

Grumbling a half-assed agreement, I get back into position on my hands and knees. "All right, go."

Lucas rests his hand next to mine for additional support while using the other to force the zipper to move farther up the track. He yanks it an inch, then comes to an abrupt stop again. *Shit*. Knowing he's right and my suitcase isn't going to shut, but not wanting to admit it, I climb off and plop myself onto the floor with a huff.

"Now what?" I ask, arms crossed.

"Now we pray for a miracle," he says, slipping his rings back on. "What the fuck do you have in there, anyway?"

"Evidence that the moon landing was faked," I deadpan. "Clothes. Toiletries. Shoes. Accessories. Hair tools. More clothes."

"Jesus Christ," he mutters, rubbing his forehead. "No wonder it's bursting at the seams."

"In my defense, this is a month's worth of clothing."

"This is most people's entire closet, Roo," he points out, although there's no judgment in his voice. "And you do know we have access to washers and dryers, right? You didn't need to pack twenty-five pairs of socks when you barely even wear tennis shoes."

"I like to be prepared," I say, pulling my shoulders back.

He'd lose his mind if he knew I have a half a year's worth of underwear in there. So what if I pack as if I'm going to pee my pants every day? I'd rather be overprepared than underprepared.

He shakes his head, glowering at my luggage like he's got a personal vendetta against it. "You need to repack."

Before I can disagree, because packing the first time was torturous enough, Lucas tugs on the zipper, undoing all our progress, and lays both sides flat on the ground. He mutters about cubes, then starts tossing things out, not even bothering to keep my clothes in their semi-folded piles. I'm too stunned to cuss him out, so I simply watch in horror as he ruins all my hard work. That may be an exaggeration since it only took twenty minutes, but those are twenty minutes I'll never get back.

Once my suitcase is as empty as the day Josie gifted it to me after my university graduation, he stands and places his hands on his hips. "Much better."

"Something's seriously wrong with you if you look at the mess you just made and think *yes, much better*." I sit taller, shifting on the floor. "And just so we're clear, you're repacking all of that."

"I know," he says, as if that was his plan all along. "We just need packing cubes."

IT DOESN'T HIT Lucas until we step through the sliding glass doors of Target that it'll be a challenge leaving here with just a set of packing cubes. None of the posts I've seen on social media about America's favorite retailer give the sprawling wonderland the justice it deserves. Just inside the doors, we're greeted with a dollar section full of adorable magnets, patterned socks, and fun frames. To the left, there's home decor galore, with plush throw pillows, stylish rugs, and elegant lamps. All the way in the back? Neatly stacked organic vegetables, brightly colored exotic fruit, and aisle after aisle of packaged goods with hanging signs above listing items like *breakfast cereals* and *international cuisine ingredients*. And don't even get me started on the beauty and personal care section to my right. Dear lord, I could buy and fill a whole new suitcase with skincare products alone.

"Do I need to get a cart?" Lucas chuckles.

I snap my mouth shut, check it for drool, and turn to him. "We have dinner in an hour," I say, already distracted by a nearby accessory display with an adorable wicker purse.

He nods. "I know."

"You brought me to America's pride and joy, knowing I won't have enough time to peruse to my heart's content." I shoot him a scowl. "That's red flag behavior, Lucas Adler."

He shrugs. "Maybe I'm just making sure you come back here with me in the future."

"America has free refills, AC everywhere, movie theatre popcorn, and Girl Scout cookies." I wave him off. "Of course I'm coming back."

"You said that was all canceled out by our use of the imperial system."

There's nothing sexier than a man who listens, especially to complaints about not knowing how many cups of sugar equate to 150 grams.

A laugh burst from my chest. "Very true, but the Boston Tea Party tips the scales in its favor."

The reason my suitcase isn't zipping is because I now own three mugs featuring American presidents I can't name.

"Now stop distracting me. We have to leave in"—I grab his arm and peek at his watch—"thirty-seven minutes."

"It's fine if we're a bit late," he reassures me, his tone soothing.

I poke him in the chest. "Your mum's been the sweetest host. I won't disrespect her by showing up late to the dinner she took the time to make."

Lucas's lips twitch up at my outburst, but he maintains a straight face when he announces, "I made dinner."

His confession has me doing a double take worthy of a slapstick comedy. "You made dinner? When?"

"I prepped it all while you were sleeping," he tells me. "My mom's just popping things into the oven and turning on the grill."

"You cook?"

Lucas willingly wakes up at five or six—practically the middle of the night—so it makes sense that he accomplished so much before I rolled out of bed, but that doesn't leave me any less impressed.

"Yep." He chuckles. "It's hard when I'm traveling, but I do it as often as I can. I could tell you all about my broccoli pesto pasta and baked salmon with grapefruit salad, but if you don't want to be late, we only have about thirty-five minutes—"

I snag his arm with one hand and a small shopping basket with the other and yank him forward. I'm like a bloodhound when it comes to finding deals and steals, but that talent extends to finding exactly what I'm looking for in a time crunch. It's one attribute of being a chronic late packer. I often realize I need a certain item the night before a trip.

"Which ones?" I ask, motioning to the shelves lined with options. Rather than grab a package and be done with it, he picks one up, turns it over, and studies the package. *Hell no*. Refusing to waste time, especially because I don't think I need cubes in the first place, I leave Lucas to his examination and wander the aisles.

He finds me in the arts and crafts aisle fifteen minutes later, my basket filled with fun finds: bronzing drops, a new primer, a black-and-white-striped jumper that may or may not make me look like a prisoner, a pair of fuzzy socks, a rosemary vinegar hair rinse, a bag of cheddar onion popcorn, a mini colander with a berry design, and a dog toy shaped like a purse that's emblazoned with *Chewy Vuitton*.

Amusement dancing in his eyes, Lucas inspects my haul, then takes the basket from my arms. "The more stuff you get, the harder it's going to be to repack, Roo. Why are you getting a dog toy? You don't have a dog."

"Tell me Champ won't love that," I say. He should be glad I didn't get the orange liquor bottle–shaped toy that said *A-Paw-Rol*, too.

With a shake of his head, he grins. "What are we doing in this aisle, anyway?"

"I need colored pencils and dual-tipped markers for an idea I have."

"Ideas are good," he says, the corners of his lips tipping up. "Are you going to tell me what the idea is, or do you want me to guess?"

I hold up a hand to stop him right there. "You're a horrible guesser, Lucas."

He reels back in offense. "No, I'm not."

"I've watched *Jeopardy* with you," I remind him.

I've discovered that when Lucas is on a plane, he does one

of three things: He watches *Jeopardy*, catches up on sports games he's missed, or plays word games on his phone. If he didn't let his competitive nature take over and blurt out the first answer that came to his head, he'd probably be decent, but alas, he doesn't. It's why he says shit like "Who is Dr. Seuss?" instead of "Who is Ralph Waldo Emerson?" I watch it with him every once in a while, not because I enjoy it, but because the show is guaranteed to lull me to sleep on the plane.

"Whatever," he mumbles, shooting me a mock glare. "So what's the idea?"

"It's easier if I show you later," I explain with a dismissive wave. "Now stop distracting me. I've got a lot of aisles to get through in the next five minutes."

He chuckles but lets me be as I pick up a few more items, then drag him to the shoe section. I've got to hand it to him; he doesn't complain, nor does he rush me, as I toss items into the basket like it's a black hole. He insists on paying and warns me that if I argue with him, it'll only make us late for dinner and he'll still end up swiping his card.

We make it back to the Adler house three minutes and forty-two seconds after the official start time for dinner. Grayson, Jaclyn, and Madison pull into the driveway moments after we do, and the rest of the Adler brothers are already snacking on hummus, pita, and veggies in the kitchen.

Lucas invites me outside with him to grill, but I decline because, well, mosquitos and Jesse. The former loves me—and it's not mutual—and the latter is avoiding me. I barely got out a full "hello" before he was hightailing it into the backyard. I don't blame him after what I'm dubbing the "pool cue and penis incident." But he deserved it. I hope. I don't know what was said during their conversation—and Lucas won't tell me—but I'm willing to bet it wasn't pleasant.

I temporarily regret my decision to stay indoors when I notice Lucas manning the grill like a pro, all while his niece hangs off his back like a spider monkey. It's a sexy sight and may replace my current favorite look—the porn pants, of course.

"We're on table duty," a deep voice says nearby, interrupting my peepshow.

Thankfully, Grayson doesn't call me out on my blatant yet respectful ogling of his brother. Instead, he simply nods in the direction of the dining room.

"I was surprised when Lucas told me you were coming to Boston," he admits, walking around the table while putting down placemats.

I look up from my phone, where I'm googling whether the fork goes on the left or the right side. I always fuck it up. *FYI: it's the left.*

"Why?" I ask, my heart jumping into my throat as I consider that maybe the surprise wasn't a good one.

"He doesn't bring people home," he replies. "Or at least he hasn't until you."

Blake, Theo, and Ella have all been to Lucas's Boston penthouse, but I read between the lines. Lucas doesn't bring single female friends home. Unsure of what to make of this information, I throw Grayson a wink, "What can I say?" I joke. "I've got a stellar sense of humor."

Chuckling, he says, "I think it's because you put him at ease."

I can't help but grin at that. I've been called loud, outgoing, vivacious, bubbly, and energetic, but I've never once been referred to as the kind of person who puts another at ease. "Um, I don't think you'd be saying that if you'd seen him trying to zip my suitcase earlier. He was anything but at ease."

"You wouldn't be disagreeing with me if you realized how much calmer and happier he is when you're around."

My cheeks heat, but before I can respond, he continues.

"He gave up a lot to get where he is today, and I respect

that, but he puts an insane amount of pressure on himself. He's always go, go, go. Lucas is so laser-focused on Formula 1 that he's forgotten there's a life outside of it. You... balance him out a bit."

"We're just friends," I tell him. It's lame, sure, using the oldest line in the book, but I don't want him to read into anything. I do enough of that myself.

"Even so." He gives me a knowing smirk. "He's been so wrapped up in racing these past few years that he's forgotten how to be a kid."

I arch a brow at him. Lucas is anything but a kid. Those muscles? That stubble? Those tattooed forearms? That's all man. "You're only, what, three years older than him?"

"Yeah, but he'll always be my kid brother," Grayson says, sounding far too much like Theo when he talks about me. I could be married with kids, and I guarantee my brother would pretend I'm a virgin.

"The two of you went to the Boston Tea Party Museum, right?" With the last placemat in position, he moves on to napkins.

I nod, curious as to where he's going with this. "Mm-hmm. Interpreters wearing costumes led the tour and everything."

He tilts his head, studying me. "And Lucas had a good time?"

"I mean, he didn't throw his arms up and say 'I had the best day ever,' but he was an active participant when we threw tea off the replica vessel, and he said he had fun."

He huffs out a laugh. "Lucas hates museums, and the only test he ever cheated on was American history."

My heart stutters, and I blink in slow disbelief. Now that's some tea.

TWENTY
CHARLOTTE

"YOU'RE BEING QUIET."

A few hours later, Lucas and I are sitting on the guest room floor, repacking my suitcase. Or, more accurately, Lucas is doing that while I supervise. It's endearing, watching him organize my clothes like he's a mini-Marie Kondo.

"Everything okay?"

"Mm-hmm," I say, bringing my water bottle to my lips.

"Blood sugar high?"

My stomach dips at the question. "Why would you think that?" I ask, twisting the cap back on. "Because I ate three pieces of sweet corn soufflé?"

Not only can Lucas drive a million-dollar car with skill and precision and sail a boat like he's a descendant of Magellan, but he can grill a ribeye that would impress Gordon Ramsay. He seriously undersold himself when he said he likes to cook. I had to stop myself from groaning multiple times during dinner.

"As honored as I am that you enjoyed it, no." He chuckles. "You get thirsty when your blood sugar spikes."

I go still at his words, and a mix of unease and maybe something like appreciation winds through me. Unless my pump makes a noise or I announce it, it's rare anyone realizes that my blood sugar is high or low. The only people in my life who recognize the symptoms are my mom, Willow, and Theo. My dad, too, before he passed. With Lucas, I now have a full handful of people.

"I'm okay," I reassure him, settling on touched by his concern. "I took more insulin halfway through dinner when I realized you could win *Master Chef*."

"If you say so." His green irises are darker than usual as he studies me with an intensity that makes me squirm. "That still doesn't explain why you're being quiet, though."

Because your brother insinuated that I make you happy and relaxed.

Rather than admit that, I merely wave off his concern. I'm a relatively confident person, but that doesn't mean I don't overanalyze and overthink absolutely everything when it comes to men I'm attracted to. *Why did he use fewer emojis in his text than he usually does? Why is he taking so long to respond? Does he sound annoyed? Why did he watch my Instagram story but not text me?* It's silly, true, and self-sabotaging, and a relationship worth its salt shouldn't cause these constant thoughts, but that's what therapy's for, right?

But I'm not dating Lucas, so the tips and tricks I usually depend on to decode a man's actions and words mean diddly squat. And I have zero clue what to make of Grayson's comment about how Lucas doesn't like museums. Because he spent four hours listening to people cosplay as colonial Americans and talk about the Revolutionary War, and he didn't complain once.

"Oh, want me to show you what I was talking about before?" I had no intention of showing him when he brought it up, but it's guaranteed to be a distraction.

A slow, shy smile spreads across his lips. "Yeah, I'd like that."

I search through my plane bag—if my purses are Mary

Poppins bags, this thing is a suitcase—until I find my sketch notebook. It was a birthday gift from my dad, and I take it with me everywhere, in case inspiration strikes, but don't use it that often. The day I run out of pages will be devastating.

I flip through designs and patterns for Theo's racing helmets until I find the design I started working on after the Canadian Grand Prix.

"Here." I hand him the notebook. "They're pants."

Lucas glances up and raises an amused brow. "I'm aware, Roo. It'd be a little worrisome if I wasn't."

He ignores my huff of laughter and turns back to the design, taking his damn time studying every detail. The custom cargo pants have one pocket that'll replicate the front left chest of an AlphaVite racing suit, another that I'll cover with patches, and a third adorned with beads I'll sew into Alpha-Vite's logo. I've thrifted tons of buttons, chains, and pendants over the years, so I'll add those as hardware and maybe a blue patterned scarf as a belt to tie the look together.

At his continued silence, my mind takes off, running like it's in a marathon. *Does he think they're stupid? The concept sounds great in my head, but can I really pull it off? I haven't sewn in a few years, and I certainly haven't constructed anything from scratch, so the end product may look like a potato sack. If Lucas doesn't see the potential—*

"These are fucking sick," Lucas finally says, breaking the silence that was bordering on unbearable.

"Sick as in 'cool and amazing' or sick as in 'these make me want to throw up like I have the flu'?"

"The first option," he confirms, biting back a smile.

My stomach clenches at his praise. "Yeah? It's kind of hard to get the full vision since I drew in pencil—hence why I needed the markers—and the concept isn't fully fleshed out yet, but it's a start. Obviously, once the lights go out, Formula 1 is all about the race, but the fashion in the paddock is becoming so much more popular. And since I've never found team merch that resonated with my style, I figured why not try it out myself?"

"It's one hell of a start." He gives my thigh a light squeeze, his warm palm seeping through the fabric of my pants. "People are going to want a pair of their own once they see these. Guaranteed."

"I don't know about that, but at least this way I can dress in my own style while supporting the team."

"Where'd the idea come from?" he asks, hand still on my leg.

"I didn't know about AlphaVite's team history until Finn told me—"

"*Finn* inspired your pants?"

"God no," I say, a laugh bubbling out of me. "After he mentioned it, I looked for Alpha Arrow or ViteRomeo shirts I'd want to wear, but to no one's surprise, I wasn't wowed by what I found. I started thinking about what you said to me during the Hot Lap, about combining style and support, and it hit me. What's stopping me from creating my own team merch? Why can't I take AlphaVite team shirts and transform and incorporate them into pieces that I'll actually wear?"

A boyish smile spreads across his lips as his eyes crinkle at the corners. "You continue to amaze me, Roo."

With a tingling warmth blossoming in my cheeks, I check my shoulder against his, and in the process, I get a whiff of his cologne. It brings me back to our *almost kiss*, which then causes me to stare at his lips. He notices quickly, his eyes widening a fraction.

Feeling awkward about getting caught *checking out his lips*, I announce, "You smell good."

Those eyes go soft instantly. "Not like a forest, right?" he teases.

"No," I laugh, rolling my eyes. "I wouldn't be sitting next to you if you did."

He chuckles, but his features turn more serious. "Thank you for visiting. Maybe it wasn't a big deal for you, but to me, it is. You made Boston feel like home again, rather than a chore."

My cheeks flush, and I straighten, not bothering to fight a smile. "Even though I knocked your brother in the nuts?"

"While I can't condone it, I do appreciate the support."

Lucas pulls me tight against him, burying his face in my hair. Then he presses a gentle kiss into my mass of curls, and I melt a little inside. That's a lie. I melt a lot. And when he pulls back, rests his hands on my face, and brushes his thumbs over my cheeks in a soothing motion? It's a miracle I'm not a puddle of adoration on the carpet.

He studies my face, his attention moving from my eyes to my lips and lingering there. I struggle to control my breathing, almost hypnotized by him. This close, I can see a small freckle under his right eye and a nearly invisible scar on his jawbone. If I had to bet, he got it while sparring. Or maybe it's a childhood battle scar from fighting with his brothers.

Lucas tugs on the end of one of my curls, and when my eyes meet his, the naked desire radiating from him crashes over me in scorching waves. Every ounce of longing in my body rushes straight between my thighs. Like we're magnets with no hope of fighting the pull, Lucas closes the distance between us, and when his breath ghosts over my face, I know there's no maybe about what's going to happen. Even so, I still let out a tiny sound of surprise as his lips finally meet mine. Looping his arms around my waist, he drags me closer, then slips his tongue between my lips, twisting and tangling it against with mine in a dance of desire.

I knew he'd be a good kisser, but boy oh boy, does he knock my expectations out of the water. As it continues, slow and sensual, I glide my hands through the soft hair at his nape, desperate for more of his touch.

The *thump, thump, thump* of footsteps on the stairs has us

pulling apart. And where I expect to find a smirk or smile on Lucas's face, like the one overtaking me, all I find is regret.

"Shit. I don't know what I was thinking," he says, his lips parted in apology. "Can we forget that happened?"

His words are a bucketful of water over the flames of need licking over my body. I press my lips together in a forced smile. "Yeah, because that's exactly what every woman wants to hear after she's been kissed."

"Shit, sorry," he says, rubbing his brow. "I like you, Roo, but I shouldn't have done that. You're Theo's sister."

Every rational thought in my minds screams at me to keep my expression neutral, to gather some shred of dignity, and miraculously, I firmly shut the door on the hurt before it escalates into something I can never recover from. Anything else—*it was the heat of the moment, you're a bad kisser, I don't like you like that, I don't want to lead you on*—would've been better than "you're Theo's sister." The title that's followed me around my whole life like a childhood bully. The title that reminds me that no matter how much I try, no matter what I do, I'll never be just Charlotte. And fuck if that doesn't sting, especially coming from him.

While I can't anatomically confirm this, I'm certain his words hurt more than a punch to the dick.

TWENTY-ONE
LUCAS

AS THEO DRIVES from the track to his childhood home, he drones on about how the reward system of his favorite coffee chain has gone downhill over the past few years, so I let myself zone out. And of course, my mind focuses on the one thing it shouldn't: Charlotte.

My words circle through my head like a merry-go-round.

That was a mistake. You're Theo's sister. Can we just forget this happened?

Like I could ever erase the memory of her lips on mine. I'm not one of those guys who likes to rush kissing and skip straight to the action. I love kissing. It may not be as intimate as other acts, but I enjoy the slow buildup, the teasing of what's to come. And fucking hell can Charlotte kiss. Her lips have haunted me for years, and now that I've had a taste, I'd give up a championship win for another.

She's off-limits.

The unspoken code among friends has me in its clutches. Charlotte is Theo's sister. Pursuing anything with her would be a betrayal, plain and simple. But that knowledge has no bearing on how I feel about her. It doesn't stop the way my heart races when she walks into a room or how my thoughts drift to her more often than I care to admit. And it doesn't keep my smile from widening when she laughs. And now that I know that a single kiss from her is better than any sex I've had, I'm screwed for the rest of my life.

The car comes to a short stop at a red light, causing my seat belt to choke me and the momentum to force a grunt from my throat. I shift in my seat, ready to badger him about forgetting how to operate a regular car, but when the worry etched into his features registers, I snap my mouth shut.

"Tell me what's wrong," he says in a stern tone. "Why have you been pouting all day?"

I take a deep breath to center myself so I don't throttle him. Despite what he thinks, I'm a thirty-one-year-old man who absolutely doesn't pout. "Nothing's wrong. I'm fine, man."

Humming, he drums his fingers against the steering wheel. "Liar. I know something happened with Jesse. Grayson told me."

Irritation flares in my chest. How is it that my oldest brother doesn't understand the concept of backing the fuck off? "He shouldn't have said anything, and I don't appreciate the two of you texting about me. It's unnecessary."

Theo's unusually stoic expression morphs into a smirk. "He didn't tell me shit, but I knew that'd get you to admit something happened."

I drop my head back against the seat. *Yup. I walked straight into that one.*

"It's not a big deal," I say, annoyance ratcheting up to agitation. "We got into an argument."

Understatement of the year. Jesse's assertion that I'm a hypocrite for calling him out while crushing on Charlotte got under my skin more deeply than a splinter. That's why I panicked after we kissed. I've successfully resisted her for two years, but watching her spend time with my family, joking and chatting like she's exactly where she belongs? I hit my breaking point. Then I told her we should forget about it. *Fucking asshole.* I keep telling myself it's for the best, but I'm not sure for whom.

"Charlotte told me you can hire a witch to curse people," Theo says, his lips pulled into a serious frown. "Just say the word, and I'll find a good one for you."

I crack a small smile at that. "I'll think about it."

"Good," he says with a satisfied smirk. The light turns green, and he speeds forward, ignoring all speed limits. "Do you think Blake's proposing to Ella tonight?"

"No." It's the same answer I gave him when he asked me this morning.

"Why else would he miss dinner tonight, though?"

"Because it's an AlphaVite *team* dinner, and last time I checked, Blake drives for McAllister."

Theo scoffs. Blake may not be part of the AlphaVite team, but Mrs. Walker considers him extended family regardless, so he still got the dinner invite.

"*Or*," Theo says, drawing out the single syllable, "he said no because he's taking her out for ice cream to pop the question. I bet he'll hide the ring in her soft serve. Oh! Or they'll put it on top with sprinkles surrounding it."

Blake bought a ring—a whopping 5.2 carat diamond from a trusted jeweler, a.k.a. my dad—but has been tight-lipped about when, where, and how he's proposing. Theo, naturally, is beside himself about not being kept in the loop, and now he's on high alert at all times. Any time Ella and Blake are alone, he's convinced it's going to happen. Grabbing a coffee? He's going to propose with the ring around the straw. Going to dinner? Surprise, there's a ring baked into the dessert. Walking Champ? He's going to be wearing a bandanna that says *Will you marry my dad?*

"Blake won't propose if her family's not in town," I point out. "And I highly doubt he'd do it with a sticky ring."

"Maybe," Theo muses. "I can't wait for the two of us to be his best men."

Cringing internally, I simply nod. Blake's going to ask Ella's younger brother to be his best man, and Theo's going to lose his ever-loving mind when he finds out he's just a regular groomsman.

Theo spends the rest of the car ride guessing how tonight's proposal will happen—ignoring the reality that it definitely isn't—including a scenario where Blake pulls the ring out of a kangaroo's pouch. He's still yammering on as we pull up to his childhood home and he expertly navigates the cobblestone driveway that winds its way up to the front entrance.

"Home sweet home," he says, drumming his hands against the steering wheel as we come to a stop.

More like mansion sweet mansion. No one in their right mind would consider the Walker's gleaming white stone house, with its tall, arched windows, dark slate roof, and views overlooking the Port Philip Bay a simple home. It's an estate.

The engine is still running when the front door swings open and Mrs. Walker waves at us. The greeting has my lips quirking of their own accord. Charlotte's looks aren't the only thing she gets from her mom. That cute little wave must be hereditary, too.

"Hey, Mrs. Walker," I say as I step out of the car. She insists I call her Laura, but I was raised to call friends' parents Mr. or Mrs., and even now, in my thirties, I can't seem to break the habit. "How are you?"

"Hi, honey," she says, pulling me into a quick hug. "Come in, come in." She leads us through the house and out onto the sprawling terrace, where she's hosting our team barbecue.

The L-Shaped outdoor kitchen island and bar-height table are covered in a spread full of foods typically found at an

American barbecue—pasta salad, potato salad, coleslaw, roasted vegetables, corn on the cob, and pineapple rings.

"Smells delicious, Mum," Theo says, reaching out to snatch a chip from a nearby bowl.

She smacks his hand away like she was expecting the move. "You're here to help, not eat before guests arrive."

"Lucas is here," Theo argues, jerking his thumb at me. "And where's Jos? You're not keeping my girlfriend hostage somewhere, are you?"

"Lucas isn't a guest; he's family." She moves in front of him to block the buffet. "Richard and Josie ran to the store to pick up a few last-minute things, so I need you to finish cleaning the grill and get the drinks from the garage. Lucas, do you mind grabbing Charlotte?"

"Sure," I reply, my heart stumbling a little at the prospect. "Where is she?"

She hasn't been around much the past few days. Though it's probably because she's catching up with friends and family, I can't help worrying that she's avoiding me after what happened in Boston. Charlotte's the queen of *forgive, but don't forget*.

If it wasn't for the brief flash of hurt in her big blue eyes after we kissed, I'd think she didn't care one way or the other how things played out between us. She's been her usual self since. Her ponytail still swings back and forth as she chats animatedly about every topic that pops into her head, whether it's where Taylor Swift gets her Amazon packages delivered while she's on tour or how it's bullshit that sunscreen isn't universally free when it's technically medicinal. It's maddening, trying to keep my feelings in check when every little thing she does makes me fall harder.

"In her room," Mrs. Walker replies, giving Theo a little shove between the shoulders to get him moving. "Upstairs, third room on the left."

I find her bedroom easily and waste no time knocking on the door. Not only because I'm eager to see her, but because I'm nervous I'll chicken out if I don't. When she doesn't answer after my third attempt, I twist the knob and push the door open.

Scanning the space, I take my time soaking in the details. The walls are adorned with a mix of *Vogue* magazine covers and art prints, while the oversized dresser is topped with collages of family photos. An unmade queen-size bed with a colorful duvet and an assortment of mismatched throw pillows takes up one side of the room, and against the opposite wall is a desk cluttered with a sewing machine, fabrics, and thread.

I double back, surveying the bed, only then realizing that one of the pillows isn't actually a pillow, but Champ Hollis-Gold. He's sprawled out and dreaming with his belly up and tongue out. At my chuckle, he lazily blinks, and when he spots me, he scrambles to his paws and lets out a small bark, his tail wiggling at rapid-fire speed. He leaps off the bed with the grace of a trained show dog, then struts around for a few moments before picking an item up off the ground and presenting it to me.

Hanging from his mouth is a thong.

A lacy lavender thong.

A lacy lavender thong that's smaller than a piece of dental floss.

Champ waits, head lifted, for me to take it from him.

Stomach churning, I shake my head. Hell no. I'm already pushing the envelope by being in here alone and uninvited. The last thing I need is to hold her fucking underwear like some sort of pervy stalker.

"Pick something else," I tell him, motioning to the plentiful options surrounding my feet. Charlotte's not what I'd call organized. The hardwood floor is scattered with socks, shirts, and pajamas. How the fuck she manages to look put together twenty-four seven when her room looks like it was recently burglarized is beyond me.

Champ lets out an annoyed bark despite the material he's still got dangling from his mouth. *Fuck.* How do I explain to a dog that there's no way in hell I'm touching Charlotte's thong? I have no way to know whether it's clean, not that it matters. Either way, this is bad.

But if I know Champ, he won't move on until I accept his present, so I take the thong from his mouth and hold it from the tips of my fingers like it's radioactive. *Christ, do those even qualify as underwear? Does it need to be made from a certain amount of material in order to make the cut?* At a loss as to what to do, I tuck them into my pocket. Only then does Champ lie on the floor and rest his face on his front paws.

Puffing out a breath, I wander over to her desk, curious about whether she's working on the design she showed me in Boston. I make myself comfortable in her desk chair—as comfortable as a six-foot man can be in a plastic swivel chair—and study the article of clothing in front of me. As I take in the details, I let out an impressed whistle. She only has one pant leg done, but already, the original design doesn't hold a candle to the real thing. Her talent blows me away. As much as I appreciate fashion, I could never in a million years design a sock, let alone clothing as detailed as this.

I pick up a pile of patches next to the sewing machine, breath catching at the Alpha Arrow design from the early '70s. How the hell did she find these? Beside the pile, there's a container of beads in an array of blues and silvers and a few ribbons in varying patterns.

A cough from behind me has me jumping up from the seat, banging my knee on the underside of the desk in the process. I turn, finding Charlotte leaning against the doorjamb, wearing a neutral expression and holding a spool of ribbon. Dressed in denim overalls and a white T-shirt, with her hair tied back in a ponytail, she's the epitome of the girl next door.

"Your mom asked me to get you," I tell her. That doesn't explain why I was sitting at her desk, but it's a start.

Charlotte nods, her eyes roving from my head to my toes. There's nothing sexual about the appraisal, but my balls tighten, nonetheless. "Mm-hmm. Did she also tell you to shove my G-string into your pocket?"

My dick immediately deflates and my stomach bottoms out. I can only guess by the heat engulfing me that my face turns fire-engine red. If my cheeks burst into literal flames, I won't be the least bit surprised. Not sure there's any way to recover from this, I blurt out, "It was Champ."

Charlotte takes a few steps into her room and scoops Champ up from the floor. He licks her cheek. I won't lie and say I'm not a tiny bit jealous of him.

She nuzzles into his furry face before turning to me. "This lil guy?"

I nod, whipping the ridiculously small scrap of fabric from my pocket and tossing it to the ground like a poisonous snake.

"I know the dog ate my homework excuse is a common one, but I've never heard anyone claim that their dog put a woman's G-string into their pocket." She hums. "It may be creepy, but I'll give you points for creativity."

"No, really," I stammer. "Champ gave it to me when I came into your room, and I felt bad not taking it—shit, that doesn't sound much better. You know how he gives presents when he greets you? Not that your underwear is a present. I'm just, um, explaining what happened. Well, he—"

"I'm fucking with you, Lucas," Charlotte says, a playful smile teasing the corners of her lips. "No dramas. I'm well aware of Champ's undergarment fetish."

"Oh, well, good," I say, my heart rate beginning to slow. "I mean, not good that he has a thong fetish, but good that you realized it wasn't me with the fetish. It was him. I don't have any fetishes. Not that there's anything wrong with a fetish. Just saying."

Shut the fuck up, man.

"What's he doing here, anyway?" I ask, wiping at the sweat that's suddenly beading on my brow, desperate to divert the conversation.

Charlotte studies me for a couple of breaths before laughing. "I volunteered to babysit him while they go out tonight. He's been a good boy, with the exception of nibbling through the back of a sandal. Well, that and giving you a pair of my underwear."

Cheeks still hot, I grimace. "Am I ever going to live that down?"

"Probably not," she freely admits. "Are people here already?"

"Not yet, but soon." I inhale deeply, then let the breath out through my nose, trying to ignore the pounding of my heart in my throat. "That's why your mom wanted me to get you."

With her lips twisted into a small frown, she presses her hands together and taps her fingers in front of her chin. "Okay. But I want to finish sewing the last pocket, so can you tell her I'll be down in a few?"

A smirk licks at my lips. I know full well that to Charlotte, *a few* can mean anywhere from five minutes to five days. Not wanting to leave her room yet, I nod, gesturing to the desk. "The pants are coming along great. Where'd you find those patches?"

She breaks into a genuine smile, her beautiful face blindingly gorgeous. With a kiss to his head, she places Champ on the floor, then shuffles over to her desk and picks up a patch. "I bought a few of them online. I was nervous it was a scam since the only other thing the storefront sold were wool socks. But I lucked out, and they showed up last night."

She opens up the top desk drawer and rifles around the clutter of buttons and hardware until she finds a small pin shaped like the Marina Bay Street Circuit in Singapore. Dropping it into my palm, she says, "Isn't that a good find?"

"Yeah." I turn it over in my hand and inspect the details. "You could use it in place of the button on the pants."

Charlotte claps, a small squeal escaping her lips. "Oh, I like that idea. I'm using an old Chanel one as the front button, but this could look good on the back pocket, maybe? Actually, it may hurt to sit on that sort of pin. I don't know. Maybe I can make a blazer and use this on the lapel and—ah, shit, I'm rambling, aren't I? Sorry."

"Never apologize, Roo," I tell her with a chuckle. "I'd happily listen to you read your grocery list."

Her smile shifts from pleased to polite, the subtle change making my heart sink. *Shit*. It's a damn good thing I didn't say what I was really thinking, which is that I'd listen to every word that escaped her simply because I like the sound of her voice and I crave being in her presence.

Desperate to break the tension that's filling the air, I ask, "Are you going to make other items, or just the pants? Not that the pants aren't impressive on their own."

Lips pressed together, she regards her sewing machine. "I don't know. These haven't been difficult, but that's because I have all my sewing equipment here. I already travel with two huge suitcases, a carry-on, and my purse, so I don't think I can get away with bringing this, too. I have a few more ideas, but I should see how these pants turn out first. When they're done, I may decide they look try-hard instead of cool."

At the mention of more ideas, I step closer. "Have you sketched anything else out yet?"

"Mm-hmm," she replies. "Do you want to see?"

I nod, but I don't speak. Irrationally, I worry that the sound of my voice will spook her out of showing me.

Charlotte opens the second desk drawer—which is somehow less organized than the top one—and takes out her sketchbook, then flips toward the middle. She explains her vision to me, her words escaping her quickly as she gets more excited by her ideas.

Despite my best efforts to keep my attention on the page, I find my focus drifting down to her lips. I take a deep breath, steadying myself so I don't give in to the urge to kiss her until she's breathless. *Fuck*. There are plenty of women out there, so why does the one I'm utterly obsessed with have to be my best friend's little sister? If keeping things platonic is really for the best, then why does it hurt the worst?

TWENTY-TWO
CHARLOTTE

ON A REGULAR DAY, I'm 100 percent a coffee slut. On a morning like this one, where I'm running on three hours of sleep because I was sewing ribbons on the outseam of what I'm calling my "paddock pants" at two a.m., I'm a straight-up coffee whore.

Willow's eyes swim with amusement as she surveys me. "You might want to ease up on groaning like you're getting railed by a ten-inch dick. People are staring."

A laugh forces its way out of me, causing coffee to dribble down my chin. "I don't think I'd be groaning at ten inches, Wills. I think I'd be running in the opposite direction."

She giggles. "Regardless, you're drawing attention."

"Whatever." Ignoring the likelihood that she's right, I take another long sip. I can't help my reaction. This coffee is crack. There's a reason this spot is ranked on several best cafés in Melbourne lists year after year.

The moment I place my ceramic coffee cup on the table, Willow slides it out of my reach.

"What the hell?" I complain with a frown. "You have your own coffee. Don't steal mine. It's rude."

"You know what else is rude?" Willow counters. "Telling me you kissed the love of your life, then failing to elaborate. I need details. And make them good. I want to feel like I was there with the two of you."

"Because that's not weird," I mumble, snatching my mug from her. I take three large gulps, relishing the roasted nut and dark chocolate flavor.

"Oh, shut up," Willow says with an unoffended laugh. "You're the one who drew a diagram of different types of penis piercings after you slept with that guy who had a frenum—"

"Here you ladies go." Our server suddenly appears with a tray full of food. If she heard the words *penis* or *piercing*, she gives no indication, which I consider ten out of ten service. Then she scurries off, leaving me alone with Willow and her unrelenting stare, which is a zero out of ten. *Ugh.*

"Talking about it isn't going to change anything," I tell her with a sigh.

Lucas isn't the first guy to reject me or tell me he's not interested, but he's definitely the first to use Theo as an excuse. And then he goes and says shit like he'd happily listen to me talk about my grocery list. Joke's on him, since I don't make a list. No, I let my cravings fill the cart.

"Maybe not, but I wouldn't be a good best friend if I didn't properly condemn him," she argues. "I can't do that without knowing all the details."

"It's embarrassing." I have no interest in rehashing my rejection. "Having to experience it once was bad enough. I don't particularly want to live through the play-by-play."

Willow rolls her eyes. "Embarrassing for Lucas, maybe. He's the dumbarse not reeling you in like the catch you are."

With a sigh, I bring my mug to my lips. I take a big sip, then spill more tea than the Boston Tea Party ever did.

Willow listens patiently, and once I'm finished, sums it up with a succinct "Well, that fucking sucks."

I huff and lean back into my seat. "You think?"

"Hmm," she says, cutting into her hotcakes. "Okay. Here's the plan. We'll go over all the reasons Lucas isn't right for you. Then you're going to go on a date with someone else to remind yourself that you're a badarse boss bitch any man would be lucky to have."

My chest tightens painfully at the idea. I hate first dates, and not because I'm bad at them. I dislike them because I'm great at them. That's the issue. I can talk to a brick wall for seven hours straight and have a great time, so it's tough for me to gauge how well a date actually went. It takes about three to five of them before I can tell whether a guy's a dud.

"For starters, he's eight years older than you," Willow says, pointing her fork at me. "That's a decent age gap."

"My dad was twelve years older than my mum," I point out.

"Sure," she says, her tone dismissive, "but they got together when people didn't even have cell phones. Now we're in the golden age of social media. It's very different. Our generation is chronically online, and Lucas is a millennial. They do weird shit like use hashtags and brag about being around when VHS tapes were a thing."

I snort. "Fair, but I'm going to need something stronger than a slight age gap to convince me to move on."

"Fine. He… um, he"—she waves her hands in front of her as if that will help her come up with a suitable reason to add to the list—"has tattoos! Lots of tattoos."

The booth shakes as I giggle. "That's a selling point, not a red flag, Wills. If anything, you're making him sound like marriage material."

Willow presses her lips together to stop her own laughter.

She's a huge Harry Styles fan and has each and every one of his tattoos memorized, so she's not really one to talk.

"He's also your brother's best friend," she says, pointing out the obvious. "And teammate."

"I'm aware," I say flatly.

"No, but think about it," she insists with a wicked gleam in her eye. "You know I love your brother, but I have no idea how Josie deals with him. I mean, I do, he's fucking hot as hell—"

"Oh, gross," I say, fighting back a gag. "Can you not say shit like that?"

She lifts a finger in an *aha!* motion. "See that reaction there? Can you imagine how weird it'd be for your brother to know his sister is fucking his best friend?"

"But explain this to me," I argue, trying not to let defeat win. "Logically speaking, wouldn't your best friend be the perfect candidate for your sibling? You already think they're great and amazing, and you enjoy spending time with them. Plus, they're vetted and close to the family."

Willow grimaces. "Yeah, but there's a level you're forgetting. If you and Lucas got together, Theo becomes a third wheel rather than maintaining two important, separate relationships. Plus, they've been friends forever. Your brother probably knows all the naughty, scandalous things Lucas has gotten into over the years. I hardly think he'd want that person dating his sister."

I sink farther into my seat. Yeah, I get her point. But understanding it doesn't make me feel any better. Why should Theo's feelings trump mine? I guess it's a moot point, regardless. Lucas would have to think I'm worth the risk to pursue anything, which clearly, he doesn't.

"All right, let's change the subject. This is getting you all espresso depresso instead of cold brew happy-roo," Willow says, stealing a piece of guava from my plate. "Show me the pants."

Heart lifting, I pull out my phone to show her the photo of my full ensemble. We're heading to the track soon, but I didn't want to risk spilling on them during brekkie, so I'm waiting until we pay the bill to change.

Her jaw drops, causing a piece of fruit to fall out and land on her plate. "Holy shit, Lottie."

Tingles of elation zip through me at her reaction. It feels really good to have my hard work appreciated.

Holding the phone closer to her face like my mum does when she's reading small text, she lets out a gasp. "Did you make a belt out of your dad's old ties?"

"Mm-hmm," I confirm.

My dad had an eclectic tie collection, and growing up, Willow and I would use them when we played dress-up. A tie would become a sash when we played Miss Universe, or we'd use it as a sling for a fake broken arm if we were playing doctor. For years after my dad passed, I considered using them, but it never felt right. If I was going to rework items he loved, I wanted to make sure I found an idea I loved just as much.

I finally made it happen.

If only moving on from Lucas could happen that easily.

WANTING to surprise Theo at his home race, I didn't mention my paddock pants beforehand. And when he spots me, I'm thankful I waited. As I approach him and Josie in the motorhome cafeteria where they're finishing up lunch, he does a double take. His eyes light up as he takes in the details of the vintage patches, the lightning symbol from the AlphaVite logo, and the pocket designed after his racing suit. By the time I'm standing beside their table, Theo's on his feet, nearly bouncing in place.

"You're finally supporting me and wearing AlphaVite," he says, his smile blinding.

Without holding back, I punch him in the arm. I don't have a lot of muscle, but he takes a surprised step back anyway. "Some would consider attending every race supportive, but far be it from me to—"

He wraps his arms around my waist and lifts me, cutting off my tirade. He spins in circles so quickly that when my feet finally touch the floor again, I have to hold a hand out to steady myself.

"They're amazing," he says, squatting to get a better look at the beading on the pockets.

My cheeks heat at his proximity to my ass. I give Josie a pleading look, but she simply laughs and rests a hand on his head, ruffling his hair.

"Those are proper fit, babes," Josie says in her posh British accent. The sound of it makes me wonder what type of accent their kids will have—British or Australian? Probably British if they live in London. Though my brother gabs a lot, so there's no doubt there'll be a little Aussie in 'em. "Where are they from?"

"Oh," I say, awkwardness seeping into me. "I made them."

Josie's eyes widen. "You *made* them?"

"I didn't make the actual denim," I clarify with a laugh. "I reworked an old pair of Levi's with materials and fabric I had on hand."

"I knew you could sew, but damn." She lets out an impressed whistle. "Are you going to make any more pieces?"

"I'd love to." I rock back on my heels, willing the heat in my cheeks to dissipate. "Wearing a new bespoke piece on each race day would be the dream."

And a difficult task. But despite my non-athleticism, I've never been one to back down from a challenge. I'd have to buy a sewing machine, have my mum ship me my collection of scrap fabric, buttons and appliqués, along with all the other baubles in my desk, *and* sketch out and design pieces I feel proud of, but it's doable.

"You definitely should," Josie says, her smile genuine and encouraging.

"You're going to make that many new pieces?" Theo's question is a legitimate one, but the skeptical tone makes my hackles rise. "Really?"

"Maybe," I say, doing my best to shrug off the sensation. "Why not?"

With an imperious brow raised, he scoffs. "There're fifteen or so races left in the season."

There's no extinguishing my irritation now. With my hands on my hips, I cock my head. "So?"

"Lottie, c'mon," he says with a casual smile, clearly clueless as to how he's riling me up. "Remember when you were super into jigsaw puzzles? And then there was the time you collected fountain pens and inks, not to mention your obsession with karate. Your interests change on a whim."

"I've always liked design," I remind him, chin tipped up. "That's not new or impulsive, Theodore."

"You could've studied it at university but chose not to," he points out with a nonchalant shrug.

That statement is like a punch to the stomach. He has no idea how deep his words cut. How could he?

"I'm not saying the pants aren't phenomenal," he continues. "I'm just saying making something new for each race is a big undertaking when your track record hasn't proven to be great."

Throat burning, I blink back tears. "That's not fair, Theodore. Not everyone magically discovers their lifelong passion at the age of six."

"I know." He holds up a hand in defense. "I'm not trying to upset you, but is spending your time designing race outfits going to help you figure out your future, your career? I don't want to see you waste time on a hobby that won't lead anywhere."

"That's enough," a peeved voice interrupts from behind me.

As if Lucas has appeared out of nowhere, he steps up to my side and glowers at Theo. "You can apologize for being a dick now."

"What?" my brother asks, his brows furrowing in genuine confusion. "I wasn't being a dick."

"Yes, you were," Lucas snaps. "Charlotte put in a ton of time and effort into creating clothing that reflects her style while incorporating something important to you. But instead of appreciating that and encouraging her to pursue her passion, you shut it down like what she's done isn't incredible. Sharing a last name doesn't give you the right to be an ass about her hobbies, whether they stick around for a short time or forever. That's fucked up, and you owe her an apology."

Theo gapes at his friend. "I—" he stutters. "That's not—"

"It's fine, Theodore," I say, wrapping a curl around my finger. "I know you didn't mean anything by it."

"That doesn't make it okay, Roo." Lucas's eyes are soft as he focuses on me. "And next time someone tries to censure you instead of support you, whether it's your brother or a random man on the street, give him a piece of your mind. Or call me and I'll do it for you."

The knot in my stomach loosens at his tone. I have no issue standing up for myself, but having someone in my corner, backing me up when I didn't realize I was in a situation that warranted it? Fuck, that's nice. Overwhelmed by Theo's criticism, but more so by Lucas's regard, I make a hasty exit, claiming I need to check my blood sugar. I don't often use my diabetes as an excuse like this, but if I'm stuck with a faulty pancreas, I might as well use it as my scapegoat on occasion.

I've just stepped into the paddock when I run into

Cooper. The red shade of McAllister's racing suit doesn't do his complexion any favors, but he's still hot as hell, with his curly auburn locks, sky blue eyes, and constellation of freckles. He looks like *Outlander*'s Jamie Fraser, which is ironic because they share a last name. I only know this because my mum fangirls over that actor like a prepubescent teen does with a boy band.

"Hey," I say, giving him a friendly wave.

"Charlotte," he replies in his rough Scottish accent. "How are ye?"

"Been better," I admit, my heart sinking a little. "Are you ready for the race?"

"Aye," he says, his shoulders back and chin held high. "How about Theo? Can't speak from experience, but I've got to imagine a hometown race can be nerve-racking."

The last thing I want to do is chat about my brother, so I shrug and go with "My whole family's here. Aunts, uncles, cousins, and all. So he's got a lot of support."

He dips his chin in understanding. "Is your boyfriend here, too?"

My first reaction is to laugh, because *what the fuck?* But when his expression remains serious, that instinct evaporates. "I don't have a boyfriend."

Cooper rears back, his eyes going wide. "Oh… I, uh, thought you were in a relationship. Maybe I heard Lucas wrong, though. Ah dinnae ken."

Spine snapping straight, I blink up at him. "I'm sorry. Did you just say that *Lucas* told you I was in a relationship?"

"Aye, in Barcelona. I asked him and Blake what your deal was, and Lucas said you had a boyfriend. He was rather adamant about it, too."

That cockblocking fucker.

My blood heats, and red crowds my vision, but I keep my tone even. "He was probably being overprotective since he's close to my brother," I say through a strained smile. "I can confirm I'm single, though."

"Hmm," he says, almost to himself. "Well, if ye want to grab drinks or something, I'd quite like that."

Affection washes through me at his unsure demeanor. "Like a date?"

His cheeks flame, and he lowers his focus to a spot somewhere near my throat. "Aye, that's what I mean."

Cooper's great on paper—sweet, sexy, and an overall good guy—but he definitely doesn't warm my chest or make my heart race simply by smiling in my direction. Thoughts of late-night conversations, shared laughter, and the way Lucas's eyes sparkle when he looks at me flash through my mind, but I quickly push those thoughts aside. Lucas made his decision, so why should I hold myself back? Willow's right: I need to remind myself that I'm a badarse boss bitch any man would be lucky to date.

With a deep breath in, I tell Cooper I'd love to grab drinks with him. Why not give him a chance? It's one date, and who knows what might come of it? I may find out whether he has a penis piercing.

TWENTY-THREE
LUCAS

THE ROAR of the crowd in Spielberg, Austria, is deafening as I pull my car into the pit lane. My engine idles down, filling the air with the smell of burning rubber and high-octane fuel. I may like the cologne I made in Èze—the one I refuse to call Velvet Desire out loud—but nothing, absolutely nothing, beats the smell of the track after a few laps.

I unclip my helmet and yank it off, my hair damp with sweat and plastering itself to my forehead. The cool air is a relief against my flushed skin. Team members rush to meet me, clapping me on the back and shouting congratulations. I can barely hear them over the pounding in my ears, caused by the adrenaline still coursing through my veins. As I climb out of the cockpit, every muscle in my body aches, but there's no stopping the wide grin spreading across my face.

"Unreal job out there, mate," a race engineer shoots over the nose, a look of pure elation on his face. "P3, man. You nailed it."

"P3?" I rasp, still trying to catch my breath.

With a harsh inhale, I peer at the big screen, where the final standings are displayed. There it is: third place. A front-row start, just behind Cooper and Harry. It's not pole position, but it puts me in a prime spot for the race tomorrow.

I peel off my gloves and wipe my forehead with the back of my hand. Sweat drips down my temple, and my racing suit feels like it's glued to my skin.

"How's the car feeling?" David asks as Mitchell hands me a water bottle.

Taking a long drink, I nod. "It feels good," I say on an exhale. "We made the right call changing to hard tires. The grip was there and the balance was spot-on."

David beams. "Great. We'll fine-tune a few things tonight, but I think you're well set up for success."

"Mm-hmm," I agree through a mouthful of water.

A heavy arm lands on my shoulders, then tightens a little around my neck, pulling me into a headlock. I elbow Theo—I know it's him; no engineer or mechanic would put me in a headlock just for fun—and he stumbles back with an *oomph*.

"P3 is great and all, but I'll be passing you in the first lap tomorrow," he taunts, wearing a mischievous smirk. "Just thought you should know."

Brow cocked, I huff a laugh. "You're going to be looking at my car's back wing until the final lap, Walker, but I love your enthusiasm."

Our ribbing continues through a few post-qualifying interviews. Blake's not good at engaging in good-natured shit talking, so as usual, he smacks Theo in the back of the head while grumbling "bugger off, wanker." This just makes Theo laugh like a maniac and double up in his efforts to get Blake to make playful remarks.

Charlotte's nowhere to be found after qualifying, and when I casually mention it to Theo, he says she's "getting ready or something." He assumes it's for the sponsor party later, but knowing her, she could also be getting ready to grab a coffee. It's a crapshoot.

Distracting myself from thoughts of Charlotte ends up being surprisingly easy, thanks to Mitchell. He catches a ride back to the hotel with me and talks business the whole way. Despite his initial concern about Theo being my new driving partner, he's now 100 percent on board. Annoyingly so.

"I don't know why I was so worried," Mitchell admits as he clacks away on one of his three phones.

"Because he likes being the center of attention," I say, using Mitchell's words from previous conversations. "You didn't want him to sideline me and turn AlphaVite into the Theo show, because I'm a powerhouse in my own right and work too hard to be outshined."

He briefly lifts his head and stares at me, the expression emphasizing the frown lines bracketing his mouth. "Yeah, well, he forces you to talk during the interviews, so forget I said any of that."

"I always talk during interviews," I defend. I act like a mediator half the time, but I'm sure to answer questions with a fucking smile on my face.

"Yeah, about the race," Mitchell replies, his expression unimpressed.

"Exactly," I say, drawing out the words. "Considering I'm an F1 driver, it's probably what I should be talking about."

With a grunt, he slips his phone into his pocket. *Shit*. When Mitchell's phone is in his hands, it means he's multitasking, so the topic at hand isn't high priority. But when he puts his phone away and focuses all of his attention on me, then the subject he wants to discuss is *serious*. He's just doing his job, but I hate when he gets all businesslike. I want to race, not talk about how signing with a brand will bring me a substantial amount of money, or the optics of partnering with another brand, or how attending a specific event will open up my network.

"Of course it is, but that doesn't help people get to know

you," he argues, straightening in the leather seat. "When Theo goes off topic, as bizarre as it is, you're forced to engage in a subject that allows your personality to shine through."

"Personality to shine through," I mutter, lowering my head. "You sound like my mother."

Ever since Netflix aired a Formula 1 documentary, the population at large wants to learn about the sport, and not just what goes on during a grand prix weekend. They want to know about *us*, the drivers. To a certain extent, I don't mind. I've always known that if I ever "made it," my life would no longer be solely my own. Not only could the decisions I make affect my family and friends, but people will always be interested in my every move, no matter how insignificant. Why a person would want to photograph me leaving a boxing session or picking up a new bottle of shampoo is beyond me, but they do, and I've come to terms with it. Like most things, I fall somewhere in the middle of Blake and Theo when it comes to my private life. I won't hire a security team to keep reporters away like Blake, but I also won't be inviting journalists over for dinner to chat about life over a fucking charcuterie board like Theo.

Sighing, I press my fingers to the corners of my eyes. Shit, does Mitchell know it's a tell? Ever since Charlotte pointed out that it gives away my irritation, I realize how obvious it must be. "I'm glad you're appreciating the good things that come along with having Theo as my driving partner."

"Hmm. I'm not the only one appreciating it. We've had quite a few brands reach out about potential sponsorships."

"Yeah?" I say, sitting a little straighter. "Anything we should pursue?"

While AlphaVite pays me a multi-million-dollar salary plus performance bonuses, a decent amount of my income comes from endorsements, appearances, licensing, and other business ventures. Forming relationships like this can lead to partnerships that'll benefit my brand—a.k.a. the money I'll depend on once my career driving in Formula 1 comes to an end.

"Yep," he says, staying suspiciously mum about it. "I want to connect with Natalie and the rest of the team before presenting you with the information, since you're a picky motherfucker. I'll set up a meeting for after the Hungarian Grand Prix next weekend."

"I'm only picky because I have no interest in working with a company whose products or clothes I don't use, wear, or know much about," I remind him. Most of the campaigns I've done and sponsors I have are directly related to racing, but I've been interested in branching out for the past few years. I've worked with Gucci and Under Armour on small campaigns. Both are brands I admire and wear often, but nothing long term came from either.

He holds up a hand to halt me. "Not saying it's a bad thing. I simply want to get all the details so we can sort through what's practical and bring it to the table."

I nod once, lips pressed together. "All right, then. Fair enough."

"Both Walkers have been good for you," Mitchell muses, tapping his fingers against his thighs. He slips his phone back out of his pocket, and just when I think he's not going to expand on what he means by "both Walkers," he hands me the device, which is open to an email from my assistant.

From: Natalie <natalie@teamadler.com>
Fwd: Potential changes to travel schedule
To: Mitchell <mitchell@teamadler.com>

Mitch - not sure if Lucas spoke to you about this, but I've gone ahead and reworked his schedule over the next few months. Everything's been changed/updated on our shared calendar, but wanted to give you the heads up, regardless. Let me know if you want to hop on a call to chat anything through!

> Begin forwarded message:
>
> From: Lucas <lucas-adler@alphavite.com>
> Subject: Potential changes to travel schedule
> To: Natalie <natalie@teamadler.com>
>
> Hey Nat,
>
> Can you please review my schedule and obligations to see if it's possible for me to extend my stay for a few extra days after the races? I'd love to have some time to explore. Since some of the Grand Prix circuits are in smaller areas, I'm open to traveling elsewhere in the country (e.g., the Italian Grand Prix is in Monza, but I'd love to visit Florence or Milan). I'm also open to arriving a few days early if that works better.
>
> If feasible, could you organize accommodations and travel, as well as put together a potential itinerary of restaurants and activities? Anything that would allow me to explore the city's highlights would be great.
>
> Appreciate it!
>
> Thanks,
> Lucas

My cheeks warm as I read the email. I've yet to bring up my interest in traveling more to Mitchell. I figured I'd see if it was doable before attracting his scrutiny. *Too little too late for that.* Natalie took my request to heart and completely reworked my calendar.

Holding the phone out to him, I shrug. "What's wrong with wanting to explore during my time off?"

"Absolutely nothing," he says. "Nat and I both think it's amazing."

"What does this have to do with Theo and Charlotte?"

Mitchell lets out a hearty laugh. "Lucas. I've known you since you were twelve years old. Want to know what happened then?"

"Is that rhetorical?" I ask with a raised brow. "Or has hitting fifty finally made your memory faulty?"

He ignores my teasing. "The moment I began managing you, and you realized that your dreams were a very possible reality if you put in the work, you stopped being a kid. You grew up like that." He snaps his fingers. "Then Charlotte shows up, and suddenly, you're finally enjoying your youth. I'm not saying it's all her, because honestly, I think this has been a long time coming, but Little Miss Sunshine definitely shined some of her light on you."

"Hmm," I murmur, simultaneously pleased and crushed. "I guess so."

His lips twitch with the barest hint of a smirk. "I know so."

I CHECK my watch for the third time in the past few minutes. To no one's surprise, time has not magically sped up. Charlotte's taking her sweet-ass time getting ready for tonight, considering we've been here for an hour and a half and she hasn't made her fashionably late appearance yet. Theo has been camped outside the kitchen doors, waiting for the servers to come out with more trays of food since we got here, so I haven't had a chance to ask him. There's no doubt in my mind that he'll complain about an upset stomach at breakfast tomorrow. There's no point trying to stop him. He'll do what he wants, regardless.

The event's sponsored by Salesforce, but from the look of the floral centerpieces covering every available inch of open space, it looks like a wedding reception. Instead of meats and cheeses, they should be handing out allergy medication. Rubbing my nose to stop myself from sneezing, I take another look around the room. Nope. Still not here.

To distract myself, I shift my attention to Blake, set on asking him if he knows what's being served for dinner, but he's staring at Ella, wearing a worried frown.

"Everything good, love?" he asks her.

My lips curl up at the pet name. He's gone from broody bachelor to best boyfriend in the span of three years, and as much as I love my friend, I wouldn't have put my money on that.

"Hmm?" Ella asks, her eyes glued to her phone. "Why wouldn't it be?"

"You're obsessively checking your phone," Blake says. "You only do that when you're waiting for news."

As if on cue, her phone buzzes with a text. Thanks to the protective screen, we can't see what's got her laughing with glee and responding at rapid-fire speed. She's been trying to get Simone Biles. It'd be incredible if the text is from her manager confirming it.

Ella finally looks up from the device, and when she finds the two of us staring down at her, impatiently waiting, her eyes widen a bit. "Oh. It's just a text from Char."

"Is she on her way?" I take a sip of my drink in an attempt to appear casual.

Blake rolls his eyes and shakes his head at me, clearly seeing through the façade. While I haven't outright told him about my feelings, he's not an idiot. He hasn't pressed me for details, although I doubt he'll give me much more time before he demands them, considering I jump to attention any time the woman's name is mentioned.

"Who?" Ella mutters, still distracted by the message. "Charlotte?"

"Yes."

"No," she says, giving her head the slightest shake. "She's on a date."

It's a miracle the glass in my hand doesn't drop to the floor and shatter into a million pieces. Nope. Only my heart shatters. I should want her happy, but I haven't yet moved on from wanting her happy with *me*.

"What do you mean she's on a date?" I ask, my tone harsher than intended.

Ella raises an eyebrow at me, unfazed. "It's been a long time since you've been out on the scene, but surely you know what a date is. It's an event that takes place when two people find each other attractive and want to see if they're compatible."

"I think Lucas means *who* is she on a date with," Blake interjects. His dark eyes meet mine in clear warning not to jump down his girlfriend's throat for simply being the messenger.

Ella brightens and pulls her shoulders back. With a grin, she sets her phone face down on the table and finally gives us her full attention.

Shit. That alone tells me I won't like her answer. Even so, I still wait with bated breath.

After what feels like millennia, she chirps, "Cooper."

My lungs seize and my throat gets tight. Still, I need clarification. "Blake's driving partner?" I croak.

Ella tilts her head and frowns, looking at me like I've lost my ever-loving mind. "Obviously. Do you know any other Coopers who happen to be in Austria right now and have a thing for Charlotte?"

Sucking in a lungful of air, I ignore her sass, and when the tightness in my chest eases a little, I ask, "Why's she on a date with Cooper?"

Ella looks at Blake for support. I can't. blame her. Clearly I'm having trouble understanding the basic details she's laid out. "Because he asked her out."

"It can't be going too well if she's texting you while out with him." Blake says it to Ella, though I have a sneaking suspicion it's to appease me.

He's right. Unless Charlotte asked him one of her cute random questions, then took out her phone to google it, it can't be going too well. Even the thought of her asking him her silly questions has my chest constricting again. Dammit.

"Oh, no. She's having fun," Ella says, nodding as if this is a good thing. "She was just keeping me appraised of the piercing situation."

I blink in confusion, and in my periphery, Blake leans forward. *Piercing?*

He finds his words first and demands, rather rudely, "What piercing?"

Rather than responding, Ella scowls.

He holds his hands up in apology. "Sorry, baby. You caught me off guard, is all. What piercing are you talking about?"

Her hazel eyes dart from Blake to me and then back again. "You know there's a rumor circulating about *that* piercing, right?"

"No, love, we don't," Blake says, using the soft and sweet tone he reserves for her alone. "What piercing?"

Across the table, Ella grimaces, looking like she'd rather swallow glass than tell us, but with a sigh, she says, "Well, um, you know Wren?"

Blake grunts out a reluctant "yes." Wren is part of McAllister's marketing team—and a good friend of Josie's—but she and Blake don't exactly see eye to eye. He recently threatened to snap her phone in half if she didn't stop asking him to learn a TikTok dance.

"Well," Ella hedges. "Wren heard from someone at Ithaca who's dating an engineer at Porsche that their friend slept with Cooper last year and that he has a piercing. Down there."

"You're yanking my chain," Blake deadpans. "Cooper fucking Fraser has a dick piercing?"

With a huff, she smacks his arm with the back of her hand. "Play nice. His Scottish accent is sexy."

Blake makes a choking noise. "That's not helping."

"I don't get why you're freaking out," she argues, lifting her chin. "It's not like *I'm* the one confirming his penis piercing. And by that, I mean confirming that it's indeed a rumor. He doesn't have one."

"Baby, for the love of all things holy, please stop talking," Blake groans, running a hand through his hair. Even with it styled like it is tonight, he rocks a messy bedhead look, and with the way it's standing on end now, he looks like he just woke up from a seventy-hour nap and doesn't know what year it is.

Ella lifts her hand to her lips and mimes zipping them shut, but I'm absolutely nowhere near done with this conversation.

"So Charlotte's on a date with Cooper," I confirm. "And while on this date, she's debunked a rumor that he has a penis piercing? Did she say *how* she discovered this?"

My stomach roils so violently I worry I might actually throw up. Ella digs her phone back out of her purse—a bag that's about a fourth of the size of Charlotte's—and slaps it into my palm. "Read it yourself."

ELLA
How's it going? I saw Cooper in the hotel lobby earlier, and he looked so cute and nervous, lol.

. . .

CHARLOTTE
So far, so good! Did you know his family lives in a castle? And his sister's married to a viscount?
I told him they should rent it out for weddings, but I think they're already rich and don't need the extra income.

ELLA
Wow. Already talking weddings on the first date!?

CHARLOTTE
LOL. You know me.
I can also confirm that Coop has jewelry-free junk.

ELLA
OMG SHUT THE FUCK UP.
I AM UNWELL.
TELL ME EVERYTHING.

CHARLOTTE
Brekkie tomorrow? I'll give you the scoop.

TAKING BACK HER PHONE, Ella shoots the two of us a dirty look. "I know you guys think of Charlotte as a little sister, but she's a grown woman. Cooper's a good guy. She could do a lot worse."

Blake palms his face, knowing full well that Ella's response isn't helping to ease my agitation.

"Where's the date?" I ask, my voice strained. I can look up her location myself, but hopefully it'll come across as less invasive if I crash her date after a friend told me about it rather than because I was stalking her like the main character in one of Willow's dark romance books.

Blake drops his heavy hand to my shoulder and gives it a squeeze. "Stop. Whatever fucked-up crazy thing you're thinking about doing, stop."

I notice then that Ella has disappeared. Frowning, I scan the space.

As if he can read my mind, Blake grunts. "You look like you're about to do something idiotic. She read the room and decided to give us some space."

"*Humph.*"

"Think," Blake says, squeezing my shoulder again.

"Think?" I twist my ring so aggressively I'm surprised I haven't given myself a rash. "All I do is think about her, man. I kissed her and then told her nothing can happen between us because she's Theo's sister, and now she's on a date with Cooper." A strangled sigh escapes me. "And yes, I'm jealous, but I'm also so in love with her it hurts to breathe sometimes, so you're going to need to give me better advice than *think*."

"Fuck," he says, puffing out a breath. He takes a long sip of his whiskey, his attention on me the whole time, and when he's finished, he flags down the bartender for a refill.

Head bowed, I massage my brow. "Yeah. You can say that again."

"Is she worth it?" he asks, his probing stare drilling into me.

"Is Ella worth it?" I snap. The second the words are out, guilt settles on my shoulders. Fuck. He's trying to help, not be a dick. "Sorry. Obviously, she is. But it's not that simple, you know?"

Blake shrugs. "You can't live your life on someone else's terms, mate, and if my assumption's right, that Theo's the only thing holding you back from pursuing her, then fuck it. What's that Taylor Swift lyric? About being a pathological people pleaser? That's you. You want everyone to be happy, but you do it at your own expense."

For the first time since Ella mentioned the word *date*, a modicum of lightness sweeps through me, and I burst out laughing. I love Taylor Swift as much as the next guy, but I can't say I know enough of her lyrics to quote a song during a heart-to-heart. "Theo will kill me. You know that, right?"

"Maybe, but it's better to die happy, don't you think?" Blake rests his forearms on the table. "Now, let's have another drink, and after tomorrow's race, once you've had some time to think, you can decide what to do. Sound like a plan?"

Still wishing I could barge in on Charlotte's date but knowing that'll only make matters worse, I nod.

Get through the race, then get the girl.

TWENTY-FOUR
LUCAS

I GET through about five hours.

Though I don't crash her date. Despite the way every bone in my body screams at me to interrupt them at dinner, I stick to Blake's plan. I have a drink, stay at the sponsor party until it's socially acceptable to leave, head back to the hotel, go through my nighttime routine, set my alarm, and get into bed.

Then I toss and turn, knowing damn well it'll be impossible to get any sleep if I don't talk to Charlotte tonight.

With the gift I had Natalie pick up for her in hand, I make my way to her hotel room. It's only two doors down from mine, but every step feels like a mile. She's a night owl, so I can almost guarantee she's up. Even so, it feels weird knocking on her door this late. Especially if Cooper's there. Our conversation's going to happen either way, but it'll be way less awkward if he's not.

I've knocked four or five times before Charlotte finally opens the door, a toothbrush dangling out the side of her mouth. I don't give myself more than the space of a couple of heartbeats to appreciate her shirt—it reads *MILF* with *man, I love frogs* written in a smaller font beneath it, surrounded by images of frogs—before skirting around her and into the room without waiting for an invitation.

"Uh, hi," she says through a mouthful of toothpaste. "Is everything okay?"

"Not exactly." Swallowing thickly, I hold the gift out to her. Despite knowing what's inside, the weight of it still shocks me, especially given the pink-striped wrapping paper and ridiculously floppy bow on top. That's what I get for having Nat wrap it; I can tie a bow tie like a pro, but I can't wrap presents for shit, much to my mother's chagrin.

She holds up a finger and shuffles back into the bathroom. When she returns, sans toothbrush, she asks, "What is it?" With her brow furrowed, she studies the box, looking more confused than curious. "Did someone drop it off at your door? Was there a creepy note? Oh my God, is it blackmail?"

With a hand cupped over my mouth, I muffle a sigh. I should've known this wouldn't go as simply as I'd hoped. "No, Roo. I got you a gift."

She scrunches her nose and turns her scrutiny on me. "Oh. Why?"

"Because I want you to have it."

"Right," she says slowly, leaning against the bathroom doorframe. "I got that part. I'm confused as to why you're giving it to me at midnight and why you're acting weird about it."

Rather than explain, I simply say, "I knew you'd be up." Placing the deceivingly heavy gift on the nearby coffee table, I add, "And race days are always busy, so I wanted to make sure you got it sooner rather than later."

She snorts. "That smells like bullshit."

Okay, breathe. You can do this. I push any and all thoughts of Theo out of my mind and focus on Charlotte. The woman who ignites a spark within me that I never knew was possible. She's the calm before the storm and the storm itself—lightning, thunder, and rain all at once. She's all or nothing, and I want every single piece of her.

"You went out with Cooper, and he's not right for you," I say, my focus never leaving her face, despite the way trepidation rolls through me. "I am. He doesn't think about your laugh twenty-four seven or replay it in his mind like it's his favorite song the way I do." Throat thick, I swallow my nerves and keep going. "He doesn't appreciate your random questions and out-of-pocket comments like I do. He doesn't obsess over your every word and smile like I do."

Charlotte's jaw drops and her arms fall to her side. "You're kidding me, right?" she huffs. "You don't get to come in here and say all that shit simply because you're jealous. You made it clear that you're not interested in more than friendship with me."

If she thinks her sassy reply will make me apologize, will make me do anything but double down, then she's in for a big surprise. Hands fisted at my sides, I stalk toward her like a lion pursuing prey. "You think I'm not interested in you?"

She throws her arms up and practically growls. "Yes. Of course that's what I think. The message was loud and clear when you said, 'Oh, shit. I shouldn't have done that. I don't know why I did. Let's pretend it never happened. You're Theo's sister.' I may not have graduated with honors, but I'm not a complete idiot, Lucas."

"That was me thinking I was doing the right thing," I correct her. "It was me putting my friend's feelings before my own, despite how much I like you."

"Right. You know what I like?" she asks, cocking her hip. "Chocolate chip cookies. Doesn't mean I'm romantically interested in them, though."

Closing the distance between us, heart pounding against my sternum, I ask, "Do you want me to spell it out for you? Tattoo it on my chest? I like you, Charlotte Grace Walker. I like you so damn much that somewhere along the way, I fell in love with you. And even if you don't want to be mine, I'll always be yours."

Her lips form a tiny, cute O. "Is that why you went to the British Tea Museum with me even though you hate museums?"

That's the last thing I expected her to ask.

"I wouldn't go there for just anyone, Roo," I admit with a helpless shrug. This may be the only time I've ever appreciated Grayson opening his big, fat trap. "Only you."

She nods thoughtfully, biting her lower lip in a way that has me clenching my fists at my sides. Slowly, she meets my eye, her expression not quite hiding her hurt. "Nothing's changed Lucas. You may say you don't care, but I'm still Theo's sister."

Taking half a step closer, I tuck her hair behind her ears. She shudders when my fingertips brush against her cheek, and I let my hands frame her face, her skin smooth and soft like silk.

"No, you're not."

She rolls her eyes. "Um, yes I am. DNA doesn't lie."

I shake my head, a grin of sincere affection and appreciation on my lips. "Not to me, you aren't. You're just Charlotte. You're a woman who's passionate and strong but not afraid to be vulnerable. You're coffee and chaos; curiosity and confidence personified. You see the world like no one else I've ever met. I'm constantly in awe of you, Roo. I want to laugh with you and learn from you and just stare at you because you're so fucking gorgeous." Chest aching, I dip a little closer, ensuring she can hear the sincerity in my words. "And I don't care what your brother, my brother, or anyone's fucking brother has to say about it—"

Warm, soft lips press against mine with hesitant urgency. The suddenness shocks me still for a moment. But soon enough, I'm threading my ringed fingers into Charlotte's curls, pressing my body against hers. Kissing her again sends a wave of relief through me. Like I was drowning and can finally breathe again. I want more, more, more of her. She tastes like minty toothpaste, and the faint smell of her lilac-scented shampoo intoxicates me more than any alcoholic beverage I drank earlier. After a moment, she pulls back slightly and murmurs something I don't quite catch.

"Hmm?" I ask, resting my forehead against hers.

"He's scared of needles."

Blinking, I zero in on her face. Now I'm paying attention. "What?"

"Cooper," she clarifies. "We were talking about my pump. His brother's diabetic, and Cooper said he doesn't know how we do it since he's terrified of needles. That's how I know he doesn't have a piercing down there."

Relief floods my system, though I do my best to school my expression.

"And after dinner, I told him I thought we were better off as friends. It wasn't fair of me to pretend otherwise when I…"

I tighten my grip on her hair, tugging her head back slightly so she has no choice but to meet my gaze. "When you what?"

Her lips part slightly, and her throat constricts, her muscles working in a smooth, coordinated effort as she swallows nervously. It's such an ordinary action, yet in this moment, it's significant, almost intimate. Because whatever she says next has the power to determine our future.

"Still wished it was you," she says, her voice unusually soft. "It's always been you."

My heart thumps wildly, and there's no hiding my grin. Not that I have any intention of trying. "Anything else you want to share? Or can I kiss you again? And fair warning, once I start, it'll be a challenge to stop."

Her eyes glisten with mirth as she giggles. "Kiss me."

I'm quick to bury my face in her neck, leaving a trail of

soft, gentle kisses beneath her ear, before making my way up her jaw until, finally, my lips connect with hers. There's no hesitancy in the way her mouth moves against mine this time, and I grunt in satisfaction as she explores with her tongue.

When she tugs the material of my shirt, I shackle her wrists above her head. "I'm not done kissing you yet."

If it were up to me, I'd never be done. But when she grinds her hips against mine in a desperate attempt for relief, I release her hands. My patience is waning, and there's a high likelihood my cock is going to burst through the thin material of my sweatpants.

Wasting no time, Charlotte slips her now-free hand beneath my waistband and into my briefs, pulling a deep groan from me. She pulls back and tucks her chin, glancing down as she gives my cock a good squeeze, her thumb quickly swiping over the tip, feeling how fucking desperate I am for her.

"Bed," I croak out between moans.

She ignores me. Instead, she grips my jaw and kisses me, slipping her tongue past my lips and swirling it against mine. Fuck. While I'd take her against this wall in a heartbeat, my desire to taste her is too strong, and for that I need her sprawled, naked, in bed. Gripping her hips, I back her toward the queen-size bed, never breaking our kiss. When the backs of her legs make contact with the bedframe, I gently push her shoulders, and she flops back onto the mattress like a rag doll.

"Naked," I demand. "Now."

I lift my shirt over my head and slip out of my sweats and briefs in record time. When I focus on her again, I find her clothed, resting back on her elbows and watching me with heavy-lidded eyes. Heat licks up my spine at the way she unabashedly appraises my body.

Then she shocks the hell out of me by saying, "You don't have a dick tattoo."

Breath catching, I rear back. "What the fuck?"

"Never mind," she says, shaking her head. "We can pillow talk about that later."

She straightens, and when she peels off her MILF shirt, my knees buckle, and all thoughts of a dick tattoo disappear as her bare breasts come into view. They're full, pink-tipped, and begging to be worshipped. I drink her in like a man dying from thirst as she tweaks her nipples, causing the weight of her breasts to quiver at the motion.

Leisurely, I stroke myself, watching her. She's got her focus fixed on me, too, as she slips off her cherry-patterned panties.

How fucking lucky am I?

Her thighs slowly part, and I groan at the sight of her glistening pussy. Like a man possessed, I lunge for the bed, dropping to my knees before it and dragging her hips to the edge.

I position her thighs on either side of my head, making myself comfortable and ignoring her audible concern that I'm going to suffocate.

"*Fuck*," she cries out as I lick her with the broad of my tongue once, twice, three times. I take my time exploring her, savoring her taste, listening to the sweet little sounds she makes as I read her body's cues. I devour her like she's my last meal, my tongue circling her clit in a pattern that has her gripping my hair so harshly I'll end up bald. Probably within a year, given how much time I plan to spend between her legs.

With an arm draped over her waist, I lock her in place and push myself nose-deep into her pussy, unrelenting as I swirl and flick the tip of my tongue against her. The motion earns me a groan that radiates through her body and mine.

Pulling back a fraction, I tell her, "I'm going to blow my load before I'm inside you if you make that noise again."

"Sorry," she chokes out, not sounding one bit apologetic. "Feels too good. Get back to work, please."

I chuckle, then obey, reattaching my lips to her core and slipping two fingers inside her. The motion is slow. I want to remember every sensation. Then I curl them until her groans sound like a chorus. She comes fast and hard, the sound so sexy I want to bottle it up like a cologne. But I don't stop my ministrations until she's pressing her knees together, forcing me to stop.

I pull back with a noisy kiss on her clit, and as I take in her blissed-out state, my chest expands with satisfaction. Her chest and neck are flushed, and she's panting as she comes down from her high. She crooks her finger at me, licking her lips while looking at my tattoo-less dick like it's the answer to all of life's questions. Leaning back on my haunches, I snag my pants and dig out my wallet.

"What are you doing?" Charlotte asks, her lower lip pushing into a pout. "It's your turn."

"It's cute that you think I'd last more than thirty seconds in your mouth," I say with a snort. It'll be a miracle if I can last more than five minutes inside her. There's no way I'll pull the trigger early, no matter how badly I'm dying to have her perfectly pouty lips wrapped around me.

"I could suck at blowjobs, you know," she teases. "No pun intended."

As I stand, I rip open the wrapper, and with my focus locked on her naked form, I slide the condom down my length. I crawl on top of her, resting my elbows on either side of her head, and gently rock my cock over her clit. She shivers at the sensation, and I revel in the power I have to make her feel so damn good. Her hair is loose and falling in a halo around her head, tangled and tousled from writhing as I brought her to orgasm. I brush my thumb against her lip, and when she nips the end of it, I can't help but groan.

Fuck, I want this forever.

"No more teasing," she says, eyes wide with need. "Please."

"Not trying to tease you, baby. I'm just taking my time."

I lower my lips to hers, kissing her deeply and lovingly, and move one hand beneath her lower back. Pushing her hips up, I ease myself inside her, thrusting until she's filled to the hilt. Fuck. I know right then and there I could spend all day inside her, fucking her until the sweet sounds that slip through her lips are more familiar to me than the roar of my car's engine.

"You okay, baby?" I murmur against her lips. Charlotte's tight, and while my dick isn't an anaconda, it's definitely bigger than average.

"Never better," she whimpers, wriggling beneath me. She clenches her pussy around me to accentuate her point.

With a throaty growl of approval, I rock inside her, then slowly rotate my hips until she's arching her back to take me deeper. Dipping my head, I lave her nipples until the sensitive skin around them pinkens from the stubble on my face.

"Perfect tits. Perfect pussy." I nip at the skin where her neck meets her shoulder. "So fucking perfect, aren't you?"

Nodding, she kisses me tenderly. "Perfect for you."

Stopping all movement, I look down at her, drink her in, soak in this tender moment. Then, with a soft kiss to her brow, I push up onto my knees, my cock slipping out momentarily as I reposition myself. Charlotte looks like a fucking Renaissance painting, lying on the stark white sheet in front of me, legs splayed, chest heaving wildly. I slip a pillow under her hips, then I slide back inside her. The changed angle instantly wipes her vocabulary of anything coherent. I thrust into her, increasing the tempo until my mind blanks of everything but her pleasure and she presses her flushed face into the fluffy pillow beneath her head.

I'm addicted to her undivided attention, so, wanting her focus back, I say, "Eyes on me, baby. Need to watch you when you come on my cock."

She obeys, and as we watch one another, I take in her every minute expression—the way her breath gets caught in her throat and comes out in short, shuddering pants, how her brows crease in pleasure every time my hips surge forward, what makes her cry out with those sinfully sweet moans. When I press my thumb against her clit and her climax overwhelms her, I memorize every detail: the way her back curves and thrusts her pert nipples into the air, how her body shudders with pleasure.

The way she clenches around me has my own release overtaking me in a blinding flash—like lightning bolts hitting my nerves in the most intolerable pleasure. Chest heaving from what was single-handedly the best sex I've ever had, I collapse onto my side and pull Charlotte against me, not wanting any space between us. I never want any space between us again.

"Damn," she mumbles into my chest.

I let out a low chuckle. "Mm-hmm."

We lie in silence for a moment, the sounds of the city drifting into the room. Despite its tempting draw, I fight the urge to close my eyes and let sleep take me. We have a lot to discuss before the sun rises tomorrow morning.

"Should we get the talk over with?" I ask, running my hand up and down her back.

This has her sitting up, hair wild, and pressing a hand to my chest. "Yes. Thank you for reminding me. Why in the bloody hell is there a rumor that you have a tattoo on your dick?"

A phantom pain slices through my groin, making me cup my deflating cock like a tattoo gun is going to appear out of thin air and attack it. "How am I supposed to know? I didn't even know there was a rumor. Did you really think I'd have one of those?" A shudder works its way through me. "Do you know how badly that would hurt? God. No. Never."

Head tilted, she studies the area in question, as if confirming, once again, that my crotch is tattoo-free. It is. She brushes her fingertips over the tattoo on my inner right thigh, causing me to flinch involuntarily. Eyes going wide, she jerks her hand back like she touched a hot stove. Clutching her wrist, I press a quick kiss against her palm.

"Sorry," I apologize, heat rising in my cheeks. "I'm, ah, ticklish there."

A bright smile blooms across her face. "That's adorable."

"Mm-hmm," I say, though I squint at her in suspicion. "Feel free to touch all you want, just don't tickle me. I'm not a fan."

She pats my knee. "There are lots of things I'd like to do between your thighs, and none of them involve tickling, babe."

The pet name has my cock twitching. "I like that."

"What?" she asks, distracted by the *Star Wars*-inspired tattoo on my upper right thigh. It's a lightsaber, though rather than a laser sprouting from it, there's a bouquet. Each flower represents a family member's birth month. "Me calling you babe?"

"Mm-hmm."

She traces my tattoos one by one, the sensation so soothing, my eyes flutter shut, and my body melts into the mattress. She takes her time, asking about the meaning behind them, but falters when she finds her own words tattooed onto my skin.

Wearing a look of intrigue and confusion, she zeroes in on my face. Then she taps the words in question. "Why'd you get this one?"

I prop myself onto my elbows and swallow past the lump that's suddenly formed in my throat. *Shit*. All I can do is hope she doesn't get freaked out by my admission. "Because you said it."

"Wait, what?" she asks, her puzzlement genuine. "What are you talking about?"

"Remember last year at the Melbourne Grand Prix?" I begin. "I was running late to dinner at your mum's house, but when I finally got there, you had saved me a spot next to you. When I thanked you, that's how you replied." I brush my thumb over the ink, heart clenching at the memory. "I was, ah… well, I was feeling pretty lonely, so it meant a lot to me. My best friends were wrapped up in their relationships, and I was actively avoiding seeing my family because of Jesse. Fuck, I was so lost. But you said that, and it made me feel like I mattered, like I was seen. I got it tattooed a week later."

Charlotte opens her mouth, squeaks, and closes it again. Then she launches herself at me, covering my body with hers and burying her face in my neck. "That's the sweetest thing I've ever heard."

"Yeah?" I say, chest tightening.

"Yes." She lifts her head so we're eye to eye. "And while I 100 percent meant what I said about saving you a seat at any table, I do feel the need to tell you that Taylor Swift said it first. I was just quoting her. It's from her song 'Lover.' It's actually really cute in retrospect, since, you know, you're now my lover."

"You're telling me I have a Taylor Swift lyric permanently inked on my body?"

"Um, yes," she says, cringing a little. "But it's really, really romantic that you'd mark yourself with the words I said to you. And technically, I did say it. I just didn't think it first. Are you mad?"

I let out a loud, booming laugh, making the bed shake. Fucking Taylor Swift. "No, I'm not mad. I'd prefer to have your original words, but I don't regret it. It's a part of our story now, even if it has a bit of a twist."

Angling closer, she kisses my jaw, then my lips. "I do have an idea for a tattoo, though."

"Yeah?" I ask, brows arched. "What is it?"

She peeks up at me through her long lashes. "I love you."

My hands still, and warmth blooms in my chest. "Is that an original phrase or another Taylor Swift lyric?"

"That one's all me," she confirms, rubbing her nose against mine.

"Say it again," I demand, tightening my hold on her.

She snuggles against me like a cat, purring with contentment. Draped over me, she feels like a weighted blanket, providing me a sense of calm. "I love you," she repeats. "And for the record, if you ever were to get a tattoo on your dick, it better be my name."

My head sinks into the pillow as I laugh. Blake was right. I'd much rather die happy and in love than live not knowing what this feels like.

TWENTY-FIVE
CHARLOTTE

I'VE DISCOVERED that mornings are tolerable when they start with coffee and multiple orgasms from Lucas Adler. Though not at the same time or in that order. Lying on his side, propped up on his elbow, Lucas watches me sip my coffee and nibble on a *krapfen*, an Austrian jam-filled doughnut. Knowing my blood sugar tends to drop after sex, he got up early to pick up sustenance and caffeine. Then he woke me with warm, sweet kisses and greedy hands.

The early morning light peeps through the curtains and catches on the curve of his jaw, highlighting the sharp lines of his face. He's breathtakingly beautiful. My eyes can't help but stray to his Taylor Swift tattoo—not that I'd ever call it that to his face. I'm still stunned. This man legitimately tattooed my words on his skin. And suddenly, I've discovered a new kink.

"Should I be worried that you've groaned more while eating breakfast than you did when I was inside you?" he asks with an easy smile.

Head tilted back, I laugh. "Nah, but the Austrians do know how to brew a cup of coffee. Want a sip?"

Lucas shakes his head. "I'm good. I'll get a cup after I work out."

"You're still going to work out?" I make a sweeping motion with one arm, motioning to the tangled bedding and his nakedness. "We've burned a minimum of a thousand calories since last night."

"There's no denying it was a great warm-up, baby."

"Warm-up?" I gasp, pressing my free hand against my chest. "Should I be jealous that you're insinuating you put in more work at the gym than you do in pleasuring me?"

He waggles his brows. "If I didn't think you'd claw my eyes out for taking away your coffee, I'd show you just how wrong you are."

I lift the to-go mug to my lips and take a small sip. "Glad you know where my priorities lie. Do you want a bite of the pastry, at least? It's delicious."

Dipping forward, he takes a big bite of the apricot-filled baked good in my hand. Licking his lips—something that has me involuntarily clenching my thighs together—he nods appreciatively. "Mmm. I have good taste."

"Well, duh," I reply. "That should be obvious, considering you're in love with me."

With a snort, he rolls out of bed. He putters around, picking up his clothes from last night. Then he does something completely unhinged. Before putting anything else on, even his briefs, he pulls on a pair of white socks.

My jaw drops, and a piece of flaky dough falls out of my mouth and onto the comforter. "What the hell are you doing?"

"Getting dressed."

"But you put your socks on first."

He peers up at me as he bends over and tugs his briefs up. "Yeah, so? I don't want my feet to get cold."

"So you put your socks on first?" I ask, holding a hand to my mouth. "That's a major beige flag."

Chuckling, he shrugs. "What's a beige flag?"

Willow's comment about our generation being chronically online and his, well, not, is starting to make sense. The beige flag trend was on all my social media feeds for weeks.

"They're neutral or mildly quirky traits," I explain. "Not a deal-breaker or dealmaker, just something that makes you pause and consider."

"Ah." He nods. "So like how you murmur in your sleep and have the cutest little snore?"

Heat rises in my cheeks. "No, that's not a beige flag, and also, I don't snore."

"Yes, you do," he says with a laugh, tugging on his T-shirt. "I promise you it's adorable, though."

"Adorable?" I huff. "That's worse than cute."

"My dad has sleep apnea and my brothers all snore like lawnmowers, so yeah, your snoring is adorable, Roo. It's rhythmic and soft, like a snuffle."

"A snuffle?" I ask, my voice pitching. "Do you know what kinds of animals snuffle, Lucas? Dogs. So thank you for comparing my sleeping habits to that of a furry four-legged creature."

His lips quirk up. "You're just one snuffly snore away from your childhood dream of becoming a detection dog, Roo."

I press my lips together to hide a smile, the corners of my mouth twitching. The bubbling sensation in my chest grows as the laughter builds. I only last a moment longer before bursting into hysterics, my stubborn annoyance dissipating into thin air.

My pump beeps, and with a groan, I snatch my phone off the nightstand to check my levels. Either the doughnut I'm eating hasn't done its job yet and I'm still too low, *or* it did its job a little too well and my levels have skyrocketed.

Lucas sits on the edge of the bed and watches me silence the alarm. "Is there a way for me to get that app on my phone?"

I lift my head and stare at him. "*This* app?"

"Yes."

"That's very sweet, but trust me, babe, you don't want to deal with it. It never shuts up."

"I wouldn't have asked if I didn't want it, Roo," he says, his expression so sincere. "I know you can manage your health on your own, and the last thing I want to do is micromanage you or judge how you handle things. I promise to respect your privacy. I just want you to know that you don't have to do it alone anymore. You have me and my support."

Tender affection fills my chest, making my heart practically float. "Okay."

Lucas opens his mouth, like he's prepared to argue, then snaps it shut. "Wow. That was easier than expected."

"I'm less combative in the mornings," I explain, then quickly correct myself. "That's a lie. I'm an absolute gremlin when I first wake up, but I'm usually too tired to put up a fight or make a good argument." I shrug. "Plus, you're sexy and I love you. Also, you said all the right things. That made the decision rather easy."

He slides back and leans against the headboard, then pulls me into his lap and presses a kiss into my mass of curls. I'm rocking a combination of sex hair and bedhead, but all morning, he's looked at me like I'm the most beautiful woman he's ever seen. "Do you want to open your gift before I leave for my workout?"

"Huh?" The sudden topic change has my brain scrambling. That's usually my MO, not his.

"The gift I brought," he reminds me. "You never opened it."

"Oh." I wiggle in his lap, making him *excited* in the process. "I can't believe I forgot about it. Although, in my defense, I got a little distracted."

To prove my point, I slip my hands around the back of his

neck and pull him in for a brief kiss. Tilting back before we get carried away and forget about the gift once again, I smile. "Present time now?"

Chuckling, he gives my arse a small smack. Then he slips out of the bed and saunters to the table. I don't bother trying to play it cool as he hands it to me. No, I go for a world record as I yank at the ribbon and tear at the paper as quickly as I can. As I peer into the box, my throat goes tight, and when I pull out the beautifully constructed professional yet portable sewing machine, my hand trembles.

"I did some research and read a ton of reviews, and this was the most highly recommended," Lucas explains, his expression a little bashful. "It has the best selection of stitches, and there's a screen where you can pick fonts to personalize things. I thought it could help with your designs while traveling."

"I-I don't know what to say," I admit, my voice thick with emotion. "Thank you."

The simple phrase doesn't feel like enough, but it's all I can get out without bursting into tears.

"What Theo said was bullshit," he continues, brushing my hair off my face. "Finding inspiration and creating more is exactly what's going to help you figure out what you want to do."

"You think?" I ask, blinking rapidly to hold back the tears pricking at the backs of my eyes.

"I know," he confirms, certainty marking his words.

While Theo apologized for being an arse at the Melbourne Grand Prix, and although I know his goal wasn't to hurt me, his words still cut. I don't know which was worse—that he believed what he was saying or that he didn't believe in me. But Lucas does. He always has. He makes me feel delicate and strong at the same time, and that's a gift no one's ever given me before.

"Not my finest segue, but how do you want to tell Theo about us?" he asks, twirling a curl around his pointer finger.

My expression must give away just how badly I *don't* want to even think about it, because he chuckles and scoots closer, grasping my chin.

"We're going to have to talk about it, baby. We can't keep this from him."

I've never been into pet names, not really, but the way Lucas calls me baby does illegal things to my body. Placing my coffee mug and half-eaten doughnut on the bedside table, I inhale, mentally preparing myself. I've got a laundry list of reasons to wait, but I have a feeling Lucas isn't going to like any of them. But I clear my throat and get the words out there. "I don't think we should."

"Um, what?" he asks, his green eyes widening like saucers. Shaking his head, he crosses his arms over his broad chest. "Absolutely not. Fuck that. I'm thirty-one years old."

"And I'm twenty-three, soon to be twenty-four," I tell him. "What do our ages have to do with anything?"

He presses his palms into his brows. "It means I'm too old to be hiding a relationship from my best friend."

"I'm not saying I want to hide it forever." I duck my head and nibble on my lower lip. "I just want to figure this out before we tell him."

He waves at the space between us. "What do you mean figure this out? It's a relationship, Roo. It's not a one-night stand or friends-with-benefits situation or a casual fling. It's real and it's us."

Warmth spreads through me at the certainty in his words. "I'd still rather take the time to make sure we're good and solid before involving anyone else."

Lucas frowns, lines bracketing his mouth. "Why? Are you having doubts?"

I rest my hands on his scruffy cheeks. "No, not at all."

Through all the chaos in my life, the one thing I've always been certain about is my feelings for Lucas Adler.

"Good, because if you were having doubts, I'd just dickmatize you until you forgot all about them." He drops a quick kiss on my lips. "The sooner we get it over with, the more time he'll have to get used to it. He's going to be upset regardless of when we tell him, but I'd rather he only be pissed that we're dating than pissed that we're dating *and* that we hid it from him."

"But what if we tell him, and then you realize that you can't date someone who's so disorganized? You're the king of schedules, and I'm the queen of doing my own thing. I'm not a cactus. I need lots and lots of attention to thrive, you know? What if—"

He holds my lips shut with his fingers. "I'm going to stop you right there."

I try to argue, but it's impossible when I'm unable to open my mouth, so I simply narrow my eyes.

Satisfied that I can't interrupt him, he says, "I don't know who made you feel like that, and if I ever find out, I'll knock them the fuck out, but you'll never be too much for me. If anything, I'm going to want more of you. Any red flags you think you have? They're beige to me, baby."

He waits a moment before removing his hand, and when he does, I once again latch on to him like a fucking octopus and bury my face in his neck.

He chuckles and hugs me tight. "So we're good?"

Angling back, I grimace. "Theo's dealt with so much change lately, and when he learns we're dating, two of his closest relationships are going to inevitably change. There's never going to be a good time to tell him, but…"

"You think now's an extra bad time," Lucas finishes for me. He doesn't sound annoyed or angry, but I can't get a read on where his head is at.

"There are only three races, including today's, before summer break," I say. "I was thinking that if we waited until then, he'll have half the season under his belt. You two usually do your own thing during the break, so he'll have plenty of time to cool off and process it before the second half of the season."

"And hopefully Josie can talk him down," Lucas adds with a considering nod.

"Exactly," I say. "If you really want to talk to him now, we can. This isn't my decision to make; it's ours."

He rests his forehead against mine. With a slight hint of warning in his tone, he says, "Summer break, then we tell him."

"Agreed." I give him a resolute nod. "And in the meantime, you can spend your free time traveling with me."

Now that his assistant has reworked his schedule, he can stay a few extra days in some of the cities he's racing in. He's not extending after today's race because he has meetings in London, but he's going to stay in Budapest after the Hungarian Grand Prix next weekend, which was my plan, too.

My plan, more specifically, was to stroll around and explore, which made his eye twitch despite his reassurance that it was "fine." He's a meticulous planner, and since I don't mind having a schedule—I just don't care to create one myself—I gave him carte blanche to create our itinerary.

"Yep," he confirms. "I'm going to start booking things tomorrow. Nat sent me a few recommendations, but I want to read reviews first."

Snorting, I give my head a shake. "You've got a serious hard-on for reviews, babe."

"Nope, only for you." He presses a lingering kiss against my neck. "Now finish your doughnut."

"Why?" Confused, I wrinkle my nose. "My blood sugar's fine now. If anything, it's a bit high."

He breaks into a wicked smile. "I need another warm-up before I head to my workout at the track, so it's definitely going to drop again."

I throw my head back and laugh. If I wasn't already in love with Lucas, this morning would have sealed the deal.

TWENTY-SIX
LUCAS

FOR ALL MY planning for our time in Budapest, I didn't foresee needing a bathing suit. Sure, there's the Danube River, but Charlotte doesn't like going into water where she can't see her toes. I could've researched the place when my girlfriend suggested we spend the day at the Széchenyi Bath, but she was excited to be involved in planning *something*, so I let her have it.

I hate the phrase "dumb blond," but assuming that the Széchenyi Bath in Budapest is anything like the Roman baths in Bath, England—tourists look but don't go in because of brain-eating amoebas—was really fucking dumb. I assumed we'd be walking around, not wading in the water. Of course, I don't realize my mistake until I'm surrounded by tourists and locals alike wearing swimsuits and holding towels as they make their way to the ticket line.

Charlotte's standing at the entrance wearing a flowing sundress and a mega-watt smile that brings her dimples to life. If gray sweatpants are girl porn, then sundresses are boy porn. They're feminine, and they're the perfect combination of cute, hot, and classy. And if Charlotte wears a dress with pockets?

The level of her excitement rivals that of a person who's just won the lottery.

"Hey, baby." I greet her with a smile. As much as I'm dreading telling Theo about us after the race next week, I will admit I'm excited that I'll finally be able to kiss my girlfriend in public.

"Hi," she says with an enthusiastic wave. "Tell me about your meeting. I've been impatiently waiting, and Mitchell's ignoring my texts, which is rather rude."

I chuckle. While Charlotte shopped this morning, I spent two hours in a virtual team meeting, discussing sponsorship opportunities. Mitchell already forwarded me screenshots of Charlotte's barrage of messages. I wanted to tell her how it went in person, but she clearly couldn't wait that long. He wasn't exactly sure what to do with her stream-of-consciousness-style messages.

CHARLOTTE **Walker**

How did it go?

Is Lucas happy? Did you make him upset?

If you did, I'll put glitter in your briefcase, and you'll be finding pieces of it for years to come.

Did Gucci invite him to Fashion Week again? And if so, can you please add that he needs a plus-one to his contract?

Is there even a contract if it's just an invite? Please confirm.

You know what? I'd rather Chanel invite him. Gucci said that a female would never run their company, and that's bullshit, so fuck them, ya know?

It's really rude to ignore my texts, FYI.

Bad karma, too.

. . .

"I'LL TELL you all about it." I tug on a curl. "But I need to figure out what to do about getting a bathing suit first. And some sandals—"

"I bought one for you this morning, just in case you forgot," she says with a proud smile. "Now tell me about the meeting, and don't hold back on the details. Spill the British colonial tea into the Boston harbor."

Yes, Charlotte has upgraded the Gen Z phrase.

"Celestial Chronos wants to be my sponsor, and they want me to be their brand ambassador," I share, a grin splitting my face.

Her face lights up, and she squeals, throwing her arms around my neck. "That's incredible, babe. I'm so proud of you. That's a huge opportunity."

Cheeks warming, I rub at the back of my neck. "Yeah. According to Mitchell, they see a lot of potential in me and think I'm a perfect addition to their family."

"Wait," she says, covering her cheeks with her hands. "Isn't the watch you restored with your grandpa a Celestial Chronos?"

Now the heat has crept all the way to the tips of my ears. "Mm-hmm. You remember that?"

"Duh." She claps and bounces in place. "Oh my God, you should do a campaign that includes your grandpa, your dad, and your brothers. Focus on the family legacy of their products. Call it Timeless Style for Every Generation or something like that. That'd be so cute."

I blink, feeling an overwhelming sense of reverence for this woman. "That's an amazing idea."

She flicks her hair over her shoulder. "I'm the queen of good ideas."

"You tried convincing me to go to an illegal gambling den with you in China," I remind her.

"Whatever," she says, rolling her eyes, the blue glinting in the sun. "My idea for Celestial Chronos is genius, though."

"I'll text Mitchell about it when we're inside."

Twining my fingers with hers and hoping no one recognizes me, I guide her to the skip-the-line entrance to start our afternoon. Széchenyi Bath is a majestic sight with its grand neobaroque architecture standing proudly against the clear blue sky. The inside is a maze filled with rooms containing pools that range from freezing to boiling.

Charlotte ends up leading me to the exclusive spa located on the building's rooftop, where we're shown to a private cabin to change. I'm so distracted by the simple red bikini she's rocking under her dress to notice that the "swimsuit" she hands me to change into is in no way, shape, or form *that*.

"What is this?" I ask her, holding the small bit of material up in front of me.

"A candle," she deadpans before rolling her eyes. "Obviously, it's a swimsuit, babe."

Not even the pet name can clear away the disdain winding through me as I let the offensive bit of material dangle from the tip of my finger. I was expecting the swim trunks to be short, given the European preference, but these? They're one step up from a Speedo.

"You're telling me that in all the shops you went in, this was the only feasible option?" I press, not buying it for one second.

"Well, it's the only feasible option *now*, since we're already here," she argues, a devious glint in her eye. There were definitely other options available, but she chose the pair that'll hug my ass like a glove and show the full outline of my dick. Cursing under my breath, I wrestle the tight elastic material of my swimsuit over my ass and thighs, all the while ignoring the way Charlotte fans herself as she watches me.

"Can I tell you how cute your arse looks in those?" she

asks, leaning to one side and blatantly ogling my butt. "Because it looks really—"

"No," I huff, wrapping myself in a fluffy robe I find hanging on a hook behind the door.

"What about—"

"No," I repeat, giving her a warning look. "Keep it up, and I'll spank you until your ass is so red it looks sunburned."

"Maybe that's my plan," she says. And with that, she tosses me a wink and sashays out of the changing room with effortless grace.

I lock up quickly, then trail behind her, an invisible thread tugging me along.

We find two empty lounge chairs and spend the next few hours snacking on fruit bowls delivered by the spa staff, checking out the saunas and pools, and relaxing in the hammocks. Well, Charlotte's relaxed. Despite the lush canopy of gleaming leaves and her warm body tucked against mine in the cocooned confines of the hammock, I can't turn my brain off.

"Babe," I say, lightly tapping her ass to get her attention.

"Hmm?" she asks, her voice lazy from the heat. "What is it?"

A soft smile passes my lips. "Can you open your eyes?"

"Why?" she asks, scrunching her nose. "They're not required for listening."

"Because I like looking at you," I admit without shame. "And I want your full attention."

"I'm purposely trying to not look at you." With a laugh, she tilts her head from where it's resting on my chest so she can see me. "Your thigh tat is extremely sexy. It's been teasing me all day, and there's nothing I can do about it."

I chuckle while willing my dick to remain calm. In this swimsuit, the last thing I need is a hard-on. There's no doubting that my girlfriend loves my tattoos. Her favorite nighttime activity is tracing them with her tongue until I lose all patience and fuck her until neither of us can think straight.

"Can I ask you something?"

She lifts a brow. "I ask you an average of seventy questions a day, so yes, you can absolutely ask me something, babe."

As always, her humor instantly makes me feel lighter. "I love when you ask me questions. It's like I'm getting an insider's view of how your brain works."

I don't know anyone else who would be chugging water and suddenly ask: *wait, do fish get thirsty? Or do they just absorb water?* Or watch an R-rated movie and wonder: *are minors who act in R-rated films allowed to watch their own movies?*

"That's the most weirdly romantic thing someone's ever said to me." She laughs, her breath fanning against my chest. "Ask away."

Puffing out a deep breath and hoping she doesn't get offended by the question, I bite the bullet. "Do you ever feel overshadowed by Theo?"

"All the time," she replies without an ounce of hesitation.

"But you're you," I sputter, thrown off by her answer. "Sorry, I don't mean you can't feel that way… I just… well, Theo doesn't overshadow you. At least not in my eyes."

"And that's part of why I love you." She cranes her neck to press a kiss to my cheek. "You're one of the few people who see me as *me*, not an extension of Theo. Most assume that being the sibling of someone famous is all glamour and perks, but they don't understand the pressure and the constant comparisons. It feels as though every one of my achievements is measured against his success, no matter how incomparable they are."

Surprise knocks me back. Her raw vulnerability is so damn refreshing while also a little heartbreaking. I've never really considered how my career could negatively impact my siblings or my parents because, for me, it's been one good experience after another. Not only am I living out my dream, but I've been able to provide for my family financially in a way that I couldn't have otherwise. I paid off my parents' mortgage, loaned Grayson money so he could go to law school—and put all the money he repays me into a college fund for Madison—bought Jesse the best of the best computer equipment so he can code to his heart's content, and funded the twins' lavish lifestyle when they studied abroad.

If Charlotte, the most outgoing, adventurous, and confident person I know, feels outshined by her brother...

A wave of sadness crashes over me. Shit. "I think Jesse feels that way."

With her lips pressed together and a small crease between her brows, she nods. "It's possible. It doesn't mean he's not proud or happy for you. But maybe he feels like he's in the background while you're in the spotlight, no matter the situation."

"Jesse's insanely smart and a major success in his field," I argue, a sense of defensiveness taking over. "He had competing offers from, like, four of the biggest tech companies in the country. Just because his path is different from mine doesn't make it any less important."

"Does he know you feel that way?" she asks, her voice as soft as her expression. "Because Theo's never once told me that."

This is what she meant when she said two of Theo's closest relationships were changing. Because I may still be his best friend, but my loyalty belongs to Charlotte. And right now? I want to smack him upside the fucking head until he realizes that he's unintentionally hurting his sister.

Taking a deep breath, I fill her in on what Jesse said during our fight. How I went after Kylie without considering his feelings, how our family's plans and events tend to revolve around my availability. How my own selfish actions caused a bigger rift between us. How I was hypocritical for breaking bro code by going after her. Then I dive into how I don't know what to do, because it's clear he wants to mend things and maybe I've been holding on to unnecessary anger.

Charlotte blinks rapidly as she processes all the details. "Oh."

I chuckle at her lame response. "Do you think I should talk to him?"

"I think it's going to be a shitty conversation, but a necessary one," she admits. "It's probably been a long time coming, but this issue with Kylie brought things to the forefront."

Sighing, I nod. "If he'd talked to me about how he was feeling rather than going behind my back, we could've avoided this entire rift."

I'd probably still be a bit pissed, but if I'd known *why* and *how* he was feeling, I would've backed away and given him my blessing rather than a black eye.

"He probably kept it to himself for the same reason I didn't tell Theo about FIT. For the same reason I want to wait to tell him about us," Charlotte admits, nibbling on her lower lip. "I know how much sacrifice it takes to race—dealing with the public, the expectations, the critics, the pressure. My own shit never seemed as important, and the last thing I ever want is to be the reason his career suffers."

With affection and gratefulness washing through me, I kiss her temple. "Let's make a deal. If I talk to Jesse, you talk to Theo."

"We're talking to him next weekend," she says, puffing out a nervous breath.

She knows damn well I mean about their own underlying issues and not about our relationship, but I don't push her. It's taken me this long to want to make things normal with Jesse, or at least a new normal, so I can't expect her to suddenly want to have a heart-to-heart with Theo when, on the surface, they're fine.

"Why don't you invite your brothers to Monaco over summer break?" she suggests. "The only things on our agenda are sailing and sex, so it wouldn't hurt to add some socialization to the mix."

It's a simple idea. One I probably should have thought of myself.

"You wouldn't mind?" I ask, tugging her closer.

I can guarantee her answer will be an honest one. One of her best attributes is that she doesn't bullshit or beat around the bush. I don't think she could even if she wanted to. Her face is too expressive. If I want an answer, all I have to do is ask.

"Of course not," she says, head tilted and eyeing me like I've just asked the most ridiculous question. "It'll work out perfectly, really, since I've decided to turn your office into my showroom-slash-workspace. If you're with your brothers, I can work on my designs in peace. Natalie sent me the room specs, so I ordered equipment to organize all my fabrics. She also found a sewing mannequin for me. It'll make it easier to construct new pieces. That's okay, right? I didn't even think to ask you, which I now realize is so entirely rude of me. But you said what's mine is yours, and I sort of took that and ran with it. You said that in reference to me eating half of your dinner the other night when I liked what you ordered more than what I did, but now I'm recognizing that sharing a steak is nowhere near renovating your office. I can have Nat return everything. It's—"

I shut her up with a kiss. When Charlotte's on a roll, it's the only way to slow her down. Not that it's any sweat off my back, since kissing my girlfriend is my favorite hobby. I reassure her that it's more than okay and shoot my brothers a quick text, inviting them to Monaco. Then, for the first time since arriving at the baths this morning, I allow myself to relax. And fuck, does it feel good.

TWENTY-SEVEN
CHARLOTTE

WITH THE EXCEPTION of hitting Jesse Adler in the nuts with a pool cue, I've never intentionally caused another person physical pain. I don't like violence. Even sanctioned fighting like boxing puts me on edge. Satin Satan—who's wearing a satin top, to no one's surprise—may push me over the edge, though. A swarm of media personnel was waiting to interview the drivers after the Italian Grand Prix podium ceremony, but, *of course*, she cornered the AlphaVite drivers the moment they stepped into the parc-femme. Granted, they're the clear go-to. Blake refuses to speak to her, and Lucas is too nice to say no to an interview. Theo, of course, will talk to anyone with a microphone.

I'd be liable to throw my shoe at her—heel-forward—if I hadn't scoured my favorite resale shops for months before finding these purple Ferragamo leather slides with bow accents at a decent price.

Lucas looks irritated, despite his win. To everyone else, he looks thrilled, but they don't know his tells. He's been fiddling with his watch nonstop since she approached him, and when he smiles, it's close-lipped, and no lines bracket his eyes.

"If you glare any harder, I think Miranda may burst into flames," Mitchell jokes with a smirk.

I'm not a jealous person by nature, but Satin Satan looks like she's about three seconds away from wiping a bead of sweat from my boyfriend's forehead with her tongue.

"That's the point," I tell him, narrowing my eyes at her until I see nothing but blobs. Whether or not he's in a relationship, it's not exactly professional for her to continually brush her tits against his arm while asking questions.

"She's harmless," he tells me, waving off my concern.

I turn my glare to Lucas's manager. "They've slept together, you knob-headed goblin."

His jaw drops. "What? How do you know this?"

"I'm a Walker, Mitchell. Are you really that surprised that I know all the paddock gossip?" I roll my eyes. "I may trust Lucas, but that doesn't mean I have to like it when he's being interviewed by a woman who's seen him naked and clearly enjoyed it, since her nipples are harder than fucking bulletproof glass."

Beside me, Mitchell barks out a laugh, the rough sound causing me to jump. I don't think I've heard him laugh before now. Maybe a little chuckle here and there, but never a hearty, motorcycle engine–sounding chortle. The noise catches Lucas's attention despite the chatter of the nearby team members and media personnel. He catches my eye and smirks.

He's been teasing me all day with soft touches and explicit promises when no one's paying attention. Lucas has a very healthy sexual appetite—one that matches my own—but it reaches new heights after a grand prix, when he has excess adrenaline pulsing through his veins. He's trying to keep me distracted as well, I'm sure, so I don't spiral into panicking about our impending talk with my brother.

I stick my tongue out at him. It's not exactly mature, but

I'm sexually frustrated and can't think straight. I find myself craving Lucas at the most inopportune times, like when he pulls off his helmet after a race, his face breaking out into a wide grin, or when he bristles if I try to open my own car door. Even now, when all he's doing is answering questions. His racing suit is perfectly tailored to his athletic frame, the sleek, aerodynamic design accentuating his broad shoulders and toned physique. He looks every bit in his element—focused, determined, and undeniably handsome. The bold blue suit boasting the team's sponsors only makes him appear larger than life. It's a major turn-on.

My phone vibrates, a welcome distraction, but the name on the screen has me letting out a strangled squeak. *Jesse Adler.* I reel back, my face flushing in confusion, as I gape at the damn thing in my hand like it's a ticking time bomb. *What the fuck?*

Both Theo and Lucas pause the interview with Satin Satan and rush over to me, certain that something must be wrong. The two of them volley questions at me. Theo thinks I'm having an allergic reaction, going on about how red my face is. Lucas worries that my blood sugar is low because I've been too nervous to eat much today.

"I got my period," I blurt out, not knowing how to explain my reaction without raising red flags.

Seriously? That was the best I can come up with?

"Um… okay," Theo says, scratching his brow and glancing around, as if that'll help. "Do you need something?"

"Tampons," I blurt out, nodding. "Or pads. Either work."

Oh my God, Charlotte. Shut the fuck up.

"Pads?" Lucas asks, staring at me like I've lost the plot. I pretty much have. He knows I don't have my period, considering he woke me up with not one but two orgasms using his mouth and didn't look like a vampire afterward.

"Otherwise known as a sanitary napkin." In case there's

any confusion. "They come in all shapes and sizes. Maxi, thin, ultra-thin, extra-long. I swear some of them are absorbent enough that if Jack had one after the Titanic went down, he could've survived by floating on it."

Knowing I need to leave before I embarrass myself further, I make a hasty exit and scurry back to the motorhome "for sanitary products." A.k.a. hiding out in Lucas's suite so I can see what the hell Jesse wants.

Within seconds of opening the message, it becomes clear that I overreacted.

Shocker.

<Jesse Adler added Charlotte Walker to the group *Fab Five (+Females)*>

JESSE ADLER

Figured it was time to start the new group text.

JACLYN ADLER

Yay! Love not being the only female. The last group text had way too much testosterone and ball chafing talk.

EZRA ADLER

Welcome, Charlotte!

The ball chafing talk was all your husband and Finn. Don't put that shit on the rest of us.

GRAYSON ADLER

Says the guy who asked if Plan B was the "medically correct name" because he was at the pharmacy and wasn't sure if they'd know what he was talking about.

FINN ADLER

I want to know why Lucas isn't answering our congratulatory texts.

Care to explain, Charlotte?

JACLYN ADLER

You didn't congratulate him, Finnegan... you said "thanks for not embarrassing the family and losing," which isn't very nice or supportive.

FINN ADLER

Ugh. Don't use your mom voice on me through text, Jac. It scares me.

EZRA ADLER

Is Lucas wearing a Portugieser Automatic 42? Been dying to get my hands on one.

GRAYSON ADLER

How the hell is anyone supposed to recognize that watch? Not all of us have a hard-on for wristwear, Ez.

EZRA ADLER

Ever heard of Google??

FINN ADLER

Didn't you know that once you become a dad, you forget how to do normal things like use Google? Duhhh.

As the texts come in one after another, I don't bother biting back a giant grin. My family group chat consists of my mum, who much prefers chitchat over the phone than text, and Theo, who uses it as his personal diary from time to time. It's nothing like this, and as cheesy as it is, I'm honored to be included.

Lucas finds me in his suite twenty minutes later, while I'm texting Jaclyn the link to an adorable baby boutique in

Melbourne and trying to explain to Finn why asparagus green and mustard yellow are indeed a horrible color combination.

He can't get a single question out before I blurt, "I got added to your family group chat. Well, your parents aren't in it, so it's not the full family group chat, but it's a stepping stone, right?"

Once the door is shut behind him, he takes a step toward me and runs a ring-clad hand through his hair. "And that made you freak out? I told Finn you'd be fine with it, but if you're uncomfortable, I can have him—"

"Jesse started the group," I interrupt, giving credit where it's due. He may not be my favorite Adler, but if Lucas is trying to fix their relationship, the least I can do is be supportive.

He goes rigid, his face frozen in shock. "Seriously?"

"Yes," I hedge, grimacing at his reaction. "Is that bad?"

His brows curve toward one another. "No, not at all, but is that why you panicked and said you need tampons? Because Jesse was the one who added you?"

"Sort of," I admit. "I saw his name on my phone and thought he was being shady, which would definitely make mending things difficult, but I now realize that may have been a tad dramatic of me. Honestly, the only downside I can see to being added to the group is that having a lot of Adler contacts in my phone may get confusing. What if I accidentally sext that I'm wetter than a water slide and not wearing anything under my skirt to the wrong person? I could never face your family again. We'd either have to break up or you'd have to cut all contact with them immediately."

When Lucas's jaw drops, I nod. Good. He understands the levity of having five new Adler contacts in my phone.

Or not. Because apparently he's stuck on another detail. "You're not wearing anything under your skirt?"

"*That's* what you're choosing to focus on?" I ask with a huff. "Seriously?"

"I don't think you realize how fucking addicted I am to you," he says, wrapping his calloused hand around my throat in a territorial move. "Doesn't matter if you're wearing a punny shirt and a grumpy pout first thing in the morning or rocking a little black dress and a flirty smile at a sponsor event. I want you. You're mine. To worship, to tease, and to fuck. So knowing you're bare under that sexy skirt you made? Yeah. That's what I'm choosing to focus on."

He slides his free hand between my legs, fingers brushing against the warmth at the juncture of my thighs. I gasp, and as he grazes my clit, a jolt of pleasure courses through me.

"Fuck, you're soaked," he groans through gritted teeth. With light, teasing strokes, he skims over the sensitive skin.

I whimper, grinding into his hand for more—more pressure, more friction, more everything.

"Tell me what you want, baby," he says, his voice deep with desire.

"I don't care," I pant, squirming and desperate for a release. "Anything."

"Gonna need more than that." He nips my lower lip. "Do you want my fingers? My mouth? My cock?"

"Is all of the above an option?"

Lucas chuckles, the sound going straight to my core. "As much as I'd love to spend the next few hours getting lost in you, I have a press conference in about twenty minutes, baby. Now choose. Tell me what you want."

What I want is for him to stop talking and do something, so I blurt out "fingers."

The word's barely out of my mouth before he sinks a finger inside me, then another, and curls them at the perfect angle. Pleasure spreads through me like lava as he plays my body like he's a Juilliard-trained violinist. I latch on to his shoulders, knees buckling.

"I love it when you're like this," he murmurs against my

skin. "Desperate for me; just how I feel about you all the time. Can't get enough of you, Roo. Want you every second, every day, forever."

He slams his lips to mine like he's a bomb liable to explode if he doesn't. The move causes the coil in my stomach to wind tighter, threatening to break free any second. I grind into his hand as his fingers work me in a measured, insistent rhythm. I palm his cock, which is straining against the tight material of his suit, pulling a grunt from him as he arches toward my fingers with an unspeakable yearning.

"I'm close," I whimper, my head falling against his shoulder as I give in to the warm waves of sensation.

"Soak my hand, baby," he says. That's it. Game over. At his command, the band inside me snaps, every nerve in my body burning white hot until a warm pleasantness settles over my skin.

As I come down, I lift my head, my gaze crashing against his.

Darkness clouds the green in his eyes, his pupils blown out, and in a deep, deliciously demanding voice, he says, "Put your hands on the back of the couch and bend over."

Lucas and I may be equals in every other aspect, but there is nothing that turns me on more than the way he dominates me inside the bedroom—or motorhome. These suites weren't made with this type of activity in mind, so it's a tight squeeze as I lean over, my knees on the edge of the cushions, and cling to the back of the small gray couch. Looking over my shoulder, I watch as he unzips the top half of his suit and muscles out of it. He's still wearing a fire-retardant shirt, but the move allows him to take out his straining cock. He strokes himself while using his free hand to rummage through my purse to find a condom. It takes a frustratingly long time, despite my directions, to pull out the leopard-print bag where I keep them, along with hand sanitizer and pain relief meds. So long that

I'm squirming in anticipation by the time he finally rolls it on, hovers over me, and lines himself up at my entrance.

No matter how ready I am to take his impressive length, there's always a slight burn as he enters me, stretching me in the most delicious way. As he fills me, I tip my head back, my mouth dropping open. The position forces my legs closer together, creating a tighter fit than usual. I curl my toes in my shoes, tucking my face into the crook of my elbow to stop myself from moaning. We may be alone in his room, but the motorhome is by no means empty, and chatter from the hallway filters through the crack beneath the door.

He starts off slow, but quickly picks up his pace, thrusting to the hilt every time he pushes forward. The angle presses against all the right spots, and I muffle my moan at the pressure, my hands digging into the couch like a lifeline as stars dance in my vision.

"That's the spot, hmm?" he grunts.

I nod absentmindedly, my walls clenching around him.

"It's so fucking hot watching my cock disappear inside you. There's nothing quite like it, baby."

He smooths a hand over the expanse of my back before snaking it under my bra and pinching and pulling at my nipples until the stimulation has me bucking against him, wildly chasing after another release as the bubble of pleasure grows in the pit of my stomach. He whispers dirty words against my neck as he pushes even deeper, covering my mouth to quiet my incoherent babbling. He's fucked the basic ability to speak right out of me.

"I'm not going to last much longer, baby," Lucas says, his hips never faltering, "so I need you to be a good girl and come for me."

At the instruction, my body complies, as if it has no other choice. I have to give him what he wants, and lucky for me, it's exactly what I want, too. My orgasm crashes over me in shuddering waves, and I pulse around him, making him grunt on every squeeze. Without slowing, he loops an arm around my waist and thrusts into me until his release hits him and he stiffens, groaning out my name. His movements slow, and when they stop completely, he remains buried inside me, air sawing in and out of his lungs.

Lucas presses a light kiss against my spine between my shoulder blades before slowly pulling out of me. While he throws out the condom and shrugs back into his suit, I freshen up my makeup and hair. Satisfied that I'm not about to walk into the conference room looking freshly fucked, I wrap my arms around his waist and rest my chin on his chest.

"You good, baby?" he asks, stroking my hair. "Need me to get you anything?"

"Nuh-uh, but thank you," I murmur lazily, releasing my hold on him. "You're the best soft top."

"What's that?"

"Someone who's dominant in the bedroom, but super nurturing outside of it." I rack my brain for an example. "Like a Sith in the sheets, and a Jedi in the streets."

Lucas bursts out laughing, clutching his sides at my *Star Wars* reference. We made a trade—he'll watch *Sex and the City* if I'll watch his favorite movie series. I agreed to this, not realizing there are eleven live-action feature films in the *Star Wars* franchise, but I'm a woman of my word.

"God, I love you," he says through his laughter.

"Love you, too," I tell him. "And not just because you gave me two orgasms in twenty minutes. I love you every day, all the time."

He kisses my forehead, then opens the mini fridge. "You ready to head to the press conference?"

I reply with a salute, then hold a hand out for the bottle of juice he has pulled out in case my blood sugar drops while we're there.

The press room is buzzing with energy. A dozen photographers tinker with their equipment while journalists type furiously on their laptops and camerapeople get set up to broadcast the interview to fans around the world. The room is sleek, with polished floors and large sponsor banners hanging on the walls. The backdrop features the iconic Formula 1 logo, and there's a long table in the front with three chairs stationed behind it, microphones and water bottles ready for the drivers.

I spot Ella's messy bun in the sea of reporters and slide into the empty seat she's saved for me. She's got her iPad in one hand, ready to take notes, and a Diet Pepsi in the other. She calls it pop, while Lucas refers to it as soda. They're both wrong, considering it's a fizzy drink, but *oh well*.

Lucas takes his seat between Theo and Blake, who placed P3 and P2 respectively, the three of them looking an equal mix of exhausted and exhilarated. The journalists immediately fire off questions, their hands shooting up into the air.

The moderator selects the first question, and Blake's asked about his controversial overtaking maneuver in the twenty-fifth lap. That's when I start to tune in and out. It's not that I don't care to listen; I simply get antsy and end up scrolling on my phone.

Everything's going well until Theo's asked about how the track limit warning he received on ten influenced his approach to the rest of the race. That line of conversation somehow morphs into one about ranking the best pasta shapes. He's claiming linguine is the clear winner—he's wrong; penne is—when my pump beeps. Grateful Lucas had the foresight to hand me a bottle of OJ, I unscrew the cap and take a few sips.

"Um... I think something's happening," Ella says, nudging me with her elbow.

"Huh?" I glance at her, but she's staring straight ahead, a look of nervous apprehension dancing across her face.

I follow her gaze and find Theo glaring at Lucas's phone,

which is face up on the table. It only takes me a split second to realize the issue.

"You have about two seconds to tell me why you have Lottie's glucose levels on your phone," Theo says, his voice tight with suspicion and booming through the microphone.

Lucas doesn't reply, instead locking eyes with me, helpless realization and regret flooding his face.

Then all hell breaks loose.

TWENTY-EIGHT
LUCAS

THEO'S not much of a fighter—he once bitch-slapped Blake rather than hit him—so I'm caught off guard when he tackles me like a WWE wrestler. I let him get in a free punch, figuring it's deserved, but when he lands a second blow to my jaw, I retaliate with a solid hit to his stomach, causing him to double over. The media room erupts into chaos as we grapple in a flurry of fists and shouts. A group of team members rushes forward to intervene as we knock over a handful of plastic chairs, but Theo's too consumed by his anger, screaming "how could you?" and "she's my sister" while slamming into me, to notice.

"Enough!" David shouts, his booming voice cutting through the room. He grabs Theo by the collar and yanks him away from me while Mitchell helps me up and shoves me to the side to avoid another tussle.

This definitely wasn't how I would have liked for Theo to find out. While I can understand his anger, he didn't need to take it this far, especially so publicly. Charlotte rushes to me, her face twisted in apology and astonishment, completely missing the brief flash of betrayal on Theo's face that her gut reaction is to comfort me.

David glares at us, his face a mask of fury. I've never seen our team principal so mad. Even after the Monaco Grand Prix when I crashed out and the Catalyst team principal went on record making disparaging comments about my driving and David's leadership, he kept it cool. Looks like we finally found the line we can't cross: brawling in a room full of reporters during a press conference.

"Go back to the motorhome." He crosses his arms over his chest while a scowl rolls across his face like a thunderstorm. "Now."

With a thick swallow, I turn to Charlotte with my own request. "Can you go back to the hotel? I'll meet you there in a bit."

The room's already buzzing with murmurs and whispers, and there's no doubt that news of the altercation will spread like wildfire. There's no need for her to deal with the fallout alone.

She ignores my request, holding up a hand to my face but stopping millimeters away from touching me. "You're bleeding."

"Maybe I can borrow one of your tampons or pads," I tease to lighten the mood. It doesn't work. Charlotte's brow furrows, and I use my thumbs to smooth out the lines creasing her forehead. "I'll be fine, baby, but I need you to go back to the hotel so I don't worry. Please?"

She nods, and Natalie, who's appeared at her side, gently guides her away from the crowd. *My assistant is definitely getting a raise.* We're all silent as we're led to a conference room in the motorhome, where two medics are waiting to ascertain the severity of our injuries. Theo takes a seat on one side of the long executive-style table while I occupy the other. The medics spend a few minutes poking and prodding us before handing out ice packs and announcing that neither of us has any broken bones.

"I'd be happy to remedy that," Theo comments, his voice harsh.

His manager, Keith, smacks him across the back of the head, forcing a grunt out of him, and mutters to keep his *bloody trap shut*. Smart advice. David is fuming in the corner of the room, his brown eyes flashing with anger. The moment the medics leave, he explodes like Mount Etna, spewing fire left and right. "Do you two have any idea what you've done?"

I shift uncomfortably. "We shouldn't have—"

"Save it, Adler," David snaps. "Fighting at a press conference? Do you realize how unprofessional and childish that is? We're a team, and you're supposed to be role models for the sport, not street brawlers."

Straightening, I rest my forearms on the table, lace my fingers, and will the anger roiling inside me to dissipate.

"You're supposed to channel your aggression on the track, not against each other," David says. "We have a good chance at winning the Constructors' Championship. The last thing we need is your personal drama messing things up. Understood?"

I wipe a trickle of blood from my nose and nod, while Theo, who's holding an icepack to his left eye, mumbles a "yeah."

"Good," he replies, his tone softening slightly. "Now. Find a way to resolve this. If it happens again, there will be serious consequences."

With those parting words, he exits the room, leaving Theo, me, and our managers alone. I reach up to rub my cheek but flinch at the contact, a dull, throbbing ache forming. Taking a deep breath, I mentally prepare myself, because although this round with Theo may not be physical, it's going to be no less painful.

"Which one of you wants to share what in the actual fuck that was?" Mitchell demands.

At the same time, Keith barks, "Start talking, you bloody idiots."

"He's fucking my sister." Theo jams his finger in my direction. The pointing is unnecessary, since there's no question he's referring to me.

I puff out a deep breath, mustering the strength to remain calm. "I'm not fucking her, I'm d—"

"Oh really?" he interrupts, his tone vicious. "You're abstaining until marriage? Spare me."

Nostrils flaring, I force another deep inhale. "What we're doing isn't *fucking*, it's *dating*," I say, tamping down on the rage he inspires. All I want to do is shake him by the shoulders, but that will only escalate the situation. "What we have isn't some casual dalliance, Theo. I care about her; I love her. I'm not using her for sex, for Christ's sake. You know me better than that."

He scoffs. "Apparently I don't know you at all because my best friend wouldn't sneak around behind my back *with my sister* for *weeks*."

"I've known you for over twenty years, man. I have a pretty good grasp on how you react to news you don't like," I say, miraculously keeping my tone even. "Whether we told you the day we got together or now, you weren't going to handle it well."

Head dropped back, he huffs a breath. "And yet, you *still* decided it was a good idea."

"Yes, because our relationship has nothing to do with you," I reply easily. My heated conversation with Jesse flashes to the forefront of my mind, the parallels of the situations glaringly obvious. "I'm not going to turn down my chance at happiness simply because you don't like the idea of us together."

Theo scowls, his blue eyes, so much like his sister's, icy. "She needs to prioritize herself and her future, not you."

That comment has my hackles raising. "She is focusing on herself," I reply, a dry edge to my voice. "If anyone's getting in the way of her future, it's you, not me. You're the one who treats her designs like they're a silly way to pass the time instead of recognizing how they have the potential to launch her into a full-time career in fashion. And before you argue that if she were serious about design, she would've studied it in school, maybe you should ask yourself why she didn't."

Theo blinks, his mouth snapping shut. "What does that have to do with anything?"

"She got into FIT and turned down the opportunity, man." I lower my head and give it a shake. "Your mom was struggling after your dad passed away, and rather than sharing the burden with you when you were already battling your own grief halfway around the world, she chose to stay local for college. She sacrificed her own dream so you could continue pursuing yours without extra stress. Now, for the first time in a long time, she's feeling inspired to create and pursue something she loves."

"I—"

"And the reason we waited so long to tell you? It was for you. She knew you'd be upset and didn't want your feelings about us to affect your racing. So fuck off about knowing what's best for her. Charlotte may be your little sister, but she's also a grown woman with an insanely bright future ahead of her. And yeah, that future now includes me, and you bet your ass I'm going to be right beside her, supporting her."

Theo doesn't reply, but any signs of anger have been wiped from his features. His brows pinch together, a forlorn frown tilting his lips downward.

Standing, I adjust my race suit. Then I head toward the door, knowing I've already said too much. There's no way for us to have a productive or meaningful conversation when we're both this heated.

Gripping the handle, I turn over my shoulder and say, "I don't want to fight with you, Theo. You're my best friend and I love you; you mean a lot to me. But Charlotte? She means *everything to* me. So when you're ready to talk, I'm ready to listen."

CHARLOTTE'S chin deep in a lavender-scented bubble bath when I step inside my hotel room an hour later. Her wrinkly toes peek out, indicating that she's been enveloped in the warm water for some time. The flickering candles on the counter cast a soft glow around the bathroom, but despite the serene atmosphere, there's a crease between her brows and a small pout on her lips.

I rap my knuckles against the doorframe. "Hey, baby."

Her eyes fly open, and she leans forward, as if to sit up, but I step forward and hold out a hand, stopping her. I kneel beside the tub and cup her face in my hands, admiring the color in her cheeks from time spent in the sun and the few small freckles that dot the bridge of her nose. I capture her mouth and nip gently at her lower lip before pulling back.

"Move forward a bit," I instruct as I stand and tear my shirt over my head.

She obeys, making room for me to join her, and once I've dipped a toe in to test the temperature, I ease into the tub. The water sloshes as I settle in behind her and rest my legs on either side of her body. As the warmth engulfs me, soothing my sore side and tight muscles, a sigh works its way out of me.

"Lean back," I murmur, wrapping my arms around her waist.

Without a word, she rests her back against my chest and her head on my shoulder. Placing her hands on my thighs, she moves her thumb in slow, comforting circles. I squirm when she passes a particularly ticklish spot, and with a giggle that lifts my spirits a little, she moves her hand.

"I talked to my mum," she says, tilting her head back.

Curiosity mixed with trepidation worms its way through me. "Yeah?" The word is rough, low. I clear my throat and try again. "What'd she say?"

The beaming smile she gives me relaxes me more than the bubble bath. "That she already considered you family, so this just cements it."

"She's not mad?"

With a snort, she shakes her head. "The only thing she's mad about is not being told sooner, but she understands why I waited."

Her assertion that her mom not know right away surprised me. The two of them are closer than any mother and daughter duo I've ever met. But she said that the more people Theo believed were keeping it from him, the more catastrophic the fallout would be.

"She also said that Theo's sensitive and doesn't like change, so it may take time for him to come around, but that once he does, he's going to realize how special our relationship is."

"Special, huh?" I ask with a chuckle, even as affection overtakes me.

"Mm-hmm," she says, giving my thigh a light squeeze. "What happened after I left?"

I tip my head back, resting it on the edge of the tub. "David reamed us out for our behavior, which we deserved, and demanded we sort it out. And then, I, um, told Theo you got into FIT and why you didn't go, and then I said a lot of other things that weren't necessarily nice but were hard truths. I'm sorry; it just came out."

Charlotte inhales deeply, her chest puffing out, before releasing it slowly. "Okay," she hedges. "I suppose it could've been worse. You could've told him that I was the one who accidentally erased his progress in *Grand Theft Auto V* or that I don't like reverse cowgirl because there's nothing sexy about staring at a man's hairy toes while trying to get off."

I bury my face in the crook of her neck, and what starts as a low rumble in my chest bursts forth in a cascade of loud laughter that echoes off the tiles. "Does this mean you're not mad?"

She sighs. "I'm definitely not *pleased*." She splashes bubbles at me. "But it's sort of hard to be upset while taking a bubble bath."

Nodding, I grab a washcloth from the basket on the ledge behind me. I lather it with soap and gently massage her shoulders and arms in slow, rhythmic circles. The soothing motion releases the lingering tension in her muscles. Within minutes, she melts under my gentle touch. As I drag the cloth against the sides of her breasts and pert nipples, a surprised hum vibrates through her chest, and despite the warm water, she shivers in my arms. There's no point in adjusting myself. I've been hard since the moment her naked body pressed against mine. But her cute, relaxed sighs only ramp up my need for her.

We stay in the bath until the water turns tepid and the bubbles on the surface have mostly dissipated. Wrapped in fluffy white towels, we collapse onto the bed, a comfortable mess of intertwined limbs. Charlotte smiles softly, her dimples popping, the blue in her eyes twinkling.

I slide both hands into her mass of curls, angling her head so I can kiss her pillowy lips. I lick hungrily into her mouth, the kiss heated, though it's nothing like this afternoon. If that encounter was a firework, then this is a campfire, burning slow and long. It's no less hot or intense, but there's a different sort of intimacy and softness to it.

Ever impatient, Charlotte wiggles out of her towel and

drapes her body over mine. Her skin, still warm from the bath, sticks to mine. With my hands pressed to her back, I tug her closer and lose myself in her taste and scent. We stay like that, trading drugging kisses, until she's grinding against me, needing friction, and I'm grabbing her ass, urging her on.

"You want to ride me, baby?" I ask, using my tongue to track a path down her neck. "You want to sink that pretty pussy down on my cock and get yourself off?"

Her chest rises and falls, her breathing picking up, and the small whimper she makes sends amusement and affection through me.

"You do, don't you? You want to wear yourself out and make a mess all over my cock."

She nods, eyes wide and hungry, desperate for me and unashamed of it.

"I'm all yours, baby," I breathe out, sinking back onto the pillows.

Straddling me, she angles to one side so she can grab a condom from the nightstand. Then she's slipping it over my throbbing erection with practiced skill. I grab her hips to help position my length at her entrance, and as she sinks onto me, the noise she makes is damn near pornographic.

"Fuck," I curse, my jaw tensing. Holy shit, I'm amazed I didn't blow my load right there and then. "You're always so goddamn tight for me."

"Ever think that maybe you're just well-endowed?" she asks through a groan.

I chuckle, but as she begins to move her hips in slow circles, her clit dragging against my pelvic bone, the sound is cut short. Resting her hands on my thighs behind her ass, she stabilizes herself, the move causing my muscles to tense automatically, as if preparing to be tickled. The sensation only lasts a moment, though, because as she starts to bounce over my cock, faster and faster, all thoughts that aren't Charlotte and her pleasure fly out of my head.

I grasp her hips and give them a firm, encouraging squeeze, though I let her keep the pace. Her breasts bounce rhythmically, hypnotizing me. Being a boob man at heart, I can't fucking help but be entranced. As heat curls up my spine, I take full advantage of my front-row seat, caressing her breasts, cupping their weight in my hands, and I tease her nipples between my index fingers and thumbs, luxuriating in the sound of her mewls.

Arching forward, I suck one into my mouth and scrape my teeth against the sensitive edges, then flick my tongue against the peak before switching to the other. Her pace stutters in response, so I pull her down, her chest meeting mine. I give her ass a small slap and thrust up into her, returning to the pace she previously set until we're both chasing that familiar high.

"Feel good, baby?" I ask, cupping her ass.

"Mm-hmm," she whimpers, fingers tangling in my hair, hazy eyes set on my face. "I'm gonna come soon."

"There you go," I praise through gritted teeth. "Fuck yes, baby. Just like that—"

"Lucas, please—"

"I know," I soothe, pounding up into her. "I got you. Keep going. Take what you need."

I disappear into the building pleasure as we keep rhythm, my lips finding hers in a passionate kiss that dampens the sound of our moans. As my deep pumps hit against that perfect spot inside her, she lets loose a soft cry of pleasure. Then she's hurtling over the edge. At the sound of my name on her lips, the word a sacred prayer, my orgasm follows, and I bite down on her left breast, marking it with my own brand of tattoo, while groaning in blissful agony.

Charlotte collapses onto me in a heap of loose-limbed bliss, her breath fanning against my chest. She's so content that she barely notices when I slip out from under her, then return a moment later with a small carton of juice from the mini fridge and a wet, warm washcloth. I place the juice on the bedside table, then get us both cleaned up before sliding under the duvet and curling my body against hers. She's soft in my arms, and I revel in how the sensation acts as a salve for all my bumps and bruises.

Usually Charlotte loves pillow talk, but she's quieter than usual. I don't blame her, given what happened at the press conference, but wanting to check in, I ask, "What are you thinking about?"

Imagine my surprise when she casually says, "Crocs."

"You hate my Crocs," I remind her, shaking with laughter.

She hides them in the back of the closet in hopes that I'll forget they're there. I never do.

"I don't *hate* them. Your love for them is just a beige flag," she explains. "I was thinking that they'd be a great partnership opportunity for you. Some of their collaborations are actually kind of cool; those slides they made with Salehe Bembery were sick."

I intertwine our fingers over my chest and press my lips against her temple. "Admit it. You've got a thing for my Crocs. Next thing I know, you're going to want me to wear them during sex."

She bursts out laughing, the sound soothing and melodious, even with the small snort punctuating it. Yeah, I may have a bruised cheekbone, a bloody nose, and sore ribs, but I'd take on Aaron "the Toybreaker" Zale if it meant being Charlotte's.

TWENTY-NINE
CHARLOTTE

LUCAS'S CÔTE d'Azur villa overlooking the glittering Mediterranean Sea is a slice of heaven. I tend to prefer the hustle and bustle of big cities, where each day is full of possibilities and curiosities, but this peace and quiet is a welcome escape after what the media's dubbing the "AlphaVite Altercation."

My time here only improved when Willow flew in yesterday to surprise me. Formula 1's summer break coincides with the Australian school system's winter break, so Lucas invited her to spend the week with us in Monaco while his brothers are here. Knowing him, he realized that some quality time with my best friend after the last few days would be good for me. I haven't heard from Theo since we left Italy. It isn't surprising; he can hold a grudge like I can, but it still hurts. I thought he'd at least send a message saying he needs some time, but nope. Radio silence.

While Lucas picks his brothers up from the airport in Nice, Willow and I head out to the terrace with a bottle of rosé and chilled wineglasses and make ourselves comfortable on the in-pool chaise lounges. The infinity pool is framed by beautifully landscaped gardens, making the area feel like a private paradise. As I soak in the warmth of the sun, it's easy to see why Lucas loves it here so much and why he's gone out of his way to make it feel like my home, too.

"Are you sexting?" Willow jokes from next to me. "Because I thought we learned our lesson."

"No," I reply with a laugh. Not even my best friend's teasing can knock the stunned smile from my face as I reread the message thread.

"Mm-hmm, sure," she says, flicking water at my leg.

I simply hand her my phone to read the conversation for herself.

> **UNKNOWN NUMBER**
> Hey. It's Cole Barrett.

> **CHARLOTTE ADLER**
> Goose's dad!

> **COLE BARRETT**
> Haha, yes. Lucas passed along your number.
> Hope that's okay.

> **CHARLOTTE ADLER**
> I suppose it depends on why you want my number.
>
> If you're trying to recruit me into your MLM, it's going to be a hard pass.
>
> If you're going to be texting me cute dog pics, it's all good.

COLE BARRETT

> Lol. I can definitely send dog pics, but Lucas gave me your contact info when I asked about the jacket you wore to the Hungarian GP. He mentioned that you made it, and I'm interested in having something like that custom made for my girlfriend to wear to my games.

> Could you create something like that for me?

CHARLOTTE ADLER

> OMG.

> Yes! I would absolutely love to make something custom for your girlfriend.

"Holy hell," Willow squeals, her eyes dancing. "This is so much better than a dick pic."

I scoff. "No one but you actually enjoys receiving those, Wills."

"Don't yuck my yum," she playfully chastises as she hands the phone over. "I knew you'd do it." Her smile is smug. "I can't say I knew how, but I had an inkling."

I study her, confusion washing over me. "What are you talking about?"

"You having a career in fashion," she says slowly, like I'm one of her small students and not a contemporary.

"It's *one* custom request."

"So?" She scoffs, bringing her rosé to her lips. "Last time I checked, one is more than zero, and I highly doubt you, me, and Cole Barrett's girlfriend are the only ones who're interested in cute clothes that rep our favorite teams."

My heart has lodged itself in my throat, and I'm trying to sputter out a response, but at the sound of voices inside the house, I give up.

"Oh, yay," Willow says, shimmying her shoulders. "I'm

ready for the new bombshells to enter the villa; I need to practice my flirting skills."

"This isn't *Love Island*," I remind her with a laugh. "And your so-called flirting might make them cry, so please be nice."

Willow's idea of flirting is roasting a man until their inflated sense of self-importance has been put through a blender and hodge-podged back together.

"That happened one time," she argues, flipping me the bird. "And I don't know why he got so offended. I told him he was cute."

"And then proceeded to tell him his personality was the issue."

As she's waving me off, Lucas steps onto the terrace. His brothers, minus Grayson, trail behind him, the group of them looking like an outrageously attractive boy band. My room would definitely be covered in Lucas Adler posters if that were the case.

"Hi," I call out, aiming what I hope is an extra friendly and nonthreatening smile at Jesse. I haven't seen him since the pool cue and penis "accident," and I'd hate for him to walk on eggshells while he's here.

"Lucas has a thing for that, you know," Willow says, her voice low.

Frowning, I turn to her. "Huh?"

"Your wave." She chuckles. "He grins every time you do it."

"Oh God. Do I wave like my mum? I always tease her about it," I groan, clutching my hands to my chest. It doesn't surprise me that Lucas noticed the habit; he's been watching me for the last few years, just like I've been watching him.

As the boys approach the pool, Finn breaks the ice by eyeing Willow and saying, "If you looked up gorgeous in the dictionary, there'd be a picture of you beneath it."

Ezra jerks his head back, and Jesse's lips twist like he's just sucked on a sour candy, but Willow cocks a brow and replies, "It's a little embarrassing that your dictionary still has pictures in it."

Lucas barely reacts to the exchange, his attention focused entirely on me. He surveys my body, his attention hotter than the sun's rays beating down on me. With a saucy wink, I stand to greet his brothers and introduce them to Wills. Finn ogles my best friend like he's a cartoon character, and I swear he almost kisses the back of her hand like she's royalty. Already, I'm certain the two of them will either kiss or kill one another by the end of the week.

The Adlers all change into swim trunks, and Lucas brings out a charcuterie board filled with French cheeses and locally made jams, a tray of wineglasses, and a six-pack of beer. He sets it all out on a table shaded by an oversized striped umbrella, but when I shuffle to a vacant chair, he tugs me onto his lap like it's the most normal thing in the world. I'm an affectionate person by nature—the number of times I've gone for a hug when the recipient is going for a handshake is embarrassing—but I didn't peg Lucas for one, too. It's a pleasant surprise.

Everyone noshes—a Yiddish word I learned from Lucas's mum that means "to snack"—while chatting, though I'm silently cursing my body instead of participating. My blood sugar's over three hundred, so while I can nibble on cheese, which is relatively low carb, I can't indulge in the crackers and jam that are calling my name like a siren at sea.

"If you don't get in on this soon, there won't be any left," Finn tells me, cracker crumbs falling out of his mouth.

Ezra shakes his head. "There won't be any left because half of it's on your fucking lap."

"Her blood sugar's high," Lucas answers for me. When I eye him, he shrugs, saying, "My phone beeped on the way back from the airport."

Willow lights up in her surprise at Lucas's revelation. The only person I've ever shared the app with was my parents, and that's when I was younger and needed their help managing my glucose levels. My face flushes at her cheeky grin, and I snuggle farther into Lucas, placing a chaste kiss on his jaw.

Despite his insistence that he wouldn't micromanage, I couldn't help but worry that he'd monitor my levels so closely that I'd have to revoke his access. Instead, he's been a silent partner, anticipating my needs, always having glucose tablets or candy handy, or suggesting we stay in and watch TV rather than going out if I'm exhausted from a low. Almost like that person who helps the queen or king remember the names of the people they encounter. He's an extra layer of support if backup is needed.

"Oh, that sucks. I'm sorry," Ezra says with a frown. "We won't eat all of it."

I wave him off. "Don't worry on my account. It's probably better if I save room for dinner, anyway, since Lucas made enough food to feed the entire principality of Monaco."

He spent all morning in the kitchen chopping vegetables and whipping up marinades. I offered to be his sous chef, but he politely declined, since he doesn't vibe with my cooking style, which consists of throwing in a little of this and a pinch of that and hoping for the best.

Chuckling at my comment, he rests his hands on my shoulders and digs his thumbs into my sore muscles. I can't help but groan at the hurts-so-good pain as he massages the knots out. For the last two weeks, I've been locked away in the office-slash-workspace, making Willow's promised Wallaby rugby corset top and turning a thrifted cream-colored, double-breasted blazer jacket into a two-piece set with the AlphaVite logo embroidered and beaded on the back. I've spent hours upon hours hunched over my sewing machine and meticulously gluing and hand-sewing the finishing details. Now my muscles are paying the price. Theo was right; I can't make a new outfit for every race. Though his reasoning was off. If anything, I have too many ideas and not enough time.

I forgot how much time and effort goes into designing a new piece—brainstorming and sketching, then finding, sourcing, and thrifting the right material before putting it all together, whether it's sewing, stitching, hemming, or fitting. Some of my ideas, like what I'm currently working on, involve restructuring and adding on to an existing piece, but others involve using old AlphaVite jumpers and shirts to construct something from scratch. But I'm not scared of the challenge; I'm ready to make it my bitch.

Willow scrunches up her nose in mock distaste. "I've only been here a night and have already heard enough of your moaning and groaning to last a lifetime."

Huffing, I roll my eyes. I've kept any *noise* to a minimum, much to Lucas's disappointment. Luckily, he likes how loud I am in bed. If he didn't, he'd be out of luck, since it'd be impossible to keep quiet with his talents.

"You can stay in one of the other rooms," Lucas says, grasping my waist. "But I have to warn you: these fuckers all snore like garbage disposals."

"Charlotte snores, too," she points out, a mischievous smile playing on her lips.

"I know," Lucas says, his grin wide. "It's cute."

"I don't snore, arseholes," I snap, sounding ridiculously petulant. "Stop gaslighting me."

On the table in front of me, my phone vibrates with a new message from Cole. When I pick it up, I can't help but wiggle in excitement.

Lucas tightens his hold on me and forces my movements to stop.

Oh. Oops. I can't help but giggle. He may not be wearing

the teeny-weeny swimwear I bought him in Budapest, but an erection would still be hard to hide in the trunks he's sporting.

> COLE BARRETT
>
> Awesome. What do you need from me? And just let me know how much I owe you.

"Did Cole just text you?" Lucas asks casually, his chin resting on my shoulder.

"Don't act all innocent, mister," I answer with a disciplining laugh. "You're the one who gave him my number, which, thank you, by the way. Why didn't you mention it?"

He doesn't get to answer before Jesse chimes in. "Cole as in Cole Barrett? Captain of the Boston Panthers?"

"Mm-hmm." I nod, though I can't confirm or deny that he's the captain. "He wants to surprise his girlfriend with a custom-made Panthers jacket."

Jesse, Ezra, and Finn toss questions at me rapid-fire, starting with "Lucas won't share his number with us; will you?" and ending with "What do you mean by custom?"

"I'm up-cycling team jerseys, shirts, pants—whatever merch there may be—and turning them into stylish statement pieces." I sit a little straighter in Lucas's lap. "I've mostly been making clothing for myself to wear to races, but my hope is that people will commission me to make them their own custom items."

"Oh, yeah. You made a pair of pants, right?" Finn says, tapping his chin. "I remember you posting on your social accounts about them."

"Of course you do," Lucas mutters.

"You have, what? Three hundred thousand followers or something like that?" Ezra adds, dropping his forearms to the table. "You should blast the hell out of yourself. Sorry, that sounded weird. I meant you should promote your work on your account since you have such a big following."

I'm well aware that if my last name weren't Walker, I'd have a few thousand followers at best, but since I post about my own travels and outfits rather than the behind-the-scenes details of my brother's life—he posts enough of that himself—I like to think that at least a small percentage of them are sticking around for me.

"Do you have a website?" Jesse asks. He crosses one ankle over the opposite knee, looking the perfect picture of relaxation. "If you don't, I'm more than happy to design one for you."

"A website?" I ask, tilting my head. "Sorry, that was dumb. Obviously, I'm aware of what a website is, but Lucas told me you focus more on consumer software than web development."

Jesse tries to play it cool, but by the way his eyes light up and dart to his brother, he's clearly thrilled that Lucas has talked about him in any capacity. I can't help but stick out my lower lip at how cute it is.

"Yeah," he says, "definitely. We can put something basic together while I'm here and then tweak it as you grow."

"That'd be amazing," I tell him, emotion clogging my throat at the genuine kindness he's showing me. "Thank you."

"Of course."

Could I create a website myself? Probably. But I'd much rather a professional do it, and if it gives Jesse and me a chance to get to know each other, that's a win-win. If my own brother doesn't want to speak with me, at least Lucas has a few to spare who do, and for right now, that'll have to be enough.

THIRTY
LUCAS

MY BROTHERS SPEND their first two days in Monaco fighting jet lag and sunburn, but by the third day, they're ready to get out on the water, and on our way to the marina, we make a stop at the local café. I've owned my place in Monaco for years, and while I've eaten here on occasion, I'm by no means a regular. Charlotte's been in Monaco for two weeks, and every employee not only knows her name and go-to order but treats her like a lifelong friend.

They know off the bat that she's Theo's sister. He's been to the café a handful of times, but he made enough of an impression that they named their special profiterole after him. Both Charlotte and Theo have the innate ability to make the person they're talking to feel like the brightest star in the night sky. Despite the pleasant thought, a niggle of discomfort gnaws at me. But with a shake of my head, I put thoughts of Theo out of my mind, not wanting to let the strained silence between us ruin my day.

"This shit is fucking good," Jesse comments, taking a sip of his honeycomb latte. "Damn."

"Mm-hmm," I respond while I check some rigging. From

there, I move to securing the sails. "Can you check the tension on the backstay?"

"On it."

While he heads to the stern to make minor adjustments on the line that connects the mast to the stern to ensure it's properly tensioned, Finn and I check on the halyard, the line used to raise and lower the sail. Ezra knows how to sail, but he doesn't enjoy it like the rest of us, so he helps Willow and Charlotte find the towels and life jackets, then set up breakfast.

Jesse, Finn, and I move around the deck with practiced ease, methodically and seamlessly going through each task. With the help of their experienced hands, it takes half as long to get the boat ready as it typically does.

Meeting me at the helm, Jesse wipes his hands on his shorts and looks out at the open water. "Feels like the perfect day."

I grin, the familiar thrill of anticipation coursing through me. "It does. Everything's in place. Weather's on our side, too."

"Clear skies and a light breeze."

"The forecast said we may get some stronger winds later this afternoon," I note, glancing at the digital navigation system. "Nothing too severe."

He squints up at the sky. "Should give us a good push toward our next waypoint."

I can't help it. I burst out laughing, the sound cutting through the almost meditative quality of the early hour. "Dude, things are bad if we're talking about the fucking weather."

Jesse grins, his laugh joining mine. "We do sort of sound like acquaintances stuck in an elevator together."

With a bit of the tension broken, we unfurl the sails, watching as a rush of wind fills the canvas. I offer to let him take her out, and he jumps at the chance. He takes the wheel, gripping it firmly as he navigates the *Blank Check* away from the dock. The engine hums softly as we glide through the maze of moored boats. Once we're on open water, he picks up speed, and the coastline on Monaco gradually recedes into the distance.

The *Blank Check*'s white hull contrasts beautifully with the deep blue of the water, especially in the light of the early morning. We sail for about an hour before we find the perfect spot to stop. The anchoring process is quick, a testament to years of sailing together, and Ezra and Finn waste no time cannonballing into the water while Willow gracefully dives in behind them.

"You don't want to cool off?" Jesse asks Charlotte. Any lingering animosity between them disappeared yesterday morning when she presented him with a signed agreement stating that she won't hit him in the nuts. It was her olive branch, and it allowed her to apologize without having to say "I'm sorry."

Yep. Definitely going to marry this woman; not that there was any doubt before.

Shaking her head vehemently, Charlotte says, "Oh, no. I don't swim."

He chokes on his coffee, the liquid staining his white shirt, and shoots me a panicked look. "What do you mean you don't *swim*?" he almost shouts, focused on her again. "You need to be wearing a life vest."

"I *can* swim. I'm simply choosing not to swim *here*," she explains. "There are sharks, deep-sea dragonfish, decomposing pirate bodies... oh, and jellyfish. I have no interest in being stung by one. What if no one has to go pee so the venom can't be neutralized? By the time one of you chugs enough water, I could succumb to toxic shock."

Jesse blinks at me, then at my girlfriend. "Um... I guess."

Charlotte shrugs, my brother's opinion in no way, shape, or form changing her views. She sets up a striped towel while sipping on her iced honeycomb latte, then slips in her earbuds and tunes out the world around her. She looks like a *Sports Illustrated* rookie in her leopard-print swimsuit with a deep-V cut that shows off her ample cleavage.

"I'm happy for you two," Jesse says with an earnest smile. "I know I said it was hypocritical of you to date her, but she's really good for you."

"Theo doesn't think so," I say with a wry smile.

He grunts and sits forward, his forearms resting on his knees and his paper cup dangling between them. "If anyone can sympathize with how it feels to be blindsided by a close friend, it's you."

Chuckling, I nod. "Touché. How have you been doing with everything post-breakup?"

I figure we may as well rip off the Band-Aid while everyone else is occupied. But based on the way he stares at me like I've grown a second head, and then a third, I don't think he agrees.

"That's what you want to talk about?"

"We've got to start somewhere." I shrug. Charlotte suggested I do a wellness check, since despite Grayson's determination to talk to me about it, I know absolutely no details regarding the breakup.

Straightening, he sighs and roughs a hand down his face. "Yeah, you're right. I'm okay, I guess. I want kids and she doesn't. We both thought the other one would change their mind, but after a while, when neither of us would budge… well, it is what it is. Breakups are never fun."

"Imagine going through a breakup and then finding out your brother's dating her," I say, keeping my tone light.

"Not my finest moment." He cringes. "I should've talked to you a long time ago. You're not a mind reader, so I shouldn't have expected you to know that I had feelings for her. I don't even think *I* realized how much I liked her until you two started dating. I really *am* sorry."

"I'm sorry, too," I tell him. "You hurt me, yeah, but it was an unfortunate byproduct, not your intention. I could've talked to you, too, and I didn't. I shut you out and made you the bad guy without taking any accountability. It didn't occur to me that you ever felt second best. That's not at all how *I* see you. You're talented and smart and successful in your own right."

"Thanks," he replies with a shy smile. "Kylie never made me feel like a runner-up, despite your history with her, so I sort of leapt at my chance. I didn't think about how much it would hurt you. You have so much going for you. I figured she wasn't all that consequential."

I take a long sip of my coffee and search my mind for the right words. "I think it was a shitty situation to begin with, and then we both fucked it up in the aftermath."

"It's my fault it happened." Jesse frowns.

"And it's my fault things got so bad that we can't have a civil conversation and are forced to talk about weather."

His responding laugh is light. "Fair enough. I've missed you, man, and not just because you have a fantastic ass—your girlfriend's words, not mine."

Dropping my chin to my chest, I give my head a shake. *Of course she said that.* "Are we good?"

Nodding, he stands and pulls me in for what Charlotte calls a "manly man hug."

Naturally, Finn ruins the moment by yelling, "Stop being pussies and get your asses in the water already."

"Calling someone a pussy is actually a compliment," Willow tells him. "Not only do they push babies into the world, but they're self-healing and self-cleaning. And they're the epitome of endurance and strength. You should pick a new word if you're trying to be derogatory." She punctuates her lecture by splashing a handful of ocean water into Finn's gaping mouth.

I turn to Jesse and pat his shoulder. "We're going to need to keep an eye on them."

"If Finn and Ezra were going to off each other, it would've happened by now," he points out.

"It's not the twins I'm worried about." I nod to the real-life Disney mermaid. "Willow's the loose cannon."

"Good point." He sets his coffee down and pulls his shirt over his head. "I'm heading in, anyway, so I can play lifeguard. Want to join?"

I tip my head in Charlotte's direction. "In a bit."

He slaps me on the back before joining the others, and I head over to where my girlfriend is lounging. I stand over her, blocking the sun, and when she notices the shade enveloping her, she pushes her sunglasses down her nose and opens her eyes.

"Oh, hey," she says, her lips spreading into a smile.

"Hey, yourself." I squat next to her and push back a stray curl. "How do you feel? Need anything?"

"My levels are reading a bit high, but I took insulin before I ate, so I'm waiting to see if it helps," she replies, squinting against the sun. "Do you mind filling up my water, though?"

"Course not." I pick up her insulated bottle and stand. In a concerted effort to not be overbearing or make her feel incapable, I rarely check her blood sugar levels and instead support in little ways like getting her water when she asks. It may not be huge in the grand scheme of things, but Charlotte's been handling her blood sugar swings and scares alone for years, so the fact that she's letting me help with anything is a win.

When I return, I squeeze in next to her, lying on my stomach but propping myself up on my elbows.

"There are more towels, you know," she tells me. "I'm sweaty and covered in sunscreen."

"I don't mind. I like being close to you."

"Hmm..." Her lips twitch. "How was your talk with Jesse?"

"Good," I reply. "Things will probably be a little awkward

and uncertain for a while because we spent so long not talking, but it's a step in the right direction."

A guilty smile washes over her face, and she blurts out "I didn't turn on any music, so I overheard everything."

Head thrown back, I bark out a laugh. Honestly, I'm not the least bit surprised. "Any feedback?"

"Nope," she confirms with a giggle. Sitting up, she picks up her phone, then she holds it out to me. "I made a list of questions in case things got awkward and you needed help, but you handled everything maturely."

⟨ Notes

Brotherly Bonding

- Are you listening to any good podcasts?
- Who would play you in a biopic of your life?
- What show are you watching on Netflix right now?
- If you were invisible, where would you go?
- Have you been on any good vacations lately?
- Would you rather have telekinesis or telepathy?
- Would you rather live in the world of Lord of the Rings or Star Wars?
- Who's your favorite person and why is it Charlotte?

My smile grows with each bullet point I read. The last one has me chuckling. She's right; she's definitely my favorite person. Leaning down, I press my lips to hers. It's a sweet, innocent kiss, but my cock throbs uncomfortably in my swim shorts regardless. *At least I'm not wearing the monstrosity she bought me in Budapest.*

"I've never had sex on my boat," I murmur against her lips.

She bursts out laughing, the sound mixing with the light lapping of the waves against the hull. "Not happening. The boat may tip over."

I pause, studying her face. "Roo, I may fuck you hard, but not hard enough to capsize a forty-five-foot sailboat."

"Clearly, you've never heard the song 'Rock the Boat,' babe, because that's exactly what they do."

As a deep chuckle rumbles through me, I rest my forehead against hers. Most definitely marrying this woman.

THIRTY-ONE
CHARLOTTE

IN WHAT FEELS LIKE A HEARTBEAT, our month of rest and relaxation in Monaco is over, and I'm at the welcome party for the Dutch Grand Prix, staring at the blinding rock on Ella's finger. It's a gorgeous cushion-cut rectangular diamond with tapered baguette diamonds on the side. Blake proposed a few days ago, and their future nuptials are already being nicknamed the "Formula 1 Royal Wedding."

The media's excitement over the announcement has, blessedly, all but stamped out any chatter about the "AlphaVite Altercation." Though it seems to still be at the forefront of Theo's mind. He didn't even bother showing up to tonight's party. It's not a mandatory event, but missing the first one back, especially after the incident, won't win him any favors.

"I think we're going to have the engagement party next month," Ella tells me. "We may have two—one in London and one in Chicago—but I'm not sure yet. It's a lot of travel."

"Just tell me where to be and when." I grin, tabling thoughts of Theo again. I've gotten good at it over the last month. "Actually, tell Lucas, and he'll make sure I'm there and on time."

The man is like a walking calendar with the memory of an elephant. The convenience cancels out how annoying it is when he rushes me to make sure we're on time.

Ella takes a sip of her wine, grinning the whole time. "How are things going with you two? I should've known he had a thing for you by the way he reacted when he found out about your date with Cooper."

"They're really good." My own smile grows. For the dozenth time tonight, I scan the crowd. This time, I find Lucas talking to Mitchell, Blake, and Blake's manager, Martin.

He looks sexy as hell in his tailored navy trousers and white button-down. His sleeves are rolled up, exposing his tattoos, and he's left the top few buttons undone, revealing his toned chest. Like he can sense my appreciation, Lucas looks over. And when he spies me, his smile ratchets up a notch. He says something to Blake, patting him on the back, and then he's striding my way like a lion stalking its prey.

"I love Blake, but damn, he is one *fine*-looking man," Ella murmurs.

I grin and clink my glass against hers. "Cheers to that."

"Hey, baby." Lucas snakes his arm around my waist and kisses my temple. "Hey, El."

She beams at his casual display of affection like it's the sweetest thing she's ever seen. "I can't wait for us to triple date."

"Once Theo pulls his head out of his arse," I grumble, much to their amusement.

"Stop stressing about it." Unlike me, Lucas is completely unbothered by Theo's absence. "The ball's in his court."

"Yeah, well the ball's about to leave the court and go straight down his—"

"And that's our cue to leave," Lucas says, plucking the wineglass out of my hand and setting it on a nearby table. "See you tomorrow, El."

She waves goodbye, her diamond ring glittering under the lights.

"Why are we leaving?" I ask, dragging my feet as he hauls me to the elevator. "I wasn't done drinking *or* socializing."

"Because I like these pants, and if we stay any longer, my dick is going to burst through the seams," he says, pressing himself against me, his hard length hitting my side. He punches the up button with more force than necessary, as if his strength alone will make the elevator arrive faster.

"Oh," I state, rather dumbly. "I don't know how I missed that. Probably because I was too focused on Ella's ring, which while not bigger than your dick, is definitely prettier. No offense. Not that you don't have a pretty dick, but in general, in a strictly aesthetic sense, I don't think anyone would describe penises as pretty. They're hot in their own way—don't get me wrong. They can be hard and veiny but also soft and squishy which—"

The elevator doors open, and as an elderly couple hobbles out, I clamp my lips together. Lucas unceremoniously drags me inside, then jabs the *close doors* button before anyone can join us. The moment the stainless-steel doors are shut, he seals his lips to mine like a bomb will go off if he doesn't. Despite the suddenness of the move, the kiss itself is sweet and sensual.

Though it doesn't stay that way for long.

By the time we're alone in our hotel suite, I'm a panting mess.

"Not that I have any objections," I say, stepping out of my heels, "but you're acting like a woman at the end of her follicular phase—uncontrollably horny for no apparent reason."

"You're the reason," he replies, cupping my jaw. "I've watched my friends find love and build relationships, always wondering when it'd be my turn. It felt like everyone was moving forward while I was stuck in mud. Until you. You came along and made all that waiting and all those doubts worth it.

You might not be a planner, but I am, and I plan on loving you for the rest of my life."

"And in the afterlife," I blurt, and when Lucas lifts a brow, I add, "We should buy a Ouija board so that after one of us dies, we can still communicate."

He stares at me for the space of a breath, then a hearty laugh spills from deep in his chest. "Deal."

"It sounded more romantic in my head," I defend through a fit of giggles. "And just for the record, I plan on loving you for that long, too."

Tilting my chin up, he assesses my face. Then he angles in, his lips meeting mine in a soft, slow kiss. I let my hands wander across his chest and abs, relishing the firmness of his curved muscles, and when I scrape my nails against his nipples, he shivers.

"I want to make you feel good." I moan against his lips and sink to my knees.

"Baby, wait." He shrugs out of his jacket and folds it neatly. Easing down, he sets it on the floor, then guides me so I'm kneeling on it. The simple, sweet act makes me wetter, if possible, when my panties are already drenched through.

His cock is hard and heavy, bulging against the zipper of his designer pants. Licking my lips, I unzip him. And when his hard length is in my hand, I tilt in and curl my tongue around the tip, teasing the prominent vein running underneath it. He groans as I alternate between covering his shaft with quick, gentle pecks and longer, lingering kisses. And when I finally wrap my lips around him and use my hands to stroke the part of him I can't fully fit into my mouth, his knees nearly buckle in relief.

He gathers my hair, forming a makeshift ponytail, so he can get a better view. I steady my breathing as best as I can and keep a quick pace. I curve my tongue along his length, making his jaw drop and his hips thrust forward of their own accord.

"Such a sweet little mouth," he moans hoarsely, tugging lightly on my hair.

His praise has me glancing up through my lashes to drink him in. His jaw works, the rapid flex of muscles there a dead giveaway that he's close. Careful to avoid brushing against his thigh and tickling him, I move one hand to his balls, and as I gently massage one and then the other, my fingers toying with the sensitive skin, his chest rises and falls rapidly.

"Shit, baby," he chokes out through gritted teeth. "Don't stop. I'm so close."

I chuckle because *duh*, and the reverberations have him thrusting his hips forward and tipping over the edge. He groans out my name as his cock pulsates against my tongue, the salty tang of his release a delicious proof of his pleasure.

Still breathing raggedly, he releases his hold on my hair and helps me onto my feet. Then he pulls me in for a long, drugging kiss, not shying away from his own taste on my tongue. I don't even realize he's unhooked the clasp of my dress until the zipper's sliding down my back and the fabric is pooling around me. His ringed fingers knead at my sensitive breasts, teasing my nipples until they're perfectly peaked.

He lifts his head, blond hair tousled and a disarmingly cocky smile on his lips. Without a word, he walks forward, forcing me to step backward until my legs collide with the bed, and I fall back with an *oomph*. Quickly, he covers my body with his and trails tender kisses across my chest, like he's tattooing my skin with his lips. When he moves down to my stomach, he spends extra time worshipping the area around my pump. Then he moves back up to my breasts. He doesn't stop, and I lose track of time as he laves my neck and collarbone with attention.

His skilled fingers finally reach between our bodies, where he finds my throbbing clit begging for attention. He teases me, working me up even though I'm more than ready to take him.

I have been since the moment I took off my heels. Lucas's refractory period is short. He could take me again now. But he loves foreplay, loves prolonging my pleasure, but I'm impatient, eager for gratification.

"Lucas," I say, my breath coming out in little gasps. I caress his chest and abs, appreciating the broadness of his curved muscles as I grind against him, the friction of his growing erection against my leg driving me crazy.

With a deep, guttural noise, he pulls me into a messy kiss. "You want my cock, baby?" he asks, his voice smoky with need.

"I don't know how I can make that more obvious," I snark, losing patience with his torturously slow teasing.

Chuckling, he rears up on his knees and snags a condom from the nightstand. His chest heaves, and his hair falls over his forehead as he slides it over his cock.

Watching him like this causes the building anticipation to spark against my skin like fireworks.

He blankets his body over mine and rolls his hips, his cock sliding against my clit, amping up my desire with each motion before positioning himself at my entrance. Focus fixed on me, he radiates pure adoration. The sensation makes my stomach flip like a coin in a winning bet. I'm starting to squirm under the intensity of it when he slides into me with ease.

He grinds his body against mine in slow, insistent circles, applying pressure to my clit with every rotation. I wrap my legs around his waist and lock my ankles at the base of his back, needing him closer. His expression bleeds passion as he moves against me, yet there's a softness to it.

I couldn't look away, even if I wanted to.

Arching upward to take him deeper, I rock my hips, my body colliding with his in near perfect rhythm. I whimper, burying my face in his neck and digging my fingers into the soft hair at the base of his neck. Heat blooms, a fever rushing over my body, as my orgasm builds, his simple touch an aphrodisiac.

"Lucas," I murmur against his skin. "I'm so close."

"Yeah?" His lips and tongue dance circles down my throat. "Good. I need to feel you squeezing my cock, Char."

He doesn't falter or change his pace. Like I knew he would, he keeps up his measured, insistent movements until the heat in my stomach explodes in a supernova and my walls pulse around him as I call out his name.

"Oh, fuck," he moans as he drops his forehead to my shoulder. "That's it."

In a matter of seconds, his cock throbs inside me as he empties into the condom, his thrusts growing languid as we ride out our orgasms. Our lips meet in a kiss that speaks a million words in a single action, a promise set in stone.

He collapses on top of me, careful not to crush me but capturing me in a cocoon of warmth. Nuzzling against me, he says, "You're my everything, Char."

The corners of my lips kick up in a smile. "Right back at you, babe."

Chuckling, he rolls to one side so he can clean us both off. Within minutes of making sure I have candy on the nightstand in case my blood sugar drops and ensuring that I'm okay and comfortable, he passes out, wrapped in a nest of peaceful slumber. I swear there could be a herd of buffalo wrestling in the room next to us and a marching band in the hallway, and still, the moment his head hit the pillow, he'd be out for the count. It's seriously impressive. On a good night, it takes an hour of creating fake scenarios before I fall asleep.

Even in a post-orgasmic haze, my body and mind are restless, so I head to the living area to work on my Boston Panthers commission. Tonight, I'm bead embroidering Goose's likeness onto a large piece of denim that I'll attach to the back of the jacket. It's a newer skill I haven't quite mastered, but I'm having fun figuring it out.

I'm in the zone, perfecting Goose's left ear, when a bang

sounds on the hotel door. I jump, dropping my needle, and a row of yellow and orange beads fall into the plush carpet, forever lost. *Ugh.* Annoyed, I pick up my needle to get back to work.

Before I can do more than that, a deep, muffled voice says, "Charlotte, Lucas, are you in there?"

There's no mistaking the visitor's identity. Theo's speaking at full volume, with no regard to the hallway full of sleeping hotel guests. I'm too confused to do anything but stare at the door.

What the fuck is he doing here?

"*Hello*," he says again, elongating the word as he smacks the door repeatedly. "Don't ignore me. We need to talk."

Scoffing, I stomp down my irritation. I've been ready to speak for the past month, but he decides *now* is the best time to have a discussion? And now that he's ready, he's impatient about it?

"If you don't answer the door, I'm going to be forced to burst in there like an AFP agent. That would suck because one, the hotel will charge me for damages, and two, there's a high chance I'll hurt myself since this door is what? Three, four inches thick? Great for security, but—"

"Be there in a minute," I call out loud enough for him to hear me. "Hold on."

I pause the movie I've had playing in the background and throw on a pair of pants. When I pull the door open, Theo is squaring his shoulders, posed like he's Bruce Lee.

"Seriously, Theodore?" I ask with an unimpressed eye roll. "I told you to give me a second."

"You said a minute," he corrects me, "and you've never been on time in your life, so I was simply being preemptive."

"It's the middle of the night," I argue, and before I can think better of it, I add, "but I suppose I'd rather you're the one showing up late and not my period."

Theo looks at me in pure horror, his face probably mirroring my own. *I seriously need to stop bringing menstruation into conversations.*

Desperate for a distraction, I cross my arms over my chest and ask, "Are you going to tell me why you're here?"

Frowning, he peers around me into the room. "Where's Lucas?"

"Asleep."

"Oh." He purses his lips, then shrugs. "I was going to chat with you at the party, but I took a nap and accidentally set my alarm to a.m. instead of p.m., so I just woke up."

Not waiting for a reply, he walks through the door as if I've extended an invitation to do so. He wanders toward the couch, eyeing the coffee table covered in beads, a few Panthers shirts and jerseys, and a denim jacket. "What are you working on?"

"Cole Barrett commissioned me to make a custom jacket for his girlfriend."

His eyes widen. "Seriously?"

"Yes," I huff, propping my fists on my hips. "Is it really that surprising that someone would ask me to make them a piece?"

"Fuck, no. That's not what I meant." He cracks his knuckles. "I meant *seriously* as in *seriously, that's amazing*, not *that's seriously stupid.*"

I narrow my eyes, not fully buying it. "Your track record sucks, so I wasn't sure."

He nods, a crease appearing between his brows. "Fair enough."

I move to sit on the arm of the couch, and he follows, seating himself on the edge of the armchair, his hands clasped tightly in his lap. He looks like a nervous student about to be lectured by the principal, but after he ghosted me for weeks, I'm happy to let him sweat a little.

"I wanted to reach out over break, but I kept chickening out," he admits, twisting his hands. "I let you down big time,

Lottie, and the shittiest part is that I didn't even realize how much until Lucas spoon-fed it to me. You gave up your dream school, and I didn't even know you applied. I wish you would've told me, but I wish even more that you hadn't felt like you couldn't or that your needs and wants weren't important as mine. They are. I need you to know that."

My eyes sting at his words. With a deep inhale through my nose, I swallow back the emotion. "This is a really good apology except for the part where you haven't actually said *sorry* yet."

Theo barks out a laugh. "I'm sorry, Lottie. I should have been there for you, supporting you like you've always supported me. Lucas reminded me that everyone's still figuring their shit out, and I need to be supportive of your dreams, not judgmental. Okay, he shoved it down my throat when he reamed me out for being an arsehole, but it was deserved. And as far as you and Lucas go… I know you don't want or need my blessing, but you have it either way."

My heart stumbles over itself. "Yeah?"

"Mm-hmm," Theo says with a resolute nod. "If he wants to spend the rest of his life with someone who snores and needs eighty alarms to get up in the morning, then more power to him."

I pick up a pillow and throw it at him, laughing at his comment. "Arsehole."

Chuckling, he tosses it back at me. "Not wanting you two together has more to do with me than either of you, which is selfish. You both deserve to be happy."

Reaching into his back pocket, he pulls out a small, slim box and holds it out with an expectant smile. I take it and carefully open it, not knowing what to expect. It's not that Theo's bad at giving gifts—he loves presents more than anyone I know—but he's just as likely to buy me an air fryer as he is a Cartier LOVE ring.

"It's a gift card to the Formula 1 shop," he blurts out, as if I hadn't already figured that out for myself. The sleek black card with the F1 logo was sort of a dead giveaway.

"Huh," I say, tilting my head to the side while pursing my lips. It's not that I'm ungrateful, simply confused.

"It's so you can buy merch," he explains, his voice hesitant. "Then you can cut it up into bits and pieces to use for new race day outfits. They also have pins and patches and stuff that could be cool to use."

My chest tightens with emotion as I take in his earnest expression. It means a lot that he took the extra step to show his support. I stand and open my arms, and he does the same, then I wrap him up in a hug. "That's really sweet, Theodore. Thank you."

When he pulls back, he grins at me, the corners of his eyes crinkling. "Course. At first, I was going to get you a gift card to that online vintage store you like, but I must've gotten the name wrong, because when I searched for it, I ended up on some website for people who have a fetish for—"

"Nope." I hold up a hand. "I don't need to know. Keep your search history to yourself, please and thank you."

He chuckles. "Whether you want to design a million outfits or never pick up a needle again, I've got your back. I want you to be happy, and honestly, you making unique one-of-a-kind shit that has people doing a double take? That makes sense."

"I don't think anyone's—"

"They are," he tells me, nodding vigorously. "I love gossip, in case you didn't know, so I'm in the loop. I know what people are talking about around the paddock. Before the break, it was your outfits, Harry's new girlfriend, and the secret love child the Porsche team principal may have."

How and where he gets his information is unbeknownst to me, but I have a feeling if I asked him about the penis piercing and tattoo rumors, he could trace them back to their original sources.

"That's nice to hear," I admit, pride rushing through me.

"It's well-deserved." Grinning, he throws two thumbs-up, which is extremely cringey. "What else are you working on?"

I locate my design journal from beneath the denim jacket and hand it to him. As he flips through, noting his favorite helmet designs from over the years, his lips quirk up. I turn to my current sketches and show him the mock-up of the jacket for Maya. Naturally, he makes some creative suggestions, and while I'd rather walk through an airport barefoot than implement most of them, I do like his idea to use a pin from the Panthers' Stanley Cup as the name tag on Goose's bedazzled collar.

He stays for a bit, and while we don't get into the details of my relationship, he does tell me he plans to talk to Lucas tomorrow morning, although he won't be apologizing for tackling him, since he thinks it was well within his rights as my older brother.

Once he's gone, I'm tired enough to go to bed, so I slip under the covers and curl up against Lucas's broad, warm body. He stirs slightly as I rest my head on his chest, pulling me closer, but his breathing remains deep, signaling that Theo's grand entrance didn't wake him. I nuzzle into him, loving the comfort of his embrace. He smells like soap and my minty whitening toothpaste—the stuff he uses even after he looked up reviews online and swears is using false advertising.

I take a moment to admire the clean lines of his freshly shaven face, the curve of his eyebrows, the way his nose scrunches slightly in his sleep, the chain he wears around his neck dangling to the side. I've never craved routine, but with Lucas, I see the beauty in waking up to the same smile every day and falling asleep next to the person whose heart beats in sync with mine. He's where I feel most like myself—I can be me without fear of being too much, too little, not enough. For all the adventures I've been on, Lucas Adler is my favorite one.

THIRTY-TWO
LUCAS

I ONLY NEED one hand to count the number of times Charlotte's woken before me. Scratch that. I don't need any hands. It's never happened. Her alarm can be blaring, and still, it takes her a minute or two to notice, after which she aggressively curses, turns off the ringing, and falls right back asleep. It's like her brain has hardwired itself to ignore it.

"Char," I say, gently rubbing her arm.

She *harrumphs* and buries her face in the pillow, hiding the text on her shirt that says *Feel Le Pain* with a cartoon baguette drawn underneath.

Keeping my voice soft, I add, "I'm going to breakfast with Theo."

She cracks open an eye, looking adorably grumpy. "Yeah?"

"Mm-hmm. Do you need anything before I go?"

The duvet rustles as she rubs her legs together like a grasshopper, something she does when she's comfortable and has no plans of moving anytime soon. "Peace and quiet."

Chuckling, I grab my gym bag. Then I head out, closing the door quietly behind me. Theo texted me late last night asking to meet before we're due at the track. I only saw it this morning, so I'm running a bit behind.

The café is a cozy, sunlit space with large windows letting in the morning light. The aroma of freshly brewed coffee and baked goods fills the air as early risers sip their drinks at small, round tables and read the day's newspapers. According to Charlotte, coffee is a big part of the Dutch culture and social life, so I'm not surprised by how busy it is, even given the early hour. I scan the room, spotting Theo seated at a corner table, sipping on what's most likely a matcha latte, lost in thought. Taking a deep breath, I steel myself and make my way over.

"Hey," I greet him, the forced casualness of my tone making me cringe.

He looks up, his expression shifting from surprise to an affability I didn't expect. "Hey, mate. Thanks for meeting me."

I swallow back my nerves and dip my chin. "Course. I'm glad you texted." It isn't until I slide into the empty seat across from him that I notice the freshly poured cappuccino with steam still rising from the top.

"I ordered for you." He shrugs. "The line was long when I got here."

"It's not poisoned?" I ask, lifting a brow.

He rolls his eyes. "No. And there's no need for me to give you any sort of big brother 'if you break her heart, I'll kill you' speech since Charlotte would just do it herself. Wouldn't be surprised if she took up tennis or golf simply so she'd have something to whack your balls with after cutting them off."

I let out a strangled laugh. He's right, but I have no intention of letting her go, so I'm not concerned about the state of my dick. I pick up the cup and take a small sip, savoring the flavor. America really needs to up their coffee game. The beans and blends I've sampled in every European country I've visited have floored me.

Theo places his own mug on the table, rests his elbows on

either side of it, and steeples his hands like we're about to enter into negotiations. "I'm sure Charlotte told you that I'm not going to apologize for punching you, but—"

"Wait, what?" I interrupt him. "When did you talk to Charlotte?"

"I stopped by your room last night to talk, but you were already asleep," he explains. "Lottie didn't tell you?"

I raise a brow. "The most Charlotte says before ten a.m. is 'turn off your fucking alarm' and 'I need coffee or I'm going to perish.'"

"Sounds about right," Theo says, chuckling. "Anyway, I told her I wasn't sorry for tackling you, but I *am* sorry about how we left things before break. It sucked, being called out for being so selfish, especially with my sister. But what you said made me realize how good you are for her. She needs someone in her corner, someone who has her back no matter what, and you proved that when you chose her."

"I'll aways choose her," I say, the admission simple but unwavering. "She's it for me, man."

He studies me, his blue eyes searching for a chink in my armor, but I can guarantee he won't find one. Eventually, he cracks a small smile and says, "Good. Blake's going to be super happy we worked things out. It'd be really awkward for him if his two future best men were fighting, you know?"

I can't help but chuckle. As chaotic and immature as my best friend can be at times, he only needed a month to come to terms with me dating his sister, while it took me three years to finally move on after I discovered Jesse was dating my ex.

"I hate to break it to you, but I think Blake's going to ask Ella's brother to be his best man." As much as I don't want to throw Blake under the bus, redirecting Theo's energy works in my favor so... *oops*.

Right on schedule, he slams his hands against the table and gasps. "He's *what*? But we're his best friends."

"Yeah, but Tyler's going to be his brother-in-law," I point out, picking up my coffee. After another sip, I add, "And they're also good friends."

Theo's pout slowly morphs into a mischievous smile. The expression immediately sets me on edge. Nothing good has ever come from a grin like that. "If you're my future brother-in-law *and* friend, that means I get dibs on being your best man, right? You are marrying my sister, after all. It only makes sense that Blake will have to be a regular groomsman."

Sighing, I shake my head. Only Theo would turn wedding parties into a competition. Not wanting to agree to anything that may bite my ass later down the line, I simply remind him that I have four brothers to consider. He scoffs and waves the response off like it's the most ridiculous thing he's ever heard.

"We don't count Jesse, so that's technically only three," he argues, waving his hands animatedly. "And it'd be rude to choose between the rest of them, so to avoid conflict, it's in your best interest to choose me."

I lower my head and laugh. "I'm glad you've moved on from pissed that I'm dating Charlotte to so happy I'm dating Charlotte that you're already jockeying for position of best man at our future wedding."

Theo shrugs. "Is that a yes?"

"Jesse and I talked over break," I tell him.

As I hoped, his attention is once again diverted. Between one blink and the next, he's laser-focused on needing *every* detail of our conversation, including what I was wearing when it went down. Apparently, this helps him "set the scene." I fill him in on the visit from my brothers, my talk with Jesse, and how we've been casually texting to stay in touch. We're by no means back to how we were a few years ago, but we're making progress.

"Does this mean I can talk to him again, too?" Theo asks, hands splayed on the table. "Because I've been dying for his help to unlock some cheat codes in this new video game I've been playing."

I shrug. "Go for it."

He grins. "I'm happy for you."

I take a sip of my drink. "We've got a lot of lost time to make up for, but I feel good about how—"

"Not about Jesse," he quickly corrects me. "I mean, yes, about Jesse; I think it's good that you two are working things out. I know you've missed him. But I mean about finding your person."

"Yeah?" I ask, lifting a brow, my heart lifting in a similar manner.

"Yup," he confirms. "Especially because it means I get to be your kid's godparent *and* uncle, and there's nothing you can do about it."

I slump into my chair and choke out a laugh. "Yeah, well, you're family. Always have been, and now always will be."

THE ROAR of the engine is deafening, but the packed crowd's cheering filters through it as I activate DRS, which opens a flap on my car's rear wing to reduce drag levels, on the straight. My car immediately picks up speed, along with my heart rate. Then I'm passing Blake's car and taking the lead with only a few laps left in the race.

"Great job pushing." David's voice crackles through the radio in my ear, calm but firm. "Just two more laps after this."

Too focused on keeping my pace outside of the straight, pushing my car to its limits, I don't reply. Two more laps. Two more chances to make sure I keep this lead. The gap isn't big, and one mistake could cost me everything.

My grip on the steering wheel is so tight that my knuckles ache. As I take another corner at a blistering speed, sweat slicks my gloves, and every muscle in my body is taut, the adrenaline coursing through me. The tires are barely holding on, the grip fading with every turn, but I can't afford to change pace now.

I focus on the track ahead, the world narrowing to just the asphalt and the sound of my own breathing. The car shudders as I push it harder, every jolt vibrating through me as I barrel down the straights and carve through the corners.

The grandstands are a blurry sea of colors and waving flags as I fly by. That's okay. I only have eyes for one spot—one person. Even though I can't see Charlotte from here, I know exactly where she is, cheering me on. She's been here for every race, every win, and every loss. I can feel her with me now, urging me forward.

The last few corners come up fast, and I take them almost perfectly, the car sliding a fraction, but not enough to slow me. The tires are screaming now, begging for mercy, but I can't relent. Not yet. I can see the checkered flag in the distance, waving like a beacon.

The moment I cross the finish line, the world around me explodes. The roar of the crowd is deafening, a mix of cheers and air horns. But all I can hear is the sound of my own breath catching in my throat. I've done it. I've won.

But I'm not done yet.

I bring the car to an abrupt stop, the brakes locking up as I pull into the pit lane. The team is there, cheering and clapping, but I barely register them as I jump out of the car and yank off my helmet, then stride in her direction.

With every step I take as I push through the crowd, my pulse quickens. My team tries to catch up, to congratulate me, but without stopping, I vault over the barrier to where she's standing next to Mitchell and a few engineers.

When I reach her, I pull her into my arms, holding her as tightly as I can. I only release her when she wiggles in my hold. I'm still in my race suit, and Charlotte may love me, but she doesn't love any sort of sweat, and after two hours in a racecar, I've got plenty of it.

"You did it," she says, a mile-wide smile on her face. "Not that I doubted you, but wow, those last few laps were stressful."

"I know. I was there," I tease, elation still coursing through me.

She playfully rolls her eyes and, squinting over my shoulder, waves her hand at someone in a *come here* motion.

Theo appears at my side a moment later, knowing better than to even attempt to hug his sister. "Great race, mate. Kicked Blake's arse," he says, slapping me on the back. Then he adds, "Um, what the fuck are you wearing, Lottie?"

Defensiveness surges inside me. I'm ready to rip into him until I realize that Charlotte's changed into a punny shirt; one I've never seen before. It says *Hopeless Bromantic* across the chest with a photo of Theo and me screen-printed beneath.

"Isn't it cute?" she asks, dimples winking as she grins. "I thought it'd be funny. I thought making light of things would help with any lingering tension. You know. Since it's the first race after break. I don't know. It was probably silly of me. I shouldn't have worn it. I—"

Cupping her face, I dip down and press my lips against her forehead. What I really want to do is pull her closer, then tangle my hands in her hair, just enough to make her gasp so I can slip my tongue into her mouth. But although I'm not planning to play down our relationship in front of Theo, I won't rub it in his face and make him uncomfortable with any major public displays of affection. And making out with Charlotte until she's dragging me up to our hotel room may cross that line.

"It's epic," Theo reassures her. "Do you have extras? I'd for sure wear this to interviews."

I give him a subtle nod, and a flicker of understanding passes between us. He may be her brother, but I'm her partner, and until the day I can no longer physically or mentally take care of her, she'll be top priority. That includes her feelings, and if he upsets her, whether over a shirt or something bigger, I'll have her back.

"He's right," I tell her. "It's great, baby."

She flushes. "It's just a shirt. No big deal."

I shake my head. "I mean thank you for being you. I've been to over fifty countries, but I've never felt more at home than I do when you're around."

A slow, uncharacteristically shy smile stretches across her face. "I love you."

"I love you, too."

Racing may be my passion, but thanks to Charlotte Walker's infectious laugh and dimpled smile, it's no longer my life. She is.

EPILOGUE
CHARLOTTE

I TIE my hair back into a ponytail in a desperate attempt to cool down. It doesn't do much. The Mediterranean heat on a July afternoon means business. Sighing, I turn back to my computer, knowing I have about twenty before the screen gets overheated thanks to the sun's harsh glare. I'm surprising Lucas with *Blank Check* merch—hats, t-shirts, and even custom Crocs—and need to approve the final mock-ups before they can go into production. I think he's going to love it, but even if he doesn't, at least I'll have a new punny shirt to add to my collection.

I've just hit send on my email to the manufacturer when a glass of orange juice appears next to my right hand.

Closing my computer, I glance up and find Lucas towering over me, his muscular arms crossed over his chest. Rather than sip the juice, I drink in the sight of him. Dressed in swim shorts, a half-buttoned shirt, and a Boston Panthers baseball hat, Lucas is the epitome of a sexy sailor.

"Stop checking me out and drink," he says, although his lips quirk up at my blatant perusal. *What can I say? My boyfriend's hotter than the sun.*

"Aye aye," I say with a salute. I had a feeling my headache and nausea were from low blood sugar rather than the sun and sea, so I chug away without complaint. Lucas waits patiently for me to empty the cup, but I'm only halfway through when something catches my attention—a massive inflatable floating in the water behind him.

Pointing to it, I ask, "What in the hell is that thing?"

"A floatie," he answers easily.

"Thanks Captain Obvious," I huff, finishing the final dregs of pulp and juice.

Lucas chuckles, the sound melding with the gentle lapping of the waves against the hull of the boat. Holding out a hand, he helps me up from my seat. The back of my sweaty legs sticks to the seat, making it a rather painful, and noisy, transition to standing.

"When did that get there?" I ask, peering over the side of the boat. It's massive. Somewhere between the size of a kid's playhouse and a garden shed. The white material of the floatie contrasts against the shimmering sea and up close, it's even more impressive—sturdy, spacious, and perhaps it's best feature: shaded.

"About two minutes after we anchored," Lucas explains with a small smile. I've tried and failed to help him anchor the *Blank Check* numerous times, but he's a micro-manager and ends up double checking everything I do and then it takes twice as long. I've learned to simply stay out of his way and let him do his thing which suits me just fine.

Pursing my lips, I follow up with another, simple question. "Why?"

"Because today's the day you're getting in the water with me."

I jerk back. "Oh, um, no thank you."

"Cute," Lucas says with a cocky grin, "but it wasn't a request. You promised."

I grumble to myself. He's a sneaky motherfucker who only got me to agree to get into the water because my orgasm was on the line. Three seconds away from earth-shattering bliss, I figured my promise would be a future Charlotte problem. Turns out the future is *right now*, and I am woefully unprepared.

"C'mon, baby," he says, nuzzling his stubbled face into the crook of my neck. "I checked the forecast earlier and the jellyfish population is vacationing down south today, so they won't bother us."

He barks out a laugh at my withering glare but doesn't back down. Instead, he slips out of his sandals and shirt and waits for me to do the same. I follow his lead, peeling my cover up over my head, but not without mumbling in protest the entire time. I may have promised I'd go into the shark and jellyfish infested water with him, but that doesn't mean I'm going to be docile and happy about it.

In only our swimsuits—and lathered in sunscreen—I follow Lucas down the steps that cascade down in a gentle slope from the deck to just above the waterline. The final step is slightly submerged, making it easy to go into the water, or in our case onto the water entry pad of the cabana-castle-floatie that's tethered nearby, gently bobbing on the surface.

Lucas immediately settles into one of the cushioned backrests, tugging me onto his lap. I settle against him and make myself comfortable, the cool water from the foot baths lapping at our ankles and the mesh shade overhead shielding us from the sun. I'm able to relax knowing that if a swordfish swims up to us, it's long, flattened bill will hit Lucas's arse first. And knowing how muscular his arse is... I don't think it's in any danger.

"Not too bad, right?" Lucas hums, resting his hand over my bikini-clad bum.

"If you don't think about the fact that there could be pirate skeletons beneath us then yes," I reluctantly agree.

"Drama queen," he chuckles. "I forgot to tell you that Mitchell texted me this morning."

I snort. "Mitchell texts you every morning, babe. If I weren't so confident in your obsessive love for me, I'd start to get a little jealous."

Lucas gives my arse a small smack. "Ha. He texted me about *you*."

My fingers—which have been tracing his newest tattoo, a small kangaroo over his heart—pause at this news. "If it was about me going behind his back and changing our flight so it's not at five a.m., I'm not apologizing. He knows I don't do mornings."

A deep rumble flows from his chest as he chuckles. "No, it surprisingly wasn't about that. He told me he has a friend who's interested in meeting you."

"Kind of weird for you to be setting up with another bloke, babe."

"*She's* a woman and wants to discuss representing you."

I blink, surprised. "What do you mean?"

His hand moves. "A manager, baby. She's seen your social media, your work... she's seriously impressed and wants to help you build something."

The jacket I made for Cole's girlfriend went viral and now I get messages every day asking if I take custom orders or where they can purchase something similar. So far, I've stuck to making pieces for me and close friends, but if I want to turn it into a profitable career, I need help, even if it's something holding my hand and mapping out my options with me.

"Holy shit," I murmur, a small laugh of disbelief escaping.

He nods, tilting my chin toward him. A smile lifts at the corner of his mouth. "You've got talent, baby. I've been saying it since day one. Now it's time for the world to see that, too."

The pride in his voice makes my heart swell, and excitement bubbles up in my chest. "So... what do I do?"

He grins. "First? You take a meeting. See what they're offering. And then? Who knows—you could be bigger than you ever imagined."

I grin, my eyes lingering on his for a moment, before I lean in, capturing his lips with mine. It starts slow, a familiar rhythm, but there's an edge to it—something hungry, like we've been holding back. He deepens the kiss, his hands threading through my hair, pulling me even closer.

He groans softly against my mouth, and the sound sends a spark through me. My heart races as his touch becomes more insistent, fingers tracing the curve of my spine, exploring with a heat that sets my skin alight. As he starts to toy with the tie on my bikini, I pull back to catch my breath.

"I'm stopping you right there," I tease, noting the mischievous glint in his eyes. "Sex on the sailboat may be great, but sex in the sea... you're not getting that lucky."

Lucas lets out a deep, rumbling. "I'm already lucky, baby. I've got you."

Swoon.

"I love you," I say softly, his words wrapping around me.

He gently brushes his thumb across my cheek. "I love you, too, Char."

Lucas makes me feel like the luckiest girl alive in ways I never expected. It's in the little things—how his smile lights up when I walk into a room, the way his hand finds mine without thinking, like we were always meant to be. Lucky for us, we finally are.

THANK YOU FOR READING!

Thank you for reading *Drive Me Home*! If you enjoyed Charlotte and Lucas's story, please consider leaving a review or sharing it with your friends.

Stay up-to-date on all of my future releases and get a bonus scene with Charlotte & Lucas by subscribing to my newsletter (www.carlyrobynauthor.com/newsletter) and following me on social media (@carlyrobynauthor).

ACKNOWLEDGMENTS

Well, here we are—the end of the Drive Me series! I'm not crying, you're crying. Just kidding. I'm definitely crying. What started as a small idea snowballed into a world beyond my wildest imagination and I'm so proud of this series.

First, a huge thank you to my amazing readers—whether you've been with me from *Drive Me Crazy* or you're just hopping in now, you're all absolute stars. Thank you for diving into this world with me, falling for these characters, and for your endless support.

To my agent, Claire Harris, **THANK YOU**. (Yes, it had to be in all caps so you know how much I mean it). You've believed in me since day one and helped bring my stories to life. I can't wait to see what's next for us.

A massive thank you to Taryn Fagerness at the Taryn Fagerness Agency and Olivia Fanaro and Mirabel Michelson at UTA, as well. I'm so grateful for all the work you do behind the scenes to help the Drive Me series get into the hands of people who love the story as much as we do. And thank you to my publishers worldwide—Fischer, General Press, Michael Joseph, and Rosman—for helping me share this story with readers near and far.

To my friends and family—your support and endless patience

have been everything. No words will ever describe how much you mean to me.

To my alpha and beta readers—Wren, Madison, Chelsey, Chrissy, Piper, Ashley—a.k.a the brave souls who saw this book in its chaotic, unedited glory. I appreciate your feedback and the time you took with my story.

Rachel—my beautiful butterfly bestie—I seriously don't think this book would've been written if it wasn't for your constant voice notes and friendship pushing me forward. Can't wait to sprint our way through more books.

And finally, to this world I've built—it's been a blast, but all good things must come to an end. Ella and Blake, Josie and Theo, Charlotte and Lucas… you've been everything. The perfect mix of romantic, funny, and emotional. I couldn't ask for a better pit crew of characters. I'll miss you… but I'm excited for whatever comes next!